Trusting Gibson

Gibson

Last Score Series

Book 2

By K. L. Shandwick

Cover Design by Russell Cleary
Editor: Jacqueline D. Kellum
Image: Colorbox
Format: Riane Holt
Beta readers : Emma Moorhead and Joanne Swinney

Disclaimer: This book has mature content and explicit reference
to sexual situations it is intended for adult readers aged 18+.

This book is a work of fiction, Names, places, characters, band
names and incidents are the product of the author's imagination
or names are used within the fictitious setting. Any resemblance
to actual person's living or dead, band names or locales are
entirely coincidental. Any actual artists are given due reference
and the situation depicted or quoted is within the fictional
imagination of the author.

OTHER TITLES BY K.L. SHANDWICK

Last Score Series
Gibson's Legacy (Last Score Book One)

Other books by KL Shandwick

The Everything Trilogy

Enough Isn't Everything

Everything She Needs

Everything I Want

Alfie Black's POV on *The Everything Trilogy*
Love With Every Beat

DEDICATION

Thank you to all my readers without whom, this book wouldn't be possible. Your constant encouragement and reviews of my work keep me going. I am constantly humbled by your support.

There is only one person this book can possibly be dedicated to and that's the person who dedicated herself to the story from the beginning. Joanne Swinney you are 'MINT!' this is YOUR book. Your support with Gibson's Legacy was invaluable but you went above and beyond in this series, and have lived and breathed Gibson with every chapter of his story as it unfolded. I know what was going on in your real life while this was taking place and you were still there for me. I suppose Michael, Joanne's husband deserves a mention too, for feeding the children takeaway food while Joanne was busy with 'KL' and didn't remember what time it was. Glad Gibson was interesting enough to make this happen for you on quite a regular basis, while the process of putting the book together was happening, Joanne. Thank you for choosing my work to support.

As an independent author, people like Joanne and others in my team are an amazing and humbling group of people who give their free time for the love of books. I am very thankful for their support and time.

Thank you to team Gibson, Emma Louise Moorhead, Ashley Heather, Jacquie Dennison, Sarah Tree, Debra Hiltz, Isa Jones, Carolyn Waddell, Angela Wallace Kawauchi, Nicola Anderson, Janet Boyd. Each of you has brought the spotlight on my work and I am truly grateful for your support and I love you all.

CHAPTER 1

ONSIDE

Gibson

Even though it was second nature to perform to tens of thousands, the night Chloe was in the wings felt different. As I walked out on stage in front of a one hundred thousand capacity crowd, the cameras reminded me that there were television monitors all over the festival and live feeds throughout South America. However, there was only one person's approval I wanted—Chloe's.

I had never been in a proper relationship. I'd never taken a girl to work with me before, but all the way through my performance on stage that night, I was aware Chloe was there. Persuading her to come with me to Rio was the best idea I'd had in a long time. She was incredible and I'd been scared that when the story about us broke that would be the end of getting to know her. I felt so wired knowing she was watching and waiting for me that I gave the performance of my life.

Playing a short acoustic set at our gigs was always the highlight of any performance from my perspective. Watching the crowd get behind me and stripping back the sound to the purity of my unplugged guitar, a single blue spotlight on one side of the stage and just allowing the music I make to touch the souls of the crowd...that always gave me a hard-on.

When I glanced over to the side of the stage; finishing the song that I had written about Chloe, my heart crushed in my chest when my eyes connected with hers. Initially there was this awesome air thickening moment between us and that had definitely been a first for me.

I slowly became aware there was something off with Chloe, changing the awesome feeling to one of fear. Tori stood next to her and by the look on Chloe's confused face, Tori had her ear. I could see from the grim expression and Chloe's lips pressed into a line, that what she was hearing wasn't pleasant.

Knowing Tori's manipulative ways, I knew she'd be shit stirring as hard as she could because having Chloe with me foiled any deluded ideas she had that I was going to fuck her. Well I was going to fuck with her at some point, but not in the way she was expecting. She wasn't going to be staying once the tour was done.

Suddenly a shocked expression on Chloe's face made her eyes pop wide open. She scanned the crowd, then her eyes flicked between me and Tori and then back at the audience. My heart crushed in my chest again but in a different aching way because I knew exactly what she was thinking. She thought I'd cheat on her and it wouldn't be long before I was looking for the next girl to hook up with. Tori, was probably giving her some slant in her favor about what happened between us.

Jumping down from the stool my ass was half way across the stage before the music for the song had died because nothing was more important at that moment than making sure Chloe continued to trust what I had told her.

Doubting thoughts were playing out on her face, her insecurities and lack of trust merging to make her reason that being with me would be the worst thing for her and it was up to me to make sure that I helped her deal with those doubts by not being anything other than honest with her. The panic I felt with that responsibility filled me with anguish.

Ten feet from her I saw Tori lean in for the kill and say something else, giving me a sly smirk as she straightened her body away from Chloe's ear, my suspicious eyes flicked back for Chloe's reaction and I was stunned by it.

Chloe's previously unassuming pose became poker straight as she turned square on to Tori as she seemed to challenge her.

When Tori's smirk froze on her face, I remember thinking I was safe with Chloe—for the moment. Whatever Tori had said had backfired and by the look of things Chloe was showing both her and inadvertently me, that she wasn't beyond advocating for herself, even with her history.

Chloe suddenly turned to face me, blowing me a

kiss and the impact on me of that was an awesome relief. The fact that Chloe had decided to dismiss whatever Tori told her about me just about knocked me on my ass. Relieved and elated at the same time, I swallowed hard in disbelief that she was giving me the benefit of the doubt instead of assuming the worst of me like everyone else did.

By the time I reached Chloe, my heart was racing because I saw a little indecision but a lot of determination. I swept her off her feet and up into my arms. Surprising me, Chloe wrapped her legs around my waist and rubbed her heat against my hard dick as I walked with her facing backwards then pressed her against a wall. Chloe's hands moved up to my hair running through it, even though it was a damp mess after being on stage.

I fought the urge to drag her around the back and fuck her hard. That was always my strongest urge coming off stage. I knew I'd never disrespect Chloe by treating her like a groupie, but it didn't mean the urge wasn't there just the same. Lowering her feet to the floor slowly, I pulled her close to my chest.

The flood lighting came on in the stadium and music blared from the sound system as most of the audience had left. "Love Runs Out" by One Republic filled the air and it was so catchy and uplifting that I found myself humming.

Making sure that we were still on the same page once I had made space away from Tori, I turned to Chloe, "Are we okay?" Holding my breath, I waited for Chloe's reaction.

Chloe's lips curled up at the sides and a soft smile appeared that reached her beautiful blue eyes. When she nodded that was my cue to kiss her, so I ran my hand into her hair, bunched it in my fist and pushed her lips harder against mine, pushing my hot tongue further into her mouth. I poured all my feelings into that moment with her. I wanted her to know that what was going on for me wasn't some fad or fucked up phase I was going through. Chloe was different. I really wanted to be with her even without the sex.

When I broke the kiss Chloe was breathless, staring up at me drunk with lust. When I saw the effect of our kiss I couldn't help but grin widely. She was a panting mess and just as worked up and needy as I was.

"Promise you won't laugh?" Chloe's brow creased as she wondered what was coming and nodded apprehensively.

"Chloe...right here, at this moment you give me reason." *What the fuck was that Gib?* I just couldn't express what was going on inside and I could hardly string a coherent sentence together with her around. All these crazy new feelings were going on inside me but I wasn't able to articulate what they were or how to express them to her.

Smiling bashfully, Chloe looked at the floor, and I could hardly bear it because doing that was one of the things that had made me mad for her in the first place. Chloe had no idea the effect her beauty had on me and I could tell she had no idea how gorgeous she was.

Placing my upturned index finger under her chin, I

lifted her head until her bashful eyes met mine. "So… Chloe Jenner, are we going to do this? Are you ready to trust me?"

Chloe pursed her lips in thought and chewed at them before answering and for a second I thought she was going to turn me down. I couldn't have blamed her after the way I put her at risk by pulling her reputation down and being careless enough to have sex with her without making sure we weren't in a place that was as private as I'd first thought. "Trust is somewhere in the future for me, Gibson. If you can accept that, then I'm here. Whatever else happens is up to you."

I knew that Chloe had just escaped an abusive relationship and was currently with me because of a careless sex session we had that had been exposed in the press—and there were my inherent ways as well, so I could accept that I was asking too much of her. Feeling sorry I had asked that of her, I pulled her close to my chest in a hug and I felt her commit to her feelings by the way she sagged into me. Effectively the ball was in my court and I had to ensure she stayed committed. At that moment the delight I felt inside was on par with when we finally got signed to Syd's record label.

Chloe had been on my mind for five long years and now I had her in my arms. Fate had thrown us together many times and neither of us had known that until after I was given her number in a one in a million chance that put us in the same frame again and that defied all logical and coincidental reason.

All I knew was that although I'd gone about arranging for Chloe to meet me in an underhand way, I couldn't be sorry for the outcome after spending time with her. My only regret was not knowing that she'd just come out of a horrible relationship with her ex-boyfriend, Kace O'Neill. If I had known that she was a victim of domestic violence I'd have never gone about it the way I had.

My strongest urge was to protect Chloe and it was my fault she was in the position she was in, so I was a little suspicious that Chloe may only be sticking with me because she was afraid to be on her own. If that was the case she was an amazing actress, because the way she responded when I was aroused didn't feel like an act at all.

Sure, I was Gibson Barclay and I'd learned how to get the best out of a sexual experience, I'd had plenty of practice perfecting that, and I know that everyone is different, but with Chloe there's a lot going on between the two of us that I've never felt before. Sex was only part of the equation.

Confused thoughts and feelings swirled around inside me that I'd never felt with anyone else. I was willing to wait with her, although, I didn't understand why. But she gave me patience and the motivation to try to slow everything down that was happening between us, "What did you think?" Smiling affectionately, I glanced at Chloe waiting for her to answer. Just being in general proximity to her made me pull this stupid looking grin all the time and when she looked up at me all innocent and wide eyed, my heart melted. Chloe was adorable.

"You have to ask, Gibson? That was an incredible performance! You get better every time I see you. Can I ask? " 'Inches From Paradise', who was that about?"

Pulling my head back farther to see if she was serious I gave her a knowing smirk, "You don't know? Seriously, Chloe? It's about you. It's about that moment in Beltz bar when I held you and you looked over your shoulder, totally disarming me with that one glance."

Chloe's innocent stare made me stop walking. She swallowed nervously which drew my eyes down to her slender neck, and appraising how sexy it was, I couldn't resist bending to press my lips to it. Switching things up, I followed that up with a quick lick and she scrunched her shoulder to her neck, shivering and chuckling infectiously in reaction.

Sweet laughter escaped from her throat and struck like a bolt of lightning that went straight down to my dick. Staring back, I was mesmerized by her lusty eyes that were looking at me in an entirely different way to the innocent questioning look that she had started out with.

"Let me show you what the words of that song made me feel about you." Closing in on her mouth, my lips touched hers and my tongue quickly penetrated through them in an urgent, passionate kiss. Chloe moaned softly into my mouth and my control was gone.

We were passing a door that was about twenty feet from the band's dressing room and I swept her off her feet and wrapped her legs around me. Cradling her fabulous firm ass cheeks in my hands I pushed her against the door. Chloe surprised me when she reached out and turned the handle and the door flew back hitting the wall.

As the door swung wide, I took in the office surroundings, ensuring it was empty and stepping inside at the same time. With a quick kick of my heel the door slammed shut and I stepped forward to place Chloe down. I spread her flat on her back on the wooden desk in there. My hands immediately fell on the fly of her jeans and I hurriedly unzipped them before dragging them roughly down past her knees then lifting her legs in the direction of her shoulders.

The urge to taste Chloe took over and I slipped my head between her legs. Licking her down the length of her pussy, the exaggerated, tortured moan made me grin widely, as the element of surprise affected her level of arousal. Her pussy was soaked with her juice. "Fuck, I can't wait darlin'. I know I should take you slow, but you're killing me with those innocent smiles and the way you just fit snugly against my body all of the time."

Dropping her slender toned legs I pulled one leg free of her jeans and pulled them back to my hips. My fingers worked fast on my belt buckle and zipper. As soon as my thick ridged dick was in my hand I was slicking my crown by dragging myself up and down her seam. Chloe looked totally disarming as she smiled nervously at me. "What do you want? Tell me," I commanded, sounding abrupt and authoritative.

When I held back to make her beg, her body hummed with anticipation and she swallowed audibly. She lifted her head to glance down at my dick then her lust-filled eyes met mine before she answered.

"You." Chloe's one word answers were becoming habitual but there was no ambiguity about this one. I positioned myself then slid the head of my dick down her seam for the last time before I stared intently at her. Nudging my dick forward, I entered her exquisitely tight wet pussy in one long gliding movement. Feeling her core hug around me was breathtaking and when she cried out, "Oh, Gibson," my throat constricted with emotion for some reason.

Chloe was the only girl I had never used condoms with and I came inside her often. The thought of doing that with any other girl would have made me sick with worry. With her it wouldn't have mattered to me at all if she got pregnant.

Chloe and I both made the same agonized moan of pleasure, "Ohhhhh," before Chloe breathed out again with another long shuddery breath and she moaned so seductively that my body was virtually vibrating with desire for her.

Drawing back almost out of her, I watched her reaction carefully and there were no nerves or any sign that she was afraid of me letting loose so I swallowed roughly, ran my hands up her thighs, gripped her hips tightly and began to fuck her hard and fast. Chloe was making soft moaning sounds that morphed into louder commands as the heat of the moment took over. "Oh yeah, oh Gibson, there, don't stop, please."

My confidence grew that Chloe was losing herself and before long her body completely attuned to mine. Soft sighs and moans, whenever I changed the pace from fast to slow, sounded so seductive, and the way she undulated in perfect synchronized moves made me work faster. When her pussy walls clenched tightly around my dick for the third time in an intense strong orgasm, I didn't fight my own and shot my load inside her, pumping in forceful spurts as my arms clung tightly around her body.

The difference in having sex with Chloe to all the other women I'd been with was that I wasn't just getting off. I was responding to the one person who got me. The only person that 'did it' for me like she did. Someone I actually wanted to please more than I wanted to please myself. These unfamiliar feelings made me continue to hold Chloe close long after we'd come.

Until Chloe, I had hated anyone touching me after sex. Usually, I just wanted to make space and recover on my own. I had no idea why she was different, but I felt happier when I was touching her than at any other time.

CHAPTER 2

MOBILE

Chloe

Pressure from Gibson's firm, possessive grip on my hip woke me as he pulled the lower half of me into his body to spoon with him. I was already lying cocooned in his arm that was around my neck and reaching down to cradle my left breast in the palm of his hand. I had woken this way every morning for over a week since I agreed to stay with him.

Inhaling heavily, his lips appeared at my ear as he whispered seductively, "I know you're not asleep, I can feel you thinking." What was really weird was, it was almost as if he could. My first thought for the past week had been when am I going to wake up from this dream? When is someone going to tell me it's time to go home?

"And I know what you're thinking. Don't. I got you, darlin', nothing bad is going to happen to you while you are with me. I told the team whatever it takes to keep you safe, darling." I prayed that Gibson was right and meant every word. As I snuggled closer his erect dick was lying in the seam of my butt and I couldn't help but give a little wriggle against him.

I was worried, we'd had sex and it was all over the media. I had escaped my abusive ex-boyfriend after a windfall and settled myself a long way from that life, and now he would know where I had gone.

Gibson growled and tightened his grip in the sexiest rub of his own in hissed response. "Fuck, Chloe. What are you doing to me?" Struggling to free myself, I turned to face him and when I looked up at him my heart raced. Just seeing him in front of me affected every fiber of my body. "Me? I was lying here minding my own business. Don't blame me for your horny thoughts, Gibson Barclay."

Grinning widely with fire and desire in his eyes, he dipped his head and kissed the end of my nose. "You know something, Chloe? You do something to me, you know that right? I can't explain it but fuck, it's like I never know what to think, or how to express myself around you. You consume me. You understand? When I'm holding you it's...it's not enough."

Gibson's pointed stare was completely serious. After he said that, we fell into this weird but wonderful silence where we just looked intensely at each other and I could see him thinking when his brow furrowed a couple of times, so I asked, "What are you thinking?" Gibson bit his lip and narrowed his beautiful grey eyes and they began to tick over my face.

"Still thinking what to say...how to explain this feeling...what's happening here between us. Fuck! I've never been stuck for words before and I feel like a babbling child around you. I dunno...when I look at you I get this tight feeling in my chest and it's...uncomfortable. Yet, I don't like it when I can't see your face. Jesus it's so damned difficult to put it into words."

So I was lying there staring silently in wonder at this mega rock star that was absolutely everything I wasn't, who was so accomplished and so stunningly handsome women fainted. Gibson was musically talented as well and I doubted there were many households in the world who didn't know who he was. On Facebook alone he had forty eight million followers, and he was telling *me* he doesn't like it when he couldn't see *my* face? That he can't explain what I do for him? The whole situation was insane.

"What are you thinking?" Gibson dipped his head and whispered sexily in my ear making my skin break out in a rash of goose bumps even though we were snug under the comforter.

I gave him a wry smirk as I paused briefly to take in how he was looking at me then I asked, "Didn't you just tell me you knew what I was thinking?"

Gibson chuckled, "Smart ass," and began tickling me. It hadn't taken much until he had me wriggling around on the bed laughing and I remember feeling happier at that moment than I had felt in a really long time.

Rolling me over, Gibson laid me on my back and crawled over me stopping dead, but still keeping me under his quiet intense scrutiny. The way he was staring at me was unnerving and my gaze toward him was more like my brain storing a mental photograph as I tried to memorize every single crease, every hair on his chin from his stubble and the way his gorgeous lips glistened when he ran his tongue over them.

Holding me like I was about to disintegrate, Gibson handled me so delicately and his fingers skimmed like feathers over my cheeks as he lightly brushed strands of hair away from my face. Leaning his forehead against mine, he pulled in a deep breath as the edge of his lips curled upwards in a smile. Suddenly, he closed the space between our mouths and gave me the most devastating kiss of my life.

A tidal wave of emotions totally engulfed me, which I can only describe as stars exploding, affecting the deepest ache in my core as his hot wet tongue pushed every erogenous button in my body. I squirmed beneath him as he positioned his body down on top of mine and pressed his hard dick against my heat.

Every time he touched me it felt like I was melting. Desire shattered all my senses and I had to fight the panic I felt when the thought crept into my mind that one day those rapturous feelings he gave me would inevitably come to an end. Gibson wanted me but fantasies only had 'legs' until they were acted out. I was certain he was acting out his and I pondered on how long until the novelty of having me around wore off.

Buzzing began to interrupt our hot-and-beginning-to-get-heavy session. Gibson broke the kiss. "Ignore it," he mumbled as he began to make his way down my body, sprinkling sensual tender kisses and nips, sucking one breast then the other and then his cell stopped.

Reaching my belly, his fingers splayed as he took in the feel of my smooth skin and his tongue had just swept into my navel, my fingers tangling in his hair, when the buzzing began again and the hotel room phone began to ring.

"Fuck! This had better be good." Gibson's cell had rung twice without letting up and his head appeared out of the cover, his face registering dark feelings of annoyance that matched his aggressive movements when he reached for the phone. "Sorry about this." Gibson swiped the smartphone and placed it to his ear, while I caught my breath.

"What the fuck is it? What's so fucking urgent that you're ringing me when I've texted you a DND and put a fucking tag on my door handle just in case you didn't know that meant do NOT disturb me, Charlotte."

Charlotte started talking and Gibson's body stiffened then suddenly he sat up, his urgent attention making my skin crawl with fear because I could see something was wrong. When his eyes flicked nervously to me for a split second his face softened, but I saw decisiveness right before he sprang out of the bed like it was on fire.

"Where? Which one? What the fuck? Did you ring Adam?"

Gibson was showing signs of stress, his arm muscles tensed as he paced the room, his fingers running back and forth through his hair. Then he held and squeezed his hard pectoral muscle before he began to rub it, as if soothing himself while he listened intensely to whatever Charlotte was telling him.

"Okay we're moving. Cabin two. My two on the door twenty four seven until the situation stabilizes. Get the jet ready, we're heading out today." How absurd was it that he had something like that at his disposal? Hearing Gibson saying that about his plane made my eyes roll as I thought how crazy his life had become, but my main focus was that he seemed to be talking in code.

Worried eyes flicked over in my direction again as if Gibson suddenly remembered I was in the room with him. "I'm sorry about this." A small smile tugged at the side of his lips, but it never changed the seriousness in his eyes. "Want to get in the shower, darlin'? We're heading out in thirty." The urgency in Gibson's voice told me not to even ask what was happening, so I slid out of the bed and quickly complied with his request. Whatever was going on was so important Gibson had let it interrupt our intimate time together.

As I showered he pushed his way into the bathroom carrying a pair of my jeans and a sweater. "Here, put these on." I looked around from the steamed up shower glass at the outfit as he laid them on the stool by the vanity unit.

Just as he was about to leave again, I stopped him. "Am I getting some panties and a bra, Gibson?"

Spinning around to face me as I stepped out of the shower, his wandering eyes perused the length of my body then met my enquiring gaze with a look of approval. "Put a bra and panties in my way Chloe, and I'll rip those fuckers right off of you when we get to where we're going. I don't do interruptions at the best of times, so interrupting me when I'm about to slide inside you darlin'...well you can imagine how pissed off I'm feeling about that right now." For the first time since Charlotte rang, I saw his face fully relax as he gave me his sexy roguish smile as his sparkling eyes still held some heat.

"So where is the fire, Gibson?" It was strange that we'd been extremely intimate with each other, yet I didn't feel I knew him well enough to ask what Charlotte was talking about on the phone and Gibson didn't volunteer what was going on either.

When Gibson's suspicious eyes instantly narrowed, he reached over pulling me into a hug. The heave of his chest at his sharp intake of breath before he spoke told me he was suppressing his true feelings. "We're just going to have a change of scenery. That's all. Some crazy fan is on the prowl so I've made a decision to move us. Taking off together will give us a chance to get to know each other better and I don't have to be at the gig until about six tonight."

From his clipped tone while he'd been on the phone, Gibson became anxious as he listened to Charlotte briefing him during their call. It seemed as if fans were just another occupational hazard to a rock star like him. Pulling me tight to his chest, his large hand gently cradled my head close to him in a strong, protective hold and I could feel all my anxieties disperse instantly.

Gibson led me out of the bathroom and I was surprised to see two trendy looking females in our hotel room pulling all his stuff out of the closet and packing up all of our things. Drawing breath I was about to ask him what was going on when he gripped my upper arms and pushed me away to look down at me. Creases in the center of his brow gave away Gibson's stressed feelings.

"Let's get out of here. I want to be alone with you and it's too damned crowded in here."

One of the girls looked up at him, giving him the most salacious smile. There was a familiarity in it and Gibson scowled at her. Instantly their little exchange made my heart sink and I had the feeling that if I continued to be with him there were going to be many more such moments.

My mind was flooded with doubt that I would ever learn to cope with running into previous conquests of Gibson's, then reminded myself what was going on between us was probably a very temporary arrangement anyway.

Weaving through hotel kitchens was becoming the norm with Gibson. One thing I was acutely aware of was that Gibson hadn't let go of me for a second. His huge protective arm held my body close to his as we made our way through another hotel kitchen in transit to the car, then stepped back to make sure I was entering the SUV first, his guiding hand ensuring that I was supported to do so.

Gibson sat heavily on the leather seat and I heard

the puffing sound it made as the air escaped. At the same time his arm slid along the back, his hand landing on my shoulder, giving me a small gentle squeeze in reassurance. "You okay, darlin'? It's takes a bit of getting used to... sneaking around like this, huh?"

Nodding at him I was impressed at his intuitive words because I was feeling a little overwhelmed again. Since meeting Gibson again my life had gone from 'shit' to 'it' to coin a phrase Kace would have said. 'It' being everything and shit being... well my lowest point ever.

The previous year had been the darkest of my life so far, and to live this surreal experience with Gibson now was beyond my comprehension. I had been stuck in an abusive relationship with my long-time boyfriend Kace, when I received an unexpected inheritance that enabled me to run away. And now I found myself being carted around by the guy I fantasized about when I was eighteen. It was the most outlandish thing that could have ever happened to me.

Gibson Barclay, a small time musician in a band called M3rCy and a secret crush of mine became a mega star. By some weird twist of fate had accidently been given my phone number five years later by his best friend's personal assistant.

Gibson had seemed to find comfort in a series of crazy little anonymous phone calls after his initial wrong number call, but when he clicked who I was, he arranged to meet me without me knowing, he knew who I was.

Strangest thing of all was that he had recognized it

was me on the phone and I'd never spoken to him back then. Once, when Gibson had heard my favorite song from one of M3rCy's albums playing in the background during our call, he asked me about it. I explained that I had once worked in a bar where M3rCy had played before they were famous.

From our conversation Gibson realized that I was the cleaner who kept walking in on him having sex with various groupies that hung around him at that time, and he then had the advantage of knowing he had been acquainted with me in the past.

Obviously Gibson didn't disclose who he really was on the phone and if he had, we probably wouldn't have continued with our phone relationship, but he didn't tell me who he was and I had thought I was talking to some random wrong number who happened to sound a bit like him.

Gibson Barclay wasn't someone I'd have been happy to associate with back then, because he was so openly promiscuous and made no excuses about his lifestyle and that shocked me. I had already seen enough—too much really—of how he treated women, but that didn't stop me from fantasizing about him.

As a male specimen I had never seen anyone that was more perfect than Gibson. Stunningly, handsome to look at with his perfect tanned skin, sensual grey eyes and roguish grin, the physique of an athlete and the intensity of the way he looked at me when he made eye contact. His combination of looks and musical talent left me breathless. I just couldn't stop staring at him. Since the first time I saw him, whenever he walked in the room he'd always made my heart stutter.

Gibson's entertainment skills both on and off the stage were charismatic, charming and funny and his forthright approach to people made him many fans. Looking back, he was always successful since I'd first known of him.

Girls literally fell at his feet and guys were in awe of Gibson. When he was in a group, everyone was riveted by his stories and the way he filled the room captivating everyone with his magnetic presence. Definitely a leader, there was no dispute who was the alpha male when Gibson was there.

Then there was me. Plain ol' Chloe that wasn't unpleasant to look at but a little quiet, the only time Gibson had ever looked like he noticed me was when I caught him giving private performances to his lady friends all over the place.

Once I had thought about it with my history of Kace and my experience of being around Gibson in the past it didn't give me confidence that I would be around him for long. So I think I was trying to mentally prepare myself that soon I'd be going back to my quiet life, and wondered how I'd cope with yet another layer of grief—this time, at the loss of someone that made me feel happier than I had in a long time.

"Come on, share. What's on your mind, Chloe?" Turning to face Gibson, I saw the serious dark look on his face as his brows creased and realized I'd obviously let my mind wander.

My confidence about my ability to keep someone like Gibson interested, already low, was waning further.

I didn't have the skills to know where to start with someone that had probably tried every position in the Kama Sutra and invented some new ones of his own.

"Just wondering what it will be like when I go home...you know...how I'll deal with everything; the media, Kace, where I'll go, what to do... boring stuff like that."

Gibson's brows frowned more and his questioning eyes narrowed. "You want to go home? Aren't you happy here with me?" I felt a pang at his question but I had to focus on my likely reality.

Jeez, of course I was happy but it felt tenuous and I had to hold something back in reserve because my gut told me there were tons of complications, mainly in the form of females. So I gave him a half smile, "Yeah, I'm happy."

I was...to a point so I stored the thought for another time.

CHAPTER 3

IN THE WOODS

Gibson

Interruptions were common place in my life, but Charlotte was pushing things to the extreme when she rang my hotel room as Chloe and I were starting to turn up the heat. My personal assistant had been told never to call me in the morning unless it was a life or death situation, so when my cell rang I tried to ignore it. When it rang again alongside the hotel room phone, I knew it wasn't good news.

As I scowled and chewed Charlotte up for her untimely call, she halted me in my tracks when the conversation included Ruby, Chloe's friend and the fact that Chloe's apartment had been vandalized. Initially it was thought to be a random act but for the fact that whoever had done it had set Chloe's college portfolio on fire.

Chloe was new to New York and only knew four people. Ruby her friend from college, a guy called Gavin who she met on the plane on the way to New

York and his roommate, Eddie. I met Ruby, and the rest of them when I had pulled a stunt to meet Chloe by saying she had won a competition with automatic entry, after purchasing a new phone. The prize was to meet M3rCy with three friends. It never even occurred to me she'd bring two guys with her.

Ruby had gone to check on Chloe's apartment and when she found that it had been trashed, she suspected Kace was involved. She had called Charlotte instead of Chloe because she knew that Chloe was delicate and she thought we were still in Rio. I think Ruby thought that I'd kept Chloe with me because of Chloe's fear that Kace would come after her, but it was much more than that.

Charlotte convinced the police that she and Ruby would be dealing with things in Chloe's absence as she was overseas with me. That was bending the truth we'd already landed back in the USA.

Ruby said the only people who were close to Chloe would know what her college work meant to her, and although there was no direct evidence to link him, she strongly suspected Kace. A local sheriff in Florida made a call to his place, but according to neighbors, Kace hadn't been seen since the day the story broke about us.

Private investigators had done a fair job of helping Chloe to be more anonymous, but with the media all over her I had inadvertently led Kace right to her door.

It was most likely that Kace had been doing some investigating of his own. It wasn't rocket science to figure out how to find her after that, because the media had been all over the hotel she was staying at when she came to see us. It wouldn't have been hard if he'd been watching on T.V. to find out where she was staying and he could possibly have found a way to access the hotel's computer system containing her home address.

Until I knew the full facts I wasn't taking any chances by telling Chloe, no point until I knew exactly what had happened. Best place for us was to stay completely out of the picture until show time. We'd flown back from Rio to Chicago the day before and were due to play at All State Venue in the evening but without knowing where Kace was, anywhere that was obvious around Chicago had to be reconsidered again.

Jerry had been flown to New York during the night at Charlotte's prompt to deal with the forensic team who were working at Chloe's place. She asked the police to make Jerry the point of contact for her because she was often in meetings during the day.

It may have seemed like we'd gone to the extremes for a girl I had been with for a week, but I had compromised her safety in the first place, and because I had gone to the trouble of keeping Chloe with me at all times, the guy was a threat to me as well. No one had woke me because they are paid to do their job and keep me safe, and Charlotte saw finding out what happened at Chloe's as part of that deal.

I knew I'd have to tell Chloe what was really going on at some point, and I had a day off the following day so I figured that I'd do it when I could spend time supporting her, because I suspected when I did it would make her feel scared. The last thing I wanted was to run off to some interview, or sit trying to be pleasant to a room full of strangers when my girl was feeling so insecure.

So I'd given Charlotte the nod to move Chloe and I to the cabin and I would commute from Michigan to Chicago. Years ago I had purchased one of the few little unassuming log cabins in a very secluded area in woods near Michigan City.

'Fret Bar' was one of two cabin getaways I had, the other being in Breckenridge, Colorado. But Breckenridge was more like my personal space and this one we were going to was a retreat for the band. Ownership of 'Fret Bar' was held in Charlotte's mother's name and I had bought it in cash to maintain my confidentiality.

Flying time from Chicago to the cabin in Michigan took no time at all in the jet, so I knew we'd be there by lunch time at the latest. Once I had settled Chloe safely in her seat and took mine next to her and exhaled heavily, relieved that I had her somewhere that I knew no one could touch her.

"Am I that much of an effort?"

Twisting my body to face Chloe's I stared into those incredible eyes of hers that I'd never been able to forget with a quizzical look. "What do you mean? You are not an effort, I told you that."

Chloe's concerned anxious stare anguish hurt my heart and I sensed she had no confidence in what we were doing. Her self-worth was so low that she only seemed to be able to process negative thoughts about herself.

That fact frustrated the fuck out of me because no matter what I said, her ex-boyfriend had beaten the trust and self-belief out of her and I was struggling to maintain a soft tone when I was so fucking over the lack of acknowledgement of the effort I was making for her.

"I know you are annoyed at me, Gibson. Hell, I'm annoyed at me. I never asked for any of this and I don't want you to keep pretending you want me here if you don't. It must be difficult for you when you are used to being around lots of women who fawn over you and you're trying to deal with me."

So there it was again, the 'groupie' reference without her actually calling them that. I never consciously did or said anything to give her the impression that I was using her, yet I got the feeling there was a gnawing thought chewing into her brain that reminded her constantly of my promiscuous past.

"Jesus, Chloe, will you ever let up with that? Tell me what is it that I have to do to convince you that it's you I want here? What the fuck have I done since you have been with me to give you the impression I was, or still am, using you?" I knew I had a point and when she didn't respond, I got pissed.

Unclipping my seat buckle and trying to temper my aggression, I heard it clunk noisily when it fell against the plane wall as I stood up. Placing my hand on the back of my head I raked my fingers through my hair then strode angrily toward the steward who was still sitting after take-off. The signal still hadn't come from the cockpit that we were cleared to move around.

"Large vodka neat on the rocks."

The steward couldn't have been more than twenty one and looked intimidated by my presence. I watched as he shifted awkwardly in his seat, then he summoned the courage to say that Johnny hadn't given clearance to remove our belts. He began advising me to sit back down and wait until it was safe to move around the cabin.

I Interrupted him, saying, "Fine, stay in your seat, I'll get the fuckin' drink myself." Turning, I disappeared into the galley and began opening and closing the metal storage cupboards noisily, briefly considering offering Chloe a drink, but when I looked out the steward and her were exchanging nervous glances, which pissed me off even more. *What the hell did they think I was going to do?*

When I found the ice and miniature bottles of alcohol, I grabbed half a dozen, stuffing some bottles in my jeans pockets before striding purposefully back down the aisle to the last seats at the back and throwing myself down heavily in the one nearest the window.

When I had passed Chloe she was looking down at her hands and my heart almost cracked at how dejected she looked, but I was pissed and didn't trust myself to speak for fear of making it worse.

Watching the back of her head I could just about see her profile and her head was still bowed down. I knew she was looking at her lap and felt so irritated

that she hadn't just shouted back at me or thrown
something or... given me any reaction really.

My throat constricted tightly when I swallowed
my frustration and my heart squeezed with emotion
because I just couldn't be the bigger person and sit
back down next to her again. I was so fucking
infuriated that the guy she had lived with had screwed
with her to such an extent, that she was probably
worried about what I would do because I was
frustrated with how he'd made her react.

Johnny briefed me while we were at the airport.
Apparently the guy who turned over Chloe's place was
almost certainly Kace. No CCTV had been installed in
Chloe's building but he'd been picked up on others in
the vicinity. Unfortunately, there were too many gaps
in the trail to track him down.

So I did what the old Gibson would have done and
drowned my sorrows. Six miniature bottles of vodka
later I wasn't drunk but I was beginning to calm down.
My judgment was a little impaired. This showed in my
general coordination, and unfortunately, the alcohol
had made me horny.

Rising out of the seat, I nodded to the steward
and inclined my head in the direction of the cockpit.
Without a word he entered it so that I could have
some privacy to talk with Chloe. I'd been quietly
watching her for about twenty minutes and the only
movement she'd made was to turn her head to the
side, apparently glued to watching the sky outside the
small window.

When I reached her seat, I stepped over her slim

legs on the foot rest and settled in the seat next to her. Chloe was now facing me, but tried to turn her head to look in the other direction and I wasn't allowing that, not when I had come to tell her how I felt. Turning her head toward me by her chin, I gave her a half smile when I was scowling inside.

"Listen, I feel we need to clear the air once and for all. You are here because that's what I want. Me: Gibson Barclay, the guy from the bar but without those other girls. Just the young dude who wanted to meet someone that he related to and wanted to be around. Only the boy I was then never knew that was possible. By spending some time with me, I kinda hoped you'd start to want this too.

"Chloe, this isn't me being arrogant, just stating a fact if I'd only wanted to fuck you I'd have done that on the beach that first night. You wouldn't have stood a chance once I got started. I know that sounds arrogant and this is going to sound shitty but it is what it is. I know all I need to know about how a woman ticks...how to turn her on...how to make her want me like I'm the *only* thing she wants.

"Trust me. I completely get how a woman's body functions and how to use it for my own gain. Showing your hand on the beach by kissing me, Chloe, if I had wanted to, those jeans would have been stripped away, your panties stuffed in my pocket like some fucking trophy and my dick inside you in a heartbeat." Watching Chloe's mouth draw in her lips, I couldn't tell if I had teased her and she was biting back a grin or stopping herself from arguing back.

Speaking to Chloe like that made me feel embarrassed for once, but I was stating a fact. When I took her to dinner as part of her prize we had both drunk a fair bit of wine. By the time I took her to the beach, Chloe's eyes were heavy with desire and I had been so desperate to have her. Every bone in my body was rattling inside my skin, aching to get a hold of her, to taste her wonderful slender body and to place my parched lips over those pert, voluptuous little breasts.

After years of thinking about that one time I had touched her, I swear I could still feel the sensation of her hips on my fingertips from that night when I held her briefly at Beltz Bar. Such a stupidly insignificant event but it was the one time that I'd never been able to shake how a girl had looked at me.

"We've been together now for how long? A week?" I stared into Chloe's vibrant blue eyes and wanted to climb inside of her. "Let me tell you something... I've *never* spent a week in any one woman's company. Or had a girl in my bed for more than two nights in a row; and that was because she was as sick as a dog from alcohol and we were grounded during a snow storm in Denver."

Chloe looked down at her lap again and I could hardly bear it. Crooking my finger under her chin, I lifted her head and those amazing eyes with the deep inky blue color very slowly rolled up my face until they locked into mine. "Chloe, I may be half way to being drunk, but what I feel in here..." Still holding the drink in my hand I tapped my chest with one finger and the melting ice made a dull clink against the glass. "And in here...and here." I lifted the glass to my head and pointed at my temple before I drew it down and pointed at my dick that was always at half-mast just by having her around.

"You do something to me and I don't have the words to explain it. I don't know what the fuck to do with these feelings and I don't know how to help you to understand it when I don't understand it myself. But get this...I don't want you to go anywhere without me. For the first time in my life, when I walk out on stage, I fucking hate it. You know why? Because I can't take *you* out there with me!"

Staring intensely at her, I knew it wasn't lust with Chloe before I'd tasted her, what was happening was much more than that. I began searching her face for her reaction. Chloe licked her beautiful sweet lips and worked a swallow before bringing her soft hand to my face in a touchingly tender move with her slim fingers caressing my jawline at one side. One word slipped from her lips as she whispered softly, "Okay."

"Okay what?" My voice was a husky broken question. I had dragged my heart out of my throat and laid it in front of her and all she had to say was, okay?

"That's it? Okay? O...fucking kay? I just told you how I felt and you hit me with that? Are you getting some kind of kick out of mind-fucking me Chloe? What the fuck does 'okay ' mean?" I couldn't hide the frustrated angry tone any longer.

Chloe's hand slipped from my chin around the back of my head and she leaned forward to kiss me softly on the lips, her eyes registered relief but never broke their intense inspection of mine. "Okay, I understand you feel something for me. I accept that it's something that you want to explore, Gibson. I'm just protecting myself from becoming involved with this...huge rock star that everyone wants a piece of...that kind of adulation, I can't compete with." Chloe pulled the sleeve of her sweater down and clung tightly to it.

Of course, Chloe was right everyone did want a piece of me apart from her. That's what had attracted me to talk to her on the phone in the first place. She was a stranger at that point and my anonymity meant she had treated me with the normalcy I craved in a world where everyone said yes to me.

Staring at the glass in my hand, I quickly brought it up to my mouth and tossed the rest of the clear liquid down my throat then dropped the glass on the floor. Taking her face in my hands, I held her in head still and gave her a solid stare, hoping my face conveyed everything the seriousness of my declaration warranted.

"Chloe, you don't have to compete. I'll say that again for you. You. Do. Not. Have. To. Compete. I am declaring you the winner. That may sound obnoxious, but if that's what you need to hear or however you need to hear it, then I'm willing to say or do whatever it takes to stop this circular self-doubt you have going on."

Gazing into my eyes with her innocent, unaffected beauty and vulnerability she made me breathless and I inhaled deeply and swallowed hard, but I was determined to finish this conversation once and for all.

"Chloe, there is no one I'd rather be with. No one compares...nothing compares to the feelings you give me when I'm with you. I want to take care of you. I'm not proud of my past, just as you are not proud of yours." Chloe's hurt eyes broke contact and I could have kicked my ass by bringing Kace into this.

"Doesn't that give us a fighting chance? Whatever is going on in your head, please learn to ignore it. Despite what you think I am not going to walk away from you and I do not want any other girls. I want only you."

Removing her warm hands from me, Chloe placed them back in her lap then began fiddling with a gold ring on the middle finger of her right hand before giving me a soul searching look with those huge wide eyes of hers before they ticked slowly over my face as if she was waiting for an answer to a question before she'd asked it. Taking a deep breath, she began shaking her head and speaking softly to me.

"Gibson, I refuse to be a victim any more. What Kace did to me...I never saw that coming. Not for a minute. I'm not sure exactly when it started and my mind is cloudy on the actual phases that started the whole thing off with him but what went on... I...I just don't ever want to revisit those feelings in another relationship."

My heart felt like Chloe was ripping it in two when I saw how tortured she was by what that- shit-excuse-for-a-man did to her. Sighing heavily, I pulled her into my chest, fighting the urge to get pissed and vent about how, what she had with him is nowhere near what is going on and that his past behavior is fucking up what is happening between us now. "Now we're getting somewhere. You think I'm violent or abusive Chloe? You think I'd ever treat you like he did?"

When I saw her waver before she replied, I almost lost it. Between that and what had happened to her apartment I was feeling the pressure that if she decided not to be with me, how was I going to keep her safe? Everything pointed to Kace being on the prowl and from what Chloe had told me already, he sounded like he wasn't the type of person that gave up easily.

"Well fuck, Chloe. Do I scare you? Do you feel threatened by me? Do you think I'm going to kick you to the curb? Come on, you've started to open up, get it out. I want to hear what you really think about what's going on here."

Just as I was getting to the crux of the matter, Johnny buzzed to alert us we were descending and about to land, the seat belt light came on and the skinny steward appeared and sat in the seat opposite.

Feeling my jaw tick with frustration as I clenched my teeth, I knew my adrenaline was beginning to flow. A knot formed deep in my stomach, but I knew I would have to continue the conversation at the cabin because there was no way we could iron everything out in front of a stranger in a brief conversation.

Chloe was going to need time and an uninterrupted flow with no prying eyes, to enable her to disclose all the suppressed personal feelings about our situation. So I let it go and took her hand in mine, lifting it to kiss the back of it.

Glancing back at Chloe, I could still see her confusion. Her stilted smile gave away how nervous she was about opening up and her hesitancy showed me how skittish she was about being in a new relationship. Giving her hand a gentle squeeze of reassurance I said, "No worries Chloe, take your time. We have however long it takes, just promise me this…you won't just take off without a word."

CHAPTER 4

UNBELIEVABLE

Chloe

Thank goodness the cabin bell sounded from the cock-pit. The lanky steward reappeared immediately, checked we had our seatbelts on, then sat down buckling himself into his dropdown seat in readiness for landing. By the look on Gibson's face, he wanted answers and he wasn't going to let the topic of Kace drop. Expressing how I felt and what I had to offer wasn't really easy when I couldn't articulate what it was that I wanted to say.

One thing was for sure, I was developing feelings for Gibson that I couldn't afford. Everything about him was pulling me in and all the thoughts whirling around in my brain and the fact that he was drawn to me as well, wasn't making much sense.

Fantasies I had about Gibson sweeping me off my feet and giving me this happy ever after kept being disrupted when my head still carried vivid images of the fascinating, hypnotizing rock star on stage with fans literally dropping at his feet as others stood with wild expressions of lust and want painted on their faces. That part of Gibson's world scared me to death.

Other images played heavily on my mind, like ones I had of Gibson the boy/man at nineteen that was screwing every woman that was willing and wore a short skirt for easy access. Those gave me a raw, sick feeling in the pit of my stomach, because I knew those scenes would forever play out in my mind, no matter what happened between us.

Every day I was falling into Gibson a little more. No, if I am honest a lot more and that brought another wave of fresh worries to my mind. Most red blooded women would have stared in disbelief and advised me to get with the program and take all he was willing to give me.

Gibson was a smoking hot rock star who said all the right things and tried so hard to make me feel special. *Why?* Apart from Gibson's reputation making me cautious, Kace had once said all those things to me as well, and look at the outcome of that relationship.

Relieved that Gibson didn't push me for an answer on the plane, I forgot myself and exhaled heavily with relief, but his pointed comment about waiting until we were at the cabin hung between us like stale cigarette smoke. Falling into an awkward silence, Gibson continued to hold my hand tightly and I got the feeling he thought I was going to take off the first chance I got.

Honesty is high on my list of attributes in someone close to me. If I am wrong, I expected to be told and I also expect to be told the truth, even if it hurts. Going with my gut thus far, I had given Gibson a certain degree of trust, but that had been me trying to live in the 'now.' Conscious of Gibson's close scrutiny of me, I became self-aware and tried to smile at him. Gibson eyed me with suspicion and I figured that he didn't fall for that.

Blocking the past was becoming an acquired skill, but I knew that burying the trauma of what had happened would only make it worse in the long term. Whenever feelings began to surface, I could feel myself shy away from facing anything painful.

The plane taxied to a stop at the gate and the whine of the engine stopped. Rising out of his seat, the cabin steward began preparing for our exit. Gibson unbuckled his belt, stretched, then stood and stretched in front of me again. Mesmerized by his muscles flexing and rippling under his tight bottle green t-shirt, I had a flashback to the time I hid in my campus dorm building watching him make those same actions shirtless after an early morning run.

Fighting my feelings, I lowered my eyes, feeling slightly embarrassed and focused on the small screw that held one of the plane's paneled walls together to the side of him. Luckily, Johnny opened the cockpit door, taking Gibson's attention away from me. It was frightening how he could disarm me so easily, so I was thankful for the breathing space.

"Sean, can I get a hand out here?" Johnny waited for Sean to unseal the door and push it open before lowering the stairs with the thick cord. Both men began to descend onto the runway.

Straightening his stance, Gibson bent forward and unbuckled my belt, pulling me to stand by my hands. "Come here, darlin' you look like you need a hug." I did.

Luckily, as we got out of the car Gibson was distracted by Johnny for a moment and I slid into the backseat of the Mercedes saloon car that was waiting for us, noting that Gibson must like Mercedes cars, because this was the second time I'd been in a similar one.

For several minutes I watched the two men talking through the window and judging by the look on Gibson's face, whatever was being said was vexing him because his brow was bunched and he was talking animatedly, pointing downward as if he was emphasizing each point he was making. Again, I had one of those moments where I couldn't believe what was happening to me and that Gibson would step forward, open the door and explain that this whole deal between us was a mistake.

Six weeks ago I had been preparing to leave Kace and when I'd had the courage to run away to my new life, there had been no respite to recover emotionally before Gibson came on the scene. Barely recovering from the physical aspects of domestic violence, I knew the mental scars had to take much longer. Time wasn't the only factor affecting how I was feeling either.

Being around Gibson would take a lot of confidence and mental preparation. Confidence I didn't have, most of it had been beaten out of me.

Would being able to face the press and the loss of my anonymity, be beyond my capability? While I was thinking about all of this, I must have spaced out a bit because I never saw the men conclude their discussion before Gibson slid into the driver's seat. He turned as the ghost of a smile tugged at his lips but he fought it and stared seriously at me.

"So Chloe, are you going to sit in the back and strip naked for me like a groupie, or are you going to climb up front and sit beside me like a normal girlfriend would do?" *Whoa! Girlfriend?* The label someone like Gibson with all his bad-boy history was honoring me with was like a shock in the center of my chest and his words made my heartbeat race wildly.

Whatever I had thought was going on between us, Gibson defining it with that title was completely unexpected. Recognizing that he was obviously serious about being with me, I wondered if he'd feel the same once I'd spoken about Kace and he realized what a mess I was.

"Well? What's it to be?" Gibson had turned his head and was staring at me with a raised eyebrow in question. "Go on Chloe, you already told me you won't be one of my groupies, so what do you say?"

When I reached for the handle and missed because I was still staring at him in disbelief, his roguish smile played on his lips right before he started to laugh. "Get that sexy ass up front here, I'm missing you already and I told you I want you beside me."

Once I was settled in the front again, I was aware

of the care Gibson took when he was driving. "You want to put some sounds on?" Reaching over I hit the on button for the radio and "Because of You" by Kelly Clarkson was just starting and as I listened to the words I wondered if they were another omen for me. *"Because of you I'm afraid to let anyone else in."*

Turning to look at Gibson, I knew by the look he gave me those words had also registered with him, because he had slowed down and was pulling the car in at the side of the road. "Hear that, Chloe? You want to let the bastard win or you want to take a chance on me?"

Nodding, I had to give him something to let him know that I at least wanted to try. "Yes." Being with Gibson had made me feel alive and although he was straight talking and brash at times, I felt safer with him than with anyone else at that point. I wasn't sure about trust when I had said yes to him. I doubted whether I'd ever trust anyone again.

My attachment to Gibson was ambivalent. On one hand my heart was already aching because I knew that I could fall so hard for him that I'd never recover. And on the other, my indecision was fuelled by what happened in the past and would affect how we were around each other.

"Fuck Chloe, you're doing it again. What does yes mean?" Gibson had turned to face me, his scowling eyes ticking over me with a worried look on his face as traffic whizzed past us on the busy freeway. Luckily, we had blacked out windows and the world couldn't see who was in the car or he'd have been mobbed.

"Yes Gibson, I can't believe I'm saying this, but yes, I do want to take a chance on—" Gibson's eye brows shot up as his eyes checked me out then his lips crushed mine before I could finish the sentence. When he broke the kiss he was slightly breathless and looked relieved. Smiling that sexy panty-dropping smile of his, Gibson made my heart melt and for a moment I he made me feel like I'd given him the stars.

"Damn, you're smarter than I thought you were. You won't regret it. All of me…that's what you'll get, darlin', no fucking half measures…I promise. You'll have to travel with me, but after the tour I'm taking a month off. I'm not letting you go anywhere without me. We're taking a month off. And I've already told Lennox we're scaling back. I'm tired and I need to find time for the causes I want to support, besides I've met this new girl and I'm really into her, ya know?"

Glancing quickly at him I saw a look that I can only describe as embarrassment, an unusual look on Gibson and it elevated him to an even sexier status in my mind. "Sorry Chloe, of course I need to fit some stuff around what you want to do. That sounded selfish, me going on like that, but I was only thinking out loud about what Lennox and I spoke about before you came on the scene."

"Mm-hm, glad you said that, Gibson, you may just have redeemed yourself towards the end of that little speech right there." Smiling at him I could see he was mulling over what I said but he didn't respond.

Turning to face the front, he pressed the button to start the car and began to drive again. Then indicating, he gave his full attention to setting us back on the road safely. When he achieved that he glanced fleetingly at me and grinned widely.

"Jesus Chloe, you just made me one happy man, darlin'. " Grasping the steering wheel, his fingers gripped and relaxed a couple of times and that little action didn't go unnoticed. "We'll be there in about ten minutes, then we'll eat and talk properly."

Nerves bubbled inside as my belly flip flopped at how excited Gibson sounded and his declaration made me feel a little more confident that he really was happy about being with me, so I tried to think of the positives, such as the trouble he took to meet me and hiring the yacht to spend time with me after I won the competition. So I made it my silent promise to try to accept that Gibson wasn't playing games, and for some unfathomable reason was choosing me out of millions of women to be with.

Gibson had neglected to fill me in on where we were going, and maybe because I was worried about the fans coming after him or maybe because I had been so self-absorbed, I hadn't got round to asking him. I know how stupid it sounds but also, the way Gibson behaved on the plane took my mind off of everything else for a while because to be honest, I was a little freaked by that.

Minutes later, he turned off the beaten track and down a windy dirt track towards a tree lined lake. I was pretty sure we were close and suddenly we reached a clearing and he pulled up in front of a fabulous little rustic log cabin, complete with a terracotta tiled roof, brick built pillars and a crooked looking chimney going up the side.

Gibson turned off the engine and smirked wickedly. "Welcome to my love shack in the woods, and before you say anything, I'm messing with you, no one has ever been here apart from the band, Johnny and Charlotte and one friend outside of the band."

Tapping on the passenger door window made me jump and turn my head. My heart sped up with the fright of it. Johnny was staring at the two of us and I hadn't heard him arrive at the cabin, but when I saw a motorcycle it registered that he had been riding alongside of us. Thinking about it, I'd seen that Ducatti a few times on the way here, I just hadn't known it was him.

Gibson held the door open and I stepped inside ahead of him. Entering the cabin, I was surprised at how big it was on the inside. Completely unassuming from the outside, its outward appearance from the front was deceptive because inside was very spacious and comfortable. An open plan layout was filled with one huge three sided sectional of about twenty seats in beige colored leather, which was placed in front of a huge open fire that had already been started and was roaring invitingly.

The bronze, lime and dark green scatter cushions complemented the decor. A wall of windows brought nature into the bright room. Cartwheels hung on the walls and an animal skin was stretched and hung over the fire mantle. Not the kind of place I expected a guy with Gibson's image to own at all.

Looking out of the walled window I noticed the back of the cabin was on stilts and there was a wraparound veranda in heavy pine wood with steps leading down to the lake's edge below. The setting was very secluded and idyllic, and the cabin was big without being ostentatious. Gibson snuck up behind me and wrapped his arms around my waist, pulling my body close to his. "You like it?" I did.

Turning, I could feel a smile stretch my lips and I tilted my head to look up at him. Feeling his warm breath on my face and inhaling how he smelt so good in his expensive cologne, I felt like I was home. I swallowed hard and fought against the strong feeling I had to kiss his mouth. "I do."

"Cool 'cause this is home for the next five days, Chloe." Johnny appeared from the kitchen with a tray with some amazing hot snacks and sandwiches and I wondered how he managed to pull such a feast together so quickly, but Gibson explained the details of how food was delivered at a time when he was running each day when he was here and that everyone thought the place belonged to Johnny who did all the ordering.

Gibson bent with a soft look in his eyes and a wicked smile as he kissed my nose and then stared longingly as I stared back in adoration. We forgot Johnny was there in that moment. Gibson's seductive stare made me forget myself and I stretched up on my toes to press my lips to his. Immediately Gibson's grip tightened around my waist and he pulled me tight against him, sliding his hand to my butt and pressing me tight to his erection.

"Gib, eat the entrée before the dessert, dude. It's getting cold and there is fish in some of this stuff so you won't want to reheat it later." Gibson snickered against my mouth before setting me away from him and taking my hand. Glancing at me, he looked really embarrassed by what Johnny said and sat down, fiddling awkwardly with the sleeve of my sweater.

"Yeah Chloe we better eat, we don't want Johnny to be chain eating with the excitement of us getting hot and horny in full view of him, do we?" Feeling mortified, my head immediately dropped in shame and I wanted the floor to develop woodworm or something so that I could just disappear.

Gibson's voice was clipped when he addressed me. "And you can stop that right now, darlin', lift your fucking head up. You have nothing to be embarrassed about. We're a couple Chloe, you think Johnny thinks we go to bed and play the alphabet game?" When he saw that I didn't respond, he continued to talk.

"Hey, there's an idea, A is for...arousal, b is for blindfold, c is for... cunnilingus. I knew that wasn't the word he was thinking of as soon as he and Johnny shared a knowing smirk between them, but Gibson was on a roll and he gave me a roguish smile as he continued, "D is for dick, obviously, e is for erogenous, f is for fucking, g is for ...Gspot, h is for handcuffs... fuck Chloe, maybe we should give this a go after all. I'm pretty good at it." Smirking at Johnny again, Gibson sat on the sofa and picked up an egg roll and squashed it into his mouth.

Johnny glanced at me and shook his head when he saw I was smiling but a little uncomfortable at their discussion, "Chloe, I told you before honey, if you're fucking the boss you're going to have to toughen up." Gibson's face instantly grew dark as he stared at Johnny. He had been about to take another egg roll but threw it back on the plate.

"You said what? You said that to her?" Turning his head quickly to me he asked, He really said that to you, Chloe?"

I pursed my lips, not really wanting to get involved and not wanting to get Johnny into trouble so said nothing, but I was worried about Gibson's reaction and instinct made me rise to my feet because I didn't want to witness the confrontation.

"Johnny, you may be one of my closest friends, but you ever address my lady like that again, I'll beat the shit out of you, understand me?" Johnny stared at Gibson then his apologetic eyes met mine and I felt my face flush with all the attention. I felt sorry for him because Gibson was choosing me over their long standing relationship.

"Sorry Chloe, that was below the belt." Gibson pulled me down beside him on the sofa and took my hand in his, resting them quite close to his groin. My eyes dropped down as I lost confidence and focused on where my hand was, then I could see that Gibson was still quite aroused and I was conscious that Johnny was watching every move Gibson made.

"Hear this Johnny, and listen well because I won't repeat it. Chloe is my priority. *Mine*. What's mine you never fuck with... remember that. She will have respect and I won't compromise on her happiness or her safety, got it?"

CHAPTER 5

AWKWARD

Chloe

Part of me expected Johnny to sneer or snicker, then come back at Gibson during their disagreement. I was relieved when Johnny said nothing further. I was thankful when Gibson's cell phone rang because it was a welcome interruption to their altercation. Being around conflict made me nervous, so when he took the call I excused myself and asked for direction to the bathroom.

Staring in the mirror, I was willing myself to stay strong, whatever way it played out with Gibson. He was showing those important to him that I was important as well and even though I felt humiliated for part of it, the way Gibson had jumped to my defense against his long standing and trusted friend touched my heart.

Mine. The way Gibson said that word about me sounded so possessive and that would have been a heart stopping moment for me, if the rest hadn't been happening. I hadn't had the time to internalize his words because I was so focused on the conversation and how both men were reacting, but standing in the quiet of the restroom, the impact of his defense was being absorbed slowly.

Trusting Gibson was going to be difficult but he had just demonstrated that he was willing to put his relationship with Johnny on the line for me, and that said a lot about how much he really wanted me around. "My lady." In public—declaring ownership of me. That particular confession was beyond my comprehension.

Soft tapping on the bathroom door brought me out of my reverie, and I turned the handle to unlock it at the same time as Gibson pushed his way inside.

Instantly his arms were around me, almost knocking me off balance as he backed me up against the countertop and pressed his big strong body firmly against my small frame. "Hello, darlin', I was missing you."

Gibson gave me his slow, sexy, roguish grin and licked his lips, then curled his head down to press them against mine in what started out as a soft sensual kiss, but ended with him relieving me of all of my clothing in a tantalizing steamy disrobing ceremony. Everywhere he exposed, he kissed and my skin detonated goose bumps where each kiss landed.

Turning me around, he positioned me in front of the long ornate silver gilt mirror and his hand swept down my belly, his finger disappearing between my legs, worshiping my body. I think Gibson kissed every inch of me, sending ripples of pleasure through my veins and into my core.

Taking his time, his slow assault on my body made me scream in anticipation. Deliciously slow traced touches made my skin react in a rash of goose bumps that made the tiny hairs on my arms and the back of my neck stand on end. Rapturous feelings enslaved me to him as he continually delighted my nerve endings. Shivers from the sensations he was instilling made my pussy clench with need and my juices flowed between my legs at the impact his sensory overload had on me.

"Ah, Chloe. What the fuck are you doing to me?" Gibson's voice was thick with lust, husky and slow. He had my leg in his hand, peppering tiny kisses up the back of it, his big hand wrapped around my whole ankle. Sensual sweeps from his other hand gently skated over my skin in a soft caress. If I hadn't experienced it, I would have doubted someone with Gibson's reputation would have been capable of such a gentle touch.

Eyes heavy with lust perused my body with a reverence I've only ever seen delivered by Oscar winning actors in the movies. Gibson was studying my body in great detail and I was mesmerized by his response to his observations. When his sensual gaze dropped to my breasts he licked his lips then rubbed them together. Tilting his mouth nearer he drew in a deep breath then his tongue darted out. When he allowed himself the first taste of my breast his searching eyes glanced up to lock into mine as his mouth sucked deeply and we shared a quiet, intense moment. I gasped at the feel of his hot wet tongue lathing over my nipple. Breaking the seal of his mouth over my nipple, he smiled slowly.

"So beautiful. You are so beautiful, Chloe." Gibson's voice was a raspy whisper, and his sensual, Southern twang was an octave lower and thick with desire, it had a dizzying effect on me.

"Come on, I refuse to take you in the bathroom on our first time here. I'm saving that for another time." Gibson smirked devilishly at me. I was about to speak but was interrupted when he stooped to pick me up in his arms and held me close to his chest. Strong arms wrapped around my back and cradled my legs under the knees.

"You're going to need the comfort of a soft mattress after what I have in mind for you, darlin'. Don't worry, Johnny has made himself scarce." Gibson smiled slowly—seductively, as he carried me naked down the hallway, each pace, getting quicker the nearer we got to the bedroom.

As I stared hypnotically into his eyes Gibson's were sparkling with wicked intent, filling me with excitement of what was to come. He smiled sexily and it looked so salacious it took my arousal to another level.

Gibson dropped me naked on the bed and crawled over me, pinning me to the bed with his arms and knees. He stared motionlessly at me for long seconds in quiet reflection until he finally pulled air into his lungs and spoke in a frustrated tone.

"Fuck, Chloe, I'm trying to take it slowly but just

seeing you like this tests my patience and control to the maximum. I know you need soft and gentle, but every ounce of my craving is to create chaos in your mind by fucking you so hard it erases every bad memory you have right out of you." My mouth went dry and I was quickly reminded of Gibson's notorious reputation and bit my lip. Something inside of me should have been warning me off but it wasn't. Gibson was trying to respect me by considering what I might need over his own wants.

Still fully clothed, Gibson was shaking with restraint as I reached for his belt buckle. Snickering knowingly, he raised an eyebrow and looked delighted that I was forward enough to go after what I wanted. Leaning forward, he licked and nibbled my ear, making me shiver, then whispered, "Tell me what you want, Chloe."

Instantly my flesh became alive and my excited reaction was to curl up in ecstasy bunching my ear to my neck at the effect of what he did to me. Gibson reached over his shoulder and grabbed a fistful of his soft white cotton t-shirt, yanking it over his head.

My eager eyes instantly fell to focus on his chest and I leaned forward, planting a soft kiss over his heart. Gibson tossed the garment on the floor. Scooping me in his arms, he rolled beneath me and I positioned myself assertively astride his hips.

Sitting squarely on his dick, he felt huge through the coarse material of his jeans. Gibson's fingers stroked my hair then flicked it behind my shoulders, tucking it behind my ears. Licking his lips, he took both breasts in the palms of his hands.

Sexy eyes stared up at me as he dragged his tongue across his bottom lip slowly and his head rose off the bed toward my chest. Cupping my breast, he rolled his tongue around the nipple, licking it and then blew softly on it before closing his mouth and engulfing a wide mouthful. He sucked it hard and I could feel the drawing sensation reach all the way down to my core. Gasping loudly in response to what he was doing to me, my breath hitched and a whispered moan escaped from my throat as I exhaled, "Ohhh."

Looking up with my breast still in his mouth, Gibson snickered and then mumbled, "You liked that, huh?" Pecking my stiff nipple again with short kisses, he placed his hands on my hips and began undulating under me, rubbing my needy pussy against his erect dick still under his rough jeans.

"Chloe, I'm mesmerized by you, darlin', those stunning blue eyes of yours make me feel helpless...speechless. Well, not speechless because I'm talking, but you know what I mean." Gibson snickered again and put his warm hand behind my head to draw me down toward his face. Stopping me an inch from his mouth, his tongue traced my lips painfully slowly.

"You know...I really want to taste you all the time? When I look at your mouth, I can't see it without wanting to lick your lips or to feel your hot tongue in my mouth. Or for you to suck mine and bite my lip. Damn, you make me so fucking hard, Chloe."

Clearing my throat, I swallowed hard. I was still an inch from his face, and taking a leap of faith, I tried to tell him how I was feeling. "Everything you just said Gibson, I understand. I feel all of that as well...and a few other things."

Beaming, Gibson's smile conveyed that he needed to hear what I'd just said, which surprised me, but before I could say anything else he rolled me on my back, my legs wrapped around his waist and his wandering hands roaming sensually down the side of my ribs. My heart was banging in my chest with excitement and I felt like I was going to explode with need.

Shifting his weight to the side, one hand pulled my arms above my head and he held them there while his other hand slid over my hip, across my thigh and down between my legs. Pushing my legs wide, his palm cupped me and his middle finger traced the seam of my pussy. "Fuck, Chloe. You are soaking wet. I love that I can do this to you."

Gibson's eyes widened in delight at the slithery warm feel of my sex and he licked his lips as he pushed his thick finger slowly past my outer lips and traced down toward my entrance. Without warning he entered me-first with one finger, then two.

His sudden infringement made me tense as I gasped for breath and even though I was lying beneath him and knew what was going to happen between us, I tried to close my legs and move away.

"Trust me." Gibson's mouth was beside mine, his voice almost like breathing, exhaling the words in such a quiet whisper which was pure but with total command. "Relax. Breathe Chloe, inhale deeply and control the urge to fight against us. I'm never going to hurt you in any way unless it's pleasurable." Believing his words, I did what he asked without hesitation and felt the lower half of my body sag in relief to allow him greater access to me.

Kissing me slowly, Gibson's fingers plunged back and forth rubbing my sweet spot until my body was humming at the hint of orgasm. His lips tugged in a half smile and he stopped, withdrawing his fingers. "Nuh-uh not yet darlin', you got to work for this one." I groaned in frustration and almost begged him not to stop.

Gibson suddenly licked my neck then pressed his lips to it and began peppering it with kisses. His onslaught was completely unexpected and the sensation was somewhere between agony and ecstasy as my body tried to deal with the conflicting sensations going on inside. As suddenly as Gibson started, he stopped, flipping me over onto my stomach and then he dragged my hips up in the air. Suddenly his mouth landed on the seam of my butt.

"Jesus, Chloe...so wet..." a guttural growl followed as he buried his mouth in between my legs, his tongue penetrating my entrance as he lapped and sucked at me. I moaned loudly, "Oh, God," hardly recognizing the sound of my own voice. Gibson broke free of my body then replaced his mouth with his fingers again. "Your legs are trembling. I fucking love how you respond to me, darlin'."

Slipping his finger to the edge of my puckered butthole, he began to massage it and I stiffened and tried to clench my buttocks together. This was completely alien territory to me.

"Trust me. Just say stop and I will. I won't do anything you don't like." Again, Gibson was whispering softly to me, reassuring me, that every move he was making was for my pleasure.

Gibson was doing insane things to my hormones but when he began to ease his finger inside, I froze again.

"No?" His question was urgent.

It felt weird and dirty. Kace had never done anything like this before and I wasn't sure that I'd ever want to reciprocate it, if that was asked of me.

He was pushing me into unchartered waters. I heard my small voice say, "This is new to me, I don't feel safe."

Curling over the back of me, Gibson whispered softly again, "Trust me Chloe, I think you'll like it and if you don't I'll stop and we'll know for sure okay?"

Swallowing hard, I nodded yes, not totally convinced but highly aware that Gibson was a rock star and was used to more than vanilla sex. Placing his mouth back on the crease of my neck from behind, Gibson licked up to my ear again. My pussy clenched and I could feel a fresh trickle of juice pool at my entrance. Gibson's fingers swept back and forth and he growled again. "Sexy girl, I just want to do *everything* to you, Chloe."

Before I could think what 'everything' meant, his

finger had teased its way inside and was gently being pushed and pulled; not deep, but just deep enough to know it was there. Gasping breathlessly and because his action was kinda taboo to me, Gibson was quick to respond in reassurance again. "Good girl. Relax I got you."

At first it felt like a weird sensation, like something was travelling in the wrong way, but his tongue was poking in and out of my pussy at the same time and then I could feel the added benefit of what he was doing.

My legs began to tremble slightly and I was becoming desperate with the anticipation of having Gibson closer. Biting the pillow, my hand clutched at the comforter and balled into a fist from how he was teasing me. "Ahh. Fuck me, Gibson. I need you inside me...please."

Wriggling away from him, I turned over and sat up to grasp at his belt buckle. Tugging, I frantically tried to access his bare skin and his smooth hard dick. Gibson rolled onto his back and stared silently up at me but I was fumbling in my hurry to hold him in my hands. "Hey. Whoa." Gibson chuckled sexily and when our eyes met I could see that he was pleasantly surprised by my impatience.

Gibson's lusty sparkling eyes were watching my hands working to free him and when I took his thick heavy dick in my hands he groaned, "Ahhh," exhaling audibly and giving me the hottest panty- melting look I've ever witnessed.

Standing up, Gibson shucked his jeans to the floor

and pulled his feet free of them, kicking them out of his way. "Damn girl, any more sudden moves like that one and you risk me blowing my load before you get my dick out of my pants."

Kneeling before Gibson, I gripped his erect dick in my hand I started to stroke him, pulling his length upwards. My thumb grazed over his apa and he hitched his breathe and rolled his head backward to look at the ceiling. I followed up his shaft with my tongue until I reached his glistening shiny head and circled my tongue over the wide brim and flicking the apa again, before he slipped it into my mouth. His body trembled with the need for more.

My other hand was teasing and scratching his scrotum, my fingertips sliding back over his perineum, before I began to stroke him in time as I sucked the head of his dick. Gibson began gathering my hair and sweeping it into a messy ponytail, but every now and again his half-closed eyes rolled and he let out another string of expletives, "Hot damn….fuck…mmmmm."

Even in the midst of what was going on, I couldn't help but notice how different Gibson was from Kace. Gibson talked all the time during sex, asking me things, whispering in my ear, being dirty. I'd never seen any of that with the girls he'd been with, or experienced it before myself, but it was so hot, he made me want to do more.

"Stroke it with two hands and look up at me when you suck my dick, Chloe." I did what he instructed and was rewarded with his pleased tone. "Ah…yeah that's it, damn." Working to pleasure Gibson with my mouth

61

wasn't a chore at all. I loved seeing how lost Gibson got with what I was doing and he wasn't slow at telling me what he liked or how he liked it.

Without warning, he lifted me and hoisted me onto his hips, backing me up against the bedroom door. "Is your pussy aching, Chloe? Do you want my hard dick filling you?" Leaning back to look at me with his lust-filled eyes and his deep voice gruff, the scene was like one from the best R movies.

My hands slid over his warm sculptured body and my stare towards him was just as intense as his was at me. "Gibson, you have to ask? I thought you were a natural at this stuff?" I teased. I didn't get to draw breath before his thick head was skimming the length of my seam and he plunged his length inside. Gibson's hands made a slapping sound on my butt cheeks as he rolled my pussy down onto him and lifted me practically off his strong hard dick.

The suddenness of his pace took my breath away and I think it had the same effect on him as he stopped stock still and buried his face in my neck as soon as I had him inside me.

"Fuck, Chloe. Jeez don't squeeze…just give me a second." I wasn't aware I was doing anything. Gibson lifted his head and gave me a sexy naughty grin, then licked his lips and leaned his forehead on me. "You are such a sexy girl, you know that? I could stay inside you forever."

My heart flip flopped at the dangerous look that followed his words, his arousal making his body hum as he leaned against mine. Strange that for all his power and prowess he didn't frighten me, instead I buzzed with anticipation while I waited to see what was coming next.

Dragging his head down my cheek he growled into my neck again and I shivered, my skin erupting in goose flesh. "Damn, Chloe I want to ride you hard but I don't want to scare you. I never want to scare you."

I heard his voice crack on the last few words and I was sure he meant it. What worried me was that he was used to women doing what he wanted and being faced with my past, I wasn't sure how quickly he'd get bored of being sympathetic when there were women throwing themselves at him every day.

CHAPTER 6

PRIVATE TIME

Gibson

"Gibson– I'm not made of glass, I'm not scared. If you do something I don't like or I feel threatened, I'll say stop. You would be able to stop, right?"

"Chloe, I've never done anything that wasn't consensual. You only have to say no, whatever is happening no means no to me, darling'.

Lifting my head to look at her again, I could see she meant every word and I couldn't describe the feeling it gave me for her to trust me like that, especially when I was dick-deep inside her.

She was giving me a solid stare and I could see that Chloe was finally giving into her feelings and wanted me to take her how I wanted. The angle her head screamed defiance and fuck if it didn't make me harder, so I started fucking her slowly and whispered, "Is this what you want?" Chloe moaned and her lips parted slightly. "Damn...sexy girl. I could lose all control with you. You know that, right?"

Chloe began undulating and grinding against me and her hands left my neck and grabbed my ass cheeks. Digging her heels in she tried to pull me closer.

"Fuck, you have a beautiful pussy. I can feel you hugging me tight in there."

Her response was to raise her eyebrow in question and I grabbed her under her legs, just above her knees and lifted them towards her shoulders. Most of her back and shoulders leaned against the door, but moving into that position meant I could slide my dick even deeper into her and I growled at the sexy way her eyes widened in surprise and she let out a breathy gasp when I did that.

With every rock of my hips, I could feel the moment she gave herself up to me completely and watched as she bit her lips. Fucking her against the door was hot, but I needed to see her and it wasn't the best position to do that, so I slid my hands under her ass and carried her to the bed, still rocking into her with every step.

When I laid her on her back, she grabbed my hair and pulled my head down, her lips crushing mine and her tongue thrust down my throat in a hungry kiss. As soon as she did that, my hips had a mind of their own and were rocking at quite a fast pace and she was handling me just fine.

"More, Gibson. Don't stop...don't stop. Give it to me. Fuck... harder." Now, missionary is all well and good, but it was a bit restrictive at times so I rolled over and pulled her up on to me. "Put your feet down, Chloe. Squat on me."

Chloe did what I asked and I saw the surprise in her eyes when she had all of me balls deep with no air in between. Instinctively she began to rise and fall, squat-fucking me, and it felt incredible.

"Oh, darlin' keep going …ohh, shit…damn." I chuckled because I was not expecting that from her at all and after a couple of minutes she began to tire. "Come here darlin'." Pulling Chloe down onto my chest I spread my legs outward and grabbed the sides of her ass.

Chloe looked so hot with her hair mussy and all over the place, her head resting on my chest and her cloudy drunk lusty look staring up at me. She was perfect. Fucking her was on another level for me. Her pussy was gripping my dick and I could feel her beginning to tighten more inside as her body began to hum with tension. That just made me fuck her harder.

Suddenly she was trying to pull away from me, but every fiber in her body was telling me she was on the edge of orgasm. So I slowed it down and could feel her sag against me, the tension of the moment ebbing, but Chloe grunted and moaned. "Not fair, Gibson… don't tease me, make me come for you."

"Well fuck, darlin' I was trying to take my time but if you insist, I'll give you what you want." Sitting up, I pulled out of her and I grabbed her legs, pulled her ass up to my chest and placed her legs over my shoulders.

Looking down over her glistening pussy, I was stunned to see an unashamed sensual smile on her lips and not a trace of fear. Dipping my head I stuck my tongue out to taste her. Chloe's breath caught, her eyes widening briefly before narrowing with the sensation and she groaned. "Oh, Gibson."

I'd have been happy to eat her out but hearing my name in that way made me want to demolish her with my dick. Rolling her onto her side, I slipped under her and turned her into reverse, positioning her over my dick again with her feet on my thighs.

"Ever had a man like this before, darlin'?"

"No. What do I do?" Chloe's voice sounded excited and slightly breathless and I loved the vulnerability of it, and yet she was willing to take a risk with me.

"I warn you, I can take you powerfully in this position, if it gets too much tell me no and we'll stop, okay?" Again, I looked for signs that she was just being brave but I saw none. "Lean back and place your hands on my chest and hang on tight."

Chloe did as I asked and I smirked behind her back at her accepting my instruction. I licked my hand and smoothed it over the head of my dick before positioning it at the entrance of her pussy. She felt soaking wet when I rubbed my dick up and down, coating myself before I began to glide deep inside. The way she hugged my dick and held it so snugly when I penetrated her was an amazing feeling.

Sliding my hands up her body, I skimmed under her arms to take her breasts in my hands. Chloe moaned and it was the sexiest noise. I felt the effects all the way down to my dick. Her feet slipped off my thighs and she ground her pussy hard on me, causing my hands to fall to her hips to control her movements.

Rotating her hips she circled her ass on me and moaned softly again, "ohhh... uh-huh."

"Fuck, grrr...mmm." I growled trying to concentrate on not losing it too soon. Taking her hands off of my chest, I pulled her back to lie on top of me, kissing and sucking her neck. She squealed with delight at the sensation, her skin erupting in goose bumps and her pussy clenching, tightly on my dick.

Seeing her skin flushed pink, I could tell she was getting more and more turned on by our hot bed session, so I began rocking in and out slowly. Chloe tilted her head and looked up over her shoulder at me. "Oh, Gibson...I could get used to this."

Every so often someone says something that just takes your breath away and affects you in a way that nothing else does. What she said wasn't anything sexy or clever or intelligent, but it was the girl I'd dreamed for five long years saying something I needed to hear, and it happened while my dick was buried deep inside her.

Reaching down, I began to talk softly in her ear and rubbing her clit. "So..." She snickered, and pouted her lips for a kiss. I obliged and was rewarded with another soft moan into my mouth.

"You want me to fuck you, darlin'?" I was taking her slowly and still rubbing her clit and she was finding it harder to speak without squirming on top of me.

"Mmm." Her breathing was becoming shallow and more breathy as she panted with desire and anticipation about when my teasing would end and I'd take her to another level of pleasure.

"Chloe?"

"Please…"

When I looked down into her eyes—drunk with lust, then saw her purse her lips and bite her bottom one, I licked mine and reached around to place her feet back on my thighs.

"Hands on my chest, darlin'." Chloe didn't hesitate. Turning her head away and I sat up heavily onto my dick then leaning back to take her weight on her hands. "Okay?"

"Kinda scared, but excited scared, ya know?" Chloe's voice was shaky and when I heard her express her true feelings, yet still willing for me to take her how I wanted, it squeezed at my heart.

"It's okay, Chloe. If you want me to stop, just tell me okay? I got you, darlin'."

"Mm-hm. Let's go." Snickering at her, because that was usually my line for stopping the conversation, I held her ass cheeks, taking her weight in my hands and started at a steady pace. Within a minute she was moaning with delight and forgetting herself, telling me what she was feeling. "Oh, yeah…keep going. I love your dick. Even the metal…especially the metal."

It wasn't long before my need began to drive me and I could feel Chloe's pussy tighten. "Don't stop, Gibson, harder….please don't stop. Puleeeez…" She shuddered and her body began to judder in spasms, so I gripped her tight and rode her harder while she screamed in ecstasy. Her hands slipped from her chest, so I pulled her flat on her back on top of me and held her body tight to mine. Turning her face up to me she kissed me hard and I swallowed her agonized noises of ecstasy slowing the pace. Chloe sat up rocking and circling, grinding herself on me. "Whew! Jeez, that was intense."

Grinning at her reaction, I was relieved that she had a healthy sexual appetite. We'd had sex quite a few times during the past week and a couple of the sessions had been a pretty good workout. I had been worried that she may not be very adventurous after what happened to her, so how she was responding told me a lot about her character and resilience.

Surprisingly, Chloe began to rock and undulate faster, then placed her feet at my side and slipped free of me. Crawling on her hands and knees, she spun around and lifted her leg across my body to position her pussy near my face.

Without hesitation my mouth was on her, licking and sucking at the tender soft petals of skin around her entrance. Licking up to her clit, I sucked in pulses while the effect and rhythm were being simulated in perfect time by Chloe's attention on my dick.

Chloe pushed my dick deep in her throat and gagged, producing a force deep down in her pussy which I felt on my tongue. Fresh juices flowed and Chloe was grinding herself on my face, like she couldn't get enough of me. Her mouth sucked me hard and she stroked my dick with just the right amount of pace and grip.

"Fuck. Oh, yeah...just like that darlin'...just like that. Damn." She was getting me beyond hot and I don't think I'd ever had as much patience or paid as much attention to how a woman was feeling emotionally about getting laid.

I'm not sure when it happened, but I couldn't hold back any longer and turned Chloe on her back, dragging her ass to the edge of the bed and pushing my dick until I was balls deep inside her again. I was done being gentle and I had to take her how I wanted her.

Standing at the end of the bed watching her body react to what I was doing and hearing her urge me on like she had... I just fucking lost it. Pounding her hard and gripping her legs on my hips, I listened to her making all the right noises and she was definitely enjoying what I was doing. "Oh God, you're making me come again."

I'd never fucked anyone so beautiful and even though what I was doing was definitely primal by that point, I was experiencing the intimacy of being with a girl that I cared for, which was a whole new world to me. So I would say the sex we had together was definitely different.

Chloe came apart shouting my name that morphed again into a silent scream as she struggled to keep her eyes open and I realized that I was just about to come as well, so I pulled out and stroked my dick hard. To my surprise, Chloe sat up and opened her mouth, then went a step further and took the head of my dick in her mouth and sucked me dry.

"Fuck." The word escaped like a whisper as I had exhaled breathlessly, and Chloe's lips were flared out around the head of my semi-hard dick still paying attention to me while I still had some small spasms working through my body from coming.

Smiling slowly, Chloe stood straight, her arms wrapping around my waist. "Thank you."

"Hot damn. You take my fucking breath away, darlin', come here." I wrapped my arms around her and pulled her up onto the bed, lifting the pillow on her side and turning it long ways behind me.

Chloe curled into my side and I reached over and pulled her side over her to keep her warm. Smiling warmly at me, she leaned forward and kissed my pec muscle, then licked my nipple before grinning up at me.

"Gibson?" Her sweet voice was kinda wobbly.

My eyes were closed while I concentrated on the feel of her as I was recovering, and I opened one to peer at her when she didn't say anything else.

"Yeah? What's up?" Chloe's face was flushed pink, her pretty pink lips bruised and her sated eyes held that just fucked look that made me want to climb on her all over again.

"Listen, I need to say something because it's on my mind and I feel myself getting lost in you, so I guess I need to put it out there."

I had both eyes open by then and was giving her my full attention. *She's getting lost in me.*

"Shoot. What's on your mind, darlin'?"

"This...situation...how long do you think we're going to do this?"

"Have sex? Stay here? What do you mean, Chloe?"

Chloe worked a swallow and looked up to meet my gaze. "This...you and me...together."

I pulled myself up the bed and pulled her along with me. Once I was comfortable, I tilted her chin to look at me and gave her a long solid stare. "Oh, we're doing this until we're not, darlin'. You mean you staying with me? Coming on tour with me?"

Shaking my head at how inarticulate she made me at times, I tried again. "What I mean is I want you with me. I love having you with me. You give me reason, Chloe. We've been there...talked about this before." Not sure what it was she needed to hear, but fuck if I could have told her anyway, the way I seemed to be tongue tied around her all the time.

Pushing away from me, she sat back on her heels to the side of me. It reminded me of when we were on the yacht and I thought about how beautiful she was in the moonlight, then compared how she looked at that point and she was even more stunning.

"You are used to women for breakfast, lunch and dinner, Gibson. I'm one woman. A girl from nowhere. I have no great sexual skills or experience to bring to you and I want to protect myself because I'm really starting to like you. I'm also worried about what will happen to me when this is over...how I'll stay safe. Kace is out there and I know he's coming for me."

Moving up on my heels to face her, I took her face in my hands. "Chloe, I'm not fucking playing at this." Making a ghosting movement with my hand between us, I continued, "This...us...I want this, I want you. I'm hoping what we have is something to build on. All I know is, I have this great, beautiful girl in my life and I'm loving every minute of being with you so far."

"As for the sex…my dick was worn smooth by groupies and sure, I guess I've done most things and had some freaky sessions which I'm not particularly proud of…but not ashamed either, you understand? I fucked women like other people eat dinner, Chloe. It was a basic need. Right down there with food, warmth, and safety. What we're doing is nothing like being with any of them."

Chloe sat silent when I spoke. I didn't see much recognition of what I was saying and wondered how to reassure her. Trying to put myself in her shoes, I probably would have run a mile instead of getting involved with someone with my reputation.

"Listen Chloe, I guess only time will tell you whether you can trust me or not, but from my point of view, you bring light to my day, darlin'. You hit me here in my chest and you are inside my head like a fucking ticker tape, the memory of your eyes and the way you first looked at me constantly running in my mind's eye. You give me reason, that's all I can tell you."

Chloe and I stared intensely at one another for a minute before she smiled slowly. "Okay." Leaning across, I took her face in my hands and kissed her tenderly and felt her body sag as she relaxed, then I knew we were really okay for a while. I had a feeling my reputation would continue to plague her, until I demonstrated to her that she could trust me.

CHAPTER 7

REVELATIONS

Chloe

Gorgeous grey eyes stared seriously into mine and I was humbled by the way Gibson had tried to reassure me that I really was what he was looking for. Tall order for me, to think about being the one he chose when there were millions of women worldwide that wanted him. I should have been elated that Gibson Barclay, mega rock star, was pursuing me when he's had so many women and now I knew for myself how much he likes sex.

How could I compete with what had gone before? A mountain of self-doubt consumed me. Gibson was used to sex and to women willing to do anything he wanted, when he wanted. What if I couldn't perform? What if I wouldn't do something he liked, because it turned me off? Would I be expected to grin and bear it?

My strong attraction to Gibson made me want to do sexual things to him I've never felt like doing before. I wondered if it was this attraction that was making me feel desperate to believe everything he said to me. Voices in my head were constantly telling me that it was impossible for a guy like Gibson to remain interested in someone like me. I wasn't super-hot or super-cool or super anything actually, and I wasn't particularly talented in any way, what did he see in me?

The truth of the matter was, I wasn't even that fun anymore. Sure, I had my moments and I could sing karaoke, dance, balance a spoon on my nose and play the guitar a little, but that was a world away from the life he was trying to make me a part of.

I couldn't imagine me at an award ceremony with him, strolling down the red carpet or posing confidently for pictures by the press. I was Chloe...mousy, quiet and preferring to blend into the background ever since Kace subjected me to domestic violence.

One thing was for sure though, since being with Gibson, I'd never experienced anything like the intense pleasure he gave me. The guy set my body on fire every time he touched me—there was no other way to describe it. What I had just experienced with him was amazing—insane. Sex with him took me to another place altogether and while I was there, it was like this incredibly erotic haze.

When Ruby gave me a lecture about different kinds of sex back in college, she rattled them off like a list, hot, urgent, make-up, intense, naughty and so on. I thought she was being crude and just trying to embarrass me. However since being with Gibson, I realize I knew nothing then, and I'd only been having sex with Kace for a few weeks at that time. But...oh boy. Ruby was right. Just clearing my mind and allowing my body to submit to the pleasure of the feelings Gibson gave me, totally changed my perspective.

Gibson was insatiable in bed I'd bet, but I could still feel him reining in his natural libido around me. We'd been with each other for a week and had sex every day... several times a day on a few occasions but I could sense he was capable of a lot more.

Even when I thought Gibson was sated after I had felt that intense build up and his body vibrated right before he spurted his hot sticky cum inside me, he'd surprised me by continuing regardless, fucking himself hard again. How he found the strength to continue to pleasure me with multiple orgasms was a revelation. I'd never experienced a whole body orgasm before Gibson and I doubt if I could live without them once I had.

Strange that Gibson could be so carnal and animalistic one minute and controlled and tender the next. Not that those two actions couldn't go together, just that it was a side to him that was very unexpected. Caressing me afterwards, he would talk quietly during our recovery, which was something that Kace never did. After being with Gibson, I realized that nothing that Kace did when we'd been intimate focused on me.

Usually, with Kace he'd go at it like he was in

another world, come, pull out and roll away. To be honest I always wanted a cuddle afterwards, but not knowing any better, just thought what Kace did was what all men did.

We had just made love and I was feeling contented in the moment as I lay with my head on Gibson's chest, listening to his strong, slow steady heartbeat. Tilting my head to look at him, I watched him sleep and my pussy clenched at the sight of the beautiful man lying sated under my cheek.

After our amazingly hot and sweaty workout, I'd spoken to him about my worries and Gibson was quick to tell me that I was what he wanted, so now I had to try to accept that. "Are you staring at me, darlin'?" A slow sexy smirk appeared on Gibson's mouth and I hardly knew how to function after seeing it.

"Might have been. It's not every day a girl gets fucked by a hot-shot rock star." I snickered at my comeback, glad that I wasn't letting his status intimidate me for the moment. We were just two young people that had 'something' going on.

"Not true, darlin', it's been every day this week— well all the days with a 'Y' in it anyway, I believe."

Licking his lips, Gibson's heated gaze dropped to my mouth and he gently pressed a kiss against my closed lips. "Damn girl, you can't look at me like that and not make me want to bury my dick deep and fuck your insides senseless."

If Gibson Barclay had said that to me five years ago, I'd have had a comeback to cut that particular train of thought dead, but the guy I was curled up with was a different animal altogether. Hot, sensual, charismatic: and dare I say—romantic...but in an alpha-male kinda way.

"You're warming to me, huh?"

Gibson had a glint of mischief in his wanton eyes and the hint of a smile at the edge of his mouth, biting back the amusement of his playful little tease.

"What the hell gave you that idea?" Wagging his finger around my face he said, "Maybe that just-fucked-glow thing you've got going on here—or it's the fact that your pussy just clenched tightly when I said that to you."

How he anticipated the effect his words would have on me I would never know, but he was exactly right and I was trying to think of a cool comeback when he spoke again.

"Don't. I know what you're thinking. You're trying to outsmart me with a bitchy comment. Save your thoughts. Whatever you come up with, I'll only counter with something equally as smart and that'll set your brain going again, but you'll never outsmart my mind darlin'. ADHD. My brain is already two paces ahead,

"Really? ADHD?"

"Yeah, multiple fucked up thoughts of irrelevant shit coming at me all the time while I try to focus on what I have to do. Speaking of which, we need to be shaking our asses, darlin'. It's a quarter to four and I need to get to the stadium by six."

I began to move away and Gibson pulled me back into him, wrapped his arm around my waist, then rolled me over to face the other direction in the bed with him, spooning close to me.

Hugging me and giving little squeezes as he spoke, Gibson's voice sounded husky. "Jesus, Chloe. I just want to lie here with you forever. Stupid of me to bring you into my bed and think I could just get up after a couple of hours and leave."

"Wait. You're leaving me here?"

Gibson exhaled heavily, and kissed the back of my head. "Yeah, just for the gig. I'll be home by one, darlin'.

"You don't want me to come with you?" Panicked that he'd brought me somewhere I didn't know and was leaving me, gave me a horrible needy feeling.

"Chloe, it chews me up when I'm on stage and I know I can't watch over you or protect you. I'd feel happier if you were here and I could just go do my job and get back to you as soon as possible. It'll be different when we know where Kace is, and the fans get used to you."

Rolling over to face him again, I could see a grave look on his face and I knew that he was being sincere. "Please darlin', I promise I'll work something out, but just for tonight, can you just do as I ask?"

Deciding he was probably right, I nodded and reluctantly agreed that I would stay at the cabin. But I wondered how I'd feel when he actually left me alone for the first time since he'd flown me to Rio at the height of the press scandal about our less-than-private sexual activity on the yacht.

Showering felt weird. Once again, Gibson left me

to get clean and sat talking on the phone to a guy called Morgan and he sounded like they went way back. Hearing Gibson speak more openly than I'd heard him with anyone else, I felt jealous that he had such a strong connection to him, which was obvious from how familiar his conversation was.

I realized that all of our conversations had been about me and his band and I knew very little else about him, but he knew tons about me already. There hadn't really been much shared about his past or general chat about his thoughts. So he seemed a bit closed off from me in that sense. Maybe as time went on, we'd get to those things and I'd feel less on the side lines.

Given what I knew about Gibson's past, I could be forgiven for worrying about the way he seemed to latch onto a female post-gig, because his hormones dictated that's what he should do. And if I am honest, it was in the back of my mind, because if I wasn't with him tonight then it may happen and really, how would I know whether it did or not?

I was wondering if, by not being there, he would have the space he needed to realize that I wasn't really all that when there were much freakier girls out there willing to do whatever he wanted. Then I thought maybe that's exactly why I was being left behind tonight.

Insecurities began to gnaw at me again but there wasn't much time for me to protest about it because as soon as I finished my hygiene routine, Gibson was out of the bed and in the shower, changed, and ready to leave. One minute he was here, the next he was gone and there was silence. Johnny had left with him and I suddenly felt vulnerable again.

My mind went into overdrive. I'd been taken to a cabin in the woods, who knew I was here? I had my phone but I was cut off from civilization until Gibson came back. His home was really warm and comfortable, but I still felt a chill and wondered if it was the loss of the guy who had been like an extension of me for the past week.

Dark thoughts started to scare me. What if the plane crashed? Who would know I was here? What if I lost Gibson. I was driving myself mad with worry and he'd only been gone for twenty-five minutes.

Pulling out my cell to check the time, I saw the emergency calls only sign. So I took on the challenge of finding a signal, so I could at least call Gibson if I needed to. After checking for a signal in various parts of the house, I finally found one out on the wraparound elevated decking at the back. It was a relief because there was no land line in the cabin.

Scrolling down the scant list of contacts, I found Ruby's and sat down on one of the fabulous redwood patio chairs, as I waited for it to connect. Ruby recognized how vulnerable I must have felt to be left there alone like that with the trust issues I had, but knew exactly what to say to support me.

"Chloe, look at it this way— if you have no clue where you are and you saw where Gibson was taking you, then Kace has no chance of finding you there."

Ruby was right. At least I wasn't going to be

looking over my shoulder to see if he was around. She was my voice of reason and once our call had ended, I was feeling much more relaxed about being on my own again. When I asked how things were with the apartment, I never got an answer to that because she moved quickly on as she was being nosy, asking me about the progress Gibson and I were making together.

The following five hours weren't bad, and I actually felt quite mellow after watching a James Bond movie from the extensive range of DVD's on the huge hundred and ten inch TV screwed to his bedroom wall. Strange thing was there was no satellite dish, cable or signal on the TV itself with the cabin being so remote.

I must have fallen asleep and stirred and when I'd begun drifting off I heard someone in the kitchen and thinking that Gibson was back already, I headed down to be with him, but I stopped in my tracks when I saw a tall leggy model-like girl with dark brown hair and glamour model breasts pulling stuff out of the fridge and placing it on the counter-top.

"Do you mind telling me what you are doing? How did you get in here? Who are you?"

As I fired one question after another, I wasn't sure what the deal was with her, but she was starting to prepare what looked like an omelet from how she was cracking all the eggs into the bowl and adding bacon, mushrooms and tomatoes.

"Oh, I know who I am, how I got in...the question is—who are you?

Staring at me with her perfectly plucked eyebrow,

raised in question, placing her hands on the granite counter top, she leaned her perfect cleavage over it in my direction and the way she responded got my back up. I'm sure I wouldn't have answered quite how I did, if it hadn't been for how familiar she seemed, making me feel more out of place.

Biting my lip and dragging my confidence from my boots to my mouth, I flicked my hair back and crossed my arms across my chest defensively. "I'm Gibson's girlfriend, Chloe. Now if you don't mind—I'd like to know what you're doing here."

Smoothing her hands back and forth on the counter she threw her head back and let out a loud harsh laugh.

"Ha! Very funny. I love your sense of humor honey, but Gibson doesn't do the whole girlfriend thing."

I wasn't sure how to respond, but I already didn't like her, and from the way she was looking at me I knew she'd made her mind up about me too. Dropping my elbow onto the countertop, I sat on one of the stools that were placed around it and tried to look casual.

"So, what *is* the deal? Since you know so much about Gibson."

Taking a stainless steel hand whisk out of the drawer, she began to whip at the eggs in the bowl and her beady eyes flicked up then she trained them on me. I was aware of how familiar she was with where everything was kept in the kitchen.

"Gibson and me..." Taking her hand off of the

bowl on the countertop, she crossed her index and middle fingers and nodded at them. "We're like *that*." I took the entwining of her fingers as she meant that they were close.

"Yeah?" I needed to know what kind of close and exactly what that entailed, but to know more I had to resist questioning her or she would just close down and I wouldn't find out what 'that' meant. My heart was banging in my chest because what she said could bring my world crashing down around me.

"Best buds, Gib and me. Gibson tells me *everything* about *everything*. We're kinda...close, he just needs to grow up and I figure there may be a bit more to us..." She looked wistful for a second then started to speak again, "Who knows? But I know I'm very important to him."

Giving me a pointed look, she began whipping the contents in the bowl again and without looking up she commented, "Chloe, you said...so you're the prize winner that's tickling Gibson's dick? I read he had taken you with him to Rio to stop the vultures from swooping. I just didn't figure on your still hanging around. So, when do you think he'll send you back?" I was devastated by her remark. She looked at me again, and my face must have conveyed the dismay I was feeling at her words, because her sarcastic smile dropped a little and she stopped whipping again.

"Aww hon, has that fucker made you think you're more to him? I keep telling him he can't play with girls forever. He needs to grow the fuck up." Shaking her head, she bent down and got an omelet pan from the low level cupboard and placed it on the stove. There was no genuine sympathy, just words.

A week. Was that my sell-by date? Why had he brought me somewhere so isolated, then just left me here? Somewhere that someone like her could just come in and trample all over my feelings. I didn't want to be around her for another minute, so I said I had just been about to take a bath when she arrived.

Eyeing me up and down again, she nodded. "Yep, he'll be coming home soon, so you should work on that hygiene hon, my experience with Gibson is all that pent up energy goes straight to his dick. Shaking her head slowly she smirked, "Actually, maybe you shouldn't bank on him being back tonight. If someone crosses his path that he thinks will take better care of him, he may just take them up on it."

Choking on the tears that were causing the lump in my throat to burn, I said nothing else, just turned and walked slowly away, trying to emanate a couldn't-care-less attitude in my stride, and questioned myself as to why I had allowed Gibson to lull me into a false sense of...not security, but a sense of him wanting to protect me, if what she was saying was true?

As soon as I was alone in the bedroom, I dissolved into a flood of tears and I just wanted to go home. But I couldn't do that either, so after feeling helpless for several minutes while the bath was running, I began snooping around in the bedroom. I knew it was wrong, but I had to see if I could shed any more light on Gibson.

CHAPTER 8

SELF-DOUBT

Chloe

Pulling the heavy antique pine dresser drawer open, I was surprised to see it crammed full of children's drawings and brightly colored pictures. Looking at the carefully detailed drawings I saw a theme developing, but it struck me as strange that someone like Gibson would have kids' artwork in his possession.

While I perused them something else hit me. Each one of them had one of three chosen scenes depicted in them; a well, a school and what I realized were mosquito nets. On the back of one was a message from a young girl to Gibson, which had neat pencil handwriting and a delicately colored African pattern around the border framing it.

Mr. Gibson, thank you for our school and our water. They are wonderful gifts you have given to our people in our village. You inspire me to work hard to learn so that I can be a doctor and help people in my village who get sick. I have to thank you for that as well, because there is much less sleeping-sickness since you have given us supplies of mosquito nets and the magic tablets that make the water from the well clean for us to drink. If my mother was still alive I think she would want to kiss you for all the help. We were all excited for your visit and we hope you come back next year. You are a beautiful man.

Jamilia.

There had to be a few hundred drawings, mainly in primary colors and all calling him Mr. Gibson. Thinking back, it had been mentioned that there was more to Gibson than his rock star hell-raising antics. Eddie, Gavin's housemate and avid fan of M3rCy, had said that Gibson gave a quarter of his salary to projects every year, and Johnny alluded to the fact that Gibson was deeper than I realized.

Who would have thought that Gibson, with his reputation, would keep things like these? And here? Was this Gibson's main home? If it was, it wasn't very luxurious or full of frivolous boy-toys like other rock stars on a par with him. Toby Francis, Gibson's best buddy, whose house I'd seen on an episode of Cribs was full of material spoils from his excessive wealth.

Closing the drawer, I had all the evidence I needed that I shouldn't look around any further. It was wrong of me to try. What did I expect to find? Sex toys? Drugs? If so then I'd been stupid to judge because all I found was a drawer full of humility.

I remembered the bath was running and waiting for me. Discarding my clothing, I slipped into the deep bath and lay back, closing my eyes, I was still trying to deal with the fact that there was a beautiful woman in Gibson's kitchen. Once I started thinking about him I pulled the memory of studying his face from earlier to the front of my mind.

Remembering Gibson's handsome face mesmerized me and for a moment I had that suffocating feeling I got when the air grew thicker because he was close to me. Weird how a thought could replicate that feeling and I could practically smell his scent all around me. The smell was like the unique one that Gibson had when he came off stage, raw and clean, his masculine smell mixed with testosterone and adrenaline from how the crowd pumped the effort into his performance.

Opening my tired eyes slowly, I almost jumped out of my skin when I saw Gibson was actually there in front of me. Sitting quietly on the toilet seat, he'd been watching me.

"Sorry, darlin', I thought you heard me come in. Then I saw you were resting for a few minutes...and the view was fucking awesome, so I just sat down and indulged in a little objectification. When your tits are covered in bubbles and the water is lapping around them, they're magnificent by the way." He flashed me his sexy roguish grin, and I couldn't help but smile back even though I was going to challenge him.

"Am I getting in or are you getting out?"

What a question. Of course I would have

preferred him to get into the tub beside me, but remembering the woman downstairs, I held myself back.

"There's a woman in your kitchen making omelets."

Gibson smiled warmly, like he was a little shy about that and shook his head. "Yeah, isn't she awesome, that's Morgan."

I almost choked when he said, 'that's Morgan.' *That's Morgan?* Suddenly my mind was in turmoil and I was in a blind panic. Hearing how he had spoken with her on the phone, all open and relaxed, I knew it had to be someone close to him, I just never figured on Morgan being a female.

When Morgan and I had our...transfer of words...because really it wasn't a conversation, she had been at pains for me to know that they could be something more, and the heavy hints she dropped told me that Gibson had slept with her on a pretty regular basis.

Sliding from my slouched position, the water slopped over the sides as I pulled myself to standing with my hands gripping both sides of the bath. A need to make space between us controlled my quick movements as I grabbed a large powder blue towel and wrapped myself in it. I had that feeling of suffocation again, but this time it wasn't pleasant and my heart was beating rapidly. Because this time, it was because I felt threatened.

Why would he bring me here, if there was a woman already here he was close to? How was I supposed to be myself with him, when there was this woman who obviously saw me as little more than someone that Gibson was merely passing his time with? Any confidence I had about being with him was ebbing fast.

I felt lost. I had nowhere to go and no way of getting there even if I had. There was no one I could call apart from Ruby— who had no clue where I was, and come to think of it, I still didn't either. First thing I could think of doing was to put clothes on and then maybe I thought I would feel less vulnerable— more able to stand up for myself.

Gibson came after me, following me from the bathroom into his room.

"What is it? What the fuck did I say?" His hands were out by his sides and Gibson continued to follow me around as I pulled out a sweater and bra, some panties and a pair of black cotton pants. Stepping into the panties, I pulled them over my butt and Gibson's hands were instantly on the waistband, his fingertips denting my flesh.

"Stop."

"Get your hands off me, *now*."

"Jesus, Chloe. Stop. This is me, Gibson. Whatever the hell I said, I'm sorry. Please. Just stop and talk to me."

I paused and stared at him silently, then lifted the bra from the bed and fed my arms through the straps. Gibson threw the towel I'd discarded over the back of the chair angrily.

"Fine. Whatever is going on in that fucking head of

yours, I'm too tired to deal with it tonight. I've been working and all I want to do is relax without any drama. I know there was nothing that I did to piss you off to this level, but my feeling is that you are in a very pissy mood, so I'm going to take a shower and go hang with my friend. You're welcome to join me...or not. It's your call. I'm never going to force you to do anything, but that doesn't mean I have to take the rap for any fucked up feelings you have over what your ex did to you."

Gibson strode over and into the bathroom, banging the door behind him and I jumped, startled by the sudden forceful action. Tears welled in my eyes, blurring my vision and I fought them back, feeling vulnerable and angry, that once again, I was in a situation where I wasn't able to just walk away. However, I knew I wasn't hanging around and pretending I felt fine with someone that was obviously his fuck-buddy and had designs on Gibson. And from the all-inclusive pass to his life that she seemed to have, I knew she would be on me like a tick on my back.

Pacing the floor, I was trying to formulate a plan to leave, but I couldn't come up with anything other than to tell Gibson straight that I wanted to go. I didn't want to... I had to go. Sitting down slowly on the bed, I swallowed noisily when the reality of leaving him in my mind caught up with the feelings in my heart. It was tearing me apart.

Gibson had been amazing with me...to me, but there was no way I was going to cheapen myself by lowering my moral standards and accepting someone hanging around who was definitely a threat to anything we had been building. Some may say I should have just been grateful for what he was willing to give me, but I'd say that after everything that had gone on before in my life, I deserved that much more.

Another thought struck me. I had come to care about Gibson. Not just lust after him, I'd gone *way* past that point, maybe even as early as the first day we spent together. What I was about to do was going to crucify me, but I wasn't going to share a man with anyone, and with Gibson we may have come to this point somewhere along the line anyway, given his history.

Maybe Gibson was on the rebound from feelings of his own as well, that I didn't know about, that thought had occurred to me several times, but the fact that he'd shown me care and tenderness, protection and said all those nice things to me, definitely said he'd enjoyed being with me and me with him. Whatever the deal was, the fact remained Morgan wasn't going anywhere so that meant I had to.

Gibson came stalking out of the bathroom and headed for his closet, his magnificently sculpted frame moving with effortless grace, muscles flexing and rippling as he walked past me. His perfect, satiny taut skin was covered in tiny water droplets that instantly drew my mind to the feel of his body under my palms as I stroked it. A small towel hung from his waist and he lifted both arms to run his hands through his dark wet hair to smooth it back. The scene was pure seduction even if that wasn't what was going on in his mind.

Watching him nervously, I cleared my throat and heard myself speak as I processed the thought. "Could you please make Johnny available to take me to a hotel, Gibson?" As soon as I spoke, my gaze lowered and I suddenly became engrossed in the emerald ring I wore on my middle finger, twisting it nervously, because I knew I was inciting conflict with him.

Gibson came out of the closet instantly and stalked over to stand in front of me, crossing his arms over his chest, his stormy grey eyes boring holes in me. When he spoke, it was a tirade of questions.

"You want to leave? Just like that? We're done? Thanks, Gibson—but no thanks? No discussion about what's pissed you off? Really, darlin'? Damn, I know you're fucked up from that gig you were stuck in with that mad bastard you lived with, but you don't think I deserve an explanation for your abrupt exit?"

Struggling to look up at him, I glanced briefly, making contact with his pained look, then flicked back and forth between him and my lap until I could choke back the tears and keep my voice sounding resolute.

"I can't be what you want me to be. I won't be what everyone expects me to be. This...this...*thing* between us, it's been insane and I'm thankful that I got to spend time with you, and got to know you...a little, but it's time for me to go and stand on my own two feet, Gibson.

"This game isn't for me. I'm way too broken to manage the stuff that's going on around me. If I thought for one minute I could be everything you want in a woman, I wouldn't hesitate to stay, but I know that I'm not, so please, let's not drag this out and can Johnny just help me leave, please?"

"This game? That's what you think this is? A fucking game?"

Gibson paced back and forth, his hand running through his hair as he gathered his thoughts and my mind was in meltdown about what was coming next. Watching his body language it radiated anger, confusion and frustration. All the while he drew in deep breaths and exhaled heavily as he formed the speech that I knew was coming.

Throwing his hand out there like he was throwing me away, Gibson then pointed at the door, "Alright. Go. Take whatever you need. Be whatever you want to be. Go and hide in that hole you need so fucking badly. Let him win, Chloe." Pausing briefly, he shook his head and continued, "I can't keep you here, but get this, I've given this my best shot and I won't come after you. If this is really what you want, then there's not much I can do about that."

There was a long moment of silence between us, neither of us moving and I was wondering whether I should get up and leave the room or whether Gibson would. I sat there staring at my hands, my heart felt crushed and feeling distressed at the thought of leaving him, every second that passed, my heart tore more with the awkward pause that hung in the air. The only thing I could hear was music coming from the kitchen. "What You Wanted" by One Republic filtered along the corridor as I tried to block it out and concentrate on what was going on.

Gibson turned on his heel and walked over to a small cooler in the corner of the room, pulling out a bottle of water. Snapping the plastic cap open, he drew my attention to him placing it to his lips, practically inhaling most of the contents. Placing the bottle down heavily on the nightstand, then he walked back around to the side of the bed I was sitting on.

"Nothing to add? Well, I have. Your little speech...what did you say? Let's break it down. Point one, 'I can't be what you want me to be.' Funny darlin', I don't ever recall asking you to be anything other than you, Chloe. I think you're pretty fucking perfect the way you are. So I don't get that particular statement at all. Point two, 'I won't be what everyone expects me to be.' Well, from my perspective I'm stoked about that, because what people expect is some blonde bimbo that's gonna get fucked and dumped by horny ol' Gibson Barclay, and we both know that's not the case here."

I glanced up and Gibson's hurt eyes instantly connected with mine, sending a tight squeeze to my heart. "You're right about one thing, 'this thing between us is insane.' Listen to that, can you hear it?" The line of the song floating down the hall had just said the same thing. "'The best love is insane.'

"There is obviously something different going on for you than there is for me, Chloe. You are my reason, this amazing heady cocktail that's made me a fucked up, babbling idiot around you. I have no idea how to make you understand that. Can't you feel what I feel for you? Can't you take it in and just *know* that what I want is to be with *you*? Be inside you? *All* the time, Chloe. That isn't me being crude or coarse. I have never felt so centered by any one person as I have with you."

Taking my hands, he pulled me to stand. "Now, I'm going to the kitchen. You can either come with me or you can take your leave. I told you before I will never force you to do anything. It's your decision, Chloe. If you choose to go, then thank you for the time you have given me and even though it's been brief, I'll remember you for the rest of my life. You have Johnny's number in your cell. That's your call to make, not mine."

Bending softly, he placed his closed mouth on mine in a painfully motionless kiss, then broke it and placed his forehead on mine. Staring sadly back at me, he held me captive for a few seconds, "You stole my soul with those eyes, darlin'."

Looking into his eyes was dissolving my fear, but he suddenly inhaled deeply and pulled away from me. Without another word Gibson turned and pulled on his jeans, zipped the fly, paused to look one last time at me, then left the room.

CHAPTER 9

DELAYING TACTICS

Gibson

Walking away from Chloe was so fucking difficult. As soon as the bedroom door closed, the crushing pains in the center of my chest at the thought she wanted to go, just about killed me. I pulled my cell from my jeans, swiped the screen and my thumbs worked quickly to send Johnny a text.

Me: You're drunk

Johnny: Uh Oh sup?

Me: Chloe.

Luckily, I had pulled my cell off the counter top in the bathroom and dropped it in the pocket of my jeans when I was carrying them back to the bedroom. Johnny never did anything unless I said so, and if Chloe thought I was giving up that easily after all that I'd gone through to find her, she'd have to think again. I was no fucking quitter and she was about to find that out.

While slipping the phone into my back jeans pocket, I racked my brain about what had set her off to the point where she wanted to leave. The only thing I could think of was Morgan turning up in the kitchen. But that wouldn't have been it, because she was just a very old friend and one of the most laid back people I'd ever known.

Suddenly the penny dropped. Chloe was intuitive, so the chances were, she'd know that if Morgan had been around me for a long time, that I'd probably fucked her. And I had...multiple times. And up to as recently as last month in fact. But to the both of us it was like going to the gym. A workout. There were no feelings involved, just two people who loved to have sex and she was a good match.

Why the fuck didn't I warn Morgan not to come to the cabin? How did she even know I was here? I couldn't remember telling her where we were going. We'd spoken when she rang just after Charlotte called me with the news that Chloe's apartment had been ransacked, but I never mentioned that I was coming here. When Morgan asked if she could come over to the hotel before we left for the cabin, I had mentioned that I was heading out because of a security issue.

Guess she knew me better than I knew myself and figured that I would come here and didn't realize that Chloe would be with me. How the hell had she got here so quickly? How Morgan had the ability to turn up in different states was beyond me. Wandering into the kitchen, my phone vibrated in my pocket. Morgan stopped, looked up at me and gave me that beautiful smile that was like a warm drink on a cold day.

Smiling warmly back, my eyes darted to my phone to check the text from Johnny.

Johnny: Roger that. You have until the morning at least. It wasn't easy talking her down from the ledge.

As soon as I saw the text, I just wanted Morgan to disappear. I had one night to convince Chloe that she should be with me and that wasn't going to be easy with a fuck-buddy hanging around. So I texted him again.

An hour. Emergency with Morgan. Take her away.

Once I'd informed Johnny that Morgan was on the scene, I knew he'd come good on figuring a way to get her out of the cabin. I didn't want to hurt her feelings, but I wasn't going to let my friendship with her get in the way of what was happening between Chloe and me.

I suppose I could have tried to speak to Morgan about Chloe, but I felt weird because I'd been fucking her for a couple of years and I'd never been in the situation where I had a girlfriend and a fuck friend in the same place at the same time.

Hell, I hadn't even thought about Morgan in the

time I'd been with Chloe. We saw each other a few times a year and spoke on the phone quite often, but she was always in some kind of drama and she did use the fact that she was 'Gibson Barclay's friend', which pissed me off sometimes. She said it opened doors for her, but I'd never have used her name if the roles were reversed.

But she was the only woman I'd met that gave me a run for my money as far as being hooked on sex and she was fun, like one of the dudes—but with a pussy. Morgan hit on me. In fact, I don't remember instigating a single session we'd ever had, those particular ideas were all on her.

"Hungry? I figured eggs were the way to go as it's late. Good gig?" Morgan had prepped everything in a bowl that she took from the fridge. She'd obviously been here some time to have managed that, but waited until I arrived to start making us an omelet. Reaching into the fridge again she took out a tossed salad and a large bottle of white wine. Sashaying past me, she placed it on the table beside the two glasses and place settings that were laid out.

Watching Morgan work around the kitchen, I looked at her and back to the table then wondered why she hadn't set it for three, because she undoubtedly knew that Chloe was here. I sat down casually.

"Did Chloe not want something to eat?" Morgan spun around with a confused look on her face.

"Chloe?"

Morgan may have thought she was being smart,

but I was way too clever to fall for the bullshit I felt was coming.

"Chloe...is that the chick you've been boning? Must say I was surprised you brought her back to your personal space Gibson, she looks a little needy. I tried to converse with her but she was pretty pissy with me. You know the funniest part? She called herself your girlfriend." Morgan was smirking with her eyebrows raised, like Chloe had said something incredulous to her.

Pushing back the chair with my legs I stood and began walking down the hall again. Morgan called out after me. "Hey, where are you going, Gibson? The eggs will get cold." Ignoring her, I pushed the bedroom door open and I saw Chloe lying on my bed. She'd been crying, her tear stained face all blotchy, and I wanted to scream in frustration that someone else had hurt her while I wasn't around.

Being mindful of not startling her again, I murmured softly. "Chloe...are you awake, darlin'? Her eyes fluttered open slowly and they were dull with sorrow, it almost destroyed me. To think how she was feeling was somehow my fault made my heart ache. Walking slowly toward the bed, I said, "Morgan is a friend, Chloe. Nothing more."

"Not true, Gibson. Women don't just appear in cabins in the wood miles from anywhere with a key to let themselves in and know where everything is instinctively in your home. It seems pretty clear to me that she's well versed at being here. You told me you didn't have a girl, but as far as I can see Morgan is as near to one without the title as you could call it."

Fuck. Chloe was right. Maybe I just wasn't paying attention to how Morgan had snuck more and more into my life. But, I didn't think there was anything 'together' about us. We were just two people who got together now and again, had fun and fucked each other's brains out. So when I looked at it that way, I knew that ultimately I was going to have to choose between Chloe and Morgan.

Another thing that I had only just realized during our conversation was that Morgan hadn't tried to welcome Chloe, she'd tried to ostracize her by making me dinner so that I'd spend time with her, knowing that Chloe was elsewhere in the cabin.

"Get up, Chloe. Get the fuck out of that bed and come with me. Let's get this sorted out. What did Morgan tell you? I know what you're thinking and you're wrong. Morgan is a friend but she's not indispensable. Not when she comes between us, darlin'."

Chloe stood up and I could see the hesitancy and insecurity on her face, so I tugged her tight to my chest. Smelling her hair and that awesome feminine smell she had affected my dick like no other woman ever had. I was still horny from the gig but I had to deal with this with my other head and not the one on the end of my dick.

She was tense in her stance and I couldn't stand the resistance, so I squeezed her tighter and waited to feel her body relax enough to submit to me hugging her. Once she did, I felt it was salvageable but it depended on how I treated both women.

There was no way I wanted to humiliate Morgan, but I had to make it clear that Chloe was the girl that was going nowhere. Actually, I was fooling myself because being with her meant that Morgan and I were never going to be in the same place again... if I was serious about being with Chloe.

Leaning back to look up at me, her eyes full and brimming with tears, Chloe's soft broken voice sounded hurt.

"I can't bear that you've been sleeping with that woman Gibson. She's different than all the others. This one has a name...and a voice and knows her way around your place. Please don't make me go out there."

Chloe pleading with me gave me a tight feeling in my chest. On the one hand, she was telling me she was hurt and that would have ripped my heart out, but there was this excited little skip that happened, like it missed a beat and that made me feel elated because she was jealous. If she was jealous, she was definitely feeling some of what I was feeling.

Bending forward, my lips brushed her ear and I whispered in a calm voice. "Trust me, Chloe. I got you, darlin'.

Initially she looked hesitant then I felt her tiny hand slip into mine. I squeezed it to reaffirm that I had her and there was nothing anyone was going to do to change that. At that moment, Chloe dug deep and started to walk with more confidence although I saw that waver when her eyes dropped in the direction of the floor. I lifted her chin and kissed her softly on the cheek then slipped my hand from hers, slid it around her waist and drew her close.

By the time we reached the kitchen her hand was around my waist in return and the picture we presented was one of unity. As soon as I saw Morgan's face, I felt sorry for her. The shocked look she had told me that maybe she had begun to think there was more going on with us than there was.

Maybe it was me that was in the wrong and strung her along? From my perspective, I had never once said anything that even hinted we were more than friends with benefits. Morgan had done all the chasing but I never saw it that way until tonight. I just thought she had more time on her hands, so had been the one that kept the contact between us going.

"So Morgan honey, what's in this omelet you made?" Walking past her, I reached into the cupboard and got a plate and began to put together a place setting for Chloe.

"You must be starving after all that energy you expelled this afternoon, Chloe." Seeing the pink tinge on Chloe's cheeks was always a turn on, especially when it was me that put it there, so I smiled and leaned in to kiss her slightly parted lips. Chloe's eyes flicked in Morgan's direction and I placed my hands on her cheeks, knowing that it would block her line of vision from Morgan, and took her mouth in a hungry kiss.

Part of me felt shitty for doing that to Morgan, since Morgan was maybe the one girl I did have some thoughts about, but not in the way I thought about Chloe. Thoughts were one thing but my feelings... they were all for Chloe, so I couldn't afford to be that considerate with so much at stake between us. I'd speak to Morgan another time and explain my feelings and apologize if I had ever given her the wrong idea.

Chloe surprised me by sitting down at the table and chatting as if nothing had happened and Morgan, who was usually very extrovert, in her conversation, was practically silent. I had to hand it to her, as tiny as she was...Chloe could do sassy when it mattered.

At one point near the end of the meal, Morgan seemed to rally and tried to put Chloe down by not remembering her name then saying she was sorry, because she'd seen that many girls with me. I could have kicked her ass about that and scowled at her because I knew she was trying to raise my temper and embarrass me.

Morgan should have known better. Nothing embarrassed me about the women I had been with. I just had a few regrets about it now that I knew Chloe. Chloe had been there and seen me at my worst for herself. The fact that she was still with me, and had taken a chance, showed the strength of character that was somewhat buried beneath the timid way Chloe conducted herself most of the time, but I had no doubt about the awesome woman she was inside.

Chloe pushed her chair back and carried her plate and mine to the counter top.

"Morgan, that was beautiful, I'm stuffed. You make a mean omelet. It was nice of you to come all this way to cook for Gibson after his concert."

Morgan raised an eyebrow at Chloe and got up with her plate, wandering around the counter to place hers in the sink.

"Gibson has a huge appetite, Chloe. I know that all too well. He's kind of insatiable when it comes to putting things in holes."

Morgan's challenging smirk to Chloe was delivered to intimidate and shock her. Chloe's irritation was clear in her eyes when they flicked to mine and I saw a fleeting look of annoyance before she bit her lip. For a second I thought she was going to cave, when she brought her forefinger to her lip and tapped it and adopted a kind of dreamy look.

"Mmm… doesn't he just. And he does it with incredible precision and skill as well."

Chloe had a slightly pink tinge in her cheeks again, but this time she was smirking knowingly and there was a look of defiance as she wandered over to me. Snaking her hand up my bare abdominal muscles to rest over my heart, she landed a quick kiss on my mouth.

"I don't know how I got through that entrée when dessert was in full view, Gibson."

A smile tugged at the corners of her mouth and I knew she knew she'd delivered a corny line of her own, but Morgan's face was ashen and there was a kind of panicked look about her, as if she had finally realized what Chloe was to me.

We heard the outside door close, and Johnny called out, "Where is everyone?"

Pretending to be surprised, I called back before he came into view, "Johnny, what are you doing here at this time of night?"

Johnny stepped appeared from the hallway with a grim look on his face, and I made a note to give him a raise, he was playing the part.

"Jerry is a mess, he's in the van. He's in a real state. He found out his wife was having an affair and he's been drinking heavily, but so have I. He won't stay with me and insists on driving. I need someone to drive him to a hotel."

Johnny turned and addressed Morgan, "Oh, Morgan. Hey, honey, I didn't know you were here. Can someone give me a hand? You were drinking with me at the gig, Gibson, so I know you can't help. You haven't been drinking have you, Morgan?

Morgan threw the towel on the side. Johnny knew she had a sweet spot for Jerry. They were great mates, but I don't think she ever fucked him.

"I've had a glass of wine but I should be okay to drive. Let's see if we can talk him in here first, I'd rather he stayed with us if he's as emotional as you say he is."

Morgan pulled on her long black leather boots and her black faux fur jacket, flicking her long shiny brown hair over the collar, then headed for the door. Johnny winked at me and turned to follow. I fucking loved that guy almost as much as Chloe at that point for coming up with a clever plan to remove Morgan from the scene with minimum drama. *Wait. Do I love Chloe?*

CHAPTER 10

SPEECHLESS

Chloe

When Johnny told Gibson about his wife, my heart went out to Jerry. I knew how he felt from the first time Kace cheated on me, but after he'd hit me a few times his affairs were a distraction and a welcome relief for me.

What was strange was that Gibson didn't seem to be interested in Jerry's welfare, and that Johnny had looked to Morgan for help and not from him. How did Johnny know to ask her? There was more to Morgan than just her relationship with Gibson. What was it about her that all these guys were looking to her? Johnny hadn't looked drunk when he turned up at the cabin either. And he was definitely in a better state than when he'd spoken to me on the phone an hour before.

Gibson cleared his throat, bringing me out of my reverie, and I turned to look up at him. Smiling down at me, he had a strange expression on his face and I was as confused as ever about the whole deal with him. I mean he just can't smile at me that way, it makes me fall apart inside and my thoughts go to hell.

"Jerry's fine, Chloe. Johnny isn't drunk. He never drinks on duty and when I'm on tour, Johnny is always on duty. You think I'd let you walk away like that? Just let you get up and leave me without a fight? You have a lot to learn about me yet, darlin'. I've been a fighter all my life. Done what I needed to do to get by."

Wagging his long finger between us, Gibson continued, "This—you...me...for the first time in my life, I don't feel like I'm doing that at all. It's like I've been in a smoke-filled room where everything was hazy and grubby...sleazy. Then you breeze into my life and out again in a flash, and fuck it's... it's like I'm different in here," Gibson pointed to his head as he spoke, "The smoke and smog clears and everything is crystal clear. You imprinted instantly with that look you gave me and damn, suddenly my mind's eye is full of that image. Full of you. Consumed and controlled by you."

Gibson led me to one of the huge sectionals and lay down, then pulled me down beside him, rolling me on top of him. He grabbed a large cushion and tucked it under his head and placing his hand on my head pulled it down to his chest. Listening to his heartbeat steady and strong and the feel of his satiny warm skin against my cheek made my heart sync with his and my panties became soaked with desire. Gibson smelt all masculine from his gig and the contact between us sparked pheromones, raising both our levels of arousal.

Tugging at my sweater, Gibson pulled the hem up to my chest, and I rose up from him as he tugged it over my head from the back. Pulling the cashmere garment from between us, he threw it long and high to land at the bottom of the sectional.

As soon as his warm hands skimmed over my skin in a sensual touch, he let out a guttural groan and moved them to my butt, pulling me tighter against him and grinding his hard bulge against my pubic bone.

"Chloe, oh...what you do to me."

I lay silently, waiting for him to speak, then wondered if he had said something else and I'd missed it, but I heard his heartbeat increase in pace and he worked a swallow, then took a deep breath. When he still said nothing I got the feeling he was struggling with something. What was he going to tell me? Why was this amazing man who was afraid of nothing and no one, who spoke his mind constantly and didn't care who he upset, struggling to talk to me?

Raising my head, I studied his handsome face and I could see that there was a 'big think' going on for him. He was mulling something in his head and he didn't know how I'd take what he wanted to tell me. Was he going to say that Morgan was important and I had to suck that up? I doubted that after the way he'd dismissed her, but in my warped mind the thought did cross my mind and I almost got off of him, but he chose that moment to speak.

"Chloe. You know that place in my head I just told you about. Like I'd been living my life in some kind of...anyway, what I want to say is...you are my clean air, Chloe. Have you ever been to the mountains? Like Denver or Wyoming or anywhere and stood at the top of a mountain?"

I hadn't, but I could still relate to what he was saying.

"I once stood at the top of a mountain in Breckenridge and the feeling...anyway I digress, but the feeling I had was something else. When I travelled up the mountainside in that open chair lift my head became more light headed with the thinner less oxygenated air, but when I stood at the top and looked down on the town there was a kind of spiritual feeling and everything was so fucking pure. The white powder beneath my feet, the air was clean and no one else was breathing the same air as me...you know what I mean? Virgin."

What was going on for Gibson was some kind of expression of words in relation to us, but I was yet to understand fully where he was going with it all.

"Chloe. You give me that feeling. Like I'm in pure air. Everything is insignificant as long as I can stand on that mountain."

Gibson snickered and the wonderful sound of laughter that rumbled from his throat was a real turn on. "Not that I'm saying you look or feel like a mountain." Gibson shuffled me around so that I was in the back of the sofa and he was in front of me, lying side by side facing each other. He took my chin in his hand and tilted my face up toward him.

"Morgan isn't coming back, Chloe. I texted

Johnny. I had no fucking idea she'd turn up here. Our friendship is terminated tonight." Gibson stared silently at me for a minute, then he inhaled deeply. "I like her, Chloe. Morgan I mean. But I think I love you. No, scratch that—I fucking know I love you. It's taken me a few days to figure out what all the thoughts running through my head meant, all the feelings that were so different to anything I'd felt before and I know without a doubt I'd die for you. So I guess that's love, right?"

My external reaction was to remain completely still and stare wide eyed back at him. My mind was in meltdown. My heart was beating so wildly in my chest I thought it would pack up at any second. All of my body's shock receptors were at full capacity and I trembled with the words that I never thought I'd hear someone like Gibson say to someone like me.

Struggling for words, I couldn't say it back to him. That would make it real. And I wasn't sure I really knew what to do with those words he'd given me, at this stage of my recovery from the mess of Kace. If I loved Gibson then I'd be leaving myself at risk of being hurt, and I wasn't sure my heart could take much more of that. I couldn't leave myself wide open like that.

There was no doubt in my mind that I cared about him. And, when he left to perform, the ache in my chest I felt from that separation was almost unbearable, but it had only been a short time since I'd escaped the hellish life I'd been captive in, so it was understandable that I didn't know exactly what I was feeling. I was fascinated, mesmerized, captivated and charmed by him, but my brain wouldn't go to feelings beyond those.

Gibson made my heart light, he made me feel special, valued and cherished and he made me feel protected. Sharing his heart with me was a one-off for him, so I had to make sure that if I took it, I wasn't going to give it back somewhere down the line.

I knew many women would think I was crazy and if Gibson Barclay was offering, I should take whatever he was willing to give me. But they would be fools to commit to a life in Gibson's crazy world where everyone thought I was a whore with some magic vagina, and that I had managed to be enough of a sex freak to keep his interest.

A few times I had overheard some conversations about us to that effect. Those kind of remarks are the ones that stick when you've been where I have. Throwing caution to the wind when I was still emotionally fragile could leave me desolate, and although he had never given me reason personally, to doubt him, my barriers were on autopilot as far as men were concerned. There was a saying that I was determined to stick to because of those conversations. "Fool me once, shame on you. Fool me twice, shame on me." Unfortunately for Gibson, I was no fool, so trust wasn't coming easy for me.

Gibson tilted my face up and kissed me tenderly on my lips. "It's okay, Chloe. I know. This is hard for you. As long as you are with me, I can wait. Take as long as you need. I got you, darlin'. I'm going nowhere, and I know I have a lot to prove to you. The world I live in doesn't help. I realize that, but we'll work past all the shit together to get you to that happy place."

Gibson smiled again, and brought his mouth to my ear. "I love you, Chloe Jenner and I'm gonna make you love me back." Hearing his breathing, his seductive, low whispered words sparked pangs of pleasure again and my pussy clenched, but his voice cracked even in barely-there voice. Leaning back, he worked a swallow, watching my reaction then he licked his lips and bent his head to kiss my neck.

"Fuck, Chloe. I'm so fucking head over heels about you, and I don't know how to express that to you adequately except to shred your panties and bury myself in your pussy until I can't see straight. I never knew how tight and suffocating the feeling of wanting someone so badly could be, until I had you in my arms."

Without another word, Gibson scooped me up in his arms with my legs around his waist and began walking towards the bedroom. We made it about half way before his mouth took mine in a soft kiss that turned so passionate our tongues were soon dueling with each other.

The sensation of that kiss sent goose-bumps cascading across my skin, my flesh sensitive to his touch and my core weeping with the sticky essence of our passionate embrace. As Gibson broke the kiss, I dipped my head and sucked his neck for a second and Gibson growled and pushed me hard against the wall, my legs moved around him and he stared lustily at me.

"Don't fucking tempt me, Chloe." Again he almost

turned away from the wall, but slammed me back against it, not in a scary way, but overcome with passion. Pushing his hard length against my heat, he growled again and spun around purposely, kicking the bedroom door wide and throwing me on the bed. What he was doing excited me and I panted, still breathless from the kiss as I watched him unbuckle his worn leather belt and free himself from the constraints of his faded jeans.

"You have no idea, have you?"

Shaking his head, Gibson was talking to me but didn't expand on what I had 'no idea' about. As soon as he was naked, his big strong hands were fumbling with the ties of my sweatpants. Then, he lost patience and pulled them down, in one strong fluid, almost rough movement below my knees.

One forearm hooked just below my knees and pushed my legs towards my chest while his mouth was sucking at my entrance and clitoris through the lacy material of my panties. "Mmm...fuck, your pussy is incredible."

Gibson suddenly became more urgent and stood up from the bed, hugging my jeans the rest of the way off, then grabbed at my panties. "What I'm about to do... trust me okay?" When I didn't answer he said it again. "Trust me, Chloe, I got you." His face was serious and he was watching me intently for any signs that I wasn't invested. I was.

"Okay." My voice sounded confident, more confident than I was feeling at that moment.

The sound of lace tearing was quite erotic

actually, and Gibson's mouth was on my pussy, his hands splaying my legs in the air as his mouth was working on my clitoris, then his tongue began sliding into my warm wet pussy. "Holy...damn, you are so fucking wet. I can't get enough of this...of you."

Gibson began licking me from front to back, then focused on my butthole. It freaked me out at first then I kind of got overtaken by the passion and eroticism of it and forgot about the dark side of what he was doing.

"One day, Chloe. One day you'll trust me enough to let me bury my dick here."

As soon as he said it, my butt clenched in a never-in-a-million-years gesture. Gibson must have felt me tense and chuckled, breaking away from me and flipping me over onto my stomach. The next thing I knew, he lay down on top of me from behind, pushing my breasts further into the mattress, his dick thrusting up at the entrance of my pussy. The pressure of his hard body felt powerful—almost oppressive and my first thought was Kace had done this. Fighting the flashback, I concentrated on the way that Gibson was holding me and that felt safe.

"Does the thought of me taking you like this scare you?"

It did. There was never any consideration from Kace, but this was different. Gibson was talking me through it and I could hear the control in his voice as he positioned himself completely square on to my entrance and suddenly thrust himself in to the hilt and kissed my neck from behind at the same time. We both grunted loudly and the excitement I felt at being taken by him was thrilling. Any fears I had disappeared as his gentle hands stroked the sides of my face in his non-verbal reassurance.

Staying still for a moment, Gibson cussed and adjusted then placed his hands either side of my head on the mattress and rose up onto his hands to put some force behind the rocking movements in his hips. "Can you feel that, Chloe? Can you feel what you do to me? I'm desperate for you."

Knowing he needed permission to let go I said, "Fuck me, Gibson. Do it." Gibson repositioned himself on his knees, grabbing both my hips, his fingers digging into my flesh and he pulled me further up onto him. Once he began to grind into me I felt him retract a little before he took me with a force and pace he never had before.

"I. Love. You. I. Love. You. God. Damn...God..."

He chanted at the same pace as he was pounding into me, then he fell silent when the speed at which he was taking me became almost punishing. Gasps and loud moans tore from my throat as Gibson took me to a place that was beyond comprehension.

Every fiber in my body was on alert. Sharp pangs of pleasure coursed through my veins.

"I fucking love doing this to you."

Gibson's low voice was sexy, thick with lust and so overpowering. I couldn't think as I absorbed the pleasure he was giving me. I felt tears roll down my cheeks as Gibson freed my mind from anything except the way he was making me feel.

CHAPTER 11

CAPTIVATING

Gibson

Feeling her beneath me like that was incredible. Trying to describe what emotions were running through me, and the connection that was going on between us, was impossible, I was beyond words.

My mind was completely devoid of thoughts other than the need to give her pleasure, to tease and punish her body in the place that was somewhere between pleasure and pain. Absorbing the pace and erotic sounds of our bodies merging, the soft sounds of me inside her and the fact that all of that essence coating my dick was for me was amazing. It was an incredible feeling. Being together in that way...no one had ever come close to touching me—mind, body and soul—in the way I felt when I was with Chloe.

Chloe was zoned out. She came so many times, it was hard to know how many. At one point it felt like my dick was in a vice, her pussy clenching relentlessly with the almost constant state of orgasmic releases as her body became more and more attuned to what I was doing to her. I'd never focused as much on pleasuring someone as much as I had on her that time. It was as if we were in a self-induced hypnotic state, whereby our bodies were almost fused in our pleasure.

Morgan was right. I was insatiable at times, but by the time we were finished and I was worn smooth, I wondered whether my dick would ever be hard again.

Lying face down, her body limp and heaving with effort from the energy she had expelled, I sat back on my knees and took in how she looked. The vision before me was amazing. Chloe's soft silky skin glistened with sweat, her hair tousled in all directions around the pillow and reaching onto the sheet. Her legs were parted and I could see her red, swollen pussy in contrast to the paler skin between her thighs. She was perfect.

I smiled at the image before me, and became aware of the smell of pure sexual ecstasy that hung in the air. My heart was bursting in my chest with the alien feelings I had about my beautiful woman. Bending to place my face between Chloe's legs I kissed her pussy softly and inhaled deeply again. She smelt so fucking intoxicating. Chloe moaned softly and lifted one leg, bending it at the knee in protest, so I smiled and sat back before making my way off the bed.

Padding barefoot into the bathroom, I washed myself in the sink then took a small white wash cloth and ran it under the hot water coming from the faucet. I made my way back to bed and began to wipe her clean. Chloe rolled over to give me a glazed stare and a tired but sated smile. As tired as I was after our session, my dick stirred and twitched on my leg.

"Did I hurt you, darlin'?" Chloe shook her head and smiled again, but remained speechless so I continued to wash her to make her comfortable. I had come twice inside her and her pussy was overflowing with my cum.

"Why do you do that?"

Looking up to meet her curious eyes, I wasn't sure whether she meant me cleaning her or something else. "Do what?"

"Take care of me...make me comfortable."

"Don't you like it?"

"It feels weird. I'm not used to such care and attention."

I stared at her for a long moment. Why wouldn't anyone take care of her? She was absolutely perfect and washing between her legs just didn't seem enough for me.

"Well you're going to have to work on that, darlin', because I'm planning on giving you everything you need to make you love me back. And when you do, I'll just have to keep finding ways of keeping that love going."

Turning away from her, I balled the cloth in my hand and threw it towards the bathroom door at force. It landed just inside the door. So I turned and waggled my eyebrows at her, pretending I was trying to impress her.

Chloe giggled and I lay down beside her, pulling

her close, while dragging the comforter up the bed to cover us both. When I did, Chloe relaxed into my arms and sighed heavily.

"A girl could get used to this."

"What about Chloe, you think she can, darlin'?

Chloe didn't speak, just lifted my hand and placed a kiss in the center of my palm then closed it and wrapped hers over mine, giving it a tight squeeze. I took that as a 'just maybe'.

We both passed out and when I woke I had turned away from her, but found her sound asleep, clinging on to me like a monkey climbing a tree. I smirked because this was the first time that Chloe had found the need to do that. Usually, it was me that was doing the hugging in bed.

Basking in the warmth of Chloe's little body flush against mine and my leg between hers. She had turned to cuddle me in the night, her arm draped over my hip and her soft fingertips brushing against the hardness of my morning wood.

A lazy smile stretched my lips when I thought about that, knowing that if she were awake and I had said anything she'd have flushed pink at her little inadvertent grope. Chloe stirred and I turned to face her. "Morning, darlin', sleep okay?"

Slowly her mouth opened and she licked her lips.

"Um... don't remember, I may have slipped unconscious after earlier."

"Alright, if you ever find yourself with insomnia Chloe, I'll knock you unconscious any day of the week."

A slow smile creased the corners of her closed eyes, before they opened in a dazed stare. She was an awesome sight first thing in the morning. Her tousled blonde hair and her half open come-to-bed eyes, along with her croaky sexy voice and her tongue that kept licking her lips made my dick hard. All of that added together made a pretty impressive sum and I just wanted to devour her.

Leaning in, I licked her lips with my tongue and kissed her softly on them, catching her bottom one between my teeth and tugging it gently. Chloe moaned and buried her face in my shoulder, protesting that she had to brush her teeth.

My hand slipped between her legs and I cupped her pussy. Sliding my middle finger along the seam, I could feel it being covered with her leaking juices.

"You have the most awesome pussy, Chloe. No...I have the most awesome pussy because it may be on your body, darlin', but from now on it's definitely mine."

Chloe grinned and wiggled a little, "Really? You're laying claim to it?"

Placing my other hand on her ass, I squeezed her cheek while inserting my middle finger inside her at the same time. Chloe's grin froze and her eyes widened, her eyelids became heavy and that pink tinge of lust clouded look replaced the clear sparkle that was normally there.

"Chloe, you can sit on it, wear it...you can even play with it, but at the end of the day when I'm horny and time permits and with your permission of course,

I'll take this wherever I want...or whenever you want."

Winking at her playfully because I knew I was being assertive about my claim on her. It was her body to do whatever she wanted with, and I knew that, but I wanted her to make no mistake about what I was saying, she was mine and I'd want her as often as she'd let me.

We spent the next ninety minutes in a vigorous sexual workout, then I showered and left Chloe to bathe while I made some calls. Johnny told me that Morgan had made a helluva scene when he explained that I wanted her removed from the cabin. At first she didn't believe him, but then Johnny showed her the text I sent and she was livid. I did feel bad about that, but she was a friend and Chloe was...well, I was in love with her.

The update on Kace was that he had gone to ground. All leads had gone stale. If he was around, he was using cash. We knew that he'd made a large withdrawal two days before Chloe's apartment was turned over and he'd boarded a flight from Miami to New York. Not being able to find him was frustrating the fuck out of me, because I knew that Chloe wouldn't fully relax until that was resolved.

Placing my cell phone into the back pocket of my dark jeans, I wandered over to the bank of windows in the cabin where Chloe was standing. It was the most beautiful morning...well, a rock star's morning at 11.56am, and my girl was wearing some lacy boy-short panties and the sight of her perfectly hard little ass was enough for me to nestle myself behind her and curl my arms around her waist. I stared out over the trees to the lake, which was a beautiful azure blue in the sunlight.

"So am I allowed out with you today?"

Swallowing hard, I knew I couldn't keep her cooped up in the cabin forever. "Are you up for the shit that's going to be coming your way about me?"

Chloe's body stiffened slightly, then it seemed to sag before she turned to face me.

"No. But I'll deal with it as it happens. I'm scared, Gibson. You have to know that, right? But I am more scared of Kace coming at me than I am of any of your crazy fans. That might sound weird but I don't know what they are capable of, but I do know what he is."

I pulled her to my chest and spoke with a quiet voice, "Chloe darlin', I got you. Nothing is ever going to happen to you while you are with me. Understand? Nothing and no one is going to hurt you if I have any say in the matter."

"I believe you, Gibson. I do. I feel that...that you want to protect me, but you can't be with me twenty four seven. What about when we're apart? What about when you are working or I want to go and see Ruby?"

"Ruby can come whenever you want her to, Chloe."

"Gibson, Ruby has a real job and bills to pay. Her students depend on her. She can't just drop everything because I want to see her. If we get together, the most likely scenario for that is for me to go to New York."

"Then Jerry or Johnny goes with you. I won't have

your safety compromised."

It wasn't hard to feel the vibe of how petrified she was about everything, and it made me fucking sick to think that she was in the position she was, with Kace, because of me.

"Tell you what, Chloe. Let's flush the bastard out. I might not be able to do much about the fans, but my security will take care of that. I'm getting you a couple of female bodyguards. Jerry and Johnny can hardly follow you into a ladies room, but I can do something about getting Kace to show up and we'll make sure he's out of the picture." Chloe smiled but swallowed hard and the nerves were clear on her face.

Standing back from her, I smacked her ass lightly and the noise made my dick twitch but now wasn't the time to pin her to the floor. Serious planning had to be done to catch that fuckwad of an ex-boyfriend of hers.

During our many little conversations about Kace, I had gleaned that he was a hot-shot sound engineer. Well fuck...I was a hot-shot rock star, so all I had to do was make the right project and draw him to me like a camel to whatever.

While Chloe was getting dressed, I rang Charlotte. Then I called Syd Jones the CEO at Zuul, the record company where we got our break. Ol' Syd and I had a rocky start to our friendship when he turned us down at his first scout outing but he came back and signed us six months later. M3rCy never looked back from that point.

Syd had his own personal studio...but it wasn't just a recording studio, it was a whole retreat with nine small houses set around a massive infinity pool complex and golf course. Boys and their toys.

Syd was mega wealthy, a billionaire entrepreneur and music mogul who made his money from shrewd property investments, football teams and for the past twenty years from the music industry.

Always cutting himself amazing deals, he had managed to hang on to some of the world's leading artists who made him the biggest bucks. Fortunately, we had branched away with our own label and were able to cut a deal on the second signing to be released after producing three more albums with him.

After spending forty minutes on the phone with Syd, he was sold on supporting me to get Chloe's life in order. Strange how he commented that it only takes one pussy to capture the imagination of a man and it sounded like I'd finally discovered that. Syd always knew just how to squeeze my balls from a distance.

Next call was another to Charlotte again, Syd gave me an idea. I never had the need to court publicity, but I figured it was time to take the bull by the horns and stand up for my girl and fight any fucker that got in my way.

By the time we were ready to leave Charlotte had set up two face to face interviews and a radio one to get us started. Explaining to Chloe that we were going on TV had her in meltdown. Jerry laughed out loud at her reaction when I told her in the car we were on the way to be interviewed by Matt Loder.

She had nothing to worry about. She looked incredible and I knew the cameraman would be as mesmerized as I was. Chloe was confused when we headed to a hotel suite instead of a television studio. I pointed out that everything was done digitally so we could be anywhere for the interview as long as we could hear Matt talking to us in a link up. We didn't need to be physically in the same room. The way things were edited made all the difference, and Chloe's relief was clear on her face.

Matt didn't pull any punches when it came to questioning what was different about Chloe to all the other girls I had been with and when he asked me, I was careful to keep my pose relaxed and smile affectionately toward Chloe. She made my heart swell because she was obviously very nervous but hid it very well.

"Hmm… well, I wasn't in love with any of those girls. I used to think that women were there to have fun with, until I met Chloe."

Matt shook his head and snickered.

"Gibson Barclay, I never thought I'd see the day when you felt that one girl was enough for you and you were publicly declaring your love for her." Turning to Chloe he asked, "Chloe, how does it feel to know your boyfriend is lusted after by most of the women on the planet? I mean, you are the envy of women the world over, doesn't it worry you that you're the one to put Gibson out of circulation?"

Chloe turned and looked confused for a moment, and I thought she was going to crumble. Then a slow smile curved at the edge of her lips and she crossed her slender legs and squeezed my hand in a don't-worry-I-got-this gesture.

"Wow Matt, good questions." Chloe looked as if she was considering for a second and then uncrossed her knee and turned to touch my cheek affectionately with her hand. "Mmm, let me see. To answer your first question, it feels...pretty awesome that my guy is adored by so many women. It means I have great taste in men. I mean, look at him. What's not to lust after? I know Gibson is pretty near perfect, so it's something I'd expect and I know I'm a pretty lucky lady for him to have chosen me.

"As for being the envy of women, well again, Gibson had to begin to settle down at some point. Lust is one thing, but his true fans ultimately want him to be happy, so they'll be glad he's found a girl that makes him that way."

Grinning up at me like a pro, Chloe had given him the perfect answer, which acknowledged my fans for supporting me, and sounding confident that I had chosen well. I knew as soon as I heard that first answer that we were going to be a pretty invincible couple, as far as the media were concerned.

CHAPTER 12

ANALYSIS

Chloe

Trying to come to terms with being Gibson Barclay's girl wasn't easy. In my head it all felt weirdly surreal. One minute we'd be talking like a regular couple, then he'd smile his sexy roguish smile that hinted wickedness was only a heartbeat away, and I'd be off fantasizing and fangirling about him for a good ten minutes at a time.

Every now and again I'd get this feeling like whoa! How did we get here? Am I really here? Then I'd look at him and he'd already be staring back at me with an expression on his face that made my heart squeeze. How did he pick me? I have to admit I'd never seen him smile so much since we'd been together. Don't get me wrong, he grinned a lot but it used to look kind of...salacious. Now though, he just looked happy.

"I know what you're thinking, Chloe."

Smirking, I raised my eyebrow and shook my head, confident that he'd never fathom the mixed up thoughts running through my mind. "Don't think so, Gibson...not this time."

"Uh huh, I think I do, darlin'." We were sitting side by side in the car on the way from the hotel to meet some people that Gibson wanted to introduce me to. Giving me his mega-watt smile with those perfect teeth and lips that I just wanted to bite and suck and press mine against all the time, I wasn't quite sure what I was thinking from that point on.

"Alright smart pants, what am I thinking?"

"You're thinking how did I get to fuck a rock star, then thinking what are we having for dinner, then thinking damn is this happening? You know how I know that?"

Damn, he was good. His guess was almost spot on.

Without conceding that was the case, I smirked, feeling pretty impressed at how intuitive he was. I kept my face passive and encouraged him to continue.

"Enlighten me."

"*How?*"

Looking at Gibson for clarity, I was puzzled at what he meant by 'how.'

"Think about it, Chloe. How did I find you? I mean, how did I get given *your* number? How many phone numbers are there out there? How did I manage to persuade you to give *me* a chance? How did you persuade yourself to take the risk with me? How am I going to keep you happy with all the shit that goes on in my daily life? So darlin'... 'how' is pretty important and I figure if you are feeling anything like I'm feeling for you, you'll be having a couple 'hows' of your own.

How is it that we're so different but so alike? As soon as I thought that I snickered again, because I had just thought of another 'how'.

"Don't analyze this thing between us, Chloe. Just be thankful. I'm so fucking thankful, I've become religious. Every time I look at you I can't help thinking divine intervention made Toby's PA send me the wrong number. I thank God I found you and the heavens for my chance with you. When I look at you I think, sweet Jesus you're my beautiful savior...my amazing timely angel. So you're kind of my new religion, Chloe."

Gibson smirked bashfully at his romantic, cheesy admission just as we pulled off the road and through some very imposing black steel security entrance gates, and although I was touched by what he just said, I became curious as to where we were going.

A dense tree lined road stretched for about half a mile with close circuit cameras scanning our every move from both sides of the road and I was curious as to where the hell we were going. Every so often I noticed spiked bars running across the road, like the kind I've seen in airport rental places to stop cars driving off the lot without permission by puncturing the tires, and the only thing that came to mind was whoever lived here took their safety pretty seriously.

Glancing back up at the sky, it was a grey afternoon in contrast to the beautiful morning. And the air was oppressive, there was a storm brewing by the look of the heavy black and grey clouds in the sky. Heavy splashes of rain spattered on the windshield just as we cleared the tree lined driveway and turned left, confused when I saw a derelict depository, a bank and an apartment block then a row of three houses with another three backing onto them.

The scene looked like a mocked up street— an abandoned street with no people. A plumber's van, a bus, an old UPS van, a station wagon and an SUV were parked strategically outside some of the buildings on both sides of the road.

"Gib, you want me to stay here or go deal with that other matter and have Johnny come back for you?"

Glancing at his heavy platinum wrist watch, Gibson looked thoughtful, then looked back at Jerry. "Send Johnny over, I want you to check in with Syd. We'll be done here by three and we'll eat at the venue. Can you call Charlotte to call ahead and tell them Chinese food." Gibson suddenly turned to look at me. "That alright with you, Chloe?"

Nodding in agreement, my gaze switched between the two of them, and wondering what was going on with Syd, because I thought they didn't work with Zuul Records any more.

"Why are we here, Gibson? Where are we? What are we doing here?"

"Protection, Chloe. I told you. We're here because Jerry and Johnny shortlisted some candidates to keep you safe. Charlotte arranged some interviews. You can't go to the restroom with Jerry in tow, and I figured that you'll want to see your parents and Ruby without me at some time or other. I mean, as much as

I want you with me all of the time, I know that's not possible, so I'm being pragmatic about it and just making sure you're going to be safe when you're not." Gibson saw the concern on my face and his eyes softened as he took my hand.

"I decided coming here would be the easier option. It was only a ten minute drive from the hotel and it would have taken longer to arrange for the candidates to come to us, with security checks and everything." Gibson had really been thinking things through and his aim was to make sure I felt confident in the role of his girlfriend.

Stepping out of the car onto the wet sand colored gravel driveway, my querying eyes scanned up the antiquated red brick building. Turning my head, I glanced back at the dilapidated buildings that looked even drearier for the rain; the shell of a ghost town stood there and I tried to take it all in as I digested what he was saying to me.

Turning back, I tipped my head and stared at the building in front of me. Arched, lead lined windows donned the upper level and rectangular ones at the bottom, all uniform and the twin block turrets at either end gave the building an imposing look. Intricate stone moldings ran up the sides of the massive black gloss painted double doors at the entrance hall situated in the center of the building.

Walking slowly inside, it smelt of cleaning products. Gibson held my hand and kissed my head, then pulled his head back to look at me. "This is the downside of being with me. I know it has to be daunting for you, Chloe, but you'll get used to having them close by. They'll become your friends.

At that moment, I wasn't sure that I wanted someone to come to the bathroom with me or have someone pick my friends for me, for that matter. Panic crept up from the depths of my belly and began to suffocate me, but Gibson instinctively knew I would be starting to freak out and slid his strong hand along my back and around my waist, pulling me close to his body.

"Trust me, Chloe. I got you, darlin', nothing bad is gonna happen to you. We're going to make sure of that."

The strong smell of wood polish distracted me as soon as we entered the grand hallway. Oak panelled walls and hardwood parquet flooring in a herringbone pattern stretched the length and width of the huge space. A wide staircase on the left hand side swept up and around at the top with a wrought iron banister railing running the length of the next floor to the other side of the hallway. An art deco chandelier hung from the center, which looked very incongruent given the very conservative paneled walls.

The clipped sound my stiletto heels made on the floor echoed even after I had stopped walking. The structure of the place felt cool and uninviting. The austere appearance gave me the feel of entering an institution of some kind.

Distant footsteps echoed in and became louder until we heard a door latch being sprung as one of the doors to our right creaked open and the door hinges squeaked, then a tall middle aged, military-type guy walked purposely towards us.

"Mr. Barclay. Good to meet you." A tight smile on his face, he regarded me briefly before introducing himself. "Terrance Blake at your service. Follow me, please." Spinning on his heel, he began walking back towards the door he'd just appeared from. Gibson and I made eye contact and he raised his eyebrow, smirked then shook his head in reaction before smiling wider as we walked behind him.

Ushering us through the door we realized this must be Terrance's office. A picture of him with a short brown-haired woman and an awkward looking teenager in braces donned his desk. Again, like the rest of the building we'd seen it was purely functional, but with a large cherry red Chesterfield sofa over on one side of the room.

As soon as we were seated Terrace gave us a file and told us that the first candidate was an Iraqi veteran and had worked security detail with al-Jaafari, the temporary Prime Minister selected directly after the fall of Saddam Hussein. Her file was pretty impressive and at thirty seven she had been in the military for twenty years before retiring earlier in the year. Her picture looked kind of intimidating.

"Brilliant career...too old." Gibson closed the file and placed it back on the large mahogany desk. "Chloe is going to clubs and events, we need someone that slots into her world and looks the part. I don't want it to be instantly recognizable who her bodyguard is. Don't get me wrong, thirty seven is no age, but ten years from now that woman's appearance will stand out in places like that. We want someone that's got longevity for Chloe. Trust is extremely important, so the less change in her circle the better."

Initially, I had thought he was being ageist and harsh, but when he explained the reason for dismissing such a heroine out of hand, I had to admit that it was a sound decision and there was no malice in it.

Terrance looked through a pile muttering to himself, I, j, k... then slipped the file that Gibson had given back in order and patted the pile square again. Gibson reached over and pulled the next buff card file from the smaller pile and began thumbing through with a bunched brow scanning the pages quickly. "Yup, we want to see this one." Placing the file back on the desk, he swiped the next and continued the process until he had two that we were going to meet.

Feeling more than a little bowled over by Gibson's assertiveness, I had to speak up or I felt I'd be in too deep to do it later. "Could you excuse us a minute please Terrance, I'd like to have a private word with Gibson?" Terrance pushed his chair back, stood and pushed it in again, smoothing the back of it before turning and leaving the room.

"What's wrong, Chloe?" Gibson stared at me with a concerned expression.

"If you are picking someone to be around me, don't you think it might be an idea if I had some input? Don't I get a say in what people I have to spend so much time with?"

Gibson tugged my hand and patted his thigh and I moved over and sat on his lap. Smiling softly in reassurance, he tucked my hair behind my ear. "Chloe, that's why you're here with me. This selection process...I know what I'm looking for." Leaning over, he tapped the first of the two files.

"This one—she's in, there's no negotiation on that. Right age, right appearance, right credentials. I don't care if you like her or not, she has all the skills we need to keep you safe."

"How do I know that, Gibson, if you haven't even discussed her with me?"

Swiping the file off the desk, he opened it and started reading aloud. "Emma Scott, twenty seven years old, six years military, decorated for active service, Intelligence Expeditionary Service medal, state kick boxing champion, Tae Kwon Do champion, platoon cross country champion, has rural surveillance and close surveillance training and looks fucking bad-ass enough to be your friend."

Gibson turned the file around and the four by two inch picture staring back at me was a sweet looking dark haired girl with huge green eyes and the sweetest smile. He was right, no one would ever think of her being my bodyguard. She could be one of the girls on a night out.

Trying to lighten the mood I asked, "So you get to pick this one. Is the second choice mine? Can I have a huge guy with a ripped body and bad-boy tattoos please?"

Gibson scowled and his face took on a dark look.

"You're having females, Chloe, I'm your ripped, tattooed bad-boy—the only guy taking care of my woman from now on is me. I watched that movie, 'The Bodyguard.' I'm taking no chances with a male living at close quarters with you."

Expecting to see a smirk after he said it, I was surprised to see him staring at me straight faced and I realized he was completely serious. Luckily, I managed to bite back a grin and was saved by a knock on the door interrupting us. Terrance Blake re-entered with a small female. Gibson stood and addressed her.

"Good afternoon, Lois. Take a seat, we'll be with you in a moment."

Turning to me, he raised an eyebrow. "Are we done with the discussion? Are you going to trust me to know what's right for you, darlin'?"

Nodding yes, I figured that if something came up during the next hour with them, I'd be confident enough to put my ten cents worth in if I felt it necessary.

In fact, by the time we were done with the interviews and I'd met both women, I was feeling more positive about having two female companions. It was pretty tough being around the band when the only female to speak to was Tori.

My assessment of Tori hadn't changed since her comments toward me in regards to Gibson being a 'lot of man.' The way she tried to warn me off got my back up and I should thank her really, because she helped me make my mind up to take a chance on him.

Johnny turned up and the decision was made that

Emma and Lois were going to be my 'minders' for the duration. As we were leaving the room, Gibson asked to use the restroom. This prompted me to do the same. Terrance nodded at a door directly across from us.

"Both facilities are through there."

Gibson took my hand and I was conscious of how much noise my heels were making, walking across the hallway with him. Smirking wickedly at me, he placed his mouth close to my ear and whispered, "Get you, attention-seeker."

Pulling back, he smirked wickedly then turned and pulled the black latch to open the door. Inside was a short corridor with both restrooms next to each other. I barely registered this before Gibson swung me around and pressed into me, kissing me with so much passion I was in no doubt he'd missed the closeness we shared.

Peppering kisses down my neck, he was delivering a kiss every few words and I was giggling at how worked up he was.

"Fuck. Chloe. The noises. You made. Encouraging. Those women. Made me so horny. I nearly asked for a fuck break."

Chuckling close to my ear, he ran his warm hands up and into my hair at the side of my face. "After the gig tonight, you are going to be so worn smooth. Make sure you stock up on your energy with that Chinese food, because I won't be responsible if you pass out with what I have planned for you."

Shaking my head, I swatted his arm and pushed

him back by his chest. "Gibson Barclay, is that all you ever think about? Getting laid?"

Gibson gave me that sexy roguish grin he does and my heart fluttered in my chest at how attracted I was to him. Smirking he stated, "Here lately, pretty much yeah. I don't hear you complaining...screaming yes...complaining..." Winking cheekily at me, he turned and pushed the door for his restroom. "The difference now is that I have my own pussy instead of random women letting me borrow one."

My jaw dropped and his words shocked me to my core. Gibson left me standing with my mouth gaping at his crude comment. I should have been horrified, but I couldn't be mad at him when what he really meant was that he had me.

CHAPTER 13

TAGGED

Chloe

Johnny drove us to the airport in Michigan after we left the security facility. I was relieved that Gibson was taking me with him to his gig, because I was still unsure about Morgan and I wasn't convinced we'd seen the last of her after our stilted interactions and Gibson's dismissal. Actually, if truth be known, I think if it had been me I'd have been devastated to be cast aside like that.

One thing had not changed about Gibson in all this time, he never made excuses for his decisions, and that worried me for the future. What might happen if and when my time was up? Would it be Johnny or Jerry's job to protect him from any backlash?

Dark twisted thoughts began to seep into my mind. If Gibson decided to throw in the towel with me, from what I'd seen of him in the past, there would be no discussion around it. I knew he'd just sever the ties. End of the story. That revelation stonewalled me and I sat struggling with yet another topic to think about. The transfer between the car and the plane became a blur, my mind preoccupied with doubts again.

Everyone expected me to be confident and ecstatic because I was Gibson Barclay's girlfriend. Women would kill to be able to say that. I knew having this label would carry a special status, especially in the world of music and the celebrity scene and even more so with Gibson Barclay's mega rock star status.

However, when everything was stripped back— the fame, his privilege, money and the excessive quirky lifestyle—underneath all of that, Gibson was just a guy who was fallible and I was... just a girl who was a tiny bit broken and scared.

The evidence so far from Gibson seemed extremely positive, with him going to lengths to ensure my protection, the attentive way he cared for me and the fact he'd told me he loved me, it all said Gibson wanted me.

I knew I'd been on the fence because Kace's negative, manipulative ways were still causing me doubts and because of my past, I expected things to go wrong in my future. Everything about us seemed too good to be true, so it was no surprise I was having trouble convincing myself that this could pan out. Fans already hated me and we were starting our fledging relationship with the world's media watching our every move.

"What?" Gibson was tugging my jacket off my shoulders and I turned my head to look at him. I had been completely preoccupied.

"Huh?" Meeting Gibson's concerned eyes, I took in his frowning face full of concern and swallowed noisily.

"You're doing it again...thinking you can't do this, aren't you?" Gibson's mouth pulled into a line.

I had no idea how he did that—knew instinctively what was going on in my head. Gibson sat down in the seat next to me and buckled both my and then his belt, turned as best he could and gently teased my hair behind my ears with gentle fingers. Cradling the sides of my face in his hands, he gave me a sexy half smile.

"Chloe, you gotta fucking stop this. All the time your mind is toing and froing, you're talking yourself out of something so incredible that's happening between us. Have you ever thought I might just be feeling what you are feeling? That any second you are going to think what the fuck—I was happier without all the attention and just take off...that I'd never see you again? Don't you understand it would fucking kill me if you were to walk out of my life like that?"

Gibson drew in a deep breath and I saw the strain my constant indecision was having on him clearly for the first time. When he let out a shaky breath and stared pleadingly at me, something shifted in my head that lightened my heart and filled my insides with relief. His words had somehow penetrated my hardened shell and touched me deep inside. Something on a spiritual level seemed to radiate between the two of us. At that very second, Kace was history.

Only when I felt free did I realize that even after

everything that had happened between us, Kace had still managed to tuck himself into a corner of my aching heart. But when I saw what that was doing to Gibson any feelings I had for Kace, good and bad, were wiped out by a strong emotional ache of need in my body for Gibson.

Concerned grey eyes stared back at me with a dark, grim expression on his face and it made my heart bleed. Suddenly I knew without doubt, Gibson was the man I really cared about. Gibson Barclay was my future if I wanted it.

Did I want this? God...I wanted it more than I knew until that moment. Trusting any man was going to be difficult with what had happened in my life, but I had learned to deal with it day by day and hopefully Gibson would keep giving me reason to believe I could have a happy ever after with him.

"Thank you for taking care of me, Gibson. I'm sorry, I haven't been fair on you. You're right. Nothing that happened to me was your fault and nothing you did when you were a teenager should affect your life today. If you were some normal guy, I'd have had no idea about your past."

Gibson was staring intensely at me and sitting stock still, holding his breath. His lips pursed together, and I became aware of his body humming as he looked at me with the same dark worried look, but this time a glimmer of hope shone in the look he gave me.

"You know how you said you like me, Gibson? Well if I'm honest with myself, I really like you as well."

Gibson's serious expression relaxed and his

tongue flicked nervously between his lips before they curved up in a smile. His eye contact was softer, then seemed to twinkle with delight.

"Oh you do? Well hot damn girl, it sounds like I just might get lucky tonight...if I play my cards right." His roguish smile was damn sexy, but there was a mixture of emotions at play on his face. Then his smile dropped as his serious glance held my gaze for a second longer before looking down as if in thought.

Leaning closer, Gibson suddenly placed his lips against mine, shutting his eyes and I could hear him have difficulty swallowing. His normal reaction to something I did that pleased him would have been for his kiss to be passionate and consuming, but there was a reverence in this one that felt like he was relieved. Just as he moved back, his gruff voice was barely audible but he whispered huskily into my ear, "Thank you, darlin'."

Reacting out of character, Gibson straightened and sagged back in his seat, but reached out to clasp my fingers in his before closing his eyes and sitting silently. Initially, I thought he was going to sleep, but as I continued to watch him I could see he was thinking and taking time out from our interaction. It dawned on me that Gibson truly wanted my acceptance, and now that I'd given it to him, he didn't really know how to deal with it.

By the time we took off Gibson had fallen asleep and with one hand I awkwardly put the headphones on to listen to some music. Ronan Keating began to sing "When You Say Nothing At All" and I sat back to listen to the words.

When I told Gibson that I really liked him, the smile he gave me lit up his face and I could see how my words had touched him. Tears welled in my eyes and one overflowed, spilling down my cheek. Emotion grasped my heart as I swallowed hard, thinking that Gibson had been patient with me.

My hand gave a tight, involuntary squeeze against Gibson's and all the emotional feelings and thoughts I had been suppressing began to bubble up into my throat, but this time I was even more scared about being in a relationship with him. This was the very moment that all his thoughts, actions and protective caring ways made me fall in love with Gibson Barclay.

Luckily, Gibson slept for the rest of the journey while I tried to regain my composure. There was no doubt in my mind that I was getting stronger. On previous occasions when my emotions were tested I had become overly emotional, dissolving into a hot, teary mess but this time it was a quiet, dignified kind of release.

Arriving in Chicago, Gibson continued to be attentive as we transferred from the plane to the car and saying that we weren't going back to the cabin because he wanted to fly straight to Seattle after the concert. I was feeling fed up being told where I was going, but now wasn't the time to bring it up.

M3rCy was playing two dates there and he reasoned if we went straight there, we'd overlap with Toby Francis and his band Gametes who were playing there as well. Toby was Gibson's childhood friend and they had both hit the big time with their music talents, but had very different tastes in music.

I had met Toby when we spent time with his band and the rest of M3rCy when I 'won' the competition. Gibson had already told me their quality time together was very rare due to their schedules, so as soon he mentioned that Toby was playing in Seattle, I knew that he'd want to get there, rest up and save his energy for after the gig, so that they could meet.

My first reaction when he told me was stilted. I wasn't sure how I felt about facing Toby again. From the first time I met him, I could tell that his opinion had already formed and he thought I was just like all the other girls Gibson had been with. That made me cringe, because I could only imagine what he thought I was doing sexually to keep Gibson's attention and float his boat.

As soon as I thought the word 'boat' I smiled affectionately, feeling a little excited inside, because when I won the prize to meet Gibson, the day trip involved boats. Various events occurred where I was accident prone or uncoordinated, and each time Gibson told me I had an issue with boats. In fact, it was because of our candid sex session on a boat that I was even invited along on tour at all.

Settling back into the car seat, Gibson pulled me tight against him and kissed my head. No words, but then again, I had none of my own to offer him anyway. I was still coming to terms with my revelation about my feelings for him.

We traveled in a comfortable silence, but he was

still holding my hand in a firm grip and as his thumb lazily grazed back and forth over the skin on the back of my hand, his little gesture gave away his secret thoughts, because it told me his thoughts included me.

Once we arrived at the concert venue, Gibson dismissed Johnny to rest because he was flying us to Seattle later, and Jerry was taking the helm from him. The ultra-modern venue was much more comfortable than the other places we'd been so far it even had a dining space in the suite with a table where we could actually sit to eat, instead of the usual buffet type stuff that was laid out for us.

The aromatic smells of the Chinese food wafted out of the room before we entered it and tantalized my taste buds. My stomach instantly growled in protest, feeling deprived of sustenance. Neither Gibson nor I had had any lunch. On the plane I had kept my eyes closed, so with Gibson asleep and me seemingly so, we had been left uninterrupted.

Lennox beckoned us over as soon as we walked through the door, but Gibson put his hand up and turned to face me, gazing with furrowed brows.

"Not you, I know you're hungry. Your belly sounded like Victorian plumbing on the way over here." Inclining his head toward the dining space, he licked his lips and smiled affectionately at me. "Get started and I'll be with you as soon as Len tells me what's happening."

Cartons of noodles, special fried rice, chili beef, lemon chicken, tiger prawns and spring rolls made my stomach growl again at having to wait a second longer

149

to devour it. As soon as I eased my way into my seat at the thick smoked glass table, Tori came over with her teenage boy attitude and climbed up on the black leather chair across from me, sitting precariously on the backrest with her biker booted feet planted firmly on the seat.

God forgive me, but I was willing the dining chair to fall over or snap. I didn't want her hurt, just to knock herself out for ten minutes so that I could enjoy my food without getting indigestion. But with all the will in the world, I knew that wasn't going to happen. Gibson was out of earshot, had his back to me and was deep in conversation with Len, so Tori was taking full advantage of this.

"Still here? Girl, your pussy must do some amazing things for Gibson's dick if he's keeping you hanging around. I thought he'd have broken you by now."

I watched her drag her gaze exaggeratedly in an up and down scan of my body, then she continued, "Sooner or later he'll tire of you. Gibson's way too much of a bad boy to keep you for much longer. You're a pretty, shiny little plaything...a novelty, and we *all* know that *they never* last."

Tori's blunt and condescending assessment of what I was to Gibson made me furious, but I knew she mustn't get a rise out of me with her snarky comments. Looking her dead in the eye, I stared her down, tired of seeing the same stupid, smug smirk on her face. I almost hoped that she'd do something like sneer, or just anything but that. The one thing I was damned sure about, was that it would take a lot more than Tori's comments to make me back down.

My training at the hands of Kace made me an expert at hiding my feelings when I was under threat. This time I would at least be able to show this skill off for my own benefit.

"Well Tori, I guess you could be wrong this time. You see, Gibson moans— *a lot* when he's inside me. And...oh girl when he comes, he just keeps right on going. Did you know that...that he fucks himself hard again? And there is just something in that incredibly dirty mouth of his that is so sexy it sets my pussy swimming. I mean for a guy, he's pretty vocal and it almost makes me insane with lust.

"Let me tell you, I've never experienced anything more erotic than the guttural sounds that come out of that man when he comes." I left a pregnant pause for her to get her head around everything I was saying, until I saw her smirk quiver, then I delivered my death nail. "So I'm not sure, but maybe you're right, maybe my pussy does do amazing things but I guess you'd have to ask Gibson about that."

Tori wasn't looking half as confident and cocksure of herself by the time I delivered my informative and rapid response to the verbal slap she had tried to deliver me. "Oh, and Tori...what's the bet that I'll *still* be here and Gibson will *still* be sticking it to *me* long after you've gone?"

Staring her out, I couldn't believe I had actually said all of that to her. If someone had told me I'd say something that crude to another woman I'd have been mortified, but desperate times called for desperate measures. And to be frank, I couldn't have cared less what she thought about me after her earlier treatment anyway.

By the look on Tori's face, I could see that she hadn't finished with me, "What does it feel like to be a groupie, Chloe? To constantly wonder when the guy that's fucking you will suddenly get bored?"

Tori was changing tact and trying to humiliate me. Breathing steadily, I busied myself dishing food onto a plate, conscious not to react to her attempt to draw me into her manipulative argument. Picking up a fork, I glanced at it and I smirked, because I was sorely tempted to flick some food at her for her bitchy behavior.

However, I knew her game so I took a deep breath and didn't do it myself, because that's exactly what someone like her would have wanted. Instead, I shuffled the food around my plate with the fork and then made another conscious effort to stuff some food in my mouth to prevent me from rising to the bait. Chewing it slowly, I had no intention of responding until I had swallowed it down. All the while I was chewing, I was figuring out what to say.

Making Tori wait was making her agitated and I noticed her knee start to bounce as one heel rose off the chair and she bounced on the ball of her foot when she became even more impatient.

"I have no idea, Tori, I would have thought you'd have more of an idea what that feels like than me. Didn't you say that Gibson had done a 'one and done' on you before? Maybe it's you that needs to share the low-down on those feelings, because having had Gibson inside me many times now, it just keeps getting better and better for us. Plus, if you factor in that we've just come here fresh from doing media interviews today about being a couple, I sense that you fall into the 'groupie' category much more than me."

Tori looked as if she was still trying to formulate her retort, her mouth opening and closing like some fish out of water, when the door to the hospitality suite opened and Emma slipped into the room. After a quick reconnaissance of the situation, she strode over like a little dynamo in my direction.

"Hey, Chloe. Finally! I made it. Mmm," Emma gushed with a familiarity that made her seem as if we were close. Turning her nose up, Emma sniffed the culinary delights in front of me. Humming in appreciation, glancing warily at Tori, and I could see Emma was obviously assessing the scene. From where I was sitting, it was easy to see that Tori was most definitely ticked off about something. "Is that Chinese food? Is there any going spare?"

Tori stood up on the chair seat and tugged at the hem of her t-shirt, straightening it down over her hips, then stepped down onto the floor. I watched Tori regard Emma, sizing her up, but she began to address me.

"Chloe, didn't Gibson tell you...*band* members only? If you want to bring your... little friends to one of our gigs, ask Charlotte to leave tickets at the door, for fuck sake. This space backstage is where we relax."

Checking out Emma's non-reaction to her comment, the sneer was back on Tori's face. "It isn't a fucking café for your mates to drop by. You just don't get it, do you?"

The only reaction from Emma was a raised brow, but before she could speak, I placed my fork on the plate and cleared my throat which got Tori's attention away from her and back on me.

"Tori, this is my friend Emma. Get used to seeing her, because I intend on taking her everywhere with me from now on. You don't like it, I suggest you take that up with Gibson."

Emma snickered back at me, her eye contact reassuring me that I had done well, before she sat on the seat Tori had been standing on and shuffled it in toward the table.

"Guess the mistress of the house has spoken, Tori. Seems to me that I have nothing better to do with the rest of my life anyway, so travelling with a band and Chloe... well, it sounds like there are loads of fun times ahead. Count me in. You think we should invite Lois as well? I hear she's hysterical to have around."

Whatever else Emma did in the future was alright with me, because at that moment I could have kissed her when I saw Tori's back straighten and her chin draw back about three inches in reaction to Emma.

Tori strutted around the table and slapped her red chipped nail polished hand in front of Emma on the table. She leaned closer to Emma's face, but side on. My eye was drawn to Tori's t-shirt, which gaped at the neck. I could see all the way down to her navel.

Tori drew breath and spat her retort at Emma, "You have no fucking idea who you're talking to, do you?"

Emma's threw me a glance and a slow half smile curled the edges of her mouth, then she pushed her seat out, sagged back against it and crossed her leg at the knee, then I saw a deliberate eye roll for effect before she stared intensely at Tori.

"Actually, I do. Tori Sparks, 26, Born February 24th 1989, state of Michigan. Parents—Ida and Stan Sparks… no siblings. Moved to the Midwest at seven years old when your father began working for Steps Engineering Company. Education: Mustang High School graduate, didn't progress to college because a private benefactor paid for your place at the New England Conservatory of Music in Boston. Flunked out of there after two years to play in a mediocre indie band called 'Wintler'. The band folded after three male band members committed a felony on a minor in a motel room and went down for a long time.

"You then toured with various B-list bands as their sessional keyboard player. But you know all that. Anyway, criminal history: seventeen parking tickets unpaid in the Boston area alone. A fine for antisocial behavior… defecating in a public place, two assaults on females in the state of Massachusetts—you want me to continue?"

Tori's terrified face was a picture—her face distorted—eyes wild. "What the fuck is this? Where did you get all this information? Who the fuck, are you?"

Emma stood slowly and swiped a spring roll off the paper plate, took her time to inspect it, then bit into it. Lifting a napkin, she wiped her mouth while chewing, then swallowed noisily. After this she turned her head to look Tori square in the eye.

"I'm Emma. I thought you'd established that already. That's *who* I am. The *'what'* this is...well like I said, I'm Chloe's friend. You fuck with my friends, you fuck with me. Got me? How do I know about you? Well, that's my job...to know who is most likely to pose a threat to my friend here. Although, to be honest from what I've seen so far, Chloe is more than a match for you. However, I doubt you are smart enough and are probably too insular, up your own ass and self-important to have figured that out for yourself yet."

Emma's knowledge stunned me in regards to Tori, she'd only been hired this morning. Pushing my chair back, I stood up in time to see Gibson watching out of the corner of my eye. Turning to look at him, I smiled warmly at him and thought he was worth the aggravation of handling Tori. Gibson smiled warmly, looking a little shy at being caught watching me. It made my heart flutter that he was seeking me out from across the room.

That little smile was all the fuel I needed to deal with Tori and her bad-ass behavior. I strolled around the table and stood next to her. Then placed my hand on her shoulder, feeling about half as confident as I wanted to, but knowing I had to make an impact on her. Patting her shoulder, I said, "Like I said, Tori, it seems like Gibson wants me around so much that he's hired not one, but two bodyguards, to make sure I'm kept safe from spiteful bitches like you. So...Tori, suck up or pack up, because your little dude attitude is going to earn you a one-way ticket home if you can't change your ways. That's not me saying that by the way, that's my observations of how tired my boyfriend seems to be of the way you're treating me."

Tori's head hung and she looked defeated, but I wasn't stupid enough to think she'd roll over and it would be all downhill after our altercation. Winning the war one battle at a time was the only way with flaws like hers.

CHAPTER 14

LUST

Gibson

Something happened on the plane, I'm not sure what but I shut down and just couldn't keep looking at Chloe. I suppose I was afraid she'd say what I've been half expecting her to and what I didn't want to hear— that she couldn't stay. I've never wanted anyone as much as I wanted her.

Chloe was amazing during the media interviews and at the time I was convinced that we were really on track as a couple, but during the transfer back to the plane her insecurity was almost palpable.

When I heard people around me in the past mention they were feeling in emotional turmoil I used to think that feeling was for insecure, weak-willed and self-indulgent people, but since I met Chloe I've had these scattered emotions and thoughts for the first time in my life, so I think I'm finally able to relate to that.

When Chloe thanked me for taking care of her, it

came out of nowhere. I wasn't expecting it and no one has ever said anything like that to me before. I've been trying to put my finger on it but she gave me this look that's too hard to describe, but it made my heart squeeze tightly inside my chest and the love I felt for her almost paralyzed me.

When she said she really liked me, I felt that admission took a lot of guts from her. She was a survivor of an abusive relationship, so when Chloe admitting to having some feelings for me, I figured that was a massive step. The relief I felt at learning she was starting to warm to the idea of us was like someone had taken a ten ton weight off my chest and I was inhaling clean mountain air.

Instinct made me want to kiss her hungrily. I fought that feeling but I had no words to describe the emotions going on in my head, so I couldn't even tell her what her words did to me. When I allowed my lips to touch hers I became choked with my feelings, so I just broke away and whispered, "Thank you, darlin'."

Suddenly my eyes stung with tears and a lump form in my throat. I wasn't ever one for getting caught up in the moment but this wave of hope, fear and love just collided somewhere deep inside and I felt that I'd say or do something to ruin it. So I remained mute, slumping back in my seat with my eyes closed. I reached blindly for her hand and willed her to understand how much she meant to me.

With all the confused, unfamiliar emotional stuff came extreme tiredness. Anything emotional seemed to drain me and I could feel it closing me down, but not before Chloe squeezed my hand tightly.

Progress had been made today and I was determined to keep building on that. I knew that I couldn't make Chloe love me, but I was going to make it fucking difficult for her not to see how much she meant to me.

Drifting off to sleep was easier than being awake trying to connect the dots about us, and when I woke the mood between us had shifted and the closeness we shared at times was back.

Arriving at the venue with Chloe before M3rCy's performance felt less worrying than at previous performances, because I had confidence in the two security guards I'd just hired, so as of now Chloe would never be left alone and it would give her girls to confide in.

Living this life can be pretty freaky at times even when people love you. I had to protect Chloe, because I know some people are fanatical, so I knew there would be a lot of negativity directed at her because of her relationship with me.

Len caught my attention as soon as we walked through the dressing suite door. I was starving but I still had to be briefed on any issues prior to our performance before I could relax and eat. Persuading Chloe to go on ahead, I enjoyed watching her tight little ass in her skin tight black jeans head off in the direction of the Chinese food we had ordered.

During my discussion with Len, I was relieved to see the first of the two women I'd hired to take care of Chloe arrive. Emma slipped into the room quietly and smiled reassuringly at me, scanning the room at the same time, she surveyed the scene. Simon almost stood but I put my hand up and looked at each of the guys while I spoke.

"It's okay that's Emma she's with Chloe." Simon raised an eyebrow because she was just his type and I smirked to myself but then scowled at him, because the last thing I needed was him fucking the hired help and taking her off her game of keeping my Chloe safe.

Following Emma's gaze I saw that she had connected with Chloe and watched Chloe's face as she smiled and looked relaxed in her acceptance of Emma and how important she would become to her. I exhaled heavily in relief, then realized I had been holding my breath for her reaction.

Len and I talked through some technical issues and a few other band related items that had crawled their way onto the agenda, and while he was talking I heard Tori's voice raised in aggression.

My immediate reaction was to get in there and chew Tori out and protect Chloe from her, but I fought that instinct because I had to see that Emma could do her job. I also knew that although Tori had a tongue like a whip and an attitude like shit, I knew for now she'd stop short of anything that got her booted from the band.

Chloe appeared to be unfazed by Tori's antics and looked like she was giving as good as she got, then when I saw Emma counting on her fingers, I moved a little closer and heard her delivering the low-down on Tori. After that my little Chloe wiped the floor with her ass, telling her that I wanted her around and that she should watch her mouth. Well...it was more 'wordy' than that but that's what it amounted to.

Watching Chloe defend herself like that made my heart swell, but it made me swell in the dick department as well. I loved the sassy side of Chloe. I was hungry for food, but watching that interaction made me hungry for her.

"Excuse me ladies, but I need a little private time with my girl here. Standing over there watching her eat has made me a hungry man." Winking, I slid my arm around her waist and drew her flush against me.

"You need to eat, Gibson, you haven't eaten since this morning."

Holding her slightly away from me, I smirked knowingly. "Exactly, Chloe. Let's go." Grabbing her hand, I tugged her back into my chest then tucked her into my side and strode towards the door.

Chloe looked flustered and her cheeks became heated, but that wasn't the only thing. As mortified as she was by my comments, I could tell that I had turned her on. Chloe's eyes were suddenly cloudy with lust and she looked absolutely fucking ravishing, as she bit her lip in anticipation of what I might do to her. Most tellingly, she didn't protest at all.

I had noticed Emma's what-the-hell expression, but she didn't move and I figured she knew exactly what I meant, because she bit back a grin, right before I pulled Chloe out of the door and back along the corridor, towards the stage. My immediate thought about Emma was that she'd do well taking care of

Chloe. She had read the situation and knew when to stand down. Chloe was mine, and no one could take care of her like I could when I was around.

As we headed backstage, I swung Chloe around and pushed hard against the wall, my body immediately following to pin her in place with her hands above her head. My mouth was devouring hers. My dick was straining long and hard against her belly, the contours of it defined through my jeans. I dipped and spread my legs so that they were either side of hers and tilted my hips until my straining dick was level with her pubic bone.

Chloe surprised me by pulling my t-shirt up and breaking the kiss. She sucked on one of my nipples and when she did that— all bets were off. Glancing around for where I could offer her some privacy, I saw that the roadies had stacked the large musical instrument storage boxes against the wall just below the stage.

There were several, each feet long with metal edging with collapsible castors all next to one another. Making short work of things, I stacked three rows and turned two of the columns left and right, then drew one in so that I had created a bit of privacy and had effectively closed us off from people straying into our little scene. A scarf was tied to one of the handles, which was obviously a reminder to someone that there was something in that box they needed to find.

Smirking salaciously at Chloe, I began grinning at the not-here look of disbelief on her face and untied the scarf from the handle. "Nothing like a little bit of spontaneity darlin'. I've been waiting all fucking day to get at you and I'm starving." Chloe giggled and shook her head in disbelief, standing speechless. Reaching out, I grabbed the hem of her t-shirt and tugged it over her head. Gripping the soft cotton material in my hand, I lifted it to my face and inhaled her scent.

Turning her around I flipped the scarf over her head, tying it around her eyes and her posture stiffened. "Trust me, darlin'." As I whispered in her ear, Chloe's shoulders dropped and I could see that she was trying. In a low slow tone I murmured how much I loved her and how she made me feel. Watching her chest rise and fall I could see that her breathing was becoming more excited for the fact that her sight had been taken and her other senses were being honed.

Reaching for her bra, I unfastened it and turned her to face me, then lowered myself to eye level. My hands skimmed her sides until they reached and cupped both ample firm breasts in the palms of my hands. Chloe's breath hitched and her mouth parted slightly in response to my touch. Starting with her left breast, my tongue circled her erect nipple which had pebbled hard. Chloe's breath hitched again and I could see the anticipation right there on her body as her strong pulse rippled the skin on her belly.

When my mouth closed over the dark rosy bud I drew hard on it and Chloe's immediate reaction was to wince, and give a breathy gasp, "Ah," followed by a soft moan from the back of her throat at the pleasure and pain sensation I had stirred in her.

"Fuck." Grating my teeth lightly on her nipple

earned me another soft moan.

"Ohh, God, more," she muttered, before I sucked again. All the while I was playing with her right nipple, tweaking and rolling it between my fingers. Chloe gasped again, this time her fingers reached out blindly to tangle in my hair as she tugged me gently toward her.

Running my arm the length of her spine, I leaned her back onto one of the metal containers and grinned when she winced at the icy steel under her bare skin. Chloe was giving me her trust lying silently blindfolded in the middle of chaos backstage. The noise of people working around us hinted at the threat of being seen, and even though she was in that situation with me, she seemed to trust me to maintain her privacy. When my eyes reached the button on Chloe's jeans, I traced the edge of her waistband with both hands, running them from her hips until they met at the button. Chloe shivered under my touch and goose bumps erupted on her satiny skin. Using both hands, I flicked the button undone before my eyes sought her reaction. Chloe licked her lips but remained still.

Pulling at the waistband, I ticked her zipper down slowly, despite everything in my body screaming at me to fuck her hard and fast. With shaky fingers I teased the sides apart. Chloe was smirking at me so I placed a hand on her belly and watched her grin drop and her mouth open in a silent "Oh," of pleasure when I slipped a finger inside her white lacy panties and began to massage the hard nub of her clit.

My reaction to watching how she responded was

no different than if she had stroked my dick with her tongue. Swallowing hard at the sight of her, I growled in a primal response to the feel and sound of her.

"Fuck." The word tore from my throat and I was almost overwhelmed with the instinct to devour her. Glancing down because my dick ached, I could see it bulging hard against my pants. I adjusted and it stretched across from my midline all the way out to the curve of the pocket, still uncomfortable but a little less painful.

Restricted by her jeans, my hand couldn't move around as I wanted it to. It frustrated me and I lost patience, pulling Chloe's jeans down her legs to her ankles. I placed her ass on the metal and this time she screamed out, "Oh, Jesus," with the shock of the freezing box. Grinning at her startled reaction, I pushed her legs up towards her chest.

"Oh— is that too cold for you? Here, let me take care of that. I'll just hold them up here and keep your ass off the steel darlin'." I was smirking but she couldn't see me. She rewarded me with a wide smile and I bent to kiss her pussy, over her panties. Chloe moaned so fucking sweetly, the sound of it almost made me lose my shit altogether.

"Damn, Chloe, this ain't ever gonna get old, darlin'." Shaking my head, I held Chloe's legs and transferred them into one hand so that I had one free. Trailing my hand from her heel to the crease where her legs met, I traced near her pussy and she was *so* responsive, she trembled under my touch.

"Hmm, you like that? Am I tickling you, Chloe?

You're wriggling your ass, darlin'." She giggled and I could tell she loved when I was playful. Caressing her calves, first one and then the other, I was taking my time, massaging them softly, while talking to her like we had all the time in the world.

"You are so beautiful, Chloe. You have no idea how you make me feel, just being in the same room. You don't even have to do anything to set my heart racing."

Voices broke into our private time, footsteps drew nearer and Chloe stiffened but didn't move.

"Who the hell piled these up high like this? Come on, help me move them back before somebody gets injured." Recognizing the crew foreman's voice at the same time as the horror of being interrupted during our illicit sexual act almost freaked Chloe out. She stiffened, but by staying still, Chloe was trying to trust me to deal with it so I reacted quickly.

"Leave them. Disappear. *Now!*" The masterful command left the roadies in no doubt about what I was doing. Fortunately for me, they knew me well, so I knew there would be no arguments.

Without waiting to see if they were going to respond, I trailed my hand down from her pubic bone over the triangular thong panties to her entrance and I slipped my finger inside them, into her wet warm pussy. I had undoubtedly regained Chloe's full attention as her chest heaved when she inhaled sharply. Complete trust was gained from her in that few minutes, when her instinct should have been to get up and bolt.

"Damn, without me having to do a thing you're ready for me." Straightening up I reached for my belt buckle and glanced up at Chloe. Her chest was rising and falling rapidly. Short shallow breaths told me Chloe's level of arousal was rising. I made short work of opening the button down fly and shucked my jeans down past my knees. Without taking her legs out of her jeans, I knelt down and licked the length of her, then pulled the thong to the side, before burying my nose in her pussy. She smelt fucking awesome and I inhaled her deeply.

"Fuck, your scent and your warm wet pussy drives me insane with want, darlin', you know that?" Chloe's back arched and her pussy pushed even closer as she moaned again and licked her lips. Watching her in that blindfold was so fucking hot.

Moving to position myself in front of her, I leaned forward, stroked my thick aching dick down her entrance, then pushed myself deep inside her in one long steady gliding motion. I felt every inch inside of her stretch and hug me, as Chloe gasped loudly. I made a low involuntary animalistic grunt and muttered, "Fuck."

Smiling slowly, I couldn't keep the words inside me a moment longer. "I love you so fucking much, Chloe. You are my reason. I told you that." Since I'd told her I loved her. I wanted to say it to her all the time. I knew I loved her once I'd held her in my arms. Chloe was perfect for me. My perfect opposite that complemented me.

Chloe's legs were in the air, running up one side of

my body and resting on my shoulder, my hand holding them tightly in place while my other cradled the globe of her ass as I began to rock her world— and mine.

Taking Chloe in a public place like this should have felt wrong because I just wanted to protect her from the world, and after what happened on the boat I should have known better. But backstage, everyone was family and this was when my legacy worked for me, because everyone was so used to me getting hot and heavy after gigs that these days no one batted an eyelid.

Besides, I'd been holding the thought of doing this since we'd tangoed a little outside the restrooms at the security selection, and it left me feeling so horny my nuts had been squeezed like they were in a vice ever since. I had been permanently hard around Chloe all day. It was one of our hard and fast sessions, but the glow on Chloe's face after she came was amazing. Walking back toward the hospitality suite left me in no doubt that it had definitely worked for her as well as me.

CHAPTER 15

NEW FRIENDS

Chloe

Walking back toward the hospitality suite, Gibson squeezed my hand as if to say, "Are you okay?" I squeezed his back in response then he turned to face me with a grin on his face and a naughty twinkle in his eye. "Damn, Chloe, you're messing with my mind, girl. I'm finding it hard to stay on task with you around. What with all these crazy, intense feelings you're making me feel."

Gibson looked genuinely happy. Slipping my hand from his, I moved closer to hug him. His strong arm immediately held me in place next to his side then he kissed my head. "I love you, Chloe Jenner. Thank you for giving me a chance." A tight feeling squeezed my heart, because for all Gibson was a massive shining star and secure in his world, he wasn't totally confident about my feelings for him.

When we re-joined the others, I saw Lennox and Tori having a quiet conversation over on the far end of the room. Tori glanced over and scowled contemptuously at me before Lennox pulled her shirt sleeve to draw her attention back to him. Simon called Gibson over to see something on his tablet and the two of them erupted in spontaneous laughter.

Gibson was holding his stomach and laughing raucously, he was breathless and just managed to squeeze out, "Damn, can we hire that guy to do that when we're not playing? I like his thinking." Laughing helplessly again, Tori looked at them laughing raising an eyebrow.

"What are you laughing at?" She swaggered over in their direction and Gibson held his hand up still chuckling and struggling to talk between kinks in his laughter.

"Not for your eyes— it's a guy thing." Ignoring him, Tori snatched Simon's tablet from his hand and turned the screen around to look at it. Her face instantly changed and became angry. Sneering she slung the tablet back aggressively at Simon and shook her head.

"Fuck you two." Stamping furiously towards the door, she opened it, stepped out and banged it closed behind her. Emma and I looked at each other in a what-the-hell-was-that-about look, and Lennox picked the tablet up and burst out laughing while Simon, who was struggling to breathe and coughing with laughter, just continued to stare at us.

"Ace!" Lennox snorted throwing his head back and began laughing loudly. Seeing my puzzled face, he waved the tablet at me to take it while still chuckling.

Emma snuck up and looked over my shoulder and we creased up chuckling at the image. Some guy had sold his story about his trysts with Tori and there was a picture of her lying on a floor in a playroom somewhere, tied up with a ball-gag in her mouth and the caption, *"Proof: Tori Sanders Isn't Always Outspoken."*

Emma and I were still giggling by the time we went to get some air, allowing Gibson and the guys time to warm up for their gig. I was glad that Emma was so relaxed and easy to be around. She suggested she should tell me a little about herself and began to describe some of the operational duties and the carnage she had witnessed during her time as a soldier, but she was careful about how much she disclosed.

Confidentiality was something that I could see she was not going to compromise during this and it gave me a further sense of security. I knew from her file she had worked in a covert capacity during her deployment and stared back in awe as this brave petite hero, chatted a bit about her previous roles and her experience.

When it was my turn, my throat constricted because Kace was a very raw subject. Emma explained that she had to gain knowledge because Kace was a "known and specific risk," and fans and the media were in the general risk category. She then went into some speech about known and unknown risks and my eyes glazing over as I stared at her, lost.

What it came down to was, as long as she knew

what the risks were, she could make accurate risk assessments to minimize any harm. After she said this, I filled her in as objectively as I could about Kace's behavior and demeanor.

Tori had reappeared, behaving pretty subdued, by the time we re-joined the group. All the other band members were ignoring her and chatting about some football player who had pulled some amazing moves to help his team to victory.

Johnny appeared and waved for Emma to leave the room and I knew he and Jerry would be briefing her about what the dangers were to me. It brought home the feeling that I wasn't free to come and go as I pleased any more. I wasn't free with Kace either, but that was different kind of prison. *Prison?* Was that how I saw this? Would I ever be anything but Gibson's girlfriend if we were going to be together?

Johnny's voice broke into my thoughts. "All set, Gibson?"

Pushing up slowly from the sofa, Gibson rocked his head from side to side before his warm gaze met mine and he walked straight toward me. With each step, his sexy roguish grin grew on his face. When he reached me his hands slid around my waist and he pulled me flush against him. When he stared lovingly down at me, my heart flip-flopped in my chest and my pussy clenched with excitement at how attentive he was being.

"Gotta go to work, darlin'. Why don't you come and hang out with me and I'll say 'hi' when I'm not too busy." Leaning back to look up at him, I smirked wickedly and crooked my finger in the V of his black soft cotton t-shirt, pulling him down to talk in his ear. "So if I come and hang out at your work, what will you give me?"

Gibson smirked and kissed my nose lightly then bent to brush it with his. "Don't worry darlin', here…" Taking my hand, he stuffed it in his pocket and rubbed my hand along his semi-hard dick running up to his pocket. He whispered intimately to me, sounding very seductive, "I'll let you play with this when I get you home…and if you're really good I might just let you sit on it."

Pulling my hand out giggling, I shook my head as Gibson winked and began to chuckle heartily. "Your face is a picture, Chloe, but I'm deadly serious, darlin', so what do you say, are you coming?" Smirking knowingly at his double entendre, he raised his eyebrow as I felt my cheeks flush. I swear if he hadn't been about to go on stage in front of 27,000 people I'd have taken the initiative and dragged him off somewhere quiet again. Gibson oozed sex from every pore and I was completely captivated.

Holding the sides of my face, Gibson kissed me softly, then pulled back and turned to Lennox, Mick and Simon saying, "Let's do this." Clasping his fingers in mine we followed Johnny through the dark passageway with bare dull light bulbs. The corridor was full of nameless people in M3rCy t-shirts, the only sign they were part of their crew.

Glancing at the M3rCy band members as we followed behind Johnny, I couldn't help but notice how attractive they all were in comparison to the motley crew of guys they had organizing their sets and running things for them. Some had unruly hair in no particular style but longer than normal, unkempt and rough looking, but I figured that they worked so hard and touring was taxing, so getting groomed was probably a lower priority than getting sleep.

Emma was standing at a junction where two other corridors met the one we were coming along. Turning my head slightly, I saw Jerry was monitoring the other. We were ushered up the stairs and into the dark where we were surrounded by black drapes and an eerie silence, considering there were thousands of people waiting out in front of the stage.

Gibson's hot minty breath fanned across my face and into my ear, sending shivers of delight down my spine and making my nipples pebble with excitement. Squeezing my butt gently, he inhaled deeply while I took in the intoxicating smell of him. "See you at the end of my shift if not before."

I never saw him move away, it was pitch black at the side of the stage, I just felt a draft of cold air where Gibson had been standing. Instantly a hand landed in the center of my back and I almost jumped out of my skin until I heard Emma's voice.

"Sorry. We need to establish some way of you knowing that I'm here if this is how dark it will be every time they are going up to the stage. I can't see anything— I think I'm going to use a night sight from now on."

Shaking my head, I stood blinking into the

darkness. It sounded incredulous that someone was going to use a military-type aid to keep an eye on me. Chloe Jenner was at a rock concert because her boyfriend was a superstar.

When the band struck the first note I was startled again, no matter how expectant it was, it still shocked me to my core when the noise of their music disrupted the momentary silence right at the beginning of their set.

Emma placed a hand on my shoulder which calmed me. "Are you okay?" Turning to face her I swallowed at the same time as the lights suddenly glared and the sound blared from the amplifier to my right startling me, before I turned back to watch Gibson and the guys perform to the masses.

It was strange to see Gibson performing now that I knew him so intimately. Every time he licked his lips, ran his hand through his sweat soaked hair or wiped his face with his hand and I'd get a flashback to something sensual he did when we had been together at one time or another. Either that or I was becoming a sex addict, because everything he did seemed to lead my thoughts back to a memory of us doing something naughty in a bed, on a work counter, on the floor, against a door or in a car.

Staring out in awe at the wonderful, larger than life rock star on stage, it was hard to believe Gibson was the same man that wrapped me in his arms so tenderly and held me as if his life depended on it in bed each night. Gone were the gentle smiles and intense eyes he gives me when we are alone, replaced by a salacious sexy smile and lust-filled eyes as he strums the strings of his guitar and stares out at the crowd like he was watching porn. There was no doubt in my mind that Gibson got off on performing to an audience.

Emma leaned in towards my ear and shouted loudly, "I know it's not my place, but fuck! Your guy is totally dripping sex out there and every female in the stadium wants to get into those jeans of his." Swallowing hard, I wasn't sure how her comment went down with me when she was going to be around Gibson daily. As quick as her comment entered my head and I'd processed it, I turned to see a soft smile on her lips.

"Come on, Chloe. I'd rather say it to you than to someone else and you overhear it. I'd have to be blind, deaf and eighty-five years old for him not to affect me. Look at him." I had been and she was right. Gibson enthralled all women and most men. Once I'd got over the shock of Emma saying it to me, I knew that she was giving me exactly what I needed to trust her with my life—brutal honesty.

Pushing everything aside, I focused on watching Gibson and the rest of M3rCy rock the house with their amazing talent and was surprised when the lights dimmed to Gibson's signature set of blue spotlights and he pulled the strap of his acoustic guitar over his head.

Mick began to strum a riff and I instantly connected with the music. They played a cover by Ed Sheeran, "Thinking Out Loud," and I fell under

Gibson's spell, totally enchanted by his ability to surprise me with something so unexpected in front of 27,000 fans.

I swear you could hear a pin drop in the electric atmosphere of the massive stadium as every female in the place swooned at the sound of Gibson's gravelly, low timbre rock sound with that oh-so-sexy Southern twang, delivering one of the most romantic songs I'd ever heard.

Feeling privileged just to witness this unplugged live performance, I was stunned when he began to move around the stage in my direction. Lost completely to the lyrics and beautiful melody of the song, Gibson's eyes were closed and he looked like he was singing as much to himself as he was to his thousands of fascinated followers who were hanging on his every word.

Moving slowly toward our side of the stage, Gibson opened his eyes and they locked into mine. His serious face briefly registered me with a small grin and a shake of his head in a weirdly shy looking way, then he sang the lines of the song directly to me, *and they connected with me instantly because of how he found me again.*

Seeing the serious look on his face, I couldn't help but recognize the plea there as he continued to deliver the lines that were so significant to our story so far in the short time we'd been together.

I noticed him sing the word darlin' instead of darling, and was bewitched by the unpredictability of Gibson Barclay. His song choice was perfect for showing me what I meant to him. And the fact he was doing this with thousands of people staring at him while he made this declaration of love to me was entirely mind-blowing to think about. The emotion in his voice was undeniable, giving him a vulnerability that I'd never seen before.

As the words finished, Gibson walked off stage and headed straight toward me, while Mick played an instrumental which sounded hauntingly beautiful. Placing his sweaty forehead on mine, he stared passionately into my wide eyes then angled it to kiss me tenderly. Breaking the kiss he said, "Tell me what else to do to prove how I feel for you, Chloe."

My heart swelled, filling my chest to capacity and was thudding in a weird uneven beat as tears stung at the back of my blurry eyes. The lump in my throat was rendering me speechless and I knew if I managed to get a sound out of it, the sobs would quickly follow.

Laying his heart on the line in that very public interaction had taken about two minutes between us, but its effect left indescribable feelings bubbling away inside my stomach. The way he delivered those lyrics had felt completely unhurried, like it had been taking place in slow motion. As quick as he was there with me, he was gone.

Rapturous applause erupted to fever pitch when the last note sounded, the tension in the house completely broken. It's a wonder it was still standing, because metaphorically speaking Gibson just brought it down with his ingenuity and exceptional candor.

Speechless, I was impressed with Gibson's

strength of character and self-assured confidence which allowed him to take an unimaginable risk of upsetting his following to declare his love for me and I hadn't even been able to voice mine back to him yet.

In the middle of a stadium full of people at a rock concert, I definitely had a new found respect for Gibson. How he had been able to sing with such depth of emotion, pouring his heart and soul into it, and to feel the words of a song like that one minute and then run and jump about on stage like he was afterward, I had no idea. Gibson was too complex a man for me to even begin to fathom.

CHAPTER 16

RAW DATA

Gibson

Len stalked his way around his drum kit and came toward me grinning. "Way too fucking romantic for a rock star, Gib, but whatever Chloe's got dude, I definitely want some. The jury is still out on whether I prefer the pussy-whipped version of Gibson Barclay or the ride-every-pussy one."

Snickering at Len, I was determined not to get pissed at him because I knew all he wanted was for me to be happy, and with Chloe I was climbing that scale. The only worries I had were making her feel secure and convincing her to believe that what I was offering her was the real deal. I also knew there were some big tests coming with that as well. Chloe still had to experience the life of a rock star at close quarters and I was all out of time for protecting her from that.

My heart almost burst out of my chest when I ran off the stage and Chloe stepped forward, instantly wrapping her arms around my neck. I was soaking in sweat, but there was no hesitation about holding me close to her. The softness of her small soft finger tips grazing on the nape of my neck felt awesome.

I was as horny as hell and still buzzing from the energy the crowd injected into me, just smelling her sweet womanly scent made my dick ache. I couldn't resist licking the silky skin on her neck and was rewarded by the sexiest erotic groan, before she leaned back abruptly to look at me.

"Hard day at the office, honey? What would you say to a shower and some downtime?"

Chloe's face beamed up at me and the wicked little twinkle in her eye and upward curve of her lips showed me she had a little sexual appetite of her own going on. I stroked her nose playfully with mine and said, "It's a date, two hours max and we're out of here."

I have to admit, I was nervous about what was coming next. Since Chloe had been on tour with me, she'd been sheltered thus far from the rawness of the lifestyle I had before, but the guys were all single and she was about to be exposed to the seedier side of being in a rock band.

Wishing I'd had longer to prepare her for what she was about to see, I knew that if we were going to do this, Chloe would have to be able to handle herself and as much as I wanted to protect her from all the excess and bitching that went on, I knew I couldn't. It was time for us to sink or swim as a couple and I just hoped I'd done enough to show her that she was it for me. Nothing else mattered.

Should I have warned her? If I 'd warned her, she'd have been second guessing me and I'd   have got frustrated with her, so I figured I'd just play things by ear and get her out of the after- party as quickly as I could.

Desperate for a shower, I gathered my stuff and left Chloe in the hospitality area with Emma, Jerry and some of our public relations team. I had a job to do and, although I was worried about her, she had to learn the ropes to survive.

So far, she hadn't been exposed to my fans much or the negative vibe that would undoubtedly surround her while we were getting established, but there was feedback all the time from people who monitored the media. Negative tweets were the worst, and I thanked God that Chloe wasn't on Twitter.

By the time I had showered there must have been fifty people in the hospitality area. Erica, Dana and Zandra, three of the regular groupies in Chicago, were busy with Lennon and Mick, while Simon was talking to Chloe. It felt good that one of the guys had my back, but the fact that it was Simon gave me a little pang of jealousy. If anyone could give me a run for my money with women, it was him.

Simon might well have been looking out for himself, because I saw the way his wandering eyes were ticking appreciatively over Chloe, and the salacious smirk he had on his face said he was having some kinky thoughts. He and I were going to have words about that. Grabbing a can of soda, I strode over towards them and slid in between them, my lips connecting with Chloe's. Kissing her passionately, I walked backwards, pushing her away from him.

When her ass hit an armchair and her body began to arch, I dropped the soda can and wrapped my arms around her, keeping her in place until I'd finished tasting her. By the time I broke the kiss she was so breathless, I grinned wickedly at how affected she was by my unexpected seduction. Chloe looked a hot mess. From the cheers that erupted from the guys in the room, I knew we'd given them a show, but there was no doubt in those guys' minds, that Chloe was mine.

Quickly scanning around the room there were eight groupies that I knew, five I'd fucked and three I wanted nothing to do with. Bad form when I was trying to impress a girl who'd only had two men in her life. Still, that was before Chloe and she was definitely keeping my interest despite her limited knowledge about sex. Being with her and inside her was different, it wasn't at all about being extreme and getting off and I was still getting to grips with this new concept.

Charlotte turned up and I could see she meant business when she pulled that ugly blue leather bound organizer out of that oversized Louis Vuitton bag of hers. "Evening, Gibson, I have a few things I need you to sign off on and there are radio competition prize winners and VIP ticket holders to meet."

Again, I was pulled in the opposite direction from Chloe and for about half an hour I wasn't even able to be in the same room as her. I should have been attentive, talking to the fans and asking them questions to put them at their ease, but all I could think about was Chloe in a room full of women that I'd boned and the thought of what might be going on scared me half to death. *What if they started challenging her like Tori had? Would Chloe have the stomach for it?*

"I told Zandra to tell the others to stay clear of Chloe." As usual Len had my back. Those words made most of my muscles from my shoulders to my knees sag in relief. Len clapped a hand on my shoulder in support because I never had to voice my worries to him, he was just always really perceptive to what I needed to hear. I knew there was going to be some bad shit happening at some point, but I would rather Chloe and I have the time to work some things out before that occurred.

"Johnny had an update on the 'fuckwad' that Chloe was with. I told him it could wait until tomorrow now. That particular issue needs to be handled in the right way, Gib. Promise me you won't lay a hand on him." Len was staring at me looking all concerned and shit, and I'd never fought with anyone, my smart mouth always whipped their asses before they even tried to throw a punch.

I'll admit to violent thoughts at the mention of Kace's name and my jaw ticked when I ground my teeth. Feeling it and doing something about it was different. I wasn't stupid enough to touch him because doing time for someone like him would only hurt Chloe more.

"Jeez, there you go again. Is there anyone in this world that believes that I can take care of things in a way that is palatable to everyone? Len, make no mistake, I will deal with this guy, and when I'm done with him his balls will be hangin' out to dry. That doesn't mean I'm gonna lay a finger on him. Watch me—I have better things planned for that fucker."

Len snickered and let the subject drop and we started shaking hands, signing t-shirts, posters and CD covers, then bid our fans goodnight before heading back to the hospitality room. My eyes roamed the room, searching for Chloe before the door was fully open. Spotting her over by the table in the other room where she had been eating earlier, I began to walk towards her.

I knew Tori hadn't been a problem for Chloe, because she had been with us. But Erica was a devious bitch and she was deep in conversation with Chloe. Erica had conned her way into my bed more than once with her wily charm and manipulative ways and she was a slut.

All that said— she was a very pretty looking woman with sleek dark brown hair cut in long layers, olive colored skin and huge brown eyes. Flaunting her sexuality and a real head turner, with her long slim frame dressed immaculately in rock chick style, fishnet stockings and six inch black patent stiletto shoes, she was most men's fantasy girl. Everyone liked Erica. Despite her manipulative ways she did have a great personality.

When Erica's eyes met mine, she smirked wickedly and instantly my heart sank to my feet. She'd been standing with one knee on a chair showing a hint of lacy garter and as soon as she noticed me, she slid her leg down off the chair, smoothed her pencil skirt down and sashayed toward me. Scowling darkly, I knew there was nothing I could do but react to whatever she said in a way that let Chloe know that I was not that guy anymore.

Reaching me, Erica invaded my body space by slapping her hands firmly on my ass and tugging me against her, so I took her by the shoulders and shoved her back at arms' length.

"What the fuck do you think you're doing, girl? Don't ever touch me like that again." My voice sounded aggressive and with hindsight my reaction only confirmed that I had something to hide, so I decided to be honest about it. "Chloe is my girl and you will do well to respect that. Whatever life was like backstage before she came on board is over, understand?"

Chloe looked hurt because my reaction told her that she had been one of my 'many'. Pushing past Erica, I began to make my way over to her but she turned and walked quickly leaving the room. I felt sick to my stomach that Erica was even there and Chloe felt humiliated because of who I was in the past. The one thing I was relieved about was that Emma had gone directly after Chloe, so I knew she had some support and Emma would be in constant contact with Jerry, so Chloe was covered.

With Chloe out of the room I could let my guard down with Erica, so I turned my attention to her and I didn't care who else was there. I thought I might as well address all of them at the same time and get it over with.

"Right. What the fuck was that?" Pointing at Erica. "You...*don't* come back. Anyone else want to out me for fucking them?" Holding my hands out, I could see the others drop their heads because they were smart enough to know that I meant business. Pointing at the door I stated, "That girl is my life. Whatever I did in the past is in the past. She's *everything* to me. If you saw the way I laid it out during the gig out there earlier, you'd fucking know that by now.

"Anyone fucks with my chances with her, I will end them, you all get me? As for you Tori, I saw the stunt you tried to pull earlier, and I nearly pissed my pants at how it backfired on you. Just because Chloe's quiet doesn't mean she's a pushover. M3rCy has eleven gigs left and I'm clarifying for everyone in the room here. Tori, I have never fucked you and never will, understand? So drop the spurned chick routine, you were never in the running. To be frank, I'm at the point where I'm ready to change the set and push your sorry ass out the door. You want to stay? Then I want no more of your bitching around Chloe. I mean it— one more word and you'll find my boot in your ass and the exit door slamming shut."

Just as I was finishing my rant, Chloe pushed the door open and strode over to me and for a moment I thought she was going to slap me, but she pushed me down on the black leather sofa and straddled me, taking my head in her hands and started speaking to the women in the room but looking at me.

"So what Gibson said? All of you better believe it, because I intend to keep this man happy for a long time to come." Bending forward, Chloe grinned naughtily, then ran her tongue sensually along the seam of my mouth and I instantly put my hand on the back of her head to take her in a hungry kiss.

With my kiss Chloe got bolder and from the heated look in her eyes, I could see what was happening was empowering her sexually. Breaking the kiss, she grinned and wiggled her crotch back and forward on my hard dick, but when my hands ran up her sides she was shaking slightly, the only sign that she was nervous about what she was doing. She was giving them a clear message, who was I to put a damper on that?

Sliding my hands under her ass, I edged forward and stood up with her, her knees next to my chest as I headed towards the door. "Excuse us but we have a plane to catch, enjoy your party, Len...see you and the guys in Seattle tomorrow at the gig."

Chloe clung to me with her face buried in my neck as I began walking down the dim blood- red painted corridor toward the exit. Emma pushed open the exit door and gave me the thumbs-up signal and Jerry was waiting immediately outside in the car.

Placing Chloe on her feet, I still held her close with my arm wrapped around her lower back. Chloe stared up at me and I sensed she had a multitude of feelings running through her head because her face was kinda registering partial expressions that morphed into other ones. I felt she was trying to shut out feelings Erica and

Tori had caused her, just because I had chosen her to be with. Before I let her go, I had to say what was on my mind.

"Chloe, I'm sorry, that must have been so fucking hard for you to deal with. If I had known this day would come I'd have never been with any of those women. The last thing I ever want is to humiliate you. I love you, and I feel fiercely protective of you, but I'm sorry to say that this won't be the last time something like that happens. You just gotta look at it like all those women were practicing runs for the time when I got to be with you." I smirked after I said it because it sounded conceited.

Chloe stared intensely at me and worked a swallow, biting her lip for a second then she took a deep breath, "It's not your fault, Gibson. What you did before we were together isn't up for debate any more, I just need to toughen up and deal with the negative side of loving you."

My heart stopped, then beat wildly in my chest at the word 'love' escaping that sweet mouth of hers. With wide eyes I asked, "You think you can do that, Chloe? Love me?" Chloe's hand tightened on my t-shirt and she twisted it in her fist, looking down at what she was doing before looking back up at me, her eyes brimming with tears. Working another swallow she was overcome with emotion and I just stood there holding her, while she struggled to compose herself enough to speak.

Clearing her throat she swallowed noisily again, then let go of my t-shirt and spoke softly, her voice cracking with emotion.

"Gibson, it's been no time at all, yet you already own my heart. Every waking thought I have you are in it or a consideration in it. You made me love you, how could I not? I'm scared Gibson, but I know that you control how my heart beats. It beats wildly when you are near and aches when you're not. When you are happy, I am happy. When you feel, I feel. Trust is hard for me and I'm trying with that, but I can't deny the feelings I have for you that are overwhelming me. You make me feel safe. You make me feel fearless to deal with the negative vibes that people give me just for being with you.

"I can accept your past Gibson, because it is what it is. You never did any of that to hurt anyone, but I think you ended up hurting yourself because you want to commit to me now and everything that's happened before continues to follow you. I love you so much it hurts, but I'm scared of what that means for me in the long term."

Chloe admitting her feelings and how vulnerable it made her suddenly became a huge responsibility for me. I prayed to God that I didn't fuck this up with her after she disclosed that she loved me. Telling me wasn't done in a romantic setting or during a time when something spontaneous might have fallen out of her mouth, but to me it was the best way possible, because of what she'd just witnessed and the shit she'd dealt with during the day. So for me she'd given me the normality I'd been desperately seeking and in my line of work that was a rarity.

CHAPTER 17

PEP TALK

Chloe

Tired of condescending remarks from beautiful-on-the-outside-ugly-on-the-inside women, I couldn't wait until it was time for us to leave M3rCy's after party. Tori had been a bitch but the final straw for me was when a groupie called Erica made a play for Gibson right in front of me. Gibson's guilty look told me she was someone that may give something away he didn't want to have to admit to. From how he reacted to her come-on it was blatantly obvious that he'd slept with her and was embarrassed about it. Either that, or he was worried that it would embarrass me. It did.

Everything that happened today suddenly caught up with me and I felt like I was suffocating again and when I saw the pained pitying look he was giving me, it all became too much. I just had to get out of there so I stupidly ran.

"Chloe, wait." Emma was running behind me and

caught me by my arm just as I was hitting the exit bar on the door leading out to an alleyway. Jerry began to step forward and the car was waiting, but Emma put her hand up in an I-got-this motion and Jerry turned and walked slowly to the front of the car, giving me the space and privacy I needed at that moment.

"Well, Chloe? What are you doing? You are just gonna hand the hottest piece of man candy I've ever seen to a whore? Because if that's your fight girl— I'd hate to see what you're like when you roll over." Emma's words incited fury in my belly like I've never felt before and I almost tore her off a strip for implying that I was weak. Especially in light of how hard I was fighting all those kind of feelings after how Kace had treated me, but that's exactly what had just happened.

"You don't know me yet, Chloe but trust me you got to go back in there because if you don't, every groupie in every town will do what Erica did. Want to know what I saw in there?" Emma's eyes searched my face waiting for me to give her the go ahead but whether I'd agreed or not, I knew she'd give me her opinion anyway.

"Gibson was mortified at her approach, Chloe. I read remorse on his face as plain as day. You know what I saw in her? Erica was someone desperate to rock the boat, but someone who was inconsequential to the man that loves you, Chloe. And, as I've stuck my neck out I may as well finish, if you don't get back in there and claim him, you'll humiliate him. As far as I can see that guy is completely knocked out by you, but is somehow still standing. You may not be aware of this, but he can't take his eyes off you. I'd give my life for a guy who looked at me like that. Gibson has this...hypervigilance around you, and a constant need to check that you are still there."

Emma was giving me a great piece of advice, even if I wasn't feeling it. I knew she was right. I had to show Gibson and those women my intentions toward him if we were going to get a smooth run at this.

So I walked back in there with renewed determination and shoved him down on the sofa, climbed over to straddle him and Gibson seemed delighted I had come back. Shortly after that, Gibson lifted me and carried me out of the room with my arms wrapped around his neck, him cradling my ass in his hands. We'd just given everyone in the room a public display of affection, but it was more than that. All those groupies knew that Gibson was mine and that I was willing to fight for him.

Just before we got into the car, Gibson and I had a moment and I admitted I needed to toughen up, then told him that his past is the negative side of loving him. Immediately Gibson jumped on this and asked if I thought I'd learn to love him. It wasn't the way I wanted to tell him but I couldn't hold it back any more, so I told him.

Staring wide eyed with a stunned look on his face, Gibson froze for a moment, then he looked thrilled at my admission, his face brightening as soon as he'd gotten over the shock of my declaration. When I slid toward him along the back seat of the car, he squeezed up close beside me and kissed me so passionately, I was worried he was going to try to get me naked for a couple of minutes.

The flight from Chicago to Seattle took about four hours and we slept for most of it. Slowly, I was beginning to know the man behind the rock star. True to his word, he passed out after being on stage and slept like a baby almost all of the way there.

Every time Gibson told me I was beautiful or called me darlin', my heart skipped a beat. Every time he held my hand, my heart swelled in my chest, and every time he told me he loved me it felt like I was going to burst. Everything Gibson had said and done since we'd first spoken on the phone had made me fall in love with him.

The transfer took no time and we had the now customary kitchen back door welcome on the way to the penthouse. Since we got in the car, I had been feeling queasy, but I thought it was because it was 5.30am and I was just overtired. The previous twenty hours had been packed with some big emotional events.

Gibson became very attentive helping me undress, giving me water and something to settle my stomach and it was as much as I could manage just to get myself into bed. Snuggling up behind me he was very careful not to put pressure on my belly and just laid his hand on my thigh. Kissing the back of my neck he whispered, "You don't think you could be pregnant do you?"

Stiffening instantly, I wondered what was going through his mind with his thought. Was he horrified?

Did he even want children? That particular subject hadn't even been a distant consideration in everything between us. I was feeling too sick to panic about that, but knew that I had already made sure that I'd never have a child by Kace, by having a Depo-Provera shot. My last one had been only seven weeks ago and I normally had it every three months, so I knew I should have the birth control aspect covered. "No." I didn't have the energy to explain, because I was fighting the nauseous feelings inside.

Kissing the back of my neck, Gibson leaned forward and murmured to me. "Darlin', whatever it is, know I love you, know that I never want you to be sick and know that I am with you for the long haul if you'll have me."

Squeezing my thigh for effect at the same time as I felt his hot breath hit the back of my neck, I felt reassured that if there were an unexpected pregnancy, he wouldn't be staying with me for the sake of the child. The normal reaction to something that profound would have been for me to turn and face him but I was too exhausted and felt so sick, I was scared to move.

Somehow, I managed to drift off to sleep, only to wake two hours later with the overwhelming feeling that I was going to vomit. Gibson was startled awake by me tearing out of bed and trying to make it the bathroom before I vomited everywhere so violently it made my head swim.

Gibson came rushing into the bathroom after me, grabbed a wash cloth and ran it under the tap. My body convulsed as I heaved, spewing the contents of my guts while Gibson placed the cold flannel cloth at the back of my neck and scooped my hair out of the way and held it. "I got you, Chloe." His soothing tone did nothing to stop the continuous retching and I wasn't even embarrassed about him seeing me that way.

After twenty minutes, Gibson turned the faucet on in the bath and steam filled the bathroom. I had stopped vomiting but my stomach ached and my guts growled sensitively, like there may be more to come. Already naked, Gibson placed me into the bath and he began wiping my face, stopping periodically to kiss the top of my head. "Damn, Chloe. That was like the vomiting scene from "The Exorcist."

Barely raising a half smile as Gibson helped me out of the bath. I was feeling so unwell I wasn't sure I was going to make it back into bed. Gibson wrapped me in a towel, then swiped his phone off the nightstand and called the hotel reception. "We need a doctor and our bathroom cleaned." Throwing the phone on the bed, he came over and began to rub me dry. "Come on darlin', let's get you back into bed, you look terrible."

Suddenly I was shivering with shock and couldn't get warm. Gibson dressed me in a t-shirt of his and lay down behind me and wrapped his arms around me. "I got you, darlin', I just want you checked out. The doctor will be here soon." Just after he said it, there was a knock on the door and Gibson pulled away from me. Wrapping a bath robe around him he went and answered the door.

After checking on me, Dr. Grant decided I had contracted food poisoning. A shot of anti- sickness medication made me feel less nauseous and he also left us some sachets of mineral salts to add to water and took a swab from my mouth for culture. The bathroom was being cleaned while the doctor was with me. There was a brief discussion about intravenous fluids, but Gibson was quick to tell the doc he'd support me to drink more and by the time the doctor left I was feeling less shocked and more able to settle to sleep.

Gibson's low voice woke me and I heard him say, "I'm not leaving her." Sitting up, I pushed myself back against the headboard and saw he was on the phone. "How are you feeling, darlin'?" Really I shouldn't have sat up because I was feeling nauseous again. "Not great."

Gibson frowned in concern. "I'm just talking to Johnny, I'm staying here with you. They'll just have to cancel the gig."

"Don't be ridiculous, Gibson, I have food poisoning. I'm not dying." Gibson looked worried, a deep crease forming between his brow.

Gibson sat on the bed and touched my cheek, "You're sick. I'm not leaving you here and going to work."

"And I am not allowing you to disappoint 30,000 people because of a touch of food poisoning. Just because you have the luxury of working for yourself, Gibson, doesn't mean you can't consider the bigger picture. I'm fine. Well I feel pretty crappy really, but I'll live. Go. Do your job, see Toby and have fun. I'm happy to stay here with Emma. I'm a big girl and as touched as I am by your caring ways, to be honest, you'll just be in the way today."

Seeing the look of rejection Gibson gave me almost made me change my mind, so I spoke in a softer tone. "Gibson, you have no idea what your gesture means to me, but really...I'm tired...worn out from vomiting, I'm no company today. I just want to sleep. Please, it's only one day and I'm fine."

Staring at me for a few minutes, I could see the conflict on his face that was playing out inside his head. Eventually he huffed a heavy breath and nodded. "Okay, but Emma comes here and stays with you."

Gibson called Johnny back and told him he'd be ready to leave in a few minutes. When he bent down to kiss my cheek I realized he had showered and gotten ready to leave while I had been passed out. Taking my hand and squeezing it he said, "I'll be home as soon as the gig finishes." I shook my head no at him, because the whole reason we had traveled during the night was so that he got to catch up and spend time with Toby.

"No. I don't want that. Spend time with Toby, please have fun, you never get to see him and the last time you did, I got in the way of that. You work so hard, Gibson. Take the time with your friend then come home, I'll still be here."

My cell rang just as I was finishing talking and Emma's ID flashed on the screen. Swiping the screen, I answered and Gibson stood waiting to hear what was going on. Emma had been sick in the night as well, so as Gibson hadn't eaten any of the Chinese food and we had, we were able to narrow down what the cause of my sickness was. Emma said she had been feeling delicate but was just about to head up to our suite in a couple of minutes. I tried to make my voice sound lighter and said I was feeling a bit better for Gibson's benefit.

Gibson's face visibly relaxed when I told him that Emma was coming to the room so he kissed me again and said that he'd call me later. I told him not to in case I was asleep, just to enjoy his time with Toby and not make too much noise when he came home. Gibson gave me a half smile, swiped his wallet and phone from the room dresser and blew me another kiss. "Keep that bed warm and get well quickly, my dick's getting cold out here all by itself."

As soon as the door latch clicked I flopped back heavily against the deep pile of the soft pillows, sighing deeply. I wasn't feeling well at all but my great act had convinced Gibson to do what I knew he had to.

Soft tapping on the door signaled the arrival of Emma, so I slipped gingerly out of bed and pulled on the bathrobe that Gibson had discarded on the chair during the night when he got back into bed. Checking my face in the mirror, I had a slightly pale yellowish tint to my skin, so I pinched my cheeks and tucked my hair behind my ears before opening the door.

Paralyzed, my heart stopped beating in my chest. Kace's face met mine and before I could think, his hand quickly gripped my forearm, like a vice and he yanked me so hard that I came right off of my feet. He placed some kind of acidic-smelling cloth over my mouth and nose, I struggled but in my weakened state was no match for him and my muffled screams went unheard.

Kace grappled with me until his arm was wrapped around my waist and he was applying pressure like he was squeezing the life out of me. My senses became dimmer with every passing second and my lungs were constricting tightly as I fought for air, but with each deep gasp I was overcome with fumes until I slipped into blackness.

CHAPTER 18

JOB TO DO

Gibson

Leaving Chloe sucked. This is one of those times I wished I was just any ordinary John Doe with an ordinary job and could throw a sick day from work to stay home and take care of her. Then again, I'd probably still have to go anyway. At least she was in the capable hands of Emma. We landed on our feet with her, she has fitted in so well and yesterday she had Chloe's back from the moment she stepped in the room. I was relieved that Chloe seemed to like her.

Once Johnny was behind the wheel and we were heading to the gig, he filled me in on the plan so far, for drawing Kace out. Every time Johnny spoke about him he was kinda cagey and I knew he was worried that I'd do something deadly to him when I finally set eyes on the piece-of-shit-for-a-man. Trust me, the thought had crossed my mind on more than one occasion and I wanted more than anything to make him suffer the way he had made Chloe suffer, but being smarter than the average bear, I'd be more inventive about getting my pound of flesh.

"Promise I won't lay a finger on him, Johnny. When I flush him out I'm thinking more in terms of making him a social leper and publicly humiliating him in a, you'll-never-get-work-in-this-industry-again type of punishment. I don't want instant gratification because it would take a lot of effort to get that from someone like him after what he did to Chloe. No, I want that fucker to suffer for the rest of his life for what he did to my girl."

Johnny turned and grinned at me, his eyes flashing wide in surprise. "Damn, Gib. Remind me never to piss you off, because you know me so well you'd cut my dick off and feed it to me, huh?"

Snickering at Johnny, I shook my head and chuckled because the most important thing to him, apart from looking after me, was getting laid. Maybe that was the reason we'd got on so well. With that thought a flash of a memory came to me. A brief visual flash of Ruby's face and I'm sure she was being fucked hard. Nothing conclusive, but her head tilted upward, face flushed like she was in ecstasy. Her eyes were filled with lust and they were staring straight at me. I must have stopped laughing abruptly, because Johnny's head snapped around in my direction and then back at the road.

"What is it? What's wrong? Gib, you look like you've seen a ghost.

"Shaking my head again, there was no way I wanted to say what I had just seen out loud. That would make it real. I'd bagged Ruby and she was so cool about it around Chloe, that I was now questioning the quality of their friendship, because she had been encouraging Chloe's relationship with me. Did Chloe know already? Had they compared notes? If Chloe didn't know, did Ruby have ulterior motives for not saying anything to me?

"Fuck!" My heart was thumping with the shock of my revelation. Chloe wasn't the only one feeling sick. Maybe Toby was right. Maybe when Chloe knew the truth, she'd turn and walk away because at the end of the day, she wanted a normal life—free from drama and she'd never get that with me. After what happened yesterday with Erica, I had felt certain that Chloe was gone when she left the room, but she came back. Now the percentage had risen on the possibility of her deserting me if I came clean with Chloe about Ruby.

Johnny sighed heavily and swung into the back lot of the concert venue. "Spill."

Breathing deeply, I held it in. I lifted my hands and swept them nervously through my hair. Exhaling in an agonizingly slow controlled way, I turned to look Johnny square in the eye. Johnny's face registered a dark, worried response before he spoke, "Oh, boy. This is a biggie Gib, huh?"

Barely nodding, I struggled to find the words that used to fall out of my mouth like I was asking for a glass of water. "I fucked her, J."

Johnny stared confused by my change of subject because when we had been laughing prior to that we'd been talking about Kace. "Ruby...I knew I'd seen her before. I fucked her back in the day."

Johnny's initial response was mute, but his face displayed his dismay. At first I thought he was disappointed in me until he started to appease me. "Okay, that's a major fuck-up, but Chloe knows what you were like. It's Ruby she's going to be more disappointed with, acting all supportive and being her best friend an' all. She'll be hurt Gib, but she'll be more hurt with Ruby than you."

Something told me that it wouldn't be that easy. Chloe already had trust issues and I had been doing well on that score, but this was now a huge elephant in the room for me, and I was going to have to shove its ass out sooner or later.

For the first time in my life, I wasn't looking forward to spending time with Toby. The last thing I wanted to do was get involved in one of Gamete and M3rCy's parties, because they were wild. It was different before I had Chloe. Now though, it felt like I was missing an arm when she wasn't with me. It was one thing to have private feelings and another to maintain a public image so if people knew we were in the same place at the same time, you could bet your ass the media were on it.

Rehearsals went well, considering my mind was elsewhere and I was itching to ring Chloe, but she'd asked me not to and I almost asked Johnny to ring Emma to check up on her that way, but Chloe was right, I needed to focus on my job and let her rest.

Up on stage I relied on the crowd to lift my mood.

Performing never got old. Seeing the pleasure on all of the loyal fans' faces was always a pick-me-up. I performed a double acoustic session because that kind of moment is the unplugged, intimate moment when I get to truly connect with every single one of those people that have paid their hard earned money to keep me doing what I do.

Without a doubt, I have the utmost respect for all of them and during the first session it came to my mind that Chloe was correct in her assessment of my responsibility to them in the anonymous partnership we shared, and today was the first time I'd ever attempted to put anything else first.

My reward for the two ten minute injections of raw music was an eruption of rapturous cheers and whistles, along with a deafening roar of appreciation. The connection in the huge dark space filled to capacity was almost palpable. If nothing else, I hoped that each one of them took that away from our performance. It made my heart so full I could hardly expand my lungs to breathe.

Toby had been playing across town and had biked over to get to the venue for the encore. At the end of the last song, when I walked off the stage he jumped out from nowhere onto my back and practically frightened the shit out of myself and Johnny. "Fuck, Gib, your man here is getting old...I could have stuck a knife in you."

Jerry stepped forward and commented. "No chance of that Toby, I saw you getting all unnecessary in the pants department when I searched you before.

It's second nature for Johnny and me to do something your guys don't. *Everyone* gets searched apart from Chloe.

"Gib doesn't like it but we got his back make no mistake on that score. You only got to do that because I let it happen."

Smirking at Toby's surprised face, I started chuckling, "See Toby, it pays to employ sexual deviants. They'll do anything to cop a feel." Johnny gave Toby a salacious smirk and tweaked his nipple and Toby yelped and held his nipple snickering before thrusting his chest at him saying, "Fuck that was hot, do it again." Johnny gave him a dark stare and Jerry, Toby and I cracked up with laughter.

Toby had arranged a visit to a local nightclub where he knew two guys who managed it and although I was reluctant to go, once we got together I knew it had been far too long since we just hung out together and had some fun. Len was on form and already sizing up which lucky women would give his dick an 'airing' and Simon picked up a piece of ass before we even reached the VIP area. Drinks flew like an open faucet and it wasn't long before I was behaving as stupidly as the rest of them. Or they were behaving as stupidly as me. Whatever.

Several drinking games later, and Matt and Jeff from Toby's band had collected a group of girls who were all out on a bachelorette party. They were also pretty drunk and couldn't believe their luck to be invited to party with us. Actually, they were really funny girls. I had to kiss the bride- to-be and normally

I'd have been all over that, but I was determined that it would be appropriate, but Len more than made up for my deficit and Toby wasn't holding back either.

Around 2.00am, I started to go downhill. We'd been drinking for a couple of hours and I was 'well oiled'. Drinking games at a party were always a bad idea if you were on your own. Jerry was there but leaving me to my own judgment, so there was no one giving me the hint that I was reaching my limit for making sensible decisions.

Things went from bad to worse, because I got up and started dancing and the girls were all over me with their hands brushing against my junk every chance they got. I guess I was wired from the gig and not being able to get laid or go to sleep and with the alcohol I'd consumed, I was feeling pretty frisky. So the dancing became a bit raunchier than I'd have liked.

Toby came over and bumped my shoulder grinning and shouted in my ear. "Damn. There's my buddy! I wondered for a while what the fuck you had done with him."

Len slapped the back of my shoulder and leaned in to talk to me after Toby had slung his arm over the shoulders of a petite brunette with hair down to her ass and a skirt that almost disappeared under it. Pulling her flush against him, they danced very closely with his hand clasping hers close to both of their chests in a very intimate way.

"Remember Chloe, dude."

Inside my head, I knew what I was doing and argued with myself that I was not crossing any lines in regards to my love for Chloe. I was just a guy in a band who was letting go with his best buddies after a long week at work.

Dancing made me thirsty and drink made me want to dance. After another couple of hours I was almost blind drunk. I hadn't eaten much and had used up what was left of my energy on the dancefloor, so I flopped down heavily on the leather padded seating to watch the others for a while.

As soon as I sat down there were three girls all over me. One girl with awful dyed-blonde hair and black roots tried to straddle me, shoving her huge tits at me and grabbing my face in her hands in her effort to kiss me. I was fending her off when Jerry dragged her away from me and told them all that I didn't want their attention, before he moved them away from me with his body and his hands out at each side, backing them up and out of the three sided area the sofas made.

That was when I realized I wasn't focusing particularly well and the room began to swim. Lying back, I closed my eyes and I must have passed out, but when I came to I was aware of a warm body snuggled up next to me. For a moment I thought it was Chloe, and pulled her closely into my side. Jerry tugged at me and when I opened my eyes he was shaking the girl to move her away from me and I sat up with a start.

"Enough, Gib. You're digging a hole here, let's get you home before you do something you'll be sorry for tomorrow." I stared at him confused and trying to cobble my thoughts together; as drunk as I was, I'd been here many times in the past and when Jerry interjected at these times, there was a warning that I was about to fuck up in some way. He always registered with me more than Johnny in these circumstances. So even inebriated, I knew that I had to do whatever he said.

All the guys in the band were annoyed that I was going home, but Jerry reminded them that Chloe was sick and that I should have been home with her already. That seemed to appease them all. Toby and I hugged tightly and he was a bit emotional, but that could have been because he had drunk too much, but we never knew when we'd see each other again.

Stupid of me to drink so much when my body wasn't used to it anymore, but Jerry was a star, getting me safely into the car. Sliding behind the wheel he pressed the automatic ignition to start the car just as buzzing sounds came from his phone in his pocket. Jerry quickly pulled it out and stared at it. When I saw the dark angry look on his face I became worried. "What?"

Jerry's jaw ticked and he turned the screen to me saying, "Trouble boss. Of course I'll back you, but with Chloe's issues, I think you might have some trouble convincing her about this one." The picture was of me and the random girl cuddling cozily on the sofa in the nightclub. She was smiling sexily and looking up at me, and in the picture I seemed to be looking down at her, except for the actual fact that I was asleep.

Nothing like shock for sobering up. Pushing my legs into the foot well of the car, I sat up straight in the seat feeling sick to my stomach and dropped Jerry's phone down the side of the seat and it rolled under so that I couldn't reach it.

"Fuck, Jerry. Get me home. I have some explaining to do, but I also have the fact that it is an innocent picture on my side. Where the fuck where you? Jesus, this is a real cluster fuck, and just when everything was falling into place with Chloe."

"Don't start that, Gib. I was there, I only went to the bathroom for less than two minutes and I'd asked Lennox and Mick to watch out for you while I was gone. If you had controlled your drinking you wouldn't have passed out."

Under normal circumstances anyone working in security that let something like this happen would never have worked again, but this was Jerry and apart from Johnny there was no one more loyal or diligent at taking care of me, I banged the dashboard in frustration but I didn't say anything else, because that would have just made a bad situation worse and I needed him to get me home as quickly as possible.

By the time we arrived back at the hotel I'd drunk a liter of water from the cooler we always kept in the car, and was dying to pee but feeling a lot more with it than when I first left the club. My heart was beating wildly against my chest wall with the worry of telling Chloe about my night and the possible hurt she'd feel when I showed her the pictures. But I knew I had to do it before someone else showed her.

Jerry swiped the key card to the suite and bid me goodnight after I stopped him from taking me inside.

Swaying a little, I tried to get my bearings in the dark before staggering toward the bathroom. Turning on the light, my head automatically looked over my shoulder to see Chloe in the bed, but she wasn't there.

Fumbling around on the wall, my hand swiping back and forth, I finally found the main switch and the room was bathed in light. *Chloe wasn't there*. Panic rose in my chest. Had Chloe already seen the pictures and fled? Knowing how fragile Chloe's trust of me was, if she had seen what Jerry showed me it would be easy for her to think the worst of me and run before I had the chance to explain. I was fearful if that was the case, I may never find her again.

CHAPTER 19

COMMUNICATION

Gibson

Where is she? Did she go to Emma's? Taking out my phone to check, I saw there was a voice message from Emma.

"Gibson—I was sick as I was about to leave earlier and tried to call Chloe again. As soon as I could I went to your suite, but there was no answer. I called Johnny and got his voicemail. Jerry was at the gig with you and I knew he'd never hear me ring so I texted him, then rang the front desk and asked the concierge to come and let me into the penthouse.

"When I got there Chloe wasn't in the room and I just want to check she's with you. Chloe said she was feeling a bit better this morning, so wondered if she'd changed her mind about going with you. Lois was coming on board today, right? So I'm hoping she's gone with her. Really, Gibson—the communication needs to be much tighter with this if we are all going to keep Chloe safe."

Oh. My. God. Pacing the room unsteadily with panic rising in my chest, I called Johnny and Jerry on speed dial and poured myself some more water, trying desperately to get my body on full alert. *Did she leave me? Just up and leave? Was she planning this? Did something happen? Did she see the pictures?* I felt as if I was suffocating, my lungs restricting with increasingly shallow breaths as I fought the dreadful feelings that were threatening to make me so fucking irrational that I'd do something crazy.

Johnny came into the room, tucking the key card he'd just swiped into his pocket. "Okay, don't panic Gibson. We need to establish the facts." He was holding his hands placed down toward the floor in his effort to pacify me.

Staring angrily at Johnny's worried face, I wanted to smash it. "Don't fucking panic? Don't panic? Where the fuck is she? Has she just upped and left me? Lulled me into a false sense of security then fucking run off into the sunset?" Flinging my arms wide I spun unsteadily around to demonstrate that Chloe wasn't in the room.

"Gibson, calm down. This isn't helping. You need to get a grip and sober up." The door latch clicked and Jerry entered the room. A red mist fell over my eyes when I saw him. Emma had texted him and he'd missed it. Just like he'd missed the girl who was now all over the fucking Internet, gazing adoringly at me. "What the hell have you all been doing? How the fuck did none of you know she was missing? Four of you and you can't speak to each other? The voicemail from

Emma was at 3:00pm this afternoon. I can understand her position, she was being sick like Chloe. Twenty-five minutes after I left her, she rang." I paced the floor unsteadily. Johnny had made some coffee in the small kitchen and poured a large strong one laying the mug down on the glass coffee table.

"Drink it. Sober up. This isn't helping. We are wasting time here, Gib. You can rant all you want, but it's not going to bring her back. What you need now is our skill set. I suggest you calm the fuck down and let us do our job."

"Do your job? I fucking trusted you all to do your job, and she's gone. How is that you doing your fucking job? You didn't see her. Chloe looked physically sick. There was nothing to suggest to me that she was capable of going anywhere. I was worrying about those pictures from the club and she had already gone, if Emma's timeline is right. Where the fuck is Lois? Where's the security detail here, because I'm at a loss as to what you all think you get paid for."

Johnny nodded at Jerry, who turned abruptly and left the suite without saying anything else. "Where is he going? He's a fucking idiot. He missed Emma's text. Where has he gone?"

Cautiously, Johnny came over and pushed me down on the chair. "Trust me. If she's up and left, we'll know that in less than an hour. You have to calm the fuck down and let us do our job. Screaming and cussing at us isn't going to bring her walking through that door, so if I were you I'd get my head in a better

215

place, because you are going to need to be on top of your game when we do find her."

Reasoning with me like that made me feel like a child, but he was right. I wasn't going to do any good by screaming at the people that needed to focus on finding out what had happened.

"Did you call her? Chloe. Did you call her, Gib?"

Johnny pulled out his phone, swiped the screen and held the cell to his ear without waiting for me to answer. I hadn't even thought of that in my drunken state.

"Harder to Breathe" by Maroon 5 started to play from somewhere in the room. I knew it was Chloe's favorite non-M3rCy song. Johnny turned swiftly, stalking in the direction of the sound and crouched down near one of the nightstands. Chloe's bag was half hidden beside the bed and he swiped it out, unzipped it and turned it upside down, emptying the contents on the bed. Rifling through the items he began picking things out, tossing them into a pile and listing them.

"Passport, cell, credit card holder..." He checked inside and pulled out the cards. "Driver's license, black visa card, bank card..." Pushing them back inside, he added them to the pile before continuing. "Wallet, keys, body spray, spare panties unused, feminine product unused, pocket book." Looking over his shoulder as he stuffed everything back in the bag except the phone, he shook his head, staring grimly back at me.

"Well wherever she is, she hasn't gone far Gib,

she's taken nothing with her." Hearing Johnny's assessment made my heart race and I was even more confused. *If she hasn't taken anything then where is she? Is she with Lois? For fuck sake think, Gibson.*

"Forgive me, I'm drunk. Give me the skinny— you need to spell this out to me. I have no idea what to think right now."

"When I know—you'll know."

Johnny made calls and barked various instructions down the line at people. The next hour and half were a blur.

Jerry let himself back into the suite. Walking nervously toward me with a hurt look on his face, it was clear to see he knew he'd made huge mistakes. Easing down slowly on the bed facing me, he had a pained look on his face.

"Gib, I'm having the hotel and nearby buildings CCTV checked. Hospitals and police stations have drawn a blank and there have been no withdrawals against her bank account or credit cards nor, car rentals in her name. I've got the whole team involved and the private investigators and public relations are working hard so that you can have some privacy while we find her."

"Jesus, she can't just have fallen off the face of the earth. Where is Lois? What the fuck happened to her?"

"The airports are being checked as we speak, Gib, but apparently there was some altercation on the flight she was on and it was diverted to Boston, the plane is still on the ground and the passengers are still in situ."

"What a cluster fuck." Running my hands nervously through my hair again, I fought against the adrenaline rush and the feeling of sickening panic in my chest. The reality that Chloe was somewhere out there without me, and possibly sick, really hit home.

Picking up the coffee from the table, I downed it in one. "Right, get me sober now! I need to think." Johnny went into the bathroom, then I heard him turn the faucet on in the shower, when he came back in the room he stood beside me with his arms folded.

"Strip, get your ass in the shower. I don't care how cold it is."

Jerry poured another big mug of coffee for me to cool while I was in the shower, then sat at the dressing table talking on his phone to someone from the team. I felt helpless.

Johnny walked into the bathroom and helped me stagger into the shower. Fast jets of ice cold water hit my skin, making it constrict into millions of goose bumps. My balls almost ran inside my pelvis to get away from the shocking cold rivulets of water that ran down and into my groin.

"Ah, *fuck,* it's freezing." Shivering against the sudden shock, my body became more alert.

"Get your head under, Gib. Don't be a pussy. You want to get sober, you'll do as you are told."

Standing naked under the shower was torturous but it reminded me why I shouldn't have let myself drink. I'm immune to recognizing when I've had enough and I'm a sloppy drunk. I'd just learned that in serious circumstances where I had to think, I was completely useless.

By the time I had showered and dried I was fully coherent and much more in control of my faculties. Jerry had established that Emma was still sick in her room and was unaware there was a problem at all, because she had done all she could in the circumstances and informed Jerry, who had inadvertently let the buck stop with him.

Padding barefoot over to the dresser, I pulled out some fresh jeans and my hand landed on the t-shirt that Chloe told me was her favorite. It was a tight white t-shirt with cotton so thin she could see my ink through it. Chloe said it reminded her of the t-shirt that I was wearing during the thunderstorm back at Beltz.

Pulling it out, I threaded my arms in to the sleeves and pulled it over my head. Johnny's phone rang as I stepped into my jeans and he headed for the door. Before I could say anything he'd left, the door banging shut behind him.

Jerry was still sitting at the table working on a laptop and glanced in the direction of the door, then at me.

"Find out what's going on. I want information. Fucking inform me." I gestured my head at the door, I was finding it hard to be in the same room as the guy. I love Jerry like a brother, but Chloe was my life and he'd fucked up big time.

I grabbed my phone and thought about calling Len but he was in a worse state than I was and I was trying to think who I could vent to. The only person I could think of was Morgan, but I knew that I couldn't do that to Chloe or to Morgan for that matter, now that I knew she'd been harboring feelings that were more than the friendship I thought we'd had.

Feeling more alone than at any time in my life, I had a stark and sobering revelation. There was not one person I knew and totally trusted apart from Chloe, that wasn't employed by me. Chloe was the only person that gained nothing from being around me and in fact, I had caused her more issues than I resolved, by highlighting where she was to Kace.

"Fuck! That's it! Fuck!" Stamping angrily toward the door, I flung it open and saw Johnny and Jerry in deep conversation. Johnny's brow was creased with worry and Jerry was rubbing the back of his neck. "He's got her, hasn't he? Kace! He's got to her! Where is he? I'm telling you, he hurts one hair on her fucking head and he's dead. I'll kill him with my bare hands."

Johnny moved swiftly toward me and enveloped me in a hug, then began to walk backward with me struggling against him until he'd taken me back into the room. He shoved me hard and I landed on the bed, surprised at how assertive he was being with me. I think he knew he was walking a fine line, and his hand was kinda vibrating on my chest with temper when he pushed me back.

"Sit down. I need to talk to you and *you* need to listen. There is CCTV footage of a guy placing something in a blanket into the car trunk in the alleyway. The guy is in a concierge suit, but the management can't identify him. We're just waiting for the footage to be streamed to us and we'll know if it is Kace."

When Johnny voiced my fears, my heart almost stopped. Jerry swiped the door key and pushed it open. And when I saw the devastated expression on his face, he didn't have to say anything. I just knew.

"Nooooo!" One glance at the look on his face and I felt like someone had taken a pickaxe to my chest. It felt like I was bleeding inside, my heart banging hard and rapidly against my breastbone, struggling for some kind of rhythm. My whole body began to shake violently in shock. Every bone in my body had been telling me not to leave her in the room by herself and I had let Chloe talk me out of the heavy feeling in my gut about that.

"I want that bastard found today, you hear me? If he harms a hair on my Chloe's head I'm gonna tear his limbs off one at a time. Do we have any concrete information? Any leads? The car? Did you inform the law? Get everyone together...the team here *now*. I want to know everything we have. Don't even think of holding back on me. This is my girl. *My girl*. My life. Remember that. Cancel the gigs. Sorry, but I can't function without her. I am not playing another note until she's back with me, y'all hear me?"

Crushing feelings both in my belly and my chest made my breathing noisy, rapid and uneven. The shock of knowing that somewhere out there Chloe was dealing with the guy that she'd been so careful to be free from, and that I had lead him right to her, almost killed me. That single thought wrecked me. Strong waves of nausea gripped me and I headed for the bathroom, just making it as far as the sink before I became overwhelmed by the involuntary heaving as I vomited everywhere.

"Shit, Gib. Come on. Let's sort you out."

Waving his arm off, I shunned him angrily. "Fuck off Johnny, I'm not a child. I'm a grown man and I did this to myself. Stop talking to me like I'm fucking stupid. I was incapacitated by alcohol, that's all. I didn't fall and give myself brain issues. So..."

Distant ringing from the other room made the two of us stop our argument dead. Both turned, in the direction of the bathroom door and headed swiftly for the main suite area. Jerry's voice trailed away as he disappeared out the door of the penthouse. I began to tell Johnny to get after him when he reappeared again as fast as he had left.

When he came back he had a grey, tired look on his face and I had a terrible relentless feeling of impending doom registering in my wildly erratic thoughts. Thinking Chloe was somewhere out there at the hands of Kace was devastating, I had never felt so guilty or helpless in my life about anything I had done, as I felt about what Chloe might be going through.

"The team are on their way, Gib. There are two detectives coming as well. We need their help to find her because the car was found abandoned behind an old warehouse, and there is no trace of them. No CCTV, no witnesses, no store for a mile or more, and it isn't a 'foot friendly' place."

Every time Jerry opened his mouth the news seemed to be worse than the last time he spoke.

"So...we had CCTV of the car and now we have nothing? No clue at all where he's taken her? What he's doing with her? Fuck! If anything happens to her..." My voice trailed off because the thoughts were too difficult to say out loud.

My fists were clenched with frustration. There was nothing I wanted more than to find and squeeze the bullying asshole's neck, but my first thought was Chloe and how petrified she must be feeling. My heart was cracking open wider with every single thought that ran through my head and I prayed that Chloe could stay strong in her weakened state and know I was looking for her.

CHAPTER 20

OUT OF MY MIND

Gibson

Five days. Five fucking days and not a word.

For the first two days I was holding it together—barely. The last three had made me sick to my stomach. Day three, we met again with the police. Charlotte and the PR team had somehow managed to keep it away from the press. The official line was that I had a virus, and as someone had wind of a doctor visiting Chloe, we had the grace of the media leaving us in private to 'recover'.

I felt a total failure that I'd let the ball drop with Chloe's safety and I had to make a call I was dreading to make. When I found the number for her parents in her phone, I felt sick. They had no idea what had happened and preferred they heard it from someone who knew Chloe, than strangers. When I dialed Chloe's parents' number I was shaking with nerves. Swiping her phone open I swallowed hard for the umpteenth time that day and prepared to deliver some news no parent should ever hear.

When I heard her mom tears stung in my own eyes and I'm not soft. By the time the call was over, I was kicking my ass all over again for the suffering I'd caused everyone by being so selfish. Cathy and George seemed lovely people, but her father was angry with me, and I deserved the venom he unleashed on the phone. Charlotte arranged to bring her parents on the first flight up and I sent Jerry to bring them over to the hotel as soon as they landed.

Ruby had to be told, but I figured Chloe's parents telling her had to be better than me having contact with her. As soon as I thought about Ruby I felt sick again. Another hurdle I'd have to overcome in the future when the penny dropped in my mind about why her face registered with me when so many girls hadn't. Maybe all this was why I never did relationships? I was a walking nightmare with a catalogue of fuck-ups to my name.

Charlotte booked her parents into another hotel to the one I was in. They needed privacy during all of this. I spoke by phone hourly as we waited for news, but I wasn't going to risk drawing attention to them by going there. Besides, I was supposed to have a virus.

Day four and I found myself ordering a bottle of Glenfiddich Malt Whiskey against the advice of everyone present. But they were only spectators in all of this, Chloe's loss was mine. I was the one going through the torture of knowing that it was me that put her in danger.

There were two camps of thought. One that

wanted the news to be made public, and to try to flush Kace into the open with the general public actively looking for him in the hope that someone would happen across where Chloe was being kept. The other camp felt if we pushed him into a corner it would become a siege situation. So we did nothing...and it was fucking terrifying to think that my hands were tied by some unstable guy with a grudge on me and my girl.

"Gib, get your ass off the bed and clean yourself up. Shower, and shave we think we've found her."

My eyes snapped open and the top half of my body sprang bolt upright. My heart beat thudding rapidly in my chest, racing like a high speed train gathering momentum.

"What? Where? Is she okay? Fuckin' tell me she's okay. What do you mean you think..." Hauling my ass out of bed, I started toward him, but leaned out and grabbed the nightstand to steady myself. I had passed out a few hours before after drinking half a bottle of whiskey. It was the first time I had slept more than twenty minutes since Chloe had been taken, and it was day five.

"Not sure Gib, all I know is that a woman has been left by the side of Lake Union in a t-shirt and a bathrobe with the hotel logo. She had a note pinned to her that said, 'Guess where I've been?' She fits Chloe's description and she has an emerald ring that matches the description of the one that Chloe wears."

Trying to swallow down the fear, my heartbeat raced, causing a throb in my temple. I was hesitant to even ask the next question. Adrenaline had begun to make my body vibrate and I was finding it difficult to fight back the tears that stung at the back of my eyes, begging to be released.

When I spoke it was so quiet...like I didn't want to say it out loud. "Chloe isn't conscious?" As soon as the words were out, it felt like my heart stopped. It probably didn't, but I know I held my breath, waiting to hear the worst.

Johnny looked at Jerry and Charlotte and rubbed his hand down his face, taking in a long, deep breath. Charlotte came over and sat down beside me, placing her arm around my neck to comfort me. She had stayed on after the meeting a few days ago and tried to make herself useful. She was also great at fending off the rest of the team.

One of the detectives wanted the rest of the band out of the loop, saying the less people that knew about Chloe being missing the better. Then no one could be overheard talking about it.

Johnny exhaled a heavy breath and slapped his hands on his thighs, pushing himself up to stand. Shoving his hands deep into his pockets, he stared sympathetically at me. "The woman they found isn't talking, Gib. Emma has gone to the hospital with Detective Mulligan to confirm that it is ...or to exclude her from their enquiries."

"Stop! Start again. Tell me *exactly* what the deal is. Why the fuck is Emma going and not me?"

"We don't want a circus, Gibson. They are pretty sure it's her which is why I'm telling you, but the PR team want to keep it as low key as possible for the both of you. George is meeting Emma at the hospital."

Jerry cleared his throat and swallowed hard, then referred to his laptop screen.

"This is what we were sent, Gibson. At 6.36am, James Farrell was walking his dog on the south side of Lake Union when he came across a young woman in a black t-shirt and white bathrobe with a note pinned to her saying 'Guess where I've been.' She's in shock and non-responsive at the moment. The guy rang 911 and she's been taken downtown to one of the Sovereign Mental Health team's facilities near the lake."

As Jerry finished speaking, Johnny's cell rang and he turned away from us, walking toward the door and speaking quietly.

"Will y'all stop leaving the fucking room when the phone rings?" I called out in frustration as I watched Johnny's shoulders bunch up near his ears like he was stressed and worried about what he was listening to. Suddenly his shoulders sagged and he spun around to face me, making eye contact.

"It's her. Chloe. The girl they found is Chloe."

Waving the fingers of my outstretched hand, I said, "Gimme me the phone. Give me the fucking phone." Snatching the phone out of Johnny's hand I held it briefly to my chest. "Get the car. Get the fucking car. What are you waiting for?" Turning my attention to the call, I asked, "Who is this?" As soon as Emma said her name I cut her off. "Emma? Is she okay? Tell me she's okay."

"She's alive, Gibson. Hopefully in time she'll be

okay. Chloe isn't talking yet, she's in shock. They're saying she's deeply traumatized right now. No one has any idea what's happened to her so they are doing all the tests and assessments to cover all possibilities."

Anxious feelings became even more debilitating to me, because whatever had happened to Chloe must have been so difficult that she was blocking everything out.

"What the fuck does that mean? All possibilities?" My question died on my lips as a jolt of electricity hit me square in the chest— they were assessing Chloe to see if she had been drugged or raped. Suddenly I was too choked to speak. I handed the phone to Charlotte to conclude the call, because the thought that he'd taken Chloe against her will was too horrendous to contemplate.

Black, angry thoughts about what I wanted to do to the guy filled the blank space that was in my mind, because I couldn't accept any thoughts that Kace had done that to her. I made a silent promise to myself not to kill the guy when I got my hands on him, but Kace was definitely going to feel my wrath for fucking with Chloe again. I hadn't even asked if he'd hit her. *What the fuck is wrong with me?*

There was no time for anything other than pulling on the clothing that had just come back from the laundry. Chloe's favorite t-shirt of mine was on the top of the pile, so I pulled it on, grabbed my wallet and my phone, and some clothing for Chloe, then Jerry took me to the car in the alleyway where Johnny was waiting.

The radio was on but I don't think Johnny noticed, he was almost as worried as I was about Chloe. Although he'd been skeptical at first, I could see that he had noted the changes in me once Chloe was on the scene. Sting was singing "Every Breath You Take" and I hit the off button on the car dashboard. My chest filled with fury.

"Fuck, the asshole must have been watching our every move."

Feeling livid and helpless at the same time is a frustrating combination. My gut felt like it was going to burst and Johnny seemed to be driving like a day-tripper out sight-seeing. Every minute that passed that we weren't there already, left me more and more frustrated. "Put your foot down for God's sake, this is taking forever."

Johnny turned his head briefly. "Stay in control Gib, I'm driving as fast as the traffic allows me. You need to get your temper in check. Chloe doesn't need someone turning up who is humming with anger. She's going to need you to be very patient and controlled to make her feel safe." He was right.

By the time we had drove up the long driveway, my heart had finally reached my mouth. I was trembling with anticipation and worry of what I was going to find when I saw Chloe. The modern building surprised me. I always figured places that dealt with mental health issues were big austere looking places and I felt embarrassed that me of all people was stereotyping like that.

Cool mint green décor and fresh flowers and the

soft furnishings made the facility feel more like a health spa and shattered the preconceived ideas I'd had on the drive over. The staff on the front desk seemed calm and super-efficient, which gave me some confidence about Chloe being in good hands.

George was gracious and told the staff that we shared next-of-kin status, and that I was to be involved in the sharing of information. I was thankful for his acceptance like that, especially given the part I played in Kace finding Chloe in the first place. I was surprised he could do that, but because Chloe wasn't in the position to give her consent it fell to George to make decisions for her.

I wanted to stay. They refused point blank to hear of it. The fact that they were so careful as to check who I was with my driver's license, even when they had addressed me by name, spoke volumes about them safeguarding my girl.

Johnny came over and sat beside me while the receptionist rang the psychiatrist who was treating Chloe. "Jerry said we had a clear run, Gib. No one knows we're here. I know you felt it took an age to get here but in these situations counter surveillance is important, the last thing we want is Chloe in the spotlight right now."

Dr. Anthony Owen, Chloe's psychiatrist, was a short balding red headed guy with thick rimmed glasses and a portly appearance. Pretty much the opposite of me to look at, but exactly the guy Chloe needed in her life right now. Within a couple of minutes he was sharing his expertize on Post

Traumatic Stress Disorder, or PTSD as he kept referring to it. He spelt out immediately that he would not allow anyone to question his judgment about what was best for Chloe in this instant. I don't think he really meant *anyone*, I think that particular comment was served to keep me in check.

So, for the following half an hour, he spoke and I sat listening, becoming more and more conscious of the seriousness of Chloe's condition. Dr. Owen explained gently that Chloe may not recognize me.

"Chloe may not remember what actually happened, while emotions experienced during the trauma may be re-experienced without her understanding why, due to repressed feelings because she is afraid of them. Or, she may disassociate herself in her mind to numb out the feelings. This can lead to the traumatic events being constantly experienced as if they were happening in the present, preventing her from gaining perspective on the experience."

When the doctor said she may disassociated I asked what that meant. From what he said, she was staring into space in a completely non-responsive state at that point. My reaction was that I wanted to tear the place apart to find her. Part of me thought if I could just take her back to my cabin in the woods, a quiet life would make everything okay. My reality was that I was eaten up with guilt because it was my selfish attitude that had put her where she was.

Understanding where Chloe was emotionally, and what that meant for Chloe wasn't easy. Dr. Owen told me the plan was for her to rest for twenty-four hours and then for them to commence a strict regimen of recovery involving cognitive behavioral therapy and an innovative and highly successful newer therapy, Eye Movement Desensitization and Reprocessing (EDMR).

All of this information was beyond someone like me, but I was going to have to be schooled in it. If this was what Chloe needed, then I had to know what it was and what to look for, to know that it was working.

The doctor's team was very conservative about their long term outlook for Chloe, but they told me that recovery would depend on Chloe's attitude and personality, as well as how good her support network was around her. *Some support network we were, when we'd all failed her.*

Everything I was being told seemed too difficult to comprehend. *How am I supposed to deal with a sick girlfriend and work?* Again, I had to dismiss the thought, because people in ordinary jobs got sick daily and they had to manage. At least I had money to pay people to help me.

"Damn. Damn. Damn." When I spoke to the doctor I behaved rationally and very matter of fact, gaining as much information as I could. When he said I couldn't see her, I almost lost it. I only wanted to see that she was okay. He was sympathetic to my suffering as well, but he said that there was a danger if Chloe saw someone she was close to, it could trigger another set of events in her mind.

Initially I refused to go home, but they were completely insistent that this was a slow process and that I would be escorted off the premises. So I had to put what was best for Chloe above what was best for me. So I found myself in the car on the way home, staring at the phone number I'd been given to call for a daily update on her condition.

"Gibson, she'll be alright. She's the strong silent type. Chloe isn't the kind of girl that is highly strung and full of drama. That's gonna help her, you understand?"

I glared angrily at Johnny and snorted. "And how the fuck, do you conclude that, Johnny?"

"Military training. Don't forget, this is some of the shit I had to learn and teach when I was training my men for operational duties in the field. We didn't just give them a gun and a badge and send them out to fend for themselves, you know. The real world isn't the fucking Wild West, Gibson."

Sitting quietly in the car on the way home, I guess I must have looked like I was having a quiet reflection, but the hatred for Kace was bubbling away in my gut and I wanted to destroy him. The doctor said that if Chloe didn't improve, that she may be given drugs to slow her mind and help her deal with her condition.

I refused to accept that because they wanted to do that to me with my ADHD, and where it is right for some, I knew it wasn't for me. I was determined to do anything that would make her feel better inside before I'd accept that. Medicine has a place in mental health— I just wanted to make sure we'd done everything else first.

Arriving back at the hotel, we had the same duck-and-dive routine to get me back into the penthouse without being seen. Lennox was waiting in the suite with Charlotte. I hadn't seen him since the night in the club. He was the first person I made eye contact with when I walked through the door.

Len pushed himself to stand and hurried across, pulling me into a tight hug saying, "Out. *All* of you. Get the fuck out and leave us!" Without speaking a word Charlotte gathered her stuff, Jerry closed his laptop and Johnny opened the door as we stood silently waiting for everyone to leave.

"Thank God. She's alright, Gibson. When is she coming back? What happened to her? Did she say where he kept her? Charlotte filled me in. You should have told me, Gibson. We're as good as brothers."

"Whoa!" Pushing Len away, I shrugged myself out of my leather jacket and let it drop to the floor, swallowing hard to fight back all the emotion that was threatening to engulf me. Since I heard what Dr. Owen said, tears had been choking me, but I had sucked it up and acted all sensible and strong. However, once it was only me and Len in the room, the emotional roller coaster had reached the end of its ride because with all the will in the world, I couldn't hold the sob that was strangling me since I'd left the hospital without her.

Len moved quickly and caught me as my legs buckled and he kinda slumped to the ground with me. Loud sobs escaped from my throat like some wounded animal and Len just held my head against his chest and rocked me, much like I had with Chloe when she had done the same.

"Gib, I promise you. Whatever has happened with her, we'll fix her. You got her, dude. Anything that happened before she was with you made Chloe what she is. Not you. Not...whatever has happened this time. Chloe had baggage before, she dealt.

"I have tons of respect for her, and you, and I know that this is going to be okay. You've got to trust yourself and find the strength to help her, but you'll come through it Gib, and so will she.
Remember...nobody died. You said that to me plenty of times when we were in the shit, so take your own advice. Chloe's alive, dude. That's all that matters."

CHAPTER 21

MEET THE PARENTS

Gibson

Somehow I had been persuaded to finish the tour because I wasn't allowed to see Chloe. No phone calls, no letters, no pictures. Nothing. Even the information I *was* getting was scant. I was not allowed to see her but even worse neither was her father. The doctor's reasoning was he was conducting research into the recovery of patients with this condition and how attachment theories could be used to help the patient feel secure. His teams' findings so far were in cases like Chloe's it could substantially increase the rate of recovery if only the primary carer, usually the mother was accessible during this process.

Charlotte arranged a house rental for George, Cathy and me and we moved in the following day with Johnny. I know that sounds weird considering I'd never met them before, but I didn't want to stay separately from them because getting to speak to me was tough at times, and they didn't need the added stress of not being able to do that if they needed to.

So Chloe's mom was working with the medical team giving them as much information as possible then even asked me to fill in some forms, then after a week, her mom was allowed a visit. That was particularly hard on her dad and me, because all we had to go on was what Cathy shared when she came home and we were desperate to see for ourselves. Chloe still wasn't talking but Cathy was excited when she came home because Chloe had given her eye contact and smiled. It was a glimmer of hope in a dark space for all of us.

During this time, Kace had gone to ground, like he'd disappeared and become a non-person. No clues to follow. He emptied his bank account on the day before he took Chloe, so there was no money trail to follow.

Kace had no credit card trail, but investigations found he'd withdrawn $31,603 from the bank. With him using cash for everything he needed, our only hope would be if someone asked him to provide his social security number or he rented a car and used his driver's license, and used either of these as forms of identity.

The two private investigators and detectives were working round the clock, and Kace hadn't slipped up at all so far, but I was leaving them to concentrate on that because Chloe was in the safest place possible. If someone like me, with my money, status and her parent's consent couldn't see her, then neither could Kace.

The night the tour ended, Len and I sat talking right into the following morning. Previously, I had already told him that when the tour was over M3rCy was taking a break. Len looked shocked when I told him that I had decided that for me, my priority was Chloe, and I wasn't going to do any band related stuff until I had a clearer idea of what she needed. What happened to Chloe was because of me, and if I hadn't arranged to meet her she'd still be safe and anonymous in New York.

"You can't keep beating yourself up about this, Gib. It happened. The important thing now is what you do next." *What do I do next?* I was still at a loss and hung around the rented house doing nothing for pretty much most of the day. Food arrived by courier and was dealt with by Johnny and Jerry because we didn't want anyone to know what was going on. During this time, when Cathy came home from seeing Chloe, George and I hung on her every word.

Three long, emotional weeks later, the pattern was still the same, except when Cathy came home she told me that Chloe was taking care of her own hygiene and dressing, and had fallen into a routine of doing this. Small steps but it was in the right direction. George and I still weren't allowed to see her, and I was almost at my wits end without her.

Every time Lennon came over I cried. Simon, Mick and him tried to take me out with them for the night, to take my mind off of her, but I was miserable company so I declined. I just lay on my bed listening to playlist after playlist coming through my ear buds.

Bruno Mars was another favorite of Chloe's and when the song "I Won't Give Up" came on I could completely relate, knowing I would hang in there for her. Some days I wondered if Chloe would ever speak or I'd ever be allowed to see her again, and my heart ached whenever I thought about that.

Week five, and the update from Dr. Owen was they had started to use music to reach Chloe. I was asked for a list of her favorite bands but the music couldn't be anything of mine or M3rCy's. Maroon 5, Bruno Mars, One republic, Daughtry and Ed Sheeran, her other favorite artists, were going to be used.

Filling her head with music, they hoped to trigger some positive responses. They had the tunes playing in the background for most of the day. The doc's assessment was that she was getting more responsive every day and the idea to use music in particular was gaining momentum.

Chloe was left a pile of CDs and a CD player because these were more visible and tactile than a playlist on a digital device. The medical team wanted to try to bring her mind back to the present time.

While all the news about Chloe was encouraging, my memories of how it felt when she touched me were beginning to frustrate me. The only thing I had, apart from some pictures, was her voicemail. I must have listened to that hundreds of times in the first few days, just to hear the sound of her voice.

When I found a little tank top in the bottom of one of my bags that hadn't been washed, I held it to my face with both hands and inhaled it deeply. It smelt of the perfume she wore. I used this during some of my darker times, and I wondered if we'd ever regain the closeness we'd started to share before her abduction.

Two days after they gave her the CD's, Chloe suddenly stood and walked over to them. Flicking through them she chose 'Baptism' by Daughtry and selected a specific track to listen to. Track two. "Waiting for Superman." My heart almost burst out of my chest when they told me that because while it wasn't significant to them, it was definitely a sign to me, because the song that she connected with me was the one she was listening to on a loop.

Five weeks and three days into her therapy, and they gave Chloe a laptop. No Internet. Just preloaded programs of art and word processing software to see what would happen. Initially, Chloe barely looked at it, then during one of her music sessions she put on Ed Sheeran's CD and played the song, "Give Me Love" and when Cathy told me that, I wondered if she was thinking of me. *Was she trying to tell them something? Was she telling them she wanted to see me?* So I listened to the words of the song and there was definitely something in that for me.

I had another meeting with Dr. Owen and Chloe's parents, and I almost lost my shit because he still wouldn't let me see her. I was so fucking frustrated about that, and after some time he suggested the medical team would take some photographs to show me that she looked well and was relaxed in her environment. Her parents had to give permission along with me to allow them to take the pictures, because Chloe was a vulnerable person and didn't have the capacity to give her consent.

When I opened the door to the rental house and stepped inside without her again, I felt so fucking angry that I rang Len. "Get me drunk. I need to get the fuck out of here. I'm hurting so bad that if I spend another night in silence with the thoughts in my head, I'm gonna go fucking crazy."

Cathy and George understood where I was coming from, and encouraged me to spend time with the guys. George was particularly kind when he rose out of his chair and hugged me tightly. I was committed to helping Chloe and I knew I had to have a strong mental attitude when she came home to gain her trust. I was up for that challenge, but at that moment I needed something to stop my mind going around in circles.

Len arrived, and he along with Johnny and Jerry took me to an exclusive club we'd been to a couple of years ago. Hearing the music lifted my heavy heartbroken mood and after a few drinks, Chloe was still on my mind, but my thoughts weren't as overbearing as they had been since she'd been taken. When I updated Len, he was of the opinion that she'd be home in no time.

Len goaded me a lot during the evening and even got me up dancing with a couple of great fangirls who couldn't believe their luck at being invited to a completely different VIP do, when they came across us by accident. I was fine until some fucker started taking pictures and then I saw red. Furious at the loss of privacy when I was trying to do something normal, I threw a punch. I'm not proud of it and at the time the dude seemed apologetic and full of remorse.

The next morning a repetitive noise dragged me from my unconscious state. I was instantly aware of the dull throb in my head, which wasn't improved when I answered the phone and Charlotte informed me about the new article posted overnight.

Is Gibson Barclay's Competition Squeeze Chloe Jenner history?

Bad Boy Gibson Barclay seemed to be back on the market last night as he partied with band mate Lennox and bodyguards late into the night in the VIP area of SPD nightclub. Sexy as sin, Gibson looked a free man without a care in the world when he celebrated his freedom with two unnamed beauties. Gibson was reportedly in a relationship with Chloe Jenner, competition winner, who caused a sensation when photographs emerged of the couple's sex antics only a day after meeting each other. After spending several hours in the company of the females, Lennox and Gibson left with their security detail alone. The unknown females were unavailable for comment.

After the altercation I thought that had been the end of it, but true to form he'd already sent the picture on to his email before he'd deleted it in the club in front of me. As if I wasn't dealing with enough and now there was even more to explain to Chloe at some point.

First I'd have to face her parents about it, so I got out of bed, stepped into my jeans and threw on a t-shirt, then padded barefooted into the kitchen. Cathy had already gone to see Chloe and George was sitting quietly on a wicker chair staring out of the large French doors at the landscaped garden. Pouring coffee into the mug, I interrupted George's thoughts and he turned his head to look at me.

"This is so draining. I'm out of my fucking head with grief about this. Sometimes my only thought is when Chloe gets out of this, I'm going hunting. The thoughts alone in my head would get my gun license revoked."

"Indeed." I knew exactly what he meant. I'd had many of those exact same thoughts myself. I placed my coffee cup down and maneuvered around the counter to stand next to his chair. Both of us stared silently out of the window for about a minute, then I heard George sniff. When I turned to face him, George put his hands over his face and began sobbing. I knew how he was feeling so without hesitation I bent down and hugged him tightly, absorbing the movement of his shaking body that wracked with distress.

Several minutes later, he was more composed and we sat talking. I told him about my night out and the news headline.

George waved it away with his hand like what I'd told him was nothing. "Gibson you have to ignore that stuff. I guess it's an occupational hazard for you to have sneaky people pull stunts to have their ten minutes of fame. In your line of work I imagine you attract attention without even trying."

Just like that, he believed me.

"Yeah, but it's Chloe I'm worried about. She had a hard time trusting anyone because of what happened to her, and there are many that would say there's no smoke without fire, especially with my reputation."

"Not my Chloe. That girl has always seen the good in people. When everyone else saw negatives, I could guarantee that she'd find the positive somewhere. Jeez, I remember when we went on vacation and were driving through an agricultural area, the smell of manure was almost knocking us out, but Chloe commented that it reminded her of flower beds because it was important to help make the plants grow."

I snickered at that because he was right, when everyone else had chosen to focus on the one thing about me, she had found another.

George then spent the morning telling me what Chloe was like as a kid and the warm feeling I had inside made me feel near to her. As he was talking, the look Chloe gave me all those years ago came to mind, and my heart was bursting with love for her again. I had been losing sight of how we went forward and George's stories were just what I needed to lift me and give me the motivation to keep going.

Several hours later Cathy came home and when she slipped off her jacket she pulled a large manila envelope out of her bag. Placing it on the table, her hand tapped it and she smiled. "Chloe." She then walked over to George and placed another in front of him, sat down beside him and took his hand.

Just hearing her name and knowing that I was going to see her, even in picture form, set my heart racing. With shaky fingers I tore at the envelope, pulling out the photographs. There were five in all and the first one I saw was perfect. Chloe was sitting cross legged with a set of earphones on, her eyes closed and she had a beautiful smile on her face. She looked perfect. More importantly, she looked at peace.

The second she was lying on her belly asleep, her hand placed on the bed level with her shoulder and a few strands of hair over her forehead. In reaction to seeing it, I held it to my heart because I missed her lying next to me.

The third photograph made me smile and I'm afraid my dick stirred and went hard, because she was looking up and the picture had been taken from a vantage point above her. Those eyes reminded me of us during foreplay, all innocent but with the potential to be corrupted.

The fourth picture she was sitting on a chair side on with her hands on her lap. She was staring ahead and Dr. Owen was staring back. This one must have been taken during a therapy session. I wasn't sure what it told me, apart from he was working with her at least.

When I got to the last picture, it took my breath away and my heart almost stopped. It was a close up of my beautiful girl and her huge, inky blue eyes were staring straight at me. Tears choked me and I swallowed continually as I fought them back.

Tracing my finger along her jaw line and then across her full lips, I lifted it and pressed mine to hers, closing my eyes. *I have to get her back.* Retiring to my room for most of the day, I lay staring at the pictures. I wasn't sure whether I felt better or worse for having them, but I consoled myself that on the outside Chloe appeared to be well and didn't look distressed.

When I emerged from my room, Cathy had made some kind of chicken pasta dish, it tasted bland—but everything seemed tasteless without Chloe.

Cathy began talking about Chloe and told me that she had been given a laptop to communicate the day before and she had suddenly started to write a story about an ordinary girl who fell in love with a rock star. The story wasn't the same as ours and the circumstances were different, but according to Cathy it was a beautiful romantic story full of emotional angst and amazing dialogues.

Dr. Owen was excited when she began to write because he said that she was channeling positive thoughts, emotions and feelings. In his estimation this was remarkable progress. When I climbed into bed that night, my heart felt a little more settled. Hearing all the positive things and having the pictures made me feel that Chloe was on her way back to me.

CHAPTER 22

TESTING TIMES

Gibson

Chloe continued to write and the staff realized it was a book, not a story. Chapter after chapter, she poured feelings and thoughts onto pages that were both brilliant and inspiring. And because she was doing this, I felt I should pen a few things of my own. So I began by writing her a love song.

> *Looking out the window,*
> *Staring at the cleansing rain*
> *Darlin' I never felt so low*
> *My tattered heart's in so much pain*
>
> *Every beat is like a shard of glass*
> *Ripping wildly at my soul*
> *I placed you in a different class*
> *And I need you here to make me whole.*
>
> *Waiting for a sign to know*

You remember that you're mine...

Used to writing lyrics that scratched below the surface, I was surprised at how difficult it was for me to put what I was feeling in my heart and the thoughts in my head, on paper. If I was having a block like this, Chloe being able to verbalize what she went through was unfathomable.

Six weeks and one day after Chloe was found, I was sitting cross legged on the floor strumming my guitar and experimenting with a new piece of music, when my cell rang. Slapping my hand against the oak wooden floorboard, I reached across my guitar and checked the caller ID and saw it was the clinic. They never rang me, so when I saw it the feeling of panic made my heart speed up and imaginary fingers closed around it, giving it a squeeze.

Working a swallow as I nervously swiped the screen to answer, my head filled with dread at how the conversation was going to go.

"Mr. Barclay?"

The sound of my name said in an official way always made me feel like I was in trouble. No one called me that. "Yes?"

"Hello, this is Patricia from Chloe's team. Please can you come over to the clinic? Dr. Owen would like to speak with you."

Cathy was there already and George was watching TV, I could hear the volume on the television in the family room. I was already slipping my shoes on and shrugging my jacket on over my shoulders. "I'll be there in twenty minutes." Johnny was in the kitchen making a pastrami sandwich. "Leave that— I need to get to the clinic."

Striding down the hall heading for the front door, I pulled it open as Johnny called in past the lounge room door and filled George in about what was happening. Johnny then came running after me, pulling his jacket on and clutching the sandwich in his right hand. I felt bad leaving George behind, but if he'd come with us, I knew it would only have torn him up more to be there and be refused access to her again.

We had done amazingly well in keeping my whereabouts private, but it took forever to get over to the facility because of all the doubling back to check we were alone. By the time we got there my hands were sweaty and I'd stroked them through my hair so much that Johnny commented for me to sort it out before we left the car.

Dr. Owen was dwarfed by his high backed swivel chair, in his office. Waving and motioning me to take a seat, he continued to dictate about Chloe into a voice recorder on his laptop. Nodding at Johnny, he stopped abruptly and commented about patient confidentiality and asked him to wait outside in the reception area.

"Sit down, Gibson. I have something to show you."

Tapping his computer keyboard for a few seconds, his head moved slightly as his eyes scanned his screen. When he found what he was looking for, he clicked on it then turned the laptop around to me. A circular icon on the screen indicated that a video was loading. It seemed slow to process and I found myself becoming frustrated that what he needed to share with me wasn't instantly available.

Suddenly Chloe was on the screen. My heart
thudded. The impact of seeing her moving image in
front of me had the maximum effect. For over six
weeks I'd been coming and going from this building
and suddenly there she was on the screen, looking so
beautiful it made my heart ache. Her level of
vulnerability was almost too much to handle. It
shredded me and I reached out, stroking my finger
down the screen at her image and swallowed back my
tears.

"Keep watching please, Gibson."

He would have had to gouge my eyes out with a
spoon to stop me. Transfixed on my girl, I waited with
bated breath to see whatever he wanted to share with
me. I didn't really care what it was, if it was only this—
then I already felt informed.

Dr. Owen realized he had muted the sound to
dictate and spun the laptop back to him again to
rectify this. My heart sank instantly when I lost sight of
her. Tapping another button, he turned the screen
again and I watched from the beginning with sound.

"Baptized" by Daughtry was just finishing and
Chloe was sitting in front of the laptop they had given
her. She was motionless, just staring at the screen. The
track ended and "Waiting for Superman" began to
play. Chloe reached up and began typing rapidly on
her keyboard, and at first I thought that the song had
inspired her to write a scene for her book. After
several minutes, she stopped and I realized the track
had finished. The video screen went blank and reset to

the beginning of the recording.

"That's good, right? That she's using a song to write, the song is stimulating her—inspiring her, yes? She's inspired by it to write something? What does this mean?"

Dr. Owen licked his bottom lip and pushed his spectacles up his nose with his middle finger, then pushed himself back in his seat. "Well, of course. Yes. But that's not it, Gibson. I wanted you to see how she was responding, but I'm now going to share the screen she was writing on."

What did she write? Was it about Kace? Was it about what happened? Adrenaline rushed through me, fearful of what he may have done and what she'd disclosed. When Chloe was found, there wasn't a mark on her. Tests were negative for force and there were no bodily fluids found that indicated that Kace had forced himself on her.

This time the doctor leaned over and clicked escape on the laptop and switched screens. All I could see was a whole document with one word, "Gibson." Chloe had entered my name over and over. Three whole pages of my name. Proof with all that had happened to her, she had, still remembered me in all of this. Another negative thought entered my head. *How does she remember me?*

I stared confused at the doctor and when he smiled, I was so fucking relieved that I could have kissed that ugly little man. Heaving out a long sigh, I then cleared the lump that had been in my throat since I watched Chloe on the screen so intently, "So what does this mean?"

"It means I want to prepare you for seeing Chloe."

Hearing those words set off a chain reaction of excited thoughts about what I was going to say to her. My adrenaline pumped even harder in my veins at the thought of finally holding her in my arms again, feeling her hair, smelling her skin and having her warm body close to mine. Then came the worry. *How do I get from what I saw on the screen to achieving that?*

"Not yet, of course...but soon. If she does this again or makes another reference to you, I'll re-introduce you to her." Reading my disappointment, he stood and stepped around his desk, placing his hand heavily on my shoulder. "I know this is frustrating for you, but we have to go at Chloe's pace. We've come a long way in such a short time, and in my view she's weeks away from talking, much faster than I could have hoped for at the start of this."

Usually that assessment would have made my heart soar, but now that I'd seen Chloe on screen and knew she was thinking about me, it was torturous. I'd seen her for myself and before that's all that I'd wanted, but now...I needed to hold her— regardless of what Chloe needed. *I* needed to hold *her*.

Opening the door, my eyes met Johnny's, who studied me with a worried look in his eyes like he was holding his breath. It dawned on me that Chloe's position had taken its toll on all of us, in one way or another.

Jerry and Johnny were close friends and he was trying to support the both of us. Jerry had handed in his resignation, and although I hadn't accepted it, I was having difficulty getting past the way he'd fucked up twice in one day.

"Take me the fuck home. No, take me to a bar. I need to get drunk." Johnny didn't answer me, just threw an arm over my shoulder in support and walked quietly back to the car beside me. When he started the car, "Fix You" by Coldplay was on the radio.

Once we were settled, Johnny took out his phone. "Len, get the boys together, we're coming over."

"I said take me to a bar."

"Nope, tell me what happened?"

After a quick run through of what had happened in the doctor's office, Johnny let out a long slow whistle. "Damn, Gib. That's tough, but I think it won't be long before you get another call. What if it's today? You want to be drunk and make her wait? Or do you want to be ready to go get your girl and sort out this fucking mess in her head?"

Johnny was always looking out for me, and this time was no different. This time I listened to his voice of reason. "Take me to Len's."

Within ten minutes of arriving, Simon and Mick turned up. I can't explain what having all the guys rallying like that did for me, but I felt like I was home. Instead of talking about Chloe, Simon and Mick started talking about a party they had gone to a couple of days ago and the wild ride they both had with some plus size model with 'tits the size of watermelons.'

Mick loves curvy women and I could actually relate, because there was something about that certain type of woman that skinny girls just couldn't compete with. Dressed in the right clothing, they oozed sex appeal.

As they were talking about their naked antics with a carton of frozen yogurt they had taken from the host's freezer, we were all cracking up laughing when Simon started telling us about acquiring a bunch of grapes and two still being missing now.

We were crying with laughter about them both being drunk and Simon stubbing his toe when he slipped on the yoghurt that the woman rubbed on his feet and was attempting to suck off. Apparently this was too tickly for Simon, who cracked up laughing and he'd attempted to run to the bathroom to take a leak in the middle of everything.

As everyone was howling with laughter, I suddenly had a flashback of Ruby's face and the grin died on my face, but this time I had a clearer vision of what had happened. Like an old news reel, the whole incident became a solid memory and I could see exactly where I fitted in.

I was rip roaring drunk. It was Mick and Len that were having sex with Ruby. Not me. I was having sex with her friend in the same room at the time. Standing up, I puffed out a huge sigh of relief and all the guys turned to face me. Johnny stood up and he could see I was emotional, I was obviously relieved. Striding across the room, I pulled Mick out of the chair and kissed him hard on the lips.

Mick struggled with me until he wrestled himself free and wiped his mouth. "Eww, what the fuck, Gib.

What did you do that for? What the fuck is wrong with you?"

Grinning at Len who was staring at me with bunched brows I said, "Ruby? Did I fuck Ruby? Nah, it was you two randy bastards." I couldn't contain my delight, and pointed at Lennox then at Mick. Mick raised an eyebrow.

"Actually Gib you got that wrong, I fucked Ruby, she gave Len head."

Len said, "She did?" Len raised his eyebrow, then stated, "Well I'd like to say it was memorable but…"

Staring incredulously at Mick I asked, "You knew? You knew I never bagged her and you never said anything?" Mick looked at Len then Johnny and finally at me.

"What am I missing here? Why did you think you'd been with Ruby? Were you with Ruby? Jeez…I'm confused, will somebody fill me in?"

Only then did I realize that the only conversation I'd had about Ruby was with Len. Communication had to improve all around within the team. Snickering, I imagined us keeping a log book of who had bagged who, to avoid this kind of confusion in the future. Not that I'd be going elsewhere.

Johnny ordered pizzas and salad and for the rest of the night we talked about music and current affairs and I have to say it was the most normal night I'd had for months. Len told me to stay the night with the others, so I did.

Waking with the sun streaming through the side of the drapes, which had been pulled too far together,

I cracked my eye open trying to focus on the time. It was 9:45am. I hadn't slept that long for months and I was feeling pretty groggy.

Proud that I'd stayed away from alcohol: my temporary crutch when life felt too much, I wandered through to the sitting room. Johnny had crashed out on the large deep-cushioned sectional with his pants draped over the back of it and his bare hairy ass mooning out toward the center of the room. Seriously, the dude was a commando in more ways than one. Not able to resist an opportunity of catching him with his pants down literally, I smacked him hard on it. Johnny flew to his feet and was ready to do battle until he realized where he was and that the person who had spanked him was me. "What the fuck, Gib you nearly finished me there."

Snickering wickedly, I smirked and shook my head. "Dude, the way you were humping that leather, I think you were trying to finish yourself."

Len came padding through bare naked and acting all ambidextrous, scratching his balls and his head at the same time, and wandered over to the fridge. "Don't let me disturb you guys, carry on." Johnny sat on the leather sofa and it made this huge farting noise as he slid his clammy skin back against the leather and Len and I were suddenly kids with toilet humor, laughing raucously at him.

Simon came through, asking what was going on because it was still the middle of the night in his world, and ended up draining a whole carton of orange juice while we said our goodbyes. Johnny and I headed back to our rental place. Only then did it dawn on me that all the guys had hung around in Seattle when they could have been at home in Cali, basking in the sun.

"When I realized Chloe was gone, I felt that I had no one in this world that loved me for me. I was wrong. You guys are family. Even you...even Jerry, the fuck up."

"Jeez, Gib, I want it known I'm adopted, I don't want people to think I have a freak in my pants like yours."

Looking at the passenger seat I gave Johnny a wry grin and he sniffed, pretending to be indignant about my comment. But I could see he was secretly pleased that I thought of him like that. I was driving because he'd been drinking with the others. I wasn't going through this torturous time with Chloe and getting so close to seeing her again, only to die in a car crash because someone who had been drinking had impaired judgment on the road the following morning.

Cathy was sitting on the sofa crying when I arrived back at the house. Alarmed when I saw how distressed she was, I rushed over and hugged her. "What's happened? Chloe? What's happened?"

Cathy was sobbing and hitching her breath, wiping her runny nose. The toll it was taking on everyone was immense. "Chloe...she...sh...Gibson."

Whatever was going on for her, she couldn't bring herself to say it.

"Is she alive." I just wanted to establish the basics, anything else I'd manage afterwards.

Cathy smiled and nodded vigorously then shook

her head, her body still wracked with sobs. "She spoke...she said, 'Gibson.' Sinking to my knees in front of her, I took her hands in mine. "Thank you, God." Swallowing audibly, I looked into eyes that were just a bit dimmer than Chloe's but there was no doubt that Chloe was made from her. "I promise you, Cathy. Your daughter will be stronger and feistier than ever by the time I'm finished. I also promise you if it takes me to my last breath, I will find Kace and he will suffer for what he did to our girl."

Cathy smiled and freed one hand, placing it to my cheek. "Gibson, you are a good man. Chloe couldn't be in better hands." My breath caught in my throat, because Cathy was the third person who had just accepted me for who I was and not what I was.

CHAPTER 23

HOPE

Gibson

Chloe said my name.

"When can I see her? Why didn't they call me? Can I go over there now?" My mind was jumping all over the place. Cathy shook her head, looking sympathetically at me and I could see the struggle on her face about giving me information I really didn't want to hear.

"They didn't call you because they knew you would go straight there, Gibson. Dr. Owen said that Chloe is undergoing her therapy sessions this morning and afternoon and they would decide from there where they take it."

Those suffocating feelings in my chest rose again and I fought to suppress them. I was in danger of losing my self-control, because I was helpless to make any decisions. In my past, everything depended on me. I answered to no one, I did what I wanted, and it was up to me to make things work. Being reliant on others wasn't in my nature, nor was waiting for someone to give me permission to do something as basic as talk to a girl.

"Gonna take a shower." I was pissed and fucking furious that my girl had asked for me and I couldn't go and comfort her. As soon as I closed my bedroom door, I kicked the wall hard then I punched rapidly into the mattress. Breathing hard, I swung around and sat heavily on the bed feeling at boiling point. Stripping my clothes off in a temper, I threw my jeans at the dresser, knocking over all the shit I'd been leaving there for days. Cups, glasses, pens, notebook...stalking towards it, I took my arm along the dresser and swiped them all to the floor before striding into the bathroom and hitting the shower faucet on.

As soon as I stepped under the shower, I slumped down the tiles and cried again. I've never cried so much in my life as I have since Chloe was abducted. Actually, I don't remember crying at all before Chloe. I had just put shampoo on my hair when I heard my cell ring. Hurriedly, I tried to rinse it off and grabbed a towel from the back of the door, wrapping it around my waist.

I had missed a call from the clinic, so hit return and waited impatiently for it to connect. "Gibson Barclay—put me through to the person who just rang this number." I wasn't in the mood for pleasantries I just wanted to see my girl.

A couple of clicks on the line and the now familiar Patricia's voice came down it.

"Mr. Barclay? Can you come over? Dr. Owen

would like you to see Chloe."

Dropping the phone on the bed, I pulled on the first piece of clothing I could find. The white t-shirt that was Chloe's favorite was lying dirty on the floor, but I couldn't have cared less, so I swiped it up, pulled it on and headed down the hallway. "Johnny move it, I'm leaving now."

Johnny appeared from his room and came walking quickly down the hall. "They called you?"

I didn't answer because I was too busy finding shoes and Cathy came from the sitting room with hands raised, "She's asked for you?"

"Sorry, Cathy, I don't know anything, just that I got a call to go in. The doc says I can see her."

The car hadn't fully stopped when I opened the door and jumped out running in front of the SUV with my hand reaching out to the hood as if that was going to stop Johnny from mowing me down. Rushing inside, the door banged hard against the wall and all the reception staff stopped dead and turned to look at me.

Breathless, I heaved deeply to fill my lungs and gasped out, "Chloe. Dr. Owen called."

The hot prim receptionist with the black rimmed glasses and top knot inclined her head in the direction of the seats. "Please sit down, I'll let them know you're here."

"Sit down?" I'd done nothing for nearly two months *but* sit down. I didn't want to sit down. All I wanted was to be in the same room as Chloe again. Patricia, the stern looking intern with her severely scraped back black hair and blue hospital pajamas, appeared and ushered me up to Dr. Owen's office. When she opened the door I could see the doc already getting out of his chair to meet me.

"Gibson. Come in, take a seat."

"No. Tell me."

"Firstly, I need you to be very calm. Second I need you to do *exactly* what I ask. If I don't think you can, then I won't risk putting you in there with her. This is about Chloe. I don't care that you are a pop star."

"Rock star."

"Whatever. Here, you are Chloe's partner. She's the one with status, not you."

Damn. Of course he was right, but wrong at the same time. I wasn't being a rock star, I was being a guy who passionately wanted to see his girl in the flesh. Nothing bullish about that.

"When you enter the room, you are not to touch Chloe. You don't speak to her for the first five minutes and you are in there for a maximum of fifteen. You steer clear of anything that is remotely a stressor for her. Talk about music. Talk about the weather…anything you think is a safe subject. I don't expect much from Chloe. You can tell her how you feel about her in general terms but you are not to discuss Kace, understand? Keep the conversation clipped. Short sentences. You start reasoning and explaining something, it will all be lost and I may as well give you a megaphone and send you out to sea in a rowing boat, because she's not going to hear you."

Smiling at me like he'd just empowered me, made me feel depressed because I felt the opposite. I was walking into a minefield and one false move could send Chloe right back into her shell. When the doc arrived, he took me down the corridor and along another with a locked door. The reality of keeping Chloe safe became even more apparent. She wasn't a prisoner, but she was locked in because she was seen as a danger to herself and others until they knew her mental status.

Every step we took sparked a reaction from my body. My pulse was throbbing in my neck and my temple. My mouth was dry, my heartbeat thready and rapid, and I was almost panting with the fear and excitement of being with her. Opening the door, Dr. Owen, crept over to Chloe who was wearing a blue maxi skirt and white fitted top and she was sitting with her back to me, staring into the corner of the room. That shocked me. I never expected not to see her face.

Placing his stubby hand on the small laminate table beside her, he said, "Chloe, I have a new person I want you to see. He has come especially to see you. I am going to leave and come back in fifteen minutes, and he will leave again."

Few things in my life have scared me, but when the door clicked shut, I don't mind saying that I felt afraid. Afraid that I'd say something that hurt her or made her react badly or worse, trigger a negative memory. So I froze, standing there with an anxious feeling making every muscle in my body solidify, my fingers opening and closing because I was itching to hold her but I knew that I couldn't do that. So trying to figure a way around everything, I took the seat and sat quietly, waiting to see what she did. When she didn't turn to look at me, I stared at the back of her head.

After five minutes I said, "Just finding some tunes for us." Reaching over, I began flicking the CD cases forward to find one that she'd enjoy. A familiar one screamed at me, which would let her know what she meant to me. It was significant but general enough and it had played once when we were in the car, "Something I Need" by One Republic.

Ryan Tedder sang to Chloe while I listened and watched Chloe intently. There was no reaction— nothing. I don't know what I was expecting and I'd been warned not to expect much, but she appeared a shell of the warm sweet girl I fell in love with. When the song finished, I checked my watch and it was seven minutes in, so I could talk to her. "Hello, darlin' how's my girl doing?"

Again there was nothing. So I just sat talking about my day and how I was doing. Any ol' shit really, because if I said what I really thinking, I'd probably have finished her off.

Ten minutes in and I was getting desperate, so I went to the CDs again and put "Waiting for Superman" by Daughtry into the CD machine. As it started playing I sat with my forearms resting on my thighs, my legs slightly open, rubbing my hands together as I continued to watch and mentally trying to prepare myself, because my time was almost up.

I figured when the song finished I'd have to stand up and leave and that brought a lump to my throat. *How would I be able to walk away from her?* Fifteen minutes and she hadn't even looked around at me. Dr. Owen showed up and said to her, "Your guest is leaving now, Chloe, but he'll come back another day."

He signaled for me to stand, but I couldn't move. I had the hardest time complying with that. Shaking slightly, I was desperate to touch her and had to fight against that instinct. How I managed to walk away from her I have no idea, but I barely made it out of the room before I leaned against the wall and pressing my back to it, slumped down to the floor.

"Sorry, Gibson. I know that was very tough for you. Come with me, I have something to show you." I followed him back to his office, feeling crushed. I had expected something to happen, but those kind of things only happened in the movies. This was real life and Chloe's mental state was fragile. Once again, the doc got his laptop and I sat waiting for the upload. It was CCTV footage of Chloe and me. Chloe to the fore with her hands on her lap, me sitting behind her to the right of the screen. I couldn't understand why he was playing it back to me. I'd been right there in the room with her and she hadn't responded.

When he started the video, I wasn't expecting anything from the debrief but as the first song played Chloe's fingers flexed and pulsed in time to the music, and stopped when the music stopped. When I told her I loved her she closed her slowly eyes and that squeezed at my heart. But near the end when I played "Waiting for Superman," silent tears rolled down her cheeks.

I was almost overcome with the emotional

turbulence, but I sucked it up. I had been in the same room and thought there was nothing coming back from her, until I saw the footage. I swallowed uneasily and stared at the doc, fighting the turmoil in my head and my heart, because I figured if he saw any weakness in me now, it would slow things down and I definitely didn't want that to happen.

Leaving the facility was fucking painful. I begged repeatedly for a room at the hospital, but they would have none of it. Chloe's beautiful eyes on the screen, with those tears rolling down, burned in my brain. The psychiatrist had viewed it all really positively, and talked excitedly about her 'remarkable progress.' Frankly, six and a bit weeks and Chloe still there and not talking didn't feel like progress from where I was sitting.

I didn't get to see Chloe the following day and no real update from Cathy other than things were pretty much the same, then at about five in the morning I had a call asking me to go over there again.

Johnny was amazing and said everything he could think of to encourage me on the way back. The ache to see her again stung my heart, she had been crying the last time when I'd been in the room with her and I hadn't even known. That screen image of her eyes and those tears of hers had been haunting me. I shook my head, trying for clarity because I had to be ready for whatever Dr. Owen wanted me to do next.

My heart felt heavy, like it was weighing down on my diaphragm and I couldn't take in air. There's no other description for it. The thought of going through what I had in that room with her again made me skittish. Visiting someone in a mental health facility wasn't something I'd ever contemplated I'd have to do, never mind visit someone who was my life.

Blinking hard, I searched the intern's face as I tried to assimilate the words I'd been waiting to hear.

"Chloe has started talking."

I almost collapsed with relief. *What did she say?* My heart began to gallop, then took on an irregular beat as my breathing got shallower and faster.

"Over and over she has been asking to see you." I was speechless. Staring silently, standing stock still in shock that this was the beginning of the end of Chloe's horrible journey. Suddenly my thoughts caught up with my mouth.

"Well, what the fuck are we standing here talking about it for? Take me to her." Patricia, the intern, turned her nose up a little and I realized that I had cussed and sounded aggressive. Actually, how I sounded was a true reflection of how I was feeling; that we were wasting time when I could have been there in front of Chloe already.

Apologizing quickly, I excused myself as a little overwhelmed by the news and she seemed to sag her shoulders, like she was relieved to hear my words. Taking me into Chloe's room, I could feel my body responding to an adrenaline rush, every nerve ending on full alert, preparing for any shock I may encounter once I saw her.

When I slipped into the room, I stood with my back to the wall. Chloe was sitting on the edge of the bed in a tiny white tank top and blue pajama shorts, and the innocence on her face along with that little tank top made me think about the times I noticed her at Beltz Bar.

Patricia signaled for me to talk to her, so I cleared my throat and pushed myself off the wall, walked slow, to the bed, then knelt in front of her to give her eye contact. "Hello darlin', I heard you wanted to see me. You have no idea how happy that makes me, because I've been waiting patiently for this day." Chloe stared into my eyes and a tiny smile played on her lips. I was a wreck, but trying to sound soothing.

What I wanted to do was reach out and scoop her up in my arms, take her home and forget the world. But she had a way to go before I could do that. "Take your time, darlin', whatever it takes, I'll be waiting." With my words, Chloe's eyes welled and a single tear spilled down her cheek. Without thinking my finger caught it, brushing her cheek. Her hand caught mine and held it against her face.

"Hug me, Gibson." Chloe's tiny, croaky voice was like the sweetest song I'd ever heard.

Fuck the rules. Gently placing my hands around her shoulders, I leaned forward and hugged her. At first she was unresponsive, then all of a sudden her body leaned into mine and I felt her relax completely. I figured it was comforting, so I squeezed her a little tighter to my chest. I wasn't expecting anything to come back at me, but her hand ran up the inside of my t-shirt and she turned her head to snuggle her face into my neck.

There was a monumental lump in my throat that I needed to clear before I could speak, so I swallowed several times and tried to keep my emotions in check. The last thing Chloe needed was me breaking down in front of her. When her other arm snaked up against my skin at the side of my body, I couldn't stop myself from talking, "I got you, darlin', It's okay. I got you."

Chloe began to cry and I thought I'd done something very wrong, but she was clinging tightly to me, her hands twisting against the material of my t-shirt. "Let it out, darlin', I'm here. I'm not going anywhere." I was rocking her back and forward and Patricia had moved behind Chloe so that I could see her. Giving me the thumbs-up sign, she slipped outside the door.

We must have stayed like that for close to an hour, but my legs had pins and needles from kneeling, so I broke away from the hug and stood up. Chloe's red-rimmed eyes followed me from the floor to regain eye contact.

"I love you, Chloe. You need to try to get well so that I can take you home, darlin'."

Chloe said nothing, but nodded and my heart almost exploded into a million pieces because of that little interaction. I had to leave her behind and go home again after that, but it was one time less until I could take her with me.

CHAPTER 24

MY TAKE

Chloe

Vaguely aware of someone rubbing the front of my thigh, I opened my eyes to see this odd looking little man telling me I was okay. The man was Dr. Owen and like his name, I owed him for helping me keep my sanity after what happened to me. Talking in a low voice, he started explaining to me where I was, and he kept telling me I was safe in a gentle voice, like I was a frightened little child. That part registered with me, but for the rest of the time he made noise.

At first, my mind was a blank about Kace and what he had done to me. My earliest conscious memories at the facility were seeing my mom's worried face and the stiff looking intern in blue pajamas who kept talking to me as if I was replying. It never occurred to me that I wasn't talking or doing anything else for that matter. Plus they kept feeding me. Why wasn't I doing that?

To be honest, my mind was numb for a lot of the time. That was, until they started playing music. Then they brought some for me to choose. The CDs and player in front of me,—like something out of the 90's—reminded me of times playing my guitar alone to one just like that my mom owned. Thumbing through the CDs most of my favorites were there: Daughtry, Bruno Mars, One Republic, Ed Sheeran, Maroon 5...the only one missing was M3rCy. *Gibson.*

Placing them on the table, I felt my heart speed up when the 'Baptized' album slid to the side. Picking it up, I turned it to look at the cover. It was a wilting flower, past its best and pretty much summing up my feelings about what might have happened to Gibson and me. Then I wondered if that's why I was here? Did something bad happen between us?

After I started playing the CDs they seemed to be everywhere in my day. When the doctor used to take me to this room that smelt like a beauty salon massage room to do some weird communication stuff by staring into my eyes, my music came with me. While talking about things like Kace were painful for me, my music came comforted me. I didn't know why he was talking to me about Kace. I wondered if he had something to do with me being here?

Those sessions started and ended with my favorite music but in the middle there was some heavy stuff going on, where he'd give me a bad thought. Then at the end of the session when I thought about it again, it didn't have the same charge of shock as it did the first time he mentioned it. Turning the CD case, I searched the song list. "Waiting for Superman" drew my eye immediately. I placed the CD into the machine and lay back on my bed. Closing my eyes, I remembered being in the park and of Paul, or Gibson, talking to me. Warm feelings coursed through me. Hearing the song made my heart ache, but Gibson felt near when I heard it. So I played it again and again.

All I wanted to know is what happened to Gibson. Thinking about him helped me to think about all the wonderful things that had happened to me since I'd met him again. Memories of happy times, the way he protected me, held me and looked at me, gave me the inspiration to write.

Suddenly words and monologues and dialogues full of angst were all locked in my head...thoughts, feelings and emotions all cramming my brain so that I couldn't think about anything else. A love story formed that needed to be put down, as the characters in my head gave their voices to the words that filled my head and gave me focus.

When they brought me a laptop, I wondered if I had asked them to...I didn't remember asking that. At first I was scared to start writing, thinking that if anyone read it they would think the female was me and there were some pretty erotic things going on with my characters. Things Gibson and I had never tried. Georgie, my female protagonist, was like me in a way, because Gibson was a rock star and I am just an ordinary girl, but she and Ollie in my story had a very different path to mine.

There was already an ending in my head for a happy ever after for their story, but it didn't seem so for me. Gibson was gone and I was somewhere safe because something had happened that I had no recollection of.

Listening to my music filled my heart with light and cleared my mind but when "Waiting for Superman" played I thought about Gibson and the lyrics he wrote, and figured that if he could do it that I should at least try. So... I wrote my book.

Every waking moment was used, except for the times when they took me for some kind of session with the doctor. My Mom came every day. *Every day.* I wondered where my dad had gone, but most of all, I worried about what happened to Gibson. As my story reached its conclusion my heart had a void again, but this time it was Gibson it was pining for. Pushing out of my chair, I automatically went to the song that made me feel close to him.

As soon as Chris Daughtry's gravelly voice began to sing, I began to write Gibson's name. Over and over until my wrist hurt then I stopped, wondering if everyone had known what I couldn't see at the time. What Gibson didn't want to see? Had I reached my expiry date like Tori warned me I would? Did he just cut me off? Why could I remember her and nothing else?

Once those questions were in my head, I couldn't shake them out again. Eventually I had to ask, but all I could say was Gibson. Sitting on my bed, my mom cupped her hand to her mouth and inside my head I was screaming what's wrong? Where is he? What happened? Suddenly my mom was ushered out the door and I was left on my own. She was in shock. Did he die?

During lunch, the urge to know what had happened to me was so strong that I blurted out Gibson's name again. The voluntary aid who was feeding me with her visitor's badge around her neck, gave me no response other than to leave the room.

Later that day I was sitting in the room, staring into the corner, I hadn't realized I was until the doctor's hand came into my line of sight. "Chloe, I have a new person I want you to see. He has come especially to see you. I am going to leave and come back in fifteen minutes, and he will leave again."

Sitting and waiting for the person to speak seemed to take an age, then I had the shock of my life when I heard Gibson's voice. There was no expectation about visitors, but my first thought was, thank god he's alive. The elation of knowing that was quickly replaced by the sensation of my heart beating erratically in my chest and pulsing up into my mouth. Two more questions emerged, Why was he here? And did something happen that brought him here out of pity?

Gibson started my music and One Republic played "Something I Need." That played once when we were in the car. It wasn't the first track on the album, so he would have had to select that to play to me. How did I think of that? Was he telling me he still needed me? I loved the song choice and I especially loved the drumbeat, it always made me tap along.

Gibson had obviously come to tell me something and when the song finished, I kind of prepared myself for him to say he was busy and had to go on tour, so he wouldn't be able to see me anymore...or similar words that let him off the hook as far as I was concerned.

"Hello darlin', how's my girl doing?" Gibson's words filled me with relief and my throat constricted as a sob stuck there. I closed my eyes to help my mind absorb his use of, 'my girl.' Gibson didn't stop talking for a few minutes, telling me about living with my mom and dad and I thought he must be making it all up and was just saying the first thing that came into his mind. My head couldn't compute my parents and Gibson in the same room, never mind living in the same house.

I heard shuffling behind me, the CD player snapped shut, then "Waiting for Superman" began to play and I wondered why he was wasting his time. Wondering why he wasn't hugging me, if I really was still his girl. I really needed a hug and by the sound of his voice, he needed one too. A tear rolled down my face, but I couldn't bring myself to move or to look at him.

Gibson cleared his throat and there was the clipped sound of footsteps advancing before I heard the door open and close softly. Dr. Owen's voice interrupted the silence.

"Your guest is leaving now, Chloe, but he'll come back another day."

In my head I was screaming. *No!* There had been no hug goodbye, just footsteps retreating and then the swish of the door opening and the soft click of it closing again.

The finality of the door closing made me feel anxious. I had no idea when Gibson would come back or even if he would. Lying awake for most of the night, I had only one thing on my mind, the image of Gibson smiling at me as he sang just for me with twenty odd thousand people out in the stadium watching his every move. I realized I could remember vividly to a certain point. I was sick.

All during the following day I had a knot in my stomach and an expectation that he may come back at any moment. When darkness fell and the staff changed shift to the evening team, I wouldn't accept that he wasn't coming. Refusing to lie down, I sat on my bed and in my head I kept saying *I want to see Gibson...I need to see Gibson*... eventually the sound came out of my mouth. I need Gibson, I need Gibson. No one was there and I repeated myself over and over.

A male nurse I'd never seen before entered the room and stood with his arms folded by the door. "Okay, Chloe. We hear you. Someone is trying to call Gibson now. It's very early in the morning." As soon as he said they were contacting him, I stopped speaking.

Gibson arrived sounding breathless and when he slipped into the room, he leaned against the wall. My pulse throbbed in my neck with my fast heartbeat at his presence and I continued to stare ahead. Knowing he was here was enough...then it wasn't. Clearing his throat, he pushed himself off of the wall then knelt in front of me, smiling a half smile that didn't quite reach his eyes. They looked nervously into mine. Gibson

K. L. Shandwick

hesitated for a moment. I wasn't used to this timid side of the alpha male I fell in love with.

"Hello, darlin', I heard you wanted to see me. You have no idea how happy that makes me, because I've been waiting patiently for this day."

My heart squeezed tightly and pumped hard and it felt like warm blood was being injected into me. Like I was coming to life and I think I smiled.

Gibson's voice was very soft as he watched me intently, "Take your time, darlin', whatever it takes, I'll be waiting." When I heard him say that, a tear fell from my eye and Gibson's hand made contact with my cheek to catch it. As soon as he touched me I didn't want him to let me go, so I clapped his hand against my face.

Finding my small gruff voice again, I demanded, "Hug me, Gibson."

Without hesitation, Gibson gave me what I needed, but I couldn't move. I was scared and holding my breath. Partly with the effect of his touch and the rest I couldn't understand. Once I got used to the feel of him, it felt so good I never wanted him to let me go.

Instinctively, I clung to his t-shirt in my effort to get closer and buried my face in his neck, inhaling his scent deeply, and my hand slipped under his t-shirt and I began to feel the warmth of his body. His smooth hard muscles strained his satiny warm skin. I can't describe the feeling I had from that. Gibson clung tightly to me in return and I heard him swallow, repeatedly telling me what we were doing was as emotional for him as it was for me.

278

"I got you, darlin', It's okay. I got you." Fat tears rolled down my cheeks as I began to cry.

"Let it out, Chloe, I'm here. Shh...I'm not going anywhere." I did, and Gibson rocked me back and forth, kissing the top of my head and whispering that everything was going to be okay. We stayed, just holding each other like that for a long time. Eventually he released me and stood up and I looked up into his serious eyes that were watching me intently, then Gibson cleared his throat again, "I love you, Chloe. You need to try to get well so that I can take you home, darlin'." I nodded weakly and thought that I needed to get well to be with him as well.

For weeks I had nothing, just an empty space in my head. Then I remembered and I woke sweating in fear. I wasn't sure if it was a nightmare or it really happened, but Kace was struggling and I had a cloth over my face with a horrible acidic smell that stole my breath until everything went black.

Slowly there were snippets of Kace and I remembered he'd taken me to this weird little shack and kept me in semi darkness. Apart from mentally abusing me, he didn't speak. I sat petrified waiting for the time when he'd force himself on me, or hit me for leaving him and being with Gibson. In my mind I was going to die, believing there was no way I was ever going to be allowed to walk away from him a second time.

During my time with him, he terrorized me. Calling me names and played his mind-fuck games that had me cowering, fearful of when the first heavy blow was going to come. I was so frightened I stayed mute. Not a word from me to him, so his assault was completely one sided. I don't know how long it went on for but there was a woman who kept showing up and I could hear the nervousness in Kace's voice. She was very flirty and as Kace is a good looking guy, she was in pursuit. It worked in my favor, but not for Kace, because if he was planning something for me she never gave him peace to follow through.

Eloise she said her name was, and she made quite a nuisance of herself, which frustrated the hell out of Kace, but it got so bad, that he got cold feet and with the same speed as I was taken, I was being bundled back into the trunk of his car and driven away.

My head said he was going to throw me in a lake somewhere or off a bridge into a river. My gut told me I'd live. We drove for twenty minutes, then he killed the engine and my heart stopped and I held my breath as I waited for him to spring the lock and face me.

When daylight flooded the trunk, strong unkind hands dragged me out and sat me on the ground. I squinted as my eyes adjusted to the light, and all I saw was the lake in front of me. I thought my time had come and my breathing became shallow and fast, as fear pushed my heartbeat up into my mouth. Pulses of shocked electric-like messages shot through my head and body and the panic began to steal my breath altogether. Then—I blacked out. That was my last memory of being with Kace. He didn't force me, he didn't hit me—he just mentally wiped the floor with me.

CHAPTER 25

CLEAN AIR

Gibson

Three weeks later, Chloe asked me to take her home. I had been staying with Chloe at the facility for ten days to learn how to deal with the issues that she may encounter, and I was given some strategies to help her cope. Forty-eight hours later, we had a plan. Johnny told me Len had told him that Simon was getting restless about not working, but I wasn't interested. He was being selfish and he knew what side his bread was buttered on. We knew he'd never leave the band. He just had to learn some patience. At least we didn't have Tori to worry about any more. Her meddling ass was kicked to the touch line as soon as the gigs were over.

After many discussions, Dr. Owen and Chloe's parents agreed that I could take her somewhere away from Seattle, where it was secluded and we'd have anonymity. Chloe needed to get stronger and we needed to keep her away from the spotlight.

So we assembled a mental health team to take with us. They worked with Chloe doing a combination of cognitive behavioral work and psychotherapy so that it could start to manage what had happened to her. Everyone was hopeful they would be able to delve into the past with Chloe, because she needed a lot of support to move forward with her life.

It was Johnny's idea to take her to my cabin in Breckenridge. The Colorado mountains are beautiful and I had a thing about cabins. Very few people knew I had this one either, because it was in Johnny's name to keep the press from hounding. The media had the idea I lived in hotel rooms. I keep a permanent one in New York. 'Strings' in Breckenridge was my number one retreat and the place I called home.

When I told Chloe we were flying to Denver, her brow creased with worry. At that point, she was afraid of her own shadow outside the facility. Once I explained my home was there and the acreage, and that I'd had managed to keep the place secret for four years from the media, I saw her visibly relax. Apart from the guys in the band, Johnny, Jerry and Charlotte, no one knew I was connected to the place.

"Trust me." When I whispered softly into her ear, I heard her swallow before she leaned back and gave me a solid look. Chloe's serious stare pierced my soul and for a few moments I held my breath, because she was my life and she held my future in her hands. Eventually she nodded and I sighed heavily and drew her back into a hug. "I got you, darlin'," I said affectionately, rubbing her back.

Travelling to the mountains was the one thing that made me really happy before I met Chloe. Summer was awesome with plenty of stuff going on, camp outs, fishing and hunting and I had some awesome mountain bike trails that I challenged myself on. It made a change from running and with the altitude there it was a tough regime, because although the air was cleaner, it was also thinner and my body had to work harder.

When Chloe saw the cabin her pretty blue eyes went wide and she placed her hand over her heart. "It's...it's beautiful Gibson." Cocking my head to the side, I had to agree. It was a magnificent 11,000 square foot, Douglas fir log home. Part brick on the bottom and elevated log at the top, it stood more than forty feet from the ground to the roof. A large wrap around deck with multiple seating areas faced the five highest peaks in the awesome mountain range that dwarfed everything before them. In the yard were massive round fire pits and a twelve person hot tub faced five highest peaks in the awesome mountain range that dwarfed everything before them.

If it looked awesome on the outside, the inside was even more impressive. Floor to ceiling windows, forty feet wide by twenty-five high, brought the mountain peaks into the great room. Impressively decorated, but with comfort and relaxation in mind, the oversized suede deep-pile cushioned couches and plush deep piled rugs in rich reds and creams made the room welcoming. The main suite had a sauna in the bathroom, a small den and an office. On the other side of the great room were five bedrooms with bathrooms and a games room. The great room was open plan with a dining room and kitchen which completed the large space.

So for three months Chloe, her counsellors and I worked on helping her regain some of her strength. The official line for the media was that M3rCy was having a break due to our grueling tour schedule. The press seemed to accept this and backed off for a while. Len and Mick were still okay about taking a break, Simon was less than impressed, but like I said, he's a pretty selfish guy, much like I was before I met Chloe.

Every day Chloe did something new to face her demons, and her strength inspired me. Every night we lay on the round patio bed watching the stars in the night sky on the decking, or while sitting close to each other in the hot tub. Sex was a mute subject. Every night I went to bed with my balls and my dick screaming at me in protest because her hot little body was snuggled close to mine, but there was no way I was pushing her for anything.

For a highly sexed guy like me, that was pretty tough to handle, so my right hand and the shower became my intimate date on a very regular basis. Len and I talked about it, because I sometimes wondered if she'd ever want to have sex again.

"Jeez, Gib...best not let the press get the scoop on this, they'll have you headlining with impotency due to wearing your dick smooth."

Len couldn't imagine going for five days without sex, never mind almost five months. Until it happened to me, it was beyond my comprehension. I had a newfound respect for monks.

It was frustrating that they never got to the bottom of the tests they did at the hospital when Chloe was brought in. Dr. Owen said that there was no evidence that Chloe had been sexually abused, and there were no physical marks on her when she was found. When he told me that particular piece of information I wanted to fist pump in celebration, but that would have been distasteful to Chloe and highly inappropriate.

I'm glad I didn't, because he then went on to say that just because Chloe had no physical signs and no semen, didn't eliminate the possibility of assault. Kace could have used a condom and she was missing for five days, so if intercourse had taken place early into the kidnap, there may not necessarily have been anything to see. They did a pregnancy test, which was negative. I hadn't even considered that outcome. Imagine the feelings involved for Chloe if that had been the case.

Chloe did tell me and her counsellors that Kace never physically touched her apart from moving her around from place to place, but they told me out of earshot of her that she could be blotting that part out in her mind.

By late September all the guys in the band were getting restless and I wouldn't let them visit for fear of knocking back the progress we were making. Len set a meeting for mid-October and I agreed to be there because although I was dealing with Chloe, I knew the time was coming when I'd have to go back to work and I still had obligations to them as well.

Some of Chloe's counselling included me, and I hadn't realized the extent to which her ordeal had affected me. I wasn't sure I'd be able to trust anyone with Chloe, but the counsellors told me that had to be tested at some point.

Emma and Lois were still on full pay and stayed with us in Breckenridge, and although they wouldn't let anyone stay at the hospital, I had figured Chloe was secure there and if I couldn't get to her, Kace certainly couldn't.

Kace—that fucker was still flying under the radar and hadn't shown himself anywhere, but I had learned through Chloe that I was a patient man. I had confidence that he would fuck up sometime and with every passing day, I got nearer to that day.

Our time in the cabin was very solemn and quiet at first, but with each passing day it got more and more normal. Music filled the space and I was even playing and writing some songs. I tried to get Chloe to play but she was too embarrassed in front of me. I didn't press her on that, but I'm not giving hope that one day she would. Sometimes when I looked at Chloe I'd see a frown form and that told me she was having intrusive thoughts about Kace, so I was still treading carefully.

Chloe went from strength to strength. Her sense of humor and quiet sassiness returned. We had fallen into a routine of running or mountain biking along the trail near our cabin. Situated on four hundred acres, the cabin was very private. Eventually the mental health team retreated and Chloe's sessions were conducted by phone.

Spending time with her team had helped Chloe talk openly about most things, and because it was just the two of us when they had gone, she began to touch me naturally. At first it was just an affectionate palm on my face, or patting my abs. It wasn't until she did this that I realized any physical contact was instigated by me. Once she started touching me I began to feel good about my world again, apart from the fact that my dick thought my brain had stopped communicating with it. It sent constant horny messages of its need to penetrate something.

My frustration began to mount and I tried hard to manage it. We'd just come back from the mountain trail and I'd been checking out her tight little ass as she struggled to place her bike wheel in the upright stand. Instantly hard, I tried to cover it by turning my hips to the side and focusing on my bike while I tried to get my dick and my feelings under control. Suddenly Chloe slid her hand over my sweat soaked back and I twisted my upper body to look at her.

"Thank you for bringing me here, Gibson. I sleep like a baby, get tons of exercise, and the company...a girl couldn't ask for more."

"No?" I was the one with a one word reply, because what I wanted to say was this isn't enough for me, I want more. I need more. Watching her smile with her healthy glow and damp hair at her hairline from exertion made me want to climb inside her. Her appearance just screamed sexual connotation to me.

Chloe's face flushed and I guess that she had heard the sexual tension in my husky one word answer. I was fighting for control when she bit her lip, so I turned back and secured the bike and we both fell into an awkward silence that continued until we reached the house. Emma was on the deck and as I made my way to the bedroom to shower, Chloe went out to talk to her.

Later that evening, after we had dinner, our previous tension seemed to have disappeared. I had other things on my mind because I was feeling a little apprehensive. I was due to leave her and fly down to LA to meet the band.

I took a couple of hours to do some work to meet obligations I had signed up for before Chloe's incident. There were a few projects I had agreed to fund overseas, and I hadn't had the chance to complete the deals with the overseas development guys to maximize the contributions. Chloe was doing some therapeutic creative writing and the house was very quiet. Everyone had gone to their own quarters and when I realized the time, I felt guilty that I'd been in my office so long.

When I opened the office door, it was dark. Someone had turned off the lights in the great room and my heart raced instantly. *Where is Chloe?* Running along the corridor with the spiral bannister to my left, I headed toward the stairs. When I saw the glow of the fire from the open plan stairs, I looked down into the great room and the sight I saw made my heart stop.

Chloe was sitting by the fire wrapped in a white sheet. Her hair was tied in a top knot, and the yellow glow of the huge open fire illuminated the soft skin on her shoulders, giving them a golden sheen.

Working a swallow, I stood for a moment committing the image to memory. She looked incredible. Chloe was making a brave decision, but one that filled me with trepidation. Gibson Barclay– scared to make a move on a girl. But Chloe wasn't just 'a girl', she was *my* girl and she had been through hell.

As I began to move down the stairs, one of them creaked. Cringing at the noise, my eyes flicked back in the direction of Chloe, who turned her head slowly to look at me. I couldn't see her face because the light from the fire was behind her, but I smiled because I wanted to reassure her. I walked toward her and the nearer I got, the more I could make out her face. Stunningly innocent, serious eyes stared back at me, making my smile stretch wider.

"Hi." Her voice was so soft, almost a whisper.

Crouching down beside her, I took her head in my hands and kissed her gently on the lips.

"Hi."

I had kissed Chloe often in the last few weeks, but it wasn't really done as a sexual overture. Breaking the kiss, I leaned back to see if she was okay, because this time it was different. Chloe smiled sweetly, leaned forward and kissed me again, this time tracing the seam of my lips with her tongue, and my world shifted on its axis.

That one little stroke of her tongue had my dick

stretching my pants to bursting point. I'll admit I struggled not to throw her to the floor and roll on top of her, but it was Chloe's next action that surprised me.

I had to untangle my legs as she pushed me on my back and reached for the buckle of my belt. Unthreading it, she pulled it clear of the belt loops, folded it in half then pulled it together, making a loud snapping noise. I almost creamed my pants, because the noise coincided with the loosening of the sheet that had been tucked in, covering her body. It cascaded around her waist, exposing her beautiful pert tits and upper body.

The torment of going at her pace was killing me and I felt terrified that I'd lose control with her, because I wasn't sure that she wasn't going to lose confidence and stop at any minute. But she reached for my pant zipper and the pressure of her hand undoing the zipper made me squirm against it and groan loudly. "Fuck, Chloe." My voice was laced with lust as I watched her seducing me.

"I need to feel you, Gibson." *What does she mean? She's undoing my belt and my zipper. She wants to feel my dick?*

"Tell me what you want, Chloe."

My body was vibrating with anticipation of her holding me in her hands and after all this time, I was worried that I'd cream right then because after five months, the thought of anyone touching me intimately was almost too much. I wanted to devour her.

"I want my life back. I want you back. I don't want

him to win."

Relief filled me and I closed my eyes, swallowing loudly, because that was what wanted for her as well.

"You got me, darlin', you've always had me. I never left you."

"I know. Thank you. But I want...I want...my Gibson, the man. The sexy, crude, cussing, highly sexy rock god seducer back. I don't need Gibson the carer anymore."

"Oh you want the rock god back now, do you? And...what about what I want, darlin'?" I sounded playful, but I was choking at her bravery and the broken words she struggled to get out. She was expressing what she wanted from me, and I knew I had to go at her pace.

"You can have anything you want, Gibson. I'm ready."

I hummed playfully, pretending to think. "Hmm...anything I want? Um, I'm not sure I know what I want. I mean I don't need a picture of your pussy...I still have that by the way." Chloe's jaw hung and I shot her a wry grin that had her giggling.

"Seriously?"

"Sure, you didn't delete my dick pic, did you? No. Don't tell me you sold it on eBay? Swapped it on Craigslist for an Adam Levine Calendar?" Chloe began laughing loudly and the sound of it was like music plucking my heart strings.

"You haven't answered me, Chloe. What did you do with it?"

Chloe smirked sheepishly at me. "Gibson...of

course I still have it. It's kept me going this last month. Every night we've gone to bed has been horrendous for me."

Before I had stopped laughing, Chloe had lurched forward and was lying across me. Completely naked and me dressed apart from my belt and my zipper undone.

"So..."

I smirked wickedly at Chloe, because her saying that took us back to our phone calls when I was Paul and she never knew me.

"So...anything?" I quizzed again playfully.

"Gibson. Tell me what you want."

"You want the tactful caring version or the honest horny Gibson Barclay one?"

"Oh, I want the full Gibson experience, please." She said with mock adulation in her voice.

"I'm not going to scare you, Chloe?" my voice lifted at the end of the question.

"Gibson—the past few months, nothing you did could ever scare me."

With that disclosure, I was off the floor shucking myself out of my jeans. Then thought I had to do one more thing. "Don't go away—I'll be right back." Stalking off in just my t-shirt, I ran up the stairs two at a time, tearing into the first bedroom. Reaching the bed, I pulled the comforter and the pillows into a pile, gathered them up and headed back to the great room. Halfway down the stairs again, I stopped at the sight of Chloe.

Chloe was sitting naked in a profile pose facing the

huge bank of windows. The moonlight illuminated her as she stared up at the snow peppered mountain tops with one leg tucked under her bottom the other bent at the knee. Silky blonde hair cascaded down to the middle of her back and the fire glowed orange behind her. She took my breath away and I became religious all over again, thanking God for the gift of her, for bringing her back safely to me, and for giving us this second chance.

Turning her head toward me, she shifted to her knees facing me in a very submissive type pose, as I walked toward her. I couldn't help thinking it's the beginning of the rest of our lives and we only live once, so I should grab it by the balls just like I always did until I met Chloe. Except this time, I'm taking her with me.

Smiling at Chloe and outwardly calm, the thought in my head was anything but. I had been a patient man but once in my life and Chloe was worth it. *Nothing and no one will ever get in the way of us again and any fucker that does...make no mistake...I will deal with them...and if I do, it won't be fucking pretty.*

CHAPTER 26

HEALING

Gibson

Chloe sat quietly, watching me intensely as I began to shake out the comforter. Every time I thought I had the measure of her, she would surprise me with something else that made me reassess my views.

I thought I knew how women ticked and what they wanted from me, but Chloe taught me that there was no doubt that I knew my way around a woman's body and how to give her pleasure, but trying to deal with what was going on in the mind of a woman was a whole different ball game.

I crawled on to the cover, sat with one knee up and patted the cover for her to come over next to me. Chloe stood up unashamed in front of me, even after what had happened. Her naked body looked incredible by the light of the fire. Kneeling beside her, I reached up and took her hands. Chloe stepped forward and her belly was next to my lips.

Moving slowly, I closed the couple of inches between us and landed a kiss on the soft skin of her belly. Chloe sucked in a deep breath and her body began to hum, a little tremor that showed anticipation and maybe there was a little fear in there as well.

Slipping her hands out of mine, she cradled my head then her fingers through my hair and I positioned myself on my knees in front of her. I rolled my head back to look at her, hardly believing this moment had come.

"Thank you, Gibson."

Chloe was bending forward, looking down at me from her vantage point, a sexy smile playing on her lips and a twinkle in her eye. "So…"

Snickering, I shook my head and clasped my hands around her ankles. Slowly, I began to tease her by skimming over the silky skin on her lower limbs and took my hands away at the knee. Flattening them out I slid my palms up her thighs and around to take the tight little globes of her ass in them. We'd done nothing but my dick was a solid straining mass, standing proud and twitching for attention.

When I pulled her close against me I could smell her sex. *Fuck.* Just the thought of being able to be with her…inside her made me feel so horny, I was fighting primal instincts to spread her flat and fuck her brains out.

Licking my bottom lip, I leaned forward and dragged my nose from her pubis, up her belly and cupped her right breast in my hand. The warmth in it radiated through my palm and I grazed my thumb over her nipple before taking it in my mouth and sucking it firmly. Chloe gave me a small moan of delight and rolled her head on her neck, extending it so that I could see the whole line of it clearly by the firelight.

Trying to go at her pace was killing me and I wasn't sure how I was going to hold out much longer after all this time without her, but Chloe must have sensed this, because she began pushing me backward and down onto my back.

Of course I complied. She could do anything she liked to me...as long as she wasn't going to draw it out. I repositioned myself on the floor, Chloe was still standing but straddled my body.

"Take the t-shirt off. I want abs."

In my half-sitting position, I smirked as I struggled to get the top over my head before I pulled it free, discarding it on the floor. Tiny crackles of electricity burst between us, which was so fitting because the atmosphere between us was electric. My body was vibrating slightly at the thought of her touching me. As soon as I felt her smooth, satiny, naked skin on her ass, I was addicted all over again.

"We need to do this my way for a while. Are you okay with that?"

The fact we were doing it at all was alright with me. I was as frustrated as fuck and desperate to push myself deep inside that sweet pussy of hers. She could have told me to do anything and I'd have been willing.

"Chloe, I thought you said whatever I want." I was teasing her but she missed that, because when I saw the hesitancy in her, I realized that all of this, no matter how much she wanted to do it, was very difficult for her.

Stroking her legs again as she stood astride me while I lay flat, I tried not to notice her pussy and concentrate on her face. "What I want is for you to be in charge, Chloe. Whatever you want. That's what I want, darlin'."

Chloe huffed out a breath and smiled, but I didn't miss the relief on her face. Kneeling down on her knees, her damp pussy skimmed across my belly. As she reached over and pulled my belt back towards her I thought that she was going to belt me, but she lifted one arm and then the other, and rested them over my head before sliding the belt leather under them and looping it through the buckle.

Pulling the belt leather tight, Chloe restrained me. My excitement went from desperately hard up to if- I-don't-fuck-something-soon-I'll-die. She was so fucking hot to watch. Tongue curved on full plump upper lip, little grunts and pants, soft moans and as she pulled the loop on the buckle her pussy wiggled against my belly leaving little warm, wet, sticky patches with her effort.

Not being able to touch her was painful. Chloe placed her hands on my pecs and pushed herself back slightly onto my thighs. *Thank you, God.* My dick bounced on my belly and Chloe glanced down at it and snickered. I was aching for her to hold it and my body was so highly strung it was vibrating slightly. If we waited much longer I felt I would disappoint her, because at this rate I was going to be a two minute wonder.

Chloe began to move and I thought, *damn this is it. The moment I've dreamed about for months. Our moment.* Pushing off me, she snaked her way up to stand and began to walk away, leaving me with my hands tied above my head. "Chloe, where the fuck are you going?"

I didn't mean to sound so aggressive, but no one leaves me with my dick as stiff as a board and my hands tied above my head. That's bad form. Chloe gave me a devilish grin and in the most seductive voice I've ever heard come out of her mouth she said, "Gibson, you've been a patient man, another minute isn't going to kill you. Lie there and be a good boy, I just need to get something."

While I was trying hard to control my feelings, I realized yet another first. No one had ever made me wait for sex like she was doing. Most women had my dick out before I was even sure that I wanted to fuck them. Thinking about her withholding in this sense, got me more excited in the anticipation of her coming back so that we could get down to it, was fucking mind blowing.

Music filled the great room and Safia, "You are the One" played seductively. Chloe reappeared with a bottle of Cristal already corked from the cooler in an ice bucket, and two glasses. Smirking, she placed them down at the side of the comforter and crawled back over to straddle me.

"So..."

I swallowed noisily, both at what was coming...and

I hoped it was me...and at how brave my girl was, to have been where she was a few short months ago, and preparing herself to take on someone like me in the bedroom again...or the floor in this case.

Leaning over, she rattled the champagne bottle in the metal ice bucket and taking it out, poured one flute of the ivory fizzy liquid. Placing the bottle back, the ice clinked noisily again. Chloe placed the flute to her lips and sipped from the glass.

"Mmmm." Her exaggerated appreciation of the flavor made my dick bounce impatiently on my belly again. Chloe looked at it, then at me and smirked. "As you've been a good boy so far, I'm going to let you taste it."

When she sipped it again, I thought she was going to kiss me and share the champagne from her mouth, but she looked up and swallowed it painfully slowly. What she was doing was killing me.

Placing her hand behind my head, she placed the flute to my lips. "Drink."

I sipped the champagne, Chloe pulling it away before I was done. It dribbled down my chin to my neck and small drops fell from the bottom of the glass onto my chest as she placed it down on the floor.

Without warning, Chloe turned and licked the spillage up my neck, my chin then traced my lips with her tongue. My ass cheeks clenched and I arched up, realizing how difficult it was to lose the use of my arms in these circumstances.

I had seen Chloe being assertive and wanting to dominate me only one other time, and as hot as this was, there was a bigger message in this. She was showing me that she was capable of moving on, and I should follow her lead. Occasionally, I didn't mind being led when I was having sex, but I much preferred to take charge.

Chloe kissed me hard and that was another surprise, because the hunger and passion in it left me in no doubt that she definitely wasn't going through the motions.

The slick juice that was coating my belly from her pussy more than backed that up as well.

When Chloe sat back, her hands on my belly, I thought that this is it...the moment where we got down to serious feelings and touching and sharing our bodies, but she leaned over and scooped a block of ice out and dropped it in the center of my chest. I shrieked at the sudden cold, and she grinned before taking it between her fingertips and trailing it down my body.

"Don't. Come sit on my face, darlin'." Chloe's eyelid drooped immediately as her she took on that sex-drunk look of lust and threw the ice back in the ice bucket.

"You want to taste me, Gibson?"

Fuck— If I didn't, I was going to die of thirst.

"Sit on my face. Do it. You smell delicious."

Chloe crawled up my body and lowered her pussy to my mouth, but without pressure. I inhaled her scent deeply and the effect was fucking sensational. Darting my tongue out, I licked her seam lightly and Chloe hitched her breath. She moaned long and low, widening her stance on her knees to bring her pussy closer to my mouth. Growling deeply into her core in response, my instinct was to hold her. My hands kept trying to react to my thought and I kept trying to carry through on that. "Open the belt. I want my hands."

Without a word, Chloe leaned forward and I sucked on her clitoris. My reward was another long moan, "Ahhhh," falling involuntarily from Chloe's lips. As soon as my hands were free I skimmed them down the sides of her body, placed them on her ass and dragged her closer to my mouth.

As soon as she was in position, I sucked hard on her clitoris, then began fucking her with my tongue until I felt her body begin to tremble. Instead of making her come, I repositioned her by laying her down and rolling over between her legs.

Sliding my palms under her ass, I checked Chloe's face and I could see she was gone. There was no question in my mind that Chloe wanted me to fuck her and she didn't appear to have any inhibitions about it either. She looked as sexy as sin and the smirk she was wearing held many improper thoughts. I would bet my life on it.

Dipping my head I licked her softly again and in response she moaned softly, whimpered and thrust her pussy into my face. So from that point on I sucked her clitoris and watched her face, adding one finger into her pussy, then two. Chloe's gorgeous huge eyes locked onto mine until they rolled back in her head.

"Eyes, Chloe. Look at me." My voice sounded stern. It wasn't a request, it was a demand.

Opening her eyes, she tried to stay focused as she came undone on my tongue. "I love you, Gibson."

Hearing her declare her love for me made me stop dead. I hadn't realized how important her saying those words again had been, until they passed her lips. It was a different declaration, because there was no argument preceding it, and I heard the love in her voice when she said it.

"Thank you." I had just been given the gift of pleasuring Chloe and she was thanking me, her manners were fucking impeccable. Crawling up beside her, I trailed the back of my fingers up her body and watched her skin detonate into millions of tiny goose bumps. Chloe shivered and wriggled and I took her face in my hands, dragged my thumbs across her beautiful plump lips and kissed her deeply, letting her taste her sex on me.

My body was screaming for her in a silent torture and my hands couldn't stop moving on her. Touching her—feeling her skin, and watching the way she reacted both by her physical body movements and the erotic sounds she made were like the most potent aphrodisiac I'd ever encountered.

Tasting Chloe was the biggest high, and the look in her eyes alone with that lust-drunk stare she was doing, made my dick ache beyond anything I'd felt before. Her hot breath was in my mouth—the smell of her. Chloe's fragrant scent, her awesome hair shampoo and the smell of her sex was driving me insane. Being there with her was a multi-sensory feast.

"What do you want, Gibson?" Stopping to stare at her, I brushed a few strands of hair away from her forehead. If I answered honestly, it might have sounded pornographic. Snickering to myself, I smiled and said what every female wants to hear.

"Whatever you want, Chloe."

"Take me." Fuck.

Two words. Take her? She didn't say to fuck her. Chloe was asking for slow and gentle. She wanted to do this but she was scared. I wanted to take care of her...handle her with care, but I was so frustrated after the last five months and finally feeling her in my hands, on my mouth, against my skin that I doubted whether I'd be able to stay in control once I was inside her.

Chloe reached down and took my dick in her hand. The feel of her small fingers circling around my dick and taking a firm grip made my eyes close.

"Eyes, Gibson."

Chloe sounded playful and I snickered as I opened them. She had a fabulous genuine smile on her face. When she began stroking me, I took a deep breath and a swallow past the lump that had formed in my throat. I was caught in the moment of the incredible turning point we'd reached. I didn't need to be played with, there wasn't going to be much time for that because I was so fucking excited, that it wasn't going to take much to get me off at all.

"Don't. I'm saving myself." Well I was trying to anyway.

Chloe's mouth stretched into a wider smile and

she licked her lips. "Gibson Barclay, I never thought I'd ever hear that come out of *your* mouth of all people."

I let out a long breath and chuckled, feeling much more relaxed for her comment.

"What can I say? You're breaking my balls here, just being in front of me." Smiling affectionately at Chloe, I figured I'd let enough time pass for her still to say 'no' but she looked relaxed and horny, was initiating and continuing to show me that she really wanted this, so I crawled on my knees between her legs and slid my hands under her ass to pull her little body closer up my legs toward my dick.

Leaning forward, I rested my forehead on hers and she swallowed, her eyes suddenly darting away nervously. "I got you, darlin', just let me take care of you." Chloe gave me a half smile and her hands landed on my hips.

Placing my dick at her entrance after sliding it down the seam of her pussy to check how wet she was, I smiled as I rocked gently into her. Chloe's eyes widened and her finger tips pressed tighter into my skin when I had slid myself up to the hilt. Stopping, I stayed still, waiting until Chloe's fingers relaxed before I made my next move.

"How does that feel?"

Chloe's eyes were glassy with lust but I could feel the apprehension radiating from her and her pussy was holding my dick like a prisoner in a secure unit.

"Good." *Well fuck, that's encouraging.*

Staring back at her, I brushed away some strands of hair from her face and placed my forehead on hers in an effort to calm her.

"Just good? Fuck, darlin', I'm losing my touch." I gave her a half-smile and sounded playful, but playful was the furthest thing from my mind at that point. I wanted her to feel safe, but inside I really wanted to ruin her for all other men. Chloe smiled and her heavy breath fanned my face, then she bit her lip before she spoke, "I'm a bit nervous."

"Darlin', it's me...I got you. Relax and let me take care of you, Chloe." When I nudged inside, Chloe's eyes went wide. "Am I hurting you?" Focusing, she watched me with an intensity that raised my awareness of the significance of where we were at.

"Only in that it's painful you're not fucking me yet, Gibson."

I rocked gently in and out and a smile played on her lips. "Mm-hm...just like that...oh, yeah...God, you're really good at this."

"Yeah? You like that? Sweet Jesus, Chloe, what you do to me." I said in a husky voice then growled loudly as I ground my dick deep into her pussy.

Chloe's eyes widened with the urgency and desperation of my movement, and was watching my face intensely, my lips only a few inches from hers.

"Well...it's alright, I suppose..."

I wiped the smirk off her face when I picked up the pace and crushed my mouth to hers and began fucking her rapidly. Neither of us lasted long. But she came apart in my arms with her body jerking violently with the force of her powerful orgasm. As soon as she started coming, my head fought with my dick not to come at that point. My dick won.

"Thank you." She whispered wistfully.

Opening my eyes I stared at her hard, swallowing past a sudden lump that formed in my throat at the love that seemed to swell my heart whenever I looked at her. I was starting to fall asleep after my twenty minute sprint to the finish line...that's how fucking Chloe had felt.

"My pleasure, darlin'...anytime." I winked at her playfully.

Thank you, God, for making this okay for us.

CHAPTER 27

FLYING THE NEST

Chloe

When Gibson left me for the first time to fly to his meeting with his M3rCy bandmates, I was worried about him leaving but I acted very relaxed about it. There wasn't one day since I'd come out of hospital that he wasn't with me, apart from when we were in the cabin.

Worry lines creased his brow and he looked like a scolded puppy when it was time to get into the SUV with Johnny, but I knew that as soon as the car left the driveway he'd be slipping straight back into his comfort zone of Gibson the rock star.

Initially, it was going to be a day trip and he'd be back in the early hours, but he called and said that something had come up and he'd be back in a couple of days. At first I felt terrified that he'd be away for two more days, but Emma and Lois were with me and they were great company.

I finally felt able to talk about Kace in the absence

of Gibson and although Emma and Lois acted like friends, they had a job to do. Part of that job was finding out as much about Kace as I could tell them.

"I know that everyone talks about Kace when they think I'm not around. He's like the elephant in the room as soon as I step in on one of those conversations. Sometimes I wonder if you all think I'm stupid, because the way you all shut up when I wander into the room makes me want to laugh out loud. I know you want to spare my feelings but nothing could make me feel as bad as he did, so just talk about it. Make it normal. Then maybe it will be less of a deal all around."

Emma kinda glided in her socks on the hardwood floor like a skater on ice from the sofa she was sitting on, to catch her balance on the kitchen counter. Taking a few grapes out of the fruit bowl, she tilted her head up in my direction. Making eye contact, she smiled with understanding at my frustration at being treated with kid gloves.

"Chloe, we all feel terrible at what happened. I had only known you a day. One day...and Lois was stuck on a plane on a runway, she never even made it to the gig. Everything we had in place wasn't enough and you suffered because of it...Gibson suffered."

I was tired of talking about Kace. All everyone wanted to talk about was Kace. He consumed my every thought for weeks there needed to be a shift away from the subject of my abduction. "I am going to say this once and we move on girls. Kace never touched me.

"To be honest with you, I wasn't talking or doing anything when I was with him either. Not talking was what got me through. I closed down to protect myself from his negative, manipulative ways. Being with him...seeing him like that again— I was scared, but Kace is no match for Gibson and he knows it. My only concern is that I have no clue if he's out there, or if he's given up. When I ask Gibson, his response is well rehearsed. Like he's trying to convince himself that he's not coming back."

Lois wandered over and placed a hand casually on her hip. "Chloe, it was our first day. We're completely up to speed now. I hope the fucker tries, because he'll get the shock of his life if he thinks your two friends are no match for him. I'm in two camps, one that says I hope he's running scared, and the other that thinks. 'Come on you stupid bastard make your move'. Emma and I will never let him near you again."

After that, I asked if we could do something else and the girls asked me what I wanted to do. Gathering my hair around from my back I pulled it over my shoulder, inspecting the ends of it. "Get my hair cut. I'm a mess...it's like rats' tails. I haven't had it cut since I met Gibson...before then, actually."

Emma twisted her mouth and Lois shot her a look. Shrugging my shoulders in confusion, I wondered what I had said.

"We're going to have to run this one past Charlotte, Chloe. The last thing you need is someone mouthing to the press that you're here. Gibson told us that there are only twelve people, including us, that know he even has this place. We're guarding that secret as well as protecting you. We need to see what Charlotte comes up with."

I was frustrated about having permission from someone I hardly knew just to have a haircut. That was a hard pill to swallow. "Well take me to a small town where no one knows me and I'll only be in there an hour at the most. No one is interested in me. I only want it trimmed, so I'll be in and out before you know it."

Lois shook her head but her eyes darted at Emma and there was this sympathetic exchange between them that made me annoyed, like I was incapacitated and they were making a decision I wouldn't like, but was best for me. "Sorry, Chloe, Emma's right. You're still recovering and Gibson doesn't want anyone drawing attention to you."

"Oh, he doesn't? And this is all about Gibson? No regard for my wishes about this? I was abducted by a fucking ex-boyfriend. Not the mafia. What are the chances he's going to be in some hick mountain town at a hair salon?"

Both girls looked like they were considering what I said, but I never let them respond because the more I thought about it, the more furious I became. I'd been controlled and manipulated by one man and Gibson may have had my best interests at heart, but I was damned if I'd be treated like some china doll in a glass cabinet, kept for best and brought out for special occasions. This was my life. *My* life, and I had to take it back or I'd forever be at the mercy of other people making decisions about me.

Pushing to the edge of the sofa, I reached over and grabbed my cell from the coffee table where I'd left it after Gibson had called me from the airport. Swiping the screen, I scrolled down looking for Charlotte's number.

"Hey, Charlotte. It's Chloe here..." Charlotte launched into a 'great to hear from you' speech and I wondered if she'd still be saying that after I let rip about my wishes and told her that we were going out—with or without anyone else's permission.

"I want to go and have my hair cut."

Charlotte hummed then I heard her cover her phone and say, "Two minutes," before readdressing me. "Chloe, Gibson won't like you going out. No one knows you're there honey—"

I interrupted her with a frustrated tone in my voice, feeling more than a little angry that some woman who worked for my boyfriend was giving me advice about what my boyfriend would and wouldn't like.

"Don't patronize me, Charlotte. Now, I'm going to get my hair cut. All I want to do is have it trimmed, I'm not running down the main street in Breckenridge with my ass hanging out and holding a banner above my head saying, 'Hey everybody look at me, I'm Gibson Barclay's girlfriend."

Charlotte tried to reason further with me and I could feel myself becoming more and more unreasonable about her protests. As far as I was concerned, they were making a mountain out of a mole hill. We were in the middle of nowhere and I was nobody, plain Jane and no one would even have given me a second glance. The paranoia was beyond my comprehension and I wondered if I'd ever be able to do anything normal again if I stayed with Gibson.

Becoming more impatient I waved the phone at Emma to take it from me. "Speak to her, I'm done. I want to go and have a haircut or I'm leaving. I may as well be in prison if I'm going to be stuck here for the rest of my life."

I knew I was becoming irrational. But the reality of being a 'kept woman' was beginning to dawn on me. I was able to take care of myself. I had done a better job of breaking free of Kace than they had of looking after me.

"Okay, Chloe. Calm down. If you need a haircut that much, then we'll have to make it happen, but you have to give Charlotte some time to get the information of where you can go, alright?"

Lois had reasoned quietly with me, she hadn't been telling me that I wasn't going even though she had agreed with Emma. It was as if she was mulling the idea and thinking of how it could happen rather than how it shouldn't.

Perching on the edge of the sofa arm, I waited silently for a moment while Emma and Charlotte concluded the call. My temper was fizzing, at the point where I could have gone either way. When Emma looked at me and waved the phone at me to take it back, I snatched it and shoved it into the back pocket of my jeans. Everyone kind of stared at each other and that made me furious. I was a grown woman and these two were acting like my babysitters.

I slapped my hands on my lap and stood up. "Right. I'm going out. Don't come with me. I need some normality. You two are suffocating me and I want some space." I stomped off in the direction of our bedroom, the noise of my bare feet slapping heavily against the wooden stairs echoing around the great room.

By the time I reached the corridor, my heart was beating wildly and my mouth was dry. Ever since Kace, I had a temper when I was pushed hard enough, and all the mollycoddling that I'd had was great in the beginning, but now it was seriously pissing me off.

Opening the closet, I fumbled around looking for two boots that matched, and mused at how messy both Gibson and I were. Our room was our private space and I had insisted that no one went through my things while I was here. Gibson's opinion was if they tidied up so that he could 'find his shit,' he was all for it.

When I heard my cell ring, I just knew it was Gibson and instantly I made a note to chew Charlotte out for reporting my wishes back to Gibson. I loved him but it was none of his business if I wanted to do something as mundane as take care of my personal appearance.

Slipping the phone from my back pocket, I saw Gibson's number with Paul's ID and the incoming signal radiating across the phone screen. Answering in a clipped tone, I bit, "Yes?"

"Fuck, you're pissed."

"I am."

"Why didn't you mention the hairdo when I was home? Why now, Chloe?"

"Jeez, Gibson— you as well? No one told me being with you would mean I have to ask fucking permission to have a hair do! I want to go out. I want to be *me* for an hour. No rock stars, no body guards, no crazy fucked-up ex-boyfriend...just me."

Sighing heavily, "Okay," he answered his voice sounded resigned.

"What do you mean, okay? Are you giving me permission now? You can go out on stage night after night and perform in front of thousands of crazy people, with all the risks that must bring, and I can't go out in the middle of a mountain town and have my hair cut?

"Gibson, I'm going to have my hair cut. I'm not going to be run over, I'm not going to fall down a sinkhole, I'm going to a beauty salon. When I've done what I intend on doing, I'll come back. Now. Either Emma or Lois drop me off at a salon or I'll call a cab. If I call a cab that's one more person that knows where your place is."

"Chloe. Stop. Fuck." Gibson huffed a huge puff of air from his lungs and sounded gruff. "Fuck, Chloe. See that mood you're in? Save it. When I get home on Friday, we're gonna do this again, you are so fucking hot when you're pissed. My dick is aching here just listening to you. I wish I was there to see that sassy little body, you sound full of attitude."

314

His comment took the wind out of my sails and I felt instantly calmer. "Is that so?"

"Bet your life it is, darlin'. Wear panties...I wanna rip them off."

"Can't wait." My core clenched at his words and I was grinning like a stupid schoolgirl. Gibson had managed to change my mood, but his sexy, playful comment made me ache for him.

"I know." I could hear the smile in his playful tone, then his voice dropped an octave. "Fuck, you're killing me here, Chloe. Just hearing you say that has the crown of my dick rubbing at my jeans...if I was there I'd sink my dick—"

Interrupting, I said, "But you're not, so..." I was starting to sound emotional but fortunately, Gibson began to conclude the call. Although I missed him, I was going out and I needed to feel in control so in a way it wasn't a bad thing.

"Listen. Gotta go right now, darlin', just promise me you'll let the girls take care of you. Don't get that hair cut short, 'cause I'll be wanting something to hold on to when I get back, it could get wild where I'll be sitting."

Gibson finished his call by telling me again how much he was missing me and how much he loved me. He was excited, Toby was in LA and he hadn't seen him since the night I was taken by Kace. I was pleased that he was getting time with him, but Gibson sounded a little apprehensive for some reason. I put it down to the fact that the last time hadn't ended well.

Less than a minute later, Emma's phone rang and I

knew it was Gibson telling her to take me. I still felt annoyed but at least I had my way at doing something very basic for myself. Emma took me to a beauty salon in town just before closing time and it was dark outside. Twenty five minutes later, we were in the car on the way back. I had a hair trim and nobody had died, as Gibson would say.

After dinner Emma, Lois and I were around the table talking and Emma stood up and walked over to the window with a frown on her face. "What's wrong?"

"There's a car coming. We're not expecting anyone."

I sniggered because the hyper-vigilant stuff they kept doing was ridiculous. If anyone should have felt afraid it should have been me. And I wasn't. We were in the middle of nowhere. No one knew we were there. No one knew Gibson's hideaway even existed and how would they know I was here?

"Maybe someone is lost?" I offered.

As the car drew up in front of the cabin, Emma turned to Lois and her eyes flicked toward the side corridor leading to the second door decking. Lois slipped the lock and went outside, closing the door softly.

Loud knocking made me jump, because I got caught up in the moment and they had me as crazy as the both of them. All I kept thinking was *Dr. Mustard in the Kitchen with the lead piping*. It was like a scene out of a murder mystery dinner I'd been to once with Kace.

Just the thought of his name in this situation made my blood run cold. Suddenly this didn't feel like a game anymore.

"Did you call anyone, Chloe?" Emma's half whispered, urgent question made me jump.

"No." Shaking my head, I watched her tense stance. Her behavior was making me nervous.

"There are two women out there. Take a look from upstairs."

Taking the stairs two at a time, I ran to the end of the corridor and looked out. The flood light over the door made it easy to see who was there. Jill and Ruby were standing freezing, Ruby slapping her arms in an effort to keep herself warm.

The shock of seeing Ruby here made me cry, I was shaking with excitement and ran downstairs saying, "Let them in, it's Ruby. Ruby's here."

Emma opened the door slowly so that I could see Ruby's face. She looked excited and smiled widely while Jill grinned as they both chimed in unison, "Surprise."

Pushing Emma aside, I hugged Ruby hard and the tears flowed. "Oh. My. God. You have no idea what your visit means to me tonight."

Jill went back to the car and reappeared with a pamper kit and massage table. "If Gibson won't let you …well, Chloe before Toby, I was a beautician. He still likes his massages and pedicures, so I have everything we need for a great night in."

Even when Gibson wasn't here, he was thinking about what I needed. Seeing Ruby was exactly the right therapy for me. I couldn't believe that Gibson had flown her in from New York. I didn't know Jill apart from the one time I met her on the beach. She seemed just like me, a little out of her depth in her man's world, but she more than anyone would understand how I might be feeling. Trust Gibson to think of her when I was feeling hemmed in. I was missing him terribly today, but his thoughtfulness was still present.

CHAPTER 28

HAIRCUT

Gibson

Finishing my call with Chloe, I tapped my cell against my mouth, thinking about how fired up she was. Fuck, she sounded sexy when she was fuming with anger. I'd never heard her so pissed, but fuck, the way she sounded sticking up for herself made me so damned hard. I was kinda glad I wasn't in the room with her. If I had been, I'd have ripped her clothes off and bent her over to teach her a lesson, stripped that hot little body naked and fucked the life out of her.

Chloe's natural aggression wasn't something she'd shown much of before, but fuck what a turn on. The only other time I saw anything like it was the morning after we'd had sex on the yacht and I found her hiding out in Gavin's room. When I got the wrong idea about them and messed with Gavin a little, she came at me with both guns blazing.

I understood her frustration at wanting to do something normal. It was the reason Chloe and I were together in the first place. Finding her at the end of the phone with the wrong number Toby's PA gave me, was everything at a time when I was starting to wonder what the point of my life was.

In actual fact, it wasn't that long after the last time I saw her at Beltz that I lost my anonymity and was able to come and go as I pleased, without anyone stalking me. Asking Chloe to step into my world was something I hadn't even considered when I planned to meet her. Selfishly, the only thing on my mind was getting her in front of me. That plan was all kinds of fucked up when I looked back at the way things had gone.

No. That was wrong, because in all that fucked-up-ness I found that Chloe had been stuck on a loop in my mind for a reason. *The* reason. She was *my* reason. When I was younger, I used to wonder why my parents hadn't just given me away. Sometimes I wondered what life was about and the reason I'd been put here to walk this earth. Deep thoughts for an 'angsty' teenager. However, as soon as Chloe gave herself to me, I knew what my life was supposed to be and the reason why I was here.

I began to feel the weight of responsibility and I wondered about being able to be what everyone wanted from me, and to try to help Chloe into my world but still keep her happy. Already, I'd been stretched in too many directions. Keeping the band, management and PR team happy, write songs, compose, tour the world, play gigs, meet fans, deal with the technical shit, make albums, sign countless

CD cases and other merchandise, attend award ceremonies, not to mention TV appearances and all the interviews for the media. I was forever in the spotlight.

This was my life. Gone were the days when I could just take off down to a store without a plan in place, just in case some crazy guy with a shotgun took exception to me because his wife or sweetheart objectified me on a calendar or in a magazine.

When I thought about all the fame and what it attracted by default, and then I put Chloe into the mix and how she'd be integrated into all of that, my head just about exploded. Chloe was fragile. Whether she knew it or not. She had been through a horrendous ordeal and I knew that she thought she was strong. There is a difference between strong and brave. And as far as I could see, Chloe tackled her days bravely.

Stepping back into the circus that was my daily life wasn't easy. It was a buzz though, nevertheless. For months. I had put almost all my focus on Chloe, not on work and it had only been the last few weeks I'd been writing again. So I had to think about getting down to some serious music with the guys.

What had happened to Chloe hadn't really been fair on them. I'd just kinda shrugged them all off to concentrate on her needs, but they had been accommodating, even Simon, but the last call I had with Len made me consider how things were for them in all of this. They were restless and without being conceited about it, I knew that I was the main pull for M3rCy, so they had all been left dangling until I could focus again, and that wasn't me acting like the team player I should have been.

I'd almost forgotten what an ordeal it could be just to go to a simple meeting. When I arrived at the offices to meet with our management, someone must have tipped off our fans that we were headed there, because the scene outside and along the street was fucking chaos.

There were six police on horses marshalling the crowds, as several squad cars blocked the road. Crazed fans screamed and jostled for position, to gain a better vantage point. There must have been at least a thousand people sprawled along both sides of the road on the sidewalk.

Breaking free of the barrier, about a dozen frenzied, screaming girls caught up with the car and banged heavily on the blacked out windows. Two got directly in front of the hood, making Johnny stop momentarily, while they stared directly at me with wide eyes across the hood, looking near to hysteria at the thought they may be able to get to me.

Johnny never let me ride up front when there was the potential for fans to mob me. He said I was more secure in the cabin at the back. There was bullet proof glass in the car and the partition was the same, so that even if they got into the front where he was, I could prevent them getting any further.

"Well, fuck! This is grand! Whoever masterminded this subtle fucking welcome is out on their ass. Find out who leaked to the press we were coming. I'm personally gonna have his balls in a stranglehold." I hated the way the PR team constantly tried to stir up shit, so that it brought the world's attention on us.

As if we could be invisible anyway. Nearly every person I had ever come into contact with called me by my first name and talked to me like they knew me from way back. From my perspective, that was a bit creepy, because sometimes they said something and I had to stop and think for a minute then I'd think. *Yeah that happened.*

Johnny was already ringing for back-up. We had three security guys on the curb outside the offices, but that wasn't enough to get me inside safely. Thank God the car was armored. We'd been given it as a gift from some Arab prince when we sang at his son's graduation a few years ago. What I liked about it, was it looked just like any other family SUV, so it didn't attract that much attention. Even with that, it was still unnerving with the pandemonium that the hysterical fans were creating.

Jerry appeared with another half a dozen guys in dark suits and earpieces. Signaling with his two fingers, he directed two guys where he wanted them to be. Turning, he pointed at another's feet to direct him to stay where he was, and then turned and motioned where he wanted the rest of them. Spinning around, he saw the three guys on the curb and deployed them to move the barriers that were already set up, until they shifted them to make a runway for me to enter the building.

Talking into his cuff of his jacket, Jerry's calm, even tone came through the intercom in the car.

"Clear to go. On my count, one and exit."

Johnny shifted across from the left where the driver's seat to the passenger seat and tapped on the window that Jerry was now leaning against.

Sliding along the leather seating, I edged forward with my heart in my mouth. No matter how many times this had happened before, I still felt scared shitless. Each time I stepped out into the crowd, the potential for something to go wrong was high.

Adrenaline made my heart pump fast, the pulse in my neck ticking rapidly as I fought the urge to run. This was an innate part of me that came with my label of Attention Deficit Hyperactivity Disorder and was a strong feature of my personality at times of stress. On those occasions— as in my current situation—I really had to fight the urge to act impulsively and trust the judgment of Johnny and Jerry to keep me safe.

Trusting Jerry was something I was trying to come to terms with after what happened with Chloe. He dropped the ball twice in less than a day, and although we'd debriefed about that until the cows came home, I was still having difficulty getting past it.

Three-two-one, exit. Suddenly Johnny unlocked my side and Jerry pulled the door open. The dull screaming from inside the car was a deafening roar as my feet hit the street. Jerry flanked my right side and Johnny my left as we walked at the same fast pace that had been rehearsed so many times, it felt like part of my set list.

I tried my best to ignore the security guy to my right, who had grabbed a girl that had been running toward me. He spun her around by her waist and in the opposite direction from me, as I waved to the crowd pretending not to notice. We gathered pace and I glanced at the entrance of the building, the smoked glass doors with the gold embossed script getting closer with every step I took.

Random voices were rising above the cacophony of screams, telling me how much they loved me and there were more than a few comments about what women would like to do to me as well as the usual offers to have my baby or proposals of marriage. To think at one point I loved that made me realize what a mess I was.

Can't say I didn't feel relieved when Jerry's hand finally gripped the long, gold metal bar that was the handle, and he yanked it open. Turning briefly I called out, "Thank you all for coming down to see me. I love you too." It was the least I could do knowing some of those girls would have travelled miles.

Moving out of the line of sight from the street, I leaned back against the wall, then bent over with my hands on my knees. "Fuck. What a fucking mess. Since when did they think it was okay to risk killing the lead singer of the band to make the headlines? I want the asshole that created that clusterfuck gone. Anything could have happened out there in that unplanned situation. There was no thought for the safety of those women and girls out there. Not one of them had the thought that someone could get mown down by a stray car trying to dodge them running across the street?"

Glancing up, I saw Jerry's nervous face looking back at me and I knew he was wondering how I felt he'd fared in that situation. By using clockwork delegation and swiftly assessing the potential risks, Jerry had dealt with a shitty situation with complete confidence and skill. He may have fucked up before, but his observation skills, risk assessment, operational and management abilities were never in question.

Once I'd recovered my composure, I took the stairs two at a time to the office.

"Jeez, Gib, when are you gonna slow down with that? I've never seen you walk up stairs like a normal person and you always jump down the last three like a kid." Snickering at Johnny because he always had the ability to inject some levity into tense situations, I glanced briefly at him and ignored the receptionist, walking over to the conference room door. I began to push it open and glanced over my shoulder again, saying, "Johnny, if I was normal I'd be like everybody else and that shit out there would be a fantasy. In case you didn't notice, I'm a fuckin' rock star— we're supposed to do stupid shit."

On entering the room, I could see that everyone else was present and Syd was over from New York. Although we weren't on his label any more we still did favors for each other, and he was trying to help form a plan to snare Kace.

Syd inclined his head. "Ah, here's the main man." I didn't like when people said that to me, even if it was somewhat true. It was demeaning to the other guys in the band. Syd had been looking out of the window at the LA skyline and turned to walk over to the table. Pulling up his jeans at the knees like he was wearing some expensively tailored evening pants, Syd sat in the leather swivel chair at the head of the table.

"There is nothing 'main' about me, Syd. I sing. That puts me at the front, but we're all in this together. Cut the shit and tell me what the plan is for this new band, what you want from us, and how you're gonna catch that warped piece of shit that took my woman."

Our heads turned when we heard the swish of the door and the receptionist pushed in a trolley with some breakfast pastries, pancakes, patties, scrambled eggs, bacon and toast. Walking over to the table she carried two large flask–like containers, one blue and one white, with coffee. "Blue is decaf."

Choosing me to sidle up to, she leaned in and placed plates, napkins and cutlery on the table. Gazing seductively at me with her eyes popping wide, she spoke in an exaggerated slow Marilyn Monroe type voice, "Anything you want Gibson, you only have to ask."

Now I knew the guys wanted Gibson back, and fuck I was kinda between a rock and a hard place, because she was a stunning looking girl and they were all watching me. She was kinda hard to ignore and I knew I'd get my ass whooped for not biting. Besides, I wasn't in the mood for the pussy-whipped jibes after what I had just experienced downstairs so I turned, grinned and pulled her onto my lap. Her hand instantly brushed over my junk on the way down, giving it a little squeeze.

"Hmm, anything I want, eh, darlin'. Well, you have no idea how much trouble that particular statement got the last girl into that said it to me." It was true the last girl was Chloe when we were on the phone, and the same the other night before she let me back inside her tight little body.

Well, fuck if I hadn't started a fire with my little show and had trouble putting the damn thing out. Instead of her accepting the flirt and shoving me back and laughing it off, she was ready to climb on me no matter who was spectating.

There was no way I could miss the full pert tits that were practically spilling out of her blouse. I was almost sure if she took a deep breath, that there wouldn't be one button left on that blouse it was straining so tightly. Adjusting herself, she wiggled her pussy right over my pant clad dick and I'll admit, it did wake me up a bit.

"So Gibson...just so that you know, I'm not a tease, I meant it, anything you want." Len was snickering and Simon had a raised eyebrow. Mick was completely disinterested and texting someone, but Syd stared straight at me, his hand skating back and forth over the highly polished mahogany table. Just waiting to see weakness in me.

Placing my hands on her waist, I stared into her pretty brown eyes and smiled. "What I want is for you to get off my dick and go do your job, honey. We're not running a brothel here and if you want to fuck, I suggest you give up your job here and go find yourself

328

a massage parlor to work in."

Loud laughter erupted and I pushed the girl off me to her feet. "Sorry honey, I don't eat take out when I have gourmet at home." I'd saved face with them, but at the receptionist's expense. Seeing the way she behaved, I figured if she only worked at a record company to fuck the musicians, then she deserved anything that was thrown at her.

Once she left, we set to work planning for the day when Kace walked back into the frame and getting ourselves ready to cut the next album. When we were done with the business side of our discussions, we all wandered into the recording studio and I played them a few of the songs and some lyrics I had written. Everyone thought they were good enough for the album, but we had to work on the drum beat and guitar riff music to go with the melodies I had down, and the kind of sound we wanted for the ones where I only had lyrics.

Several hours later we were lost in our music, the one thing that brought us all together in the first place. The last six months melted away. I'll admit it felt great to be back with them and I realized how much I had missed the joy I got out of making music.

CHAPTER 29

JILL SPILLS

Chloe

Waking up without Gibson was much harder than I imagined it would be. For the last two days I'd slept fitfully without his strong warm body wrapped around mine. Instinctively, my hand had slid across to meet the coldness of the sheet in the bed, expecting to make contact with him. When my brain caught up with my hand, I'd remember he was in LA. Each morning that finding always left me with a heavy heart well into the morning.

Tuesday wasn't too bad because I spoke to him twice during the day and again before he went to dinner, then the girls arrived and as we'd stayed up late into the night, I hadn't really noticed that he hadn't called again.

Yesterday was hard because I had a three minute phone call before he was due to record an interview for a TV program, and then he was making a video for their new single. When he told me they had overrun and he would be staying until the weekend, I had wanted to go there, but he was quick to ask me to stay on here because of how bored I'd be. The way he explained it made sense, I'd only be lonely somewhere else because he'd be working all of the time.

Ruby said it was natural for me to miss him, as it was the first time we'd been away from each other. She was wrong about that, because we had lived for weeks without each other, before Gibson insisted and they allowed him to stay at the mental health facility.

When I drew back the drapes, the most idyllic and beautiful snowy mountain range was on display before me. We'd had the first proper snow dump of the season and looking out of the French doors, over the white covered wooden deck railings, the secluded woodland scene was picture postcard perfect. From the amount of snow that was resting against the doors, there must have been at least two feet of snowfall in the night.

Loud knocking preceded Ruby invading my space as she spilled into the room whooping and hollering about the snow. "Oh, Chloe! I love the snow." Growing up in Florida, I could relate. It made it magical to me. Every time I experienced snow, it felt like the first time.

"I spoke to Emma and she's going to arrange for the snowmobiles she found in the big barn at the bottom of the hill to be brought up here, so we can have some fun in the snow."

I slowly tore my eyes away from the view and turned to meet her gaze grinning excitedly. "Let's get breakfast, I can't wait." Playing around on the snow would keep me occupied for a few hours at least and I thought it may lift the heavy feeling I had about missing Gibson. My one worry was that we didn't come equipped for the snow. Gibson talked about getting some snowsuits and ski jackets, but we hadn't got that far before this snow.

At breakfast, I voiced my concern that we wouldn't have enough warm clothing for the weather conditions. Lois grinned and shook her head. "Don't worry about that Chloe, we found a pile of really thick snow suits and snow boots. Even if they are a bit big, you're only going to be sitting on the snowmobiles in them."

Jill came in with her hair in a messy bun, wearing short pajamas, her ass cheeks barely covered by the bottoms. "Count me out. I'm a beach babe. You won't get my skinny ass on one of those death traps. Thanks for making that racket and waking me up, by the way." Gesturing her head at the window, she was referring to Emma and Lois bringing the machines up to the house.

Ruby looked incredulously at Jill, unable to understand how anyone could not like the snow. "Where's your sense of adventure, Jill?"

Jill poured some coffee and blew into the steamy cup she was cradling in both hands. Glancing up, she gave Ruby a look of disdain before smirking. "Ruby, I'm Toby Francis' girl, I have all the adventure I can manage."

Emma and I smirked at each other and looked

over at Ruby who seemed to be mulling Jill's comment over. "True. Toby looks like he's so hard to handle so—point taken."

After eating breakfast, I didn't shower because I knew I'd get sweaty in the snow suit and I couldn't wait to be out there. So I pulled on some yoga pants, a bra and a t-shirt and a beautiful mohair sweater Gibson had somehow produced for me.

Someone must have checked my attire at some point prior to arriving here, because there were several new sweaters and lots of sweat pants in my size in the closet when I arrived. Gibson only said he didn't want me to be cold in the mountain air.

By the time I was ready to go out, I had so many layers on I could hardly bend my arms. Ruby was a bit of a tomboy and I was girlie-girl, so I gave up my Ski Doo for the back of hers, after five minutes of stop-starting because the clutch on the handle bar was freaking me out.

I swear we bounced off the ground more than once and I could hear Ruby's muffled "Yeehaw" coming from the inside of her snood, scarf and helmet shielded face. I was shivering with the cold by the time we stopped. Ruby took the scarf away from her face, pulled the snood down and took her hat off.

As soon as I saw her face, I snorted with laughter because it was the first time I'd ever seen her look less than perfect. Wild frizzy hair with the damp air became static from the woolen hat she'd been wearing and her mascara had run down her cheeks where her tears from the cold had streamed down her face. Crazy as it seems, I actually think it's the prettiest she'd ever looked.

When we came back inside, the warmth of the underfloor heating and the smell of the log fire felt like heaven to me. Emma had put two bath robes in the utility room, so we changed from all the wet gear in there. One luxury that felt like an essential in the cabin was the hot tub. It was hot and ready on the deck and there was a Swedish sauna in the master suite, but I wanted to experience being in the tub with the snow on the ground and the massive mountains as the backdrop. Dressed in the robe, I padded through to the great room to see if Jill wanted to join us in the tub.

The atmosphere in the cabin was very calm. I guessed this was what drew Gibson to it in the first place. Emma was busy using a laptop and Lois was sleeping because apparently, one stayed awake all night.

Once settled in the tub, Jill filled us in on how she met Toby when she was working in a hotel as a beautician and his PA had called to arrange a massage for him. Instead of dealing with Toby in the treatment room, she went to his hotel room and they just clicked. How she described it was pretty wild, she'd covered him in thick massage oil and after a few minutes of deep muscle massage, he'd got off her massage table and insisted he return the favor. She then elaborated that Toby's was an internal deep muscle massage.

An hour into our soak, I was feeling the most

relaxed I had since college. Everything was just sublime. Sitting chatting with girlfriends was something I hadn't done much of in the past couple of years, until Jill made a comment that made my heart stop.

"I have to say, Chloe— you are handling this stuff with Gibson amazingly well. You've really surprised me...you are much more controlled than I was the first time." Jill's hand was flat and moving in and out of the water— almost absentmindedly, except it wasn't, because she was watching it drip through her fingers, like she was being measured in her delivery of what she was saying.

Ruby's brow creased as we swapped confused glances and then Ruby frowned at Jill.

"Sorry Jill, you've lost me, what is she handling better than you?"

Exhaling a tired sigh, Jill looked sympathetically at me and then glanced quickly at Ruby before looking back at me. "Gibson. The record company function...the fly-on-the-wall pictures, Toby's sister sent them to me. She thinks I'm too good for Toby."

My heart stopped with the jolt of electricity in shock. *What pictures? What was Gibson doing?*

"Strange that neither of them mentioned it. Gibson took Morgan with him and I have no idea who the leggy whore was that was with Toby."

My mind just wouldn't go where she was trying to lead it. It was clear that Jill was distressed about Toby, and I could see that she had no clue I hadn't seen the pictures or that I didn't know what she was talking about.

"All I'm saying is—well, I know how it feels. It stings and you don't have to put a brave face on it, Chloe. I've been where you're sitting now and I still remember the first time Toby cheated on me."

Gibson cheated on me? I sat silently, trying to absorb exactly what she was telling me. None of it made sense. However, Gibson was a rock star. And what rock stars did in their daily lives and the scrapes they got themselves into was nonsensical to the rest of us living in the real world.

"Guys that write love songs can play on your heartstrings Chloe, and they have the ability to say exactly what you need to hear, when you need to hear it. I was determined to leave Toby the first time he did it to me, but he talked me around with amazing words that he strung together, and I think he believed what he was saying at the time… and I loved him…"

Jill stood up abruptly in the hot tub, fighting back tears, the water slopping noisily around her thighs.

"Sorry Chloe, I really am. You have no idea how much I wanted to think that Gibson could give up that sordid part of a band's lifestyle for you. For a while there I really believed he'd changed, because he'd found someone so special in you. It gave me hope that one day Toby would realize what I was to him, and do the same."

Stepping out of the water, Jill reached over to where she had discarded her robe and shrugged it over her shoulders, rapidly blinking back tears and angrily tying the belt tightly around her waist. She walked quickly away with her head bowed and a loud sob escaped her throat. Turning to look at Ruby, I stared numbly at her.

Gibson really cheated on me? Three days away? He went to a party and never told me? Was that because he was taking Morgan? Gibson hadn't called me again and I'd thought it was because he was recording. And from conversations we'd had about that, I knew that they could be there twenty-four-seven when they were working on something.

What was strange was that Morgan was back on the scene after how Gibson responded to her at the cabin. I knew I needed to see for myself what was so damning. With Gibson I had learned not to have knee jerk reactions. Besides, there may well have been pictures, but were they current ones?

I grabbed my robe and began treading carefully through the freezing cold snow to get back inside. It was crunching under my feet and stinging my skin as it stuck and melted on my wet skin. I felt sad for Jill when I saw her curled up in the fetal position on the sofa, staring up at the snow covered peaks of the mountains. Pushing her over with my butt, I sat perched on the edge of her sofa and stroked her hair.

"Are you okay, honey?" Jill chewed the side of her mouth, and I knew that I couldn't tell her that I hadn't seen the pictures or she would have known she'd screwed up and spilled about them.

"Jill, would you mind sending me the pictures, I want to see them again? I deleted them when I was in a temper this morning." Jill looked nervously back at me, then she began to sit up on her elbows and leaned over to get her laptop.

"Sure, although why you would want to look at them again is beyond me."

Tapping some buttons on her keyboard, Jill's eyes scanned down her email, then selected and clicked the email she was looking for. "Email address?" After I shared that with her, she clicked again.

"All done. Enjoy."

Jill's tone was sarcastic but she was hurting badly. Leaning over, I slid my hands around her and pulled her close to me. I could feel the resistance in her because she was trying to protect her feelings. After a moment her body went limp and she began to cry softly.

CHAPTER 30

DANCING

Gibson

Jeez. My head is bursting. I woke up late in the day with the mother of all headaches. At first I didn't know where I was and had little recollection of the night before. Then I remembered Syd asked for a favor. So we showed up to the launch party of a new band he'd signed.

I racked my brain for some memory of what had happened to me after a certain point, but I drew a blank. There were snapshots of people in my mind, Toby, Len and a few other people I'd spoken with. Then I remembered drinking with Toby and me dancing with girls. Vague recollections of some random woman dancing naked on a table, but that's all I could remember.

What the fuck was I doing drinking? Toby had come to the launch but I couldn't remember how he got there, and I found it impossible not to drink around that guy. Stretching out, I smoothed my hand down my abs in a gesture of self-comfort and stroked my morning wood resting my hand around it. Chloe's soft, hot little body came into my mind and I instantly found myself stroking up and down my shaft slowly while her tight little ass played on my mind.

I hadn't even woken up properly and opened my eyes, yet I was horny just at the thought of Chloe. There and then I promised to make it home to her. Another day without her and I was going to be unbearable to be around. I began to think about her ass and how it felt over my hands and how good she tasted on my mouth. The more I thought about it, the wilder the fantasy and the harder I got. Within a couple of minutes I was tugging rapidly at it, but it didn't feel like enough.

When I came–my release was purely functional. There was no way my hand satisfied me. Nothing was going to appease my dick now that I'd been back inside Chloe's tight little pussy with those smooth, slick little walls completely.

Rolling to my right, I found a box of tissues on the nightstand and once I had wiped cum off my dick I stretched out restlessly again. I knew that it wasn't going to be long before I'd be fantasizing about what I was going to do to her and about getting home to Chloe. I'd only been inside her for one night in months and I wasn't sure whether that was worse now that I had been again, or if I should have waited until I had gotten back from this trip.

I rolled to my left at the same time as I heard a loud female groan. Startled I edged myself up on my elbows and looked out into the large suite. Morgan was lying on a couch about fifteen feet away, on her side; her ass, except for a thong string, was bare and facing in my direction.

Throwing myself back down heavily on the bed I was both pissed at myself and horrified at the situation, wondering what the hell she was doing back at Len's place with me. With no memory of her from the night before, I had no idea how she got there.

Nothing was coming to me, but my only saving grace was that she was asleep on the couch and not in my bed. Then I started to deduce I could have fucked her there then crawled into bed, so I dragged my ass out of bed and snatched my cell phone off the nightstand as I headed to the bathroom so she wouldn't hear me and called Johnny.

Johnny answered clearing his throat. He sounded rough, croaking, "Yep?" His tired gravelly tone pissed me off because he should have had my back. In a hissed whisper and a low angry tone, I asked, "What the fuck happened last night? Morgan is lying practically bare assed on the couch in my room. Please tell me I didn't fuck her." Raking my hand through my hair, I caught sight of how rough I looked in the mirror. My guts were in agony; twisting in knots at the potential I had done something so monumentally wrong. I prayed for everything to be a bad dream.

"Why didn't you keep her the fuck away from me? The last thing I remember is talking to Syd and the band. One minute Len was telling me that Toby had arrived and the next I'm doing shots and dancing. I'm never drinking with that fucking Toby again. Don't let me do that ever again. Promise me you'll knock me the fuck out before you let that happen again." Johnny hacked a cough and grunted while he listened and I knew he was getting his shit together before he replied.

"Gib, you were a fucking mess, dude. When I tried to have a quiet word with you, you told me...and I quote, "Mind your fucking business, Johnny. Just because I hire you to work for me doesn't give you the right to tell me I've had enough to drink. You are crossing the fuckin' line, dude.

"Five months I held my shit together while Chloe's head got straightened out, I deserve to have fun and enjoy myself with my buddies for one night. Sit back, relax, don't fucking interfere. It's not your place. You are not working tonight. Interrupt me again and you're fucking crossing the line, understand? Or words to that effect."

Whoa! Fuck. I knew I was an asshole when I was drunk but I can't ever remember saying anything close to that to Johnny before. The guy had always been reliable and practically invisible when I had nights out. Johnny usually managed my security effortlessly, so for me to behave like that I must have been feeling pretty out of my depth about something. Mumbling about being drunk and not knowing what I was doing, I struggled to apologize outright.

"Just cut me some slack and give me the short version of what went on before Morgan wakes up. Fuck this is a cluster fuck." I began pacing on the cold marble floor in the bathroom and rubbing my chest while I waited to hear the damage I'd caused. All I could think about was Chloe and how she was going to feel. I hadn't even called her last night because I got drunk before I'd even thought about it.

Johnny grunted again, like he was sitting up, I heard a noise like slapping skin and Johnny then he said, "Get up, doll you gotta leave *now*. Come on get your ass out of the bed and leave, I got a job to do. Thanks for everything, you were a great ride, honey." I heard a very disgruntled female voice telling him he was an asshole, then some rustling followed by a hard bang, which I figured was his door.

Suddenly I heard Johnny's voice slightly echoing and then I heard him passing urine. "Fuck Johnny are you gonna have a shit and a shave as well before you fill me in, dude? Tell me what the fuck happened last night."

Johnny let out a huge puff of air slowly and I could feel whatever he was going to tell me was going to be bad. "Alright are you ready for this?" I wasn't but I need to know what I was dealing with.

"So as you know you got rat-assed-drunk. Tori arrived—Syd had invited her not knowing the drama she caused when she was with us. Once M3rCy had agreed to make an appearance he thought he'd better extend the invitation to her as well, because he had no idea that she wasn't staying. Anyway, she waited until you were really drunk and made her move. To cut a long story short— her hands were all over you and I have to say Gib, the way you were dancing with her you were almost dry humping her."

"Fuck!" I was clearly off my face. There was no way I'd have gone near her had I been sober. How was I going to explain it to Chloe? If I was *that* drunk then I'm sure I made an ass of myself and let Chloe down.

"Where does Morgan fit into all of this? Sweet, Jesus, I'm utterly fucked aren't I?" My heart was aching in my chest at the thought that Chloe was going to have to deal with more shit and this time of my making.

"You owe Morgan. Apparently she saw you had arrived in LA on TV, and when she saw the footage of the chaos as you arrived at our offices, she headed down from Sacramento where she was staying with friends. By the way she is still extremely pissed at you so don't expect an easy ride when she wakes up."

"I'm not fucking her, Johnny." Starting the shower faucet running, my mind was going over everything I could possibly say to Chloe that would make what happened at the party okay. There were no positives coming to mind with that particular exercise.

"Jeez, Gib, I mean she's going to ride your ass for what you did to her at the cabin up north."

My mind was so focused on being able to get myself off the hook about my legacy that I couldn't even listen in context at that point. "All I can hear is you connecting me to riding her or her riding me so fucking change your language choices, the words you are using are making me more frustrated about this by the minute."

"Morgan wanted to talk to you so she showed up

at the offices. You were the one that gave her a swipe card to enter the building in the first place. You haven't taken that back from her. She has access all over the place. Her lanyard has shit on it that gets her everywhere. So Kiri, the big titted receptionist, gave her your whereabouts and she showed up." He sniffed down the phone and I felt he'd only given me half the story.

"So..."

"So she saw how drunk you were... you were completely trashed by the way, and she saw how Tori was behaving around you, like she was gonna whip your dick out and blow you on the dance floor, so she swooped in to save the day."

"Morgan did that? So, she dragged me away from Tori then what?"

"Then nothing. When I told Morgan not to pull a fast one and take advantage of you being drunk she said, 'I wouldn't fuck Gibson if he were dying and it could save his life'." Johnny laughed hard at that comment, then coughed and remembered who he was talking to.

"What I mean is, we got you in the car and brought you back here, she stayed with you to make sure you didn't choke...so you really didn't fuck her?"

Poking my head around the door to the couch, Morgan was still flat out. "Fuck, how can you tell if you fucked someone when they are lying unconscious?"

Johnny started to laugh again but I was having a serious sense of humor failure. None of it was remotely funny. This was my life. Chloe was my life.

The girl that was lying on my couch was someone I
used to fuck. How does that look with my history and
the fact that I don't even trust myself not to get it
wrong?

"How much did you drink last night?"

"Me? I don't drink when I'm on duty boss."

"What did you drink when you got back here?"

"Never got as far as drinking, my dick was down
that broad's throat before I'd closed the door here."

"Get the plane ready. I'm heading back to
Breckenridge."

"But you got…"

"Fuck, Johnny. Take your ass down to the airfield
and get the fucking plane ready. I'm not interested in
anything except seeing Chloe, although what the fuck
I'm gonna say to her is gonna have to be all kinds of
fuckin' inspirational." By that time my voice was loud
because I wasn't able hold back the fear of what this
looked like even to me, and I forgot that I was trying to
be quiet.

"Gibson?" *Fuck. I woke her up.*

"Morgan's awake. Get the fucking plane. I'm
leaving here in an hour."

Swiping my phone closed I tossed it on the
counter beside the white porcelain sink and stepped in
the shower. Luckily the glass was completely steamed
up by the time Morgan reached the bathroom.

"Gibson?" I closed my eyes trying to shut out the
emotion of hurting her. This was yet another thing I
didn't really want to do but there could be no mixed
messages for Morgan. Plus, what I said and her

response would tell me in no uncertain terms what went down between us.

"Thanks for what you did last night Morgan but you can't be here. I can't have you here. I'm with Chloe. You need to leave." Shit I felt bad but not half as bad as I thought Chloe might feel if she got wind of this before I got to her.

"What the fuck, Gibson? From where I was standing you'd pretty much forgotten about Chloe when you were on that dancefloor. And...that's the thanks I get for lying on that uncomfortable jagged material sofa all night to stop you from dying of alcohol poisoning?"

"Yeah and what else, Morgan. Why did you really stay?"

A loud bang rang out as the impact of whatever she threw at the toughened shower glass rocked me to my core. "Fuck! Are you insane? What was that?"

"Am *I* insane? I just saved your ass from becoming another rock-star-dies-in-bed-after choking-on-his-own-vomit headline, you ungrateful bastard."

"Oh! Do you want a thank-you-for-saving-me fuck?" Swallowing hard, I knew how callous I sounded but she had to leave.

"That's it. I'm going. Fuck you, Gibson Barclay. We're done." Morgan disappeared into the bedroom and I continued to shower hoping to stay there until she'd gone completely. I didn't want to come face to face with her again. If I did I knew she'd pull all that teary female shit and I'd say something even worse to her.

Turning the shower off I was just about to step out when her lanyard came over the shower glass and landed on my head. "Keep your fucking passes and key cards they're no good to me. You're a selfish asshole and I want nothing more to do with you."

I jumped when she banged the bathroom door behind her then heard her bang the bedroom one. Leaning back against the cold tile I sighed deeply. I liked Morgan a lot as a friend, but I loved Chloe and female friends like Morgan could only complicate things even further.

The way Morgan had responded was entirely appropriate and if I had dipped my dick in there, she'd have had my balls for the way I'd handled her this morning. So I'd had a narrow escape.

One thing was for sure. My drinking was a problem. I could only hope that Chloe believes that even though some of my more suggestive behavior reared its head with my alcohol intake, I hadn't cheated on her.

CHAPTER 31

PHOTOGRAPH

Chloe

Staring at the blurred images in front of me, there was little doubt in my mind about being able to excuse what I was looking at. Gibson was up close and personal with Tori in the picture, his hands on her hips, her ass leaning into his front. She was looking over her shoulder at him. There was no doubt in my mind that Gibson was drunk but there was lust in his eyes. I knew that look, I see it every time he looks at me.

As my stinging eyes ticked over the photograph on the screen it looked pretty damning and I was struggling to find something that made what I was looking at, a farce. Simon was dancing near Gibson and Len was grinning in the background. Johnny was standing to the side, his legs slightly parted, arms folded across his chest and with a grim look on his face. It was how *he* was looking at Gibson that made it all the more real.

Seeing how devastated Jill was downstairs made

my heart hurt—both for her and for me. Jill had been living with this feeling I had since she'd been with Toby. It felt raw for me because this was what I had expected from a guy like Gibson, but with all we'd been through and how supportive he had been of me, it had slipped my mind about this side of his personality and his horny attraction to women.

After his three minute call to me yesterday, I had been forgotten. *Was he ever going to tell me about this party? How did Tori get there?* I was sure Gibson had told me she was out of the picture when the tour ended, and her departure was personally welcomed by me, even though I said nothing to Gibson about her. Then I thought back to all their arguments and Gibson saying he hadn't slept with her. *Were all those arguments because they were attracted to each other but it wasn't good for the band?*

I kept looking again at the picture and waiting for a light bulb moment, something that would make me think, *you know what? This is old because...* unfortunately I had to concede that the image was current and Gibson had possibly begun to move on.

Slamming my laptop lid closed I hit it hard with the flat of my hand feeling angry that after everything with Kace, Gibson had asked for my trust and I'd given it to him. My instinct was to run. To get as far away from the world and the fucked up ways that people conducted themselves around me.

Knowing those pictures were out there and that everyone who was present at that party saw how Gibson was behaving with other women shattered me.

Feelings of hatred for Tori— for Gibson, even the rest of the band and toward Johnny who watched on, twisted my gut. Depression, anger and sadness overwhelmed me to the point where the best I could come up with to do, was to get into my bed and cover my head.

I wanted to block out the world because I just couldn't face anything else. Coming through the ordeal of Kace was a major hurdle, and I did that because Gibson was so strong for me, but I felt betrayed by the one person that I had let in again and it seemed like he had failed me.

Once I let the tears flow the flood gates opened I was a sobbing wet mess. I lay there from the afternoon's dusk light until it was dark. Ruby knocked softly on the door, but didn't wait for me to open it. Pushing the door just wide enough to step inside, she closed it quietly and walked over to my bed.

"Hey Chloe." I didn't answer her. I couldn't. My throat was constricted by the sob that was threatening to come to my mouth. If I spoke to her I knew I'd really lose it and I was fighting for control. I knew some point I was going to have to decide what I do next and I wasn't ready for questions.

Where do I go? How do I get there? Am I strong enough to deal with everything on my own? To be honest, I was much better than I had been for the past few months, but it wouldn't take much to push me back to rock bottom. Hell I was almost there now.

The mattress dipped at the bottom of the bed under Ruby's weight as she began to crawl up beside

351

me. Without saying anything she just stroked my hair. Her touching concern should have made me feel less distressed but it didn't. Feeling her behind me reminded me of Gibson. How could I go forward, knowing how I feel about him? Without the love I thought he had for me? How do I do that while still loving him despite those pictures? Just like I was sure Jill still loved Toby.

I must have fallen asleep and woke to the noise of "Harder to Breathe" by Maroon 5, the tune I'd downloaded as my ringtone. Ruby had left the room at some point and I was alone in the dark. My eyes still stung and I felt sick from all the crying and my head hurt. Following the direction of the sound I found my cell glowing on the dresser near the window. Opening the blinds the room was bathed in moonlight.

Gibson was calling. Almost twenty four hours after those pictures had been uploaded, he was calling. I left it unanswered to go to voicemail and sat down on the chair staring out into the bright dark night, because the snow and full moon still painted a magical scene. What I was feeling in the pit of my stomach didn't match that picture at all.

There were times when I felt I had been hard on Gibson; when I could have just gone with the flow. I thought it was just what happened with Kace that kept holding me back. Today's reality check made me realize it was an inbuilt protective mechanism at play that was designed to protect me from guys like Gibson, who were fatally attractive and highly addictive, but deadly as far as my heart was concerned.

Several minutes later there was another knock on the door. When no one opened it I walked slowly over and opened the door. Lois was standing with one hand in her back pocket and her cell in the other. She gestured by waving it at me to take it.

"Gibson's on the phone for you." Shaking my head I closed the door and leaned my forehead against it, fighting back the sob that was stuck in my throat and only a swallow away. I wasn't even sure I had anything to say to him.

My mind was in turmoil. My heart felt like it had been cut open and I had a pain in the center of my chest and the distress was overwhelming when I considered that I may have to walk away from him. There was also the question of whether he even knew that I knew about the pictures, or that he'd been partying without me. Again I wondered if I should run, but he was in LA and I was in Colorado. The distance between us would give me time to think about how I moved forward with my life.

Everyone was concerned because I had refused to eat. I didn't want to come out of my room to face anyone because apart from the pictures, finding out about them the way I had was embarrassing as well. Jill arrived at my door but didn't knock just opened the door and put the overhead light on.

"Fuck! I'm so sorry Chloe. Ruby just told me you hadn't seen the pictures. The last thing I'd ever want is for you to be walking in my shoes, but you are. You must have thought I planned that today, believe me honey, I didn't. Toby and Gibson are always dangerous when they're together. It's like they have this weakness—a collision of two alpha males in one spot and neither of them seem to realize they bring the best but also the worst out in each other.

"Alcohol has a huge impact on their decisions and they seem to fuck up effortlessly when they get into a party situation." Walking over beside her I sat down slowly on a small chair, feeling pretty pathetic that we were just two ordinary girls in extraordinary circumstances and we shared a problem that neither of us had the answer to.

Jill sat down on the bed opposite me and her puffy, tired eyes really pulled at my heart strings. Licking her lips nervously, she looked down and picked some lint off of her yoga pants before glancing up quickly, fixing her red-rimmed eyes into mine in an intensive stare.

"So what are you going to do? Are you going to have it out with him? Tell him you know?"

"It's probably a given that he knows I've seen them Jill, I just refused to talk to him on the phone."

"Have you decided what you're going to do next?"

"Probably the same as you did, front him out about it. But Gibson won't be able to sweet talk me, Jill. I need honesty. I can't say how I'll react until he shows his hand. Then I'll decide where to go from there."

Jill stood up and placed a hand on the door handle before turning back to me. "Can you do it when I'm not around because I'm more than likely to fire some insults in Gibson's direction. I know that Toby is responsible for himself, but both of them together…" Placing her hand on her hip Jill turned back to face the door and stopped, "I really am sorry, Chloe. I didn't know that you hadn't a clue about the pictures."

"Jill I don't blame you for sharing them with me. I'd rather know what I'm dealing with, than go around in a blissful ignorance. You did me a favor by telling me even if it was accidental."

Pulling the door open, Jill gave me a sympathetic smile and Ruby came into view just before she closed the door and pushed it back open again.

"Gibson's here, Chloe. His car just pulled up in front of the house, I figured you'd want to know."

My heart stopped as I sucked in a deep breath, feeling panic rising. I was completely unprepared about what I should even say to him. Spending all day crying hadn't helped. I was a wreck, emotionally and physically. I looked disheveled and I hadn't even showered. I was about to face Gibson and block out his insanely attractive looks and his beguiling ways and be determined to hear him out but not be swayed by how my heart felt.

I didn't want him to see me and my initial thoughts were that I wanted to make myself presentable, but then I thought about what I saw and decided that I'd be making a pretense of coping with what I knew when I clearly wasn't. Ruby stepped closer and hugged me.

"I'm here, okay? Whatever you need. Just text me, Chloe. If you need to get out of here just say and we'll figure something out honey." Stepping back she placed her feet back flat on the floor and smiled at me but it didn't reach her eyes. Ruby's brow was furrowed and I could see she was worried about me.

Closing the door I sat once again on the bed collecting my feelings and preparing to go down and face whatever the truth was about Gibson, and how that would shape my future. Staring down at the ring my parents gave me during a happier time and I briefly thought of them. Then I tried to take a moment to center myself before I saw him.

Suddenly there was a rush of air and Gibson was in the room beside me. "Chloe." Hearing the sound of Gibson's low velvety tone when he spoke made me close my eyes. Now that he was in the room I felt even less prepared to deal with the truth about his past few days without me. Swallowing noisily, I could feel my emotions waver because he was here and I was going to have to confront the mess I witnessed in the photos Jill had forwarded to me.

Just having Gibson near me was making my body hum, an irresistible pull that drew me to him. Magnetism. I had to fight against his presence drawing me into him, even when I didn't want it to. When I opened my eyes, I focused on the intricate gold thread in the cream comforter while I tried to keep my composure. Gibson smelt clean and seductive wearing my favorite cologne and although he hadn't actually touched me I could sense his closeness to me.

Sighing heavily his anxious broken words flew out of his mouth in a hurried way like he was protesting his innocence. "It's...the pictures...they're not what it looks like, Chloe. I mean they are but I didn't know I was doing it."

I almost laughed because it was the type of excuse a child may have said after being caught doing something they wanted to devolve themselves of responsibility for.

Dragging my eyes up his legs, past his groin, taking in his dark jeans, his familiar soft brown leather belt and up the black tight t-shirt that showed off the contours of his abs and pecs I stalled then finally made eye contact with him. Gibson knew he'd fucked up. It was all right there in his face, guilt and grief. There was no doubt in my mind that whatever had happened, Gibson was sorry for his actions.

Sorry didn't mean I could accept him with another woman. I'd been there with Kace and I'd never be able to accept that again.

Clearing his throat and swallowing, Gibson shifted on his feet and ran his hand through his hair. "I need to talk to you." His voice sounded wounded and laced with concern. I wasn't sure if that was concern for himself or for us– or just for me and how I was going to react.

"Obviously. You came rushing back here to do it, so I'm pretty interested in what you think you can say that is going make those pictures of you and Tori seem pointless to our relationship Gibson."

Gibson sat down heavily on the bed beside me and I immediately stood up, folded my arms and walked over by the window, moving behind the high backed chair then hugged myself.

"Fuck. Don't. Don't do that. Come here. I can't do this with you standing there like that." Gibson put his hand out for me to come go over to him, but ignored the gesture then shook my head.

"Just say what you want to say, Gibson." Really, I should have wanted to slap him hard, but if Kace had taught me anything it was never to show anger. Kace found it unnerving that I never got pissed at him no matter how much he goaded me, so I expected it to have the same effect on Gibson. There was no way I was going to allow anyone to manipulate me into being less of a person again.

Gibson scrubbed his hand down his face and slapped his thighs with the palms of his hands pushing himself to stand. Walking slowly to the door, he pulled the handle down and cracked the door open, turning back to look at me he shook his head looking defeated.

"Well from the general apathy of your tone I don't feel there is any point in me laying everything out, Chloe? Seems to me you've already made your mind up about me and whatever I say, will only put the final nail in the coffin for us, darlin'."

Without another word, Gibson opened the door stepped out and swung it back. The soft click signaling his departure made me feel worse than when I saw the pictures that made everything wonderful I'd been feeling about him, disintegrate.

CHAPTER 32

WALKING AWAY

Chloe

So that's it? Gibson's futile attempt at explaining what had happened with Tori was a non-starter. Since I'd seen the pictures I was a teary mess and he just swept in, made a half-hearted attempt at denying it, changed his mind and admitted it in the same sentence then when I wasn't falling at his feet, he just brushed me off and left.

Sitting down on the chair in a stunned silence, I stared out of the window and watched a rabbit bouncing around in the snow. The day had started with a magical feeling and my world was brighter than it had been in years, and all it took for everything to tumble down was for Gibson to live up to his reputation.

I thought I could trust him. Gibson had been amazing during my recovery and in the time we shared we'd grown really close. Every time I looked at him my heart almost burst into a million tiny ones. That's how much love is in my heart for him. *What do I do with that now?* Outwardly he had everything–was everything to every one...or tried to live up to that.

There was so much pain in my head and my heart that I couldn't think. Not a word would come either positive or negative. I didn't know what to do. Where to go? Who to go with? Glancing at the clock it was 8:00pm so I decided I would get ready for bed. *Do I sleep here? Should I go to Ruby's room? Will he be back?* Everything about being in the cabin, suddenly seemed unnatural. Ruby came back and told me Gibson had gone again.

Every time someone told me something it was like they were stabbing my heart with a jagged knife. Each word piercing into me and making my heart bleed more with every comment. "You need to eat, Chloe. Shower and come downstairs. There's pizza and salad. It won't do your energy levels any good to be hungry."

The last thing I felt like was eating. My apathy was slowly being eroded by fury. Gibson had screwed with my whole life and I was more confused about what I should do now than when I left Kace. I could either sink or swim. My instinct was to lie down and roll over, but if I did that I let Kace and Gibson and all men who mess with women's lives win. So I did what Ruby suggested and showered.

When I went downstairs Emma and Lois were sitting in on the far side of the Great Room. Emma on her laptop, Lois reading her Kindle, again. Whatever she was reading must have been great she could hardly drag herself away from it at times. Jill had gone.

Ruby told me she'd left with Gibson, and that left me wondering if he'd taken her back to LA with him.

After eating, Ruby asked me to watch a movie but I just wasn't in the mood for concentrating on anything like that. Emma and Lois went out and did their nightly check, although what they were checking for was still a mystery. We were so far from civilization and it was freezing out there. Anyone that made it here on foot deserved the right to do whatever they wanted to us for surviving the hazardous terrain out there.

Lois had stacked more logs on the fire and it was still burning brightly by the time everyone started to retire for the night. But my earlier nap and Gibson's appearance had left me wide awake and restless. I knew if I went to bed I'd just bawl my eyes out and feel even lower than I already was.

An acoustic guitar was displayed on a stand over in the corner by the Great Room window, I'd noticed it several times and music was something I tended to be drawn to in troubled times, so I wandered over and unclipped the holder that was securing the neck to the metal stand.

Being shy about playing, I turned all the lights off and sat by the fire, Lois was still sitting reading with just the glow of her Kindle over on the far side of the room. Sitting cross legged in the room in front of the fire, I stared up at the white covered mountains that dwarfed the cabin. They were like a large mural against the massive landscaped window giving the illusion of a panoramic view.

Absentmindedly, I began to strum some chords and a tune came to mind that was both wonderful and painful for where I was at right in my life. "Photograph" by Ed Sheeran started to transfer from my mind to my fingers. Closing my eyes I began singing quietly to myself. I was usually embarrassed to sing out loud, but there was only Lois and she couldn't really see me from where she was sitting– besides she wasn't paying attention.

Finishing the song I looked around and Lois was no longer in her chair. I thought she must have gone upstairs, but when I looked behind me the large shadow of a man began to move nearer me. My heartbeat went from a steady seventy to easily double and I could feel the blood pumping in my ears. I knew it was him before his face came into view but I was still shocked that Gibson had come back.

"You play very well." Embarrassed he'd been listening, for a split second I had forgotten why he was here listening and why I'd even picked up the guitar in the first place.

"Is that what you came back to tell me? Oh no, sorry I forgot you live here, it's me that doesn't." Sarcasm dripped from my mouth as my clipped tone shredded the words, and I chided myself for being one of those people that couldn't bite their tongue and rise above the hurt that was overtaking me.

"Chloe I deserve everything you want to throw at me, darlin'." His voice sounded both sad and tired. Gibson stood still and the fact that he wasn't protesting his innocence was both to his credit and against him.

"That's it? You do...that, and I can do what I want? Well right now Gibson I don't know what the fuck to do. You have absolutely no understanding of what it took for me to leave Kace. Some days I thought that my life would be just that. The abused girlfriend. Then I was thrown a lifeline and I clung to that and found the strength to get out. I made a life for myself in New York. I was safe. Living each day as it came and I could see blue sky through the storm that had been my life for god knows how long, Gibson. I was beginning to feel my way around everything and you came along and ripped me the fuck away from that and turned me inside out. "

Gibson took one step closer his hand gesturing his appeal.

"I'm sorry, Chloe. What happened yesterday? Fuck! I want none of that life. *You* are my life." Gibson's voice sounded frustrated and I wasn't sure if that was self-directed or at me, but he moved past the fire blocking the light, and went and sat on a foot stool in front of me. Glancing up at him, I could see his silhouette with the white backdrop of the snow covered peaks and dark sky in the distance through the massive window. It was a beautiful image in a horrible situation.

We both sat in an uneasy silence for what seemed like an age then Gibson cleared his throat and his soft tone cut into the quiet with what seemed like a very honest account of what he thought had happened.

"I'm a sloppy drunk, Chloe. I know I am. I try not

to drink. Apart from the day on the yacht, the night you went missing and last night, I haven't drunk in nearly two years, because I know I have a problem. It's not that I'm an alcoholic...that's not it at all. I don't crave the taste or need it to function, it just makes me crazy. I'm not sure whether it's how it reacts with my brain because my wiring is different, but I can't remember most of what I do when I've been drinking."

Gibson inhaled a deep shaky breath and huffed the air out in a rush like the thought of what he just said had been sitting heavily on his chest for a long time. I heard him rub his hands together and saw him raise them to his head and rake them through his hair and in watching his body language I could see how much whatever happened had affected him as well.

"Chloe, I love you. I love you so fucking much. I know I never fucked any of those women. I know that much because Morgan helped me out by blocking Tori and she and Johnny took me home."

"Morgan?" *Oh yeah, what was he doing with her after he'd told me he wouldn't see her again?*

Gibson told me everything that had gone on, from Syd's request to how Morgan and Tori had come to be at the party. When he told me Morgan had stayed the night with him I felt sick. From the moment Gibson started to talk to me I could feel the ice melting around my heart, but Jill's comments about Gibson and Toby being lyricists and clever with their words made me cautious. I wanted to believe him, but at the same time what he was telling me was not to trust him because he may well do it again the next time he was drunk.

"Chloe, do you honestly think that I'd spend five months waiting for you and the first time we're apart I'd throw what we were building into the fucking fire? Burn it like we're nothing? You've seen me with Tori? You think I'd want to fuck that? You think I'd do that in my right mind? You think I'd be here now, out of my fucking mind with grief that I've hurt you if I didn't give a shit, and just wanted to pin some horny assed chick to the wall, so she could say she got her revenge on me for not wanting to fuck her sober?"

Gibson stood up and stepped up closer to where I was sitting then knelt down beside me. Taking my hands in his, he wrapped his fingers around them and looked with sad eyes pleading at me.

"Please Chloe. I'm so sorry this happened. All I can do is lay everything that I know out honestly and I understand how it looks, and with my reputation, I don't blame you for thinking the worst of me, but none of it was planned. I got drunk, danced my ass off and got put to bed. That's what Johnny tells me anyway. When I woke feeling shitty my first thought was still you. How I missed you and wanted you next to me in that bed."

Another silence fell between us and I just stared quietly at his face in the dark. He was so near me that all I had to do was move my hand a couple of inches and I'd touch him...feel his warmth.

"I need to think Gibson. I can't just say it's okay, because everything in my life to do with men has been shrouded in complications. Living with a cheater is not the life I want. I'm not that girl any more. Chloe Jenner deserves more and if that 'more' is living with a nine to five, Monday to Friday husband who treats me like his princess at the weekend, then that's what I wish for.

"Last night, Gibson Barclay the rock star overlapped with Gibson Barclay the man. What you do; being a rock star, and who you are in private became one person. I have to figure out what that means to me and depending on how you manage that, it may be the deciding factor of whether I can stick around or not."

Gibson dropped one hand and reached out squeezing my shoulder. I shrugged him off. "Please respect what I need, Gibson. I'd like to be alone if you don't mind." I sounded harsh but I wasn't going to cave in to being with him like nothing had happened. Jill had made that mistake and look where it had got her with Toby. Besides I was really serious about not being that girl who was used and abused emotionally again, because their partner took what he wanted from life.

"I'll be in the bedroom. I hope you find it in your heart to forgive me, Chloe. You are in my heart. The only girl ever to make it there. You're there for a reason, Chloe. You *are* my reason...my life." Gibson placed one foot on the floor and pushed his weight on to it as he stood up. Without saying anything else he walked over to the stairs and headed up to the bedroom.

Watching the way he was reacting, I knew before he reached the top step that everything he'd told me, the way he had told me—the honesty in his voice—the remorse…he knew what he'd done and he was genuinely at a loss that it had happened.

Without thinking I began strumming the strings of the guitar that was lying flat on the floor beside me where I had placed it. Picking it up, I placed it across my crossed legs and an old song came to mind that had fitted the sentiment for how I was feeling.

I began to play "More Than Words" by Extreme, and although I loved the song, I didn't know all of the words. My emotions made me feel like I was on a roller coaster. Crying, singing, angry and my heart was shredded.

Singing was something that I used to do to block out Kace. When I was on my own I'd lie on the floor and sing…except it was "Inches from Paradise" the song Gibson had written about a moment that passed between us. When I sang it at the time I had no idea the song was about me.

Playing "More Than Words" again, I closed my eyes in concentration and suddenly I felt Gibson close. Warm arms slid between my body and my own as the fingers of his left hand lightly touched mine, mirroring the same chords of the song I was playing. My throat constricted instantly at his touch and I choked, a wave of emotion engulfing me because he couldn't stay away.

Gibson's right hand slid around my stomach and he wiggled himself closer until I was sitting between his legs and I couldn't fight my feelings any longer. Allowing my body to lean back I placed my head against his shoulder and he pressed my fingers onto the strings to play the song again.

Soft, low, dulcet tones filled my ear as Gibson leaned forward and sang all of the words of the song to me. Tears rolled down my cheeks that he could be so contradictory in his public and private life and showing me this side of him made him more of a man than anything he could do with aggression.

With my eyes shut, I lay back until the last note sounded then turned to look up at him by the light of the fire. "Trust me, Chloe. I got you, darlin', I'd never want to do anything to hurt you."

I did. The way he had read me today. Leaving without a fight when he had tried to tell me...he knew I wasn't in a place to hear what he had to say. Kace would have screamed and shouted— protesting his innocence and he'd have given some fast talking excuse to push me into submission. Gibson didn't go there. Instead he left and I was hurt by that at the time, but he had called it just right.

Backing off, he had given me time to breathe after seeing him. It helped me to feel that even though what he had to say may hurt me, I should at least allow him to present his side of the story that went with the pictures I'd seen. If Jill hadn't been here and had the conversation about Gibson and Toby, I wondered if I'd have been more accepting of Gibson's explanation.

Then again, if Jill hadn't been here I may never have known about the party. Shaking my head, I dismissed that. Gibson Barclay is a world-wide artist. I was sure that wasn't the only article out there about the incident.

Gibson whispered in my ear again. "Sorry, darlin', please let me show you how I feel. I promise to do better. I'm never touching another drop of alcohol as long as I have you." Nodding slowly in acceptance, I tilted my chin so that our lips were close to one another and Gibson took my mouth in a gentle, sensuous kiss, but I doubted it would as simple as that for him...or for me.

CHAPTER 33

I DON'T BITE

Chloe

Placing the guitar down, Gibson placed his hands on my body, shifted and turned me into him and he groaned deeply against my mouth. "Fuck. I'm sorry I hurt you, Chloe." His mouth began to trace down my chin then extending my head he peppered kisses all the way down to my collar bone. Shifting he stood up and pulled me by my hands to stand. As soon as I did he swept me off of my feet by cradling my legs and body in his arms.

Gibson was still placing little kisses on me as he walked up the stairs, "I need to spread you out on that bed and fuck all this pain away. You give me heartburn, Chloe. It only goes away when I'm inside you." I started laughing loudly because what he said sounded corny and absurd. Gibson smirked because he got his own joke but I knew exactly what he meant, when we weren't together the heavy pain in my heart was the worst feeling.

Passing Ruby's room "Sugar" by Maroon 5 was playing and it vaguely registered with me when Gibson kicked the bedroom door open. He strode over and dropped me onto the bed, quickly covering me with his body. A whoosh of air came out of my lungs with his weight. "Damn. Sorry, darlin', did I hurt you." Shaking my head I smiled and although I was still feeling a bit worried about the photo, I was in no doubt what I meant to him. Flying home unexpectedly told me part of that.

"You're so fucking gorgeous, Chloe. I'd never do anything that would make you leave me."

Compassion had driven Gibson to fly home. He had cared about my feelings enough not to try to fix things by phone. Grand gestures didn't impress me much because they can also be the actions of a man who was guilty. But, I really didn't think Gibson was guilty of anything except trusting people that didn't bring out the best in him. Toby, his best friend is unfortunately one of those people.

Stripping me to my underwear, Gibson's hands stroked down the front of my body, his mouth quickly followed the trail and peppering me with kisses. The way he was touching me felt comforting rather than sexual— healing hands. Using both palms he made sweeping movements over my skin avoiding my erogenous zone. Gibson's eyes changed from caring to sensuous as his gaze followed his hands as he carefully tracked what he was doing. Fingertips then traced lightly over my skin. I think that he was trying to soothe the tension from me. Even with this kind of touch by Gibson, my body was coming alive—responding to his fingertips skating over my skin whether that was his intention or not.

I melded into the mattress, and a soft moan parted my throat. Gibson's amused lust-filled eyes flicked to mine and I smiled feeling slightly embarrassed that my body had let me down by telling him how he was making me feel.

"Oh, you like this?"

When I saw Gibson's warm, gorgeous smile stretch across his face and his eyes twinkle when they connected with mine, it confirmed that he wasn't immune to what was happening either, despite his best efforts to hide his erection.

"Fuck, Chloe. You are so beautiful...so beautiful..." His voice trailed off as he swallowed roughly and licked his lips, before he bent forward to lay small kisses across my stomach, trying to control his warm shuddery breaths. As feather-light as they were, he may as well have been branding me because his scorching wet lips made my body erupt in a million goose bumps.

Edging up on my elbows, I watched his mouth move across and up my body to take one of my nipples in it. Gibson sucked it hard.

A plea fell from my lips, "Oh, please..." Gibson stood staring at me, unbuttoning his jeans one at a time in an agonizingly slow motion. As soon as he popped the last button he smiled wickedly, pushed them down his legs with both hands and grabbed mine on the way back, bending my knees to my shoulders swiftly. His possessive grip was so arousing my skin tingled where he touched and a whoosh of air came out of my lungs at how suddenly he'd restricted my belly.

Grunting, he whispered into my core through my panties, "Oh, darlin'," and then hooked his thumb inside the lacy crotch and pulled them to the side, burying his tongue deep inside me. His expert tongue tantalized my core and made juice seep from my pussy and run down my butt crease onto the bed. He began fucking me fast with his tongue and occasionally sucking again when more juice leaked from me. Soft moans turned to loud groans and gasps, while Gibson growled low and deeply into my core before sitting back, wiping his mouth with the back of his hand. "Fuck. My. God. Your taste— so sweet. So fucking sweet. I'm lost for words for how you make me feel. I just... don't have *any* words for this."

Crawling up the bed the mattress dipped deeply and I rolled into him. "Come here." Gibson pulled me against him and turned me on my side. Lifting my left leg he placed my knee over his then lifted it so that it made my legs wider. Placing his hand over my pussy between my legs and his other hand glided over my skin to cup my right breast.

"This right here..." Gibson's palm rubbed in and out of my legs, over my mound before he gave it a slap and cupped it firmly again. "This is mine. *Mine.* Chloe. The thought of never having you again made me so fucking desolate today. I don't want to live if I can't have you here with me." His tongue ran the length of his bottom lip and he nibbled my neck. Kissing the back of my shoulders, Gibson breathed out deeply on the back of my neck before biting it gently.

"I thought you said you didn't bite?" Gibson smirked and positioned himself at my entrance, drawing his dick back and forth and coating it in my juice then began nudging himself into me slowly, "I don't usually. This is a distraction technique."

"And I'd be distracted by a small bite on my neck when there is a huge dick sliding into my pussy? You think that's all it's going to take to distract me?"

Gibson smirked wickedly, "Well...to be honest I could distract you a hell of a lot more but you'd have to be pretty game for that kind of pleasure."

I had an arousal overload at Gibson's wicked taunt. It made my pussy clench tightly with need as his words set off a cascade of signals, which put my body on full alert. My heart had already been racing in effect to him being inside me, but it went into shock at the threat of even more pleasure than I was already feeling.

"Yes?"

"Oh Chloe, you have no fucking idea what I could do to you."

Gibson started kissing my neck again but didn't push himself into me any deeper. "So where were we...?"

"You were distracting me from the thick, large metal-clad object poking into my pussy." I giggled because it felt weird to be joking about that, but he was being playful and it was really hot when he did that.

"I was. So am I biting you again or you think you need more distraction? I mean...just how adventurous are you feeling, darlin'?"

Turning to look at him, and I was thinking that after seeing that picture of Gibson earlier we'd never be here again— but we were, so I had to go with my gut. "Well...of course I am. But— I warn you, it will take something pretty special to take my mind off what is happening between my legs right now."

Gibson grinned holding my stare, then poked his middle finger into my mouth. "Suck it. *Hard.*" I did and his dick twitched at my entrance and he spontaneously sunk his dick another inch into me before stopping himself. Making sexy sounds and eyeing my neck again, Gibson, growled. "Fuck." Growling longer this time, his mouth sucked on my neck while I sucked his finger. "Hot damn, girl, you are so fucking sexy, I could ruin you."

I looked away as he pulled his finger out, but he took my face in his hand and he turned my head back to stare at him. "Eyes!—keep looking at me. I want to see what I do to you." Gibson was rocking gently in me but not sinking deeper inside.

"You are it for me, Chloe. You understand that?" I nodded slowly and he grinned, "Keep looking at me just like that, darlin'." Gibson licked his middle finger again and pulled my body closer, taking it out of his mouth he placed it over my butt-hole and applied gentle pressure. Gibson must have read the fear in my eyes and was quick to respond.

"Relax, I got you. Nothing bad is going to happen." When he felt that my body was still tense he kissed my neck and whispered softly to me. "Trust me." I did and I wanted to show Gibson that even if I didn't like this, I couldn't really say it until I'd at least tried.

"I do."

Gibson pulled out of me and placed his dick at the entrance of my butt and I almost flew off the bed. Grinning wickedly his voice half laughing, he quickly reassured me. "Stop, I'm not going to stick it in your ass, I only want to lubricate you."

My body calmed and in the quiet slow way he handled me I submitted and he placed his dick back at my entrance. Without warning he pushed his dick inside me and his middle finger in my butt at the same time. My butt felt full... a weird feeling at first but not painful. Slowly he began to rock in and out and the sensation was incredible. Gibson pulled my jaw round to see my face and smiled, the sensual sounds he made were so ridiculously sexy. "Slow and easy first time round, Chloe, then the next one is for me, darlin'."

Changing position, Gibson pulled out and quickly bent to lick my pussy again, before pushing himself deeper inside me again. I could feel him in my stomach when he placed his forehead on mine. "Damn Chloe I waited so long for this and to think I almost ruined it with a few drinks."

Honest words were tumbling from Gibson while he cradled my head with one hand, telling me what I meant to him— how I made him feel, and all the time he was slowly rocking my world. When he felt I was close there was no need for words, Gibson knew instinctively when to switch it up and suddenly he was pounding into me rapidly, bringing me to a heady shaky release, the sensation reaching from my head to my toes and making me buck in his arms with the force of it.

"Oh, God, Gibson." When I screamed his name, Gibson smiled at the pleasure he'd given me, smirked knowingly, then touched my clitoris again ordering me to come again. "Do it," I couldn't have stopped myself, if I tried. When I came hard he held me tightly, talking softly, telling me how much he loved me.

As I recovered, Gibson was stroking my body again, then he lifted me so that I was sitting up and slid his head under me and pulled my pussy onto his face. I started to protest, but he drank from me and after a minute he changed tact, growling sexily as he rolled me over onto my stomach. He made eye contact with me when I looked over my shoulder then pulled me up onto my knees.

Pushing my shoulders down on the bed he slid himself inside me again. From that point on there was nothing gentle and everything alpha male in his possessive claim on my body. There was nothing tender about it, the bed squeaked and creaked noisily and we were both groaning and moaning loudly. By that point neither of us cared who heard us.

When I woke up Gibson's cell was ringing. Turning around, I saw Gibson's bare butt as he crawled towards the end of the bed to find it in his jeans pocket. I felt stiff and winced when I stretched out, quickly pulling my knees up again. Gibson noted my discomfort and slid completely off of the bed. Taking the call as he walked into the bathroom. I heard the tub filling with water.

Whatever the phone call was it must have been important because Gibson got showered while I sat in the tub and when he was done, he wrapped a towel around himself and disappeared back into the bedroom without even noticing I had gotten in there. When he came back he was buttoning down a black shirt with white stud buttons. "Gotta go out. Not sure when I'll be back, but Chloe I want you to stay home today."

Something in his voice was different from the other times he had told me to stay home. "What's going on?" Gibson was trying to act normally but he was a bad liar. I stood up and the water cascaded down my body, as I reached for the rolled up bath robe that was stacked in the pigeon holes over the bath.

"I don't have time for this, Chloe. Just do what I say, okay?" Gibson was hopping as he tried to pull his boot on and the urgency with how he was getting dressed freaked me out, but I could see that whatever was going on wasn't good, and my sixth sense told me it had to do with me.

Drying myself off as I ran in front of the door, I threw my arms wide to stop Gibson from leaving, staring up at him anxiously and needing him to tell me what the hell that phone call was about. "Chloe, darlin', you need to get out of my way. I'm in a hurry."

"No. This has to do with me...with Kace? Have they found him?"

Gibson rolled his eyes dramatically and rubbed the back of his neck, then looked me square in the eye. "They have. At least... they know where he is right now."

I felt sick at the thought that he had finally shown himself. "I'm coming." Pushing Gibson back, I made for the closet returning with a pair of black sweat pants and a grey hooded sweater, pulling them on as I ran back towards the door he had now opened.

"No! I won't take you anywhere near him. You're not fucking coming."

Panic set because I suddenly thought he was in Colorado. "He's here? In Colorado?"

Gibson shook his head and held me by my arms at arms-length. "No, Chloe. He isn't in Colorado, he's in New York."

"You're going to New York? You just sweep in here and sweep back out again? Just like that? You leave me here again, telling me not to go out and you're going to New York?" My voice was becoming more and more hysterical as I argued my case and Gibson's frown got more pronounced.

I was desperate to be heard so I delivered an ultimatum to Gibson. "I'm not fucking hiding any more. This has to stop! I've been to hell and back and now I need to take some control of the decisions made about my life. *My* life, Gibson...not my life with you. If you ignore this, then I won't be here when you come back."

Gibson looked frustrated and pulling back his shirt sleeve to look at his watch nodded then looked back at me. "Get your coat and meet me in the car."

"No, wait for me. If you go before I'm ready, I'm serious Gibson, I'm not staying. I've been shoved around by one man in my life and that's one too many. I understand about your fame and everything but this isn't the same thing."

Gibson hesitated then nodded in agreement and I grabbed my coat. Emma and Lois were standing in the great room. Gibson watched them staring at him. "What are you fucking looking at? She's leaving that means you are as well. Get your kit and get in the car."

Both women ran in the same direction and appeared back with their outdoor wear. Emma pulled a boot on and grabbed her cell from the counter. "What about Ruby?"

Gibson glanced upstairs and looked back at her. "I don't give a fuck about her. Ruby's a big girl, there's plenty of food we'll... deal with her later. Get in the car." Looking in my direction Gibson motioned to me to come to him. When I walked over he took my hand and squeezed it tightly. "You sure about this?" I wasn't but I had to see it through to the end.

"Okay, darlin', let's do this." He opened the door for us to pass. When I saw Johnny and Jerry both at the car as well, it gave me some reassurance that if Kace tried anything these guys would all have my back this time.

CHAPTER 34

CHASING SHADOWS

Chloe

Fastening the buckle of my seat, Gibson pulled the strap to check it was secure, like I was a child. Reaching around, he fastened his own then took my hand. Immediately, his thumb grazed over mine and he looked at me concerned. "You stay with Jerry and Lois every single minute you got it, Chloe? You go to the John, Jerry goes as well, do you hear me?"

The gravity of the situation we were heading toward could be heard in the tone of his voice. Delivering his order I was being told what he expected. It wasn't a request. The speed of his words gave away his own anxiety, and the way he looked at me made me offer him reassurance that I would listen and do what he said, and not what whatever came to mind the moment I came face to face with Kace. If anything came to mind.

Reality began to bite the nearer we got and I questioned whether I was strong enough to face him again. Months of painful memories seeing Gibson's worried face and how helpless he looked trying to reach me. The way his hand rose to touch me only for his fingers to crumple closed and he'd stuff it in his pocket, instead of doing what came naturally to all couples still in the fledgling stages of their relationship.

One good thing to come out of Kace's warped stunt was that Gibson and I knew the strength of our love for each other, because I had been able to overcome the fearful feelings about men and tried not process only negative thoughts like I had before. Dragging the rational side of my reasoning back to the fore was easier for having Gibson by my side. He had offered me protection and even though he was the last guy on earth I had thought I could trust. I did.

Gibson was quiet during the flight and once in a while his hand gripped mine tightly; which at times felt a tad aggressive, and if I had to hazard a guess, he was trying to deal with his own feelings about breathing the same air as Kace. Johnny and Emma were sitting up at the back of the plane pouring over a map, while Lois and Jerry discussed something on Jerry's laptop but the sound of their low voices was lost with the hum of the plane and the earbuds I was wearing.

I'd been doing great until I heard the three dings on the cabin bell, to signal our decent. We'd been in the air less than four hours. As soon as we hit 10,000ft I began to feel sick. Nerves were getting the better of me and Gibson was so attuned to me he wasn't slow to notice.

"Fuck, Chloe. I knew I should have left you back in

Colorado. I'm getting Jerry and Lois to take you to Syd's place when we're on the ground."

"No, Gibson. I don't want that. I *really* don't want that. As much as this frightens me, I need to see this through. I need to see that Kace can't hurt me anymore. If everyone else takes control of that without me, I'll still look over my shoulder every time I'm alone. Trust me...I need to see this to the end."

Gibson looked at me with frustration, his jaw ticked twice then his concerned eyes flicked over to look at Lois and Jerry, who had stopped what they were doing to listen to the conversation between Gibson and me. When he looked back at me his worried eyes softened and a silent understanding seemed to pass between us. Licking his lips, Gibson leaned forward, closing the space between us and kissed me softly on my closed mouth. "Isn't that my line?" Furrowing my brow I wasn't sure what I'd said.

"Trust me? You sure pick your moments to pull that one out of the hat, darlin'."

Giving me a soft smile, Gibson was trying to reduce the tension in me with distraction. Chewing the inside of my cheek I didn't try to hide how maybe seeing Kace was making me feel, but I was determined it had to be done. "I got you, darlin', I'm never going to let anything bad happen to you again." Inclining his head in Lois and Jerry's direction he looked back at me. "They've got you. Kace comes anywhere near you he's a dead man."

"Where is he?" My voice sounded shaky—weak. Gibson closed his eyes for a second then turned to face me. Releasing his grip on my hand he interlaced his fingers on one hand with mine again.

"Okay, there's some stuff I need to tell you. Stuff you don't know, stuff that Jerry and the team of private investigators have been working on. They were getting nowhere using all the usual channels to trace him.

"We didn't want to go public because we didn't want more media attention drawn to you, so Syd was trying to draw him out with an offer of work. The search he put out was for a specific type of sound engineer, one so specific with experience that matched Kace's credentials exactly. The package he was offering was too appealing to a guy like Kace.

"We knew he had been in New York already, and we think he turned your apartment over shortly after the story of us broke in the media. We can't prove anything with that...he left no prints. Sorry we didn't tell you about that Chloe, but you were a mess at that point."

I scowled and it was obvious to Gibson that I didn't like what I'd heard. Leaning over, Gibson tucked my hair behind my left ear and cupped my face in his hand. "Sorry, darlin', are you sure you want to hear this?"

Biting my lip I hesitated for a moment then nodded again, "Yeah I need to know what's been going on, I have loads of questions but I know this isn't the time." My heart was banging hard and rapidly in my chest that no one had told me any of this at the time. I was trying to deal with the deception and everyone keeping information about my life from me, but it wasn't the time to let those feelings get the better of me.

Drawing in a deep breath Gibson exhaled and raked his hand through his hair then began talking again. "So there was the New York connection, then he disappeared...fell off the face of the earth. Charlotte was liaising with the police and Jerry came out to speak to a couple of the detectives to give them the details about Kace and the possible connection.

"When Kace took you in Seattle that was premeditated. He had acquired a hotel staff uniform so he could move freely in the building and no one would bat an eyelid. The fact he left you after five days indicates he never intended to keep you somewhere permanent, or something happened that he had to move and it was too risky to take you as well. Or the sick bastard wanted to mind fuck all of us, as well as you. He must have known we'd be looking for you."

At that point in his conversation, the plane touched down. Gibson was distracted for a moment before he turned back to me and sighed again, then tried to speed up what he was telling me before we transferred to the car.

"Anyway, the reason it's taken so long to find him is he cleared his bank account out and didn't use any of the usual monetary and identity tools. So no credit cards, no hired cars, no social security number and no bank withdrawals. He was faceless for months working with cash."

Puzzled I flexed my fingers against Gibson's. "So

how did you find him? Smirking and looking smug he said, "Syd." I didn't understand what he meant. I knew Syd ran a record company they used to be with. I remember when they first started the guy used to do press conferences about M3rCy.

"Remember the job I told you about? Well Syd put the ad out on the websites and Music magazines, and Kacey-boy answered it. He's running out of money and needs work. Our private investigators had some tech guy figure some shit on the website to track his IP. He was clever but fell down on something that fucking basic. The IP pinpoints him to the address of a Hotel on the upper East side near your apartment, Chloe."

I froze when I heard how close Kace had stayed to where my home was. If I had left Gibson at any time and returned home alone, the thought that Kace pounced at any time, like he had in the hotel, sent shivers down my spine.

"How do you know he'll still be there?" Suddenly, my urgency of getting to Kace was as strong as Gibson's had been back at his cabin.

"We've got him covered, darlin', don't worry about that. The PI's that have been tracking him are eyeballing him as we speak. We have the two detectives working on your case already there, and the manager has been tipped to call for backup if he tries to leave the building."

Jerry turned his laptop around for me to see and interjected on our conversation. "He's in his room right now watching porn on his laptop. Been watching for just over seven minutes." Jerry smirked and shrugged his shoulders. "PI's technical guy did something..."

The cabin door opened and Gibson unclipped my belt then his. Still clutching my hand he pulled me up to stand. "I love you, Chloe. We're gonna put this baby to bed and get on with our lives together."

Giving Gibson a slow nervous smile I nodded and reached up and kiss him tenderly. "Thank, God. I can't wait."

Gibson gave it a squeeze. "Let's go."

It was raining hard when we left the aircraft, the grey sky heavy with thick dark clouds and the wind driving the icy rain diagonally at us. It was a miserable sight, after the beautiful winter scenes of Colorado. Gibson opened the door for me to slide into the back seat of a white SUV with blacked out windows, then slid along the seat beside me.

Johnny and Emma took the front seats. Emma was driving and Johnny became the passenger after piloting the flight. Jerry and Lois were in the car behind us. Gibson raked his hand through his hair, ruffling it to shake out the excess water, while I gathered my thoughts.

Johnny rang Gibson on his phone and I thought that was quite funny, considering they were only feet away from each other. Then I realized that Gibson was concentrating intensely to what Johnny was telling him, and was making sure that I couldn't hear because the radio was on. The music was interrupting my concentration. I could hear Johnny talking but wasn't able to make out what he was saying.

We pulled down an alleyway and I was getting used to passing through hotel kitchens with surprised chefs and kitchen staff staring wide eyed at my boyfriend coming and going like it was the most natural thing in the world for him. But today was different, my heart was in my mouth with fear and it had nothing to do with Gibson or his work.

Johnny and Emma left the kitchen while Jerry and Lois stayed with us. A girl in a set of chef's whites with a blue checked neckerchief came over and asked Gibson to sign her apron. Gibson's jaw ticked. This was not the time for someone to interrupt, but I couldn't believe how cool he was. He asked her name, signing quickly and handed it back, just as Johnny pushed the door open.

"Clear. Left- elevator door 50ft. Emma in situ. Gibson grabbed my hand and with the others close behind us, we walked quickly to the elevator, Gibson had his head bowed down to avoid recognition. Stepping inside, he waited for the doors to close then looked Johnny square in the eye. "Shoot."

"Same floor—opposite doors, room number eleven forty one. Exit left first. Detective Mulligan is waiting at the door." Johnny was already swiping his phone and Jerry was scrolling on his, while Lois was looking on. Emma was standing in front of us waiting for our pending arrival on the floor.

When the elevator glided to a halt and the doors opened, Emma held her hand behind her for us to wait, stepping out she looked in both directions, "Clear."

On entering the hotel room a guy of about thirty was waiting by the door and Gibson slapped his back. "Good job. I owe you. Brief me. Chloe, this is Detective Mulligan by the way."

Staring at me, he looked at Gibson and shook his head, giving Gibson an angry scowl.

"No way! Bad idea."

"Trust me, I know, but she's here. Just tell me what's going on, where is he?"

Mulligan heaved a sigh of resignation, "First, this has to be by the book once he's in the room. Any stupid moves will go in his favor. You are not to touch him, understand?"

"You have my word. My instinct is to beat the shit out of him, but for Chloe's sake I won't. That would only take me down to his level. But—make no mistake I want that fucker to suffer for what he did to my girl and locking him away is about all we have. So I won't do anything to fuck that up."

"Do this right and we'll have him for a long time. You have to wear the wire so we have it on tape. Chloe as well. Although I wouldn't even have *her* anywhere near this hotel with him in it if she were mine, given what he's already done to her."

Gibson gave him a dark solemn look, his dark, worried eyes darting to me then back to the detective. "Well she isn't yours—she's *mine*. Chloe is my world but I got her, dude. She wants to stay—she stays. This has been a long time coming for her."

Gibson squeezed my hand in reassurance and the detective rubbed his finger under his collar in annoyance before protesting further about sticking his neck out to do this. Gibson was in no mood for the uncooperative tone he was setting and managed him in pretty much the same way as he did his band. Gibson's power of persuasion was no match for the arguments that Mulligan put up and after a couple more minutes, he started to brief us on what had been happening.

"O'Neill is in the bar drinking with two women, but the last thing we want is him picking someone up and bringing her upstairs." Emma stepped forward taking her gun out of the back of her pants and placed it on the table.

"I'll bring him up."

The detective quickly swiped it from the table opened the barrel and emptied the bullets from it. Waving it at Gibson, he asked, "You don't happen to have one of these on you, do you?"

Nodding at Johnny and Jerry, he replied, "No I don't have a fucking gun, these guys are my protection."

Gibson then nodded at Johnny to have Emma covered by Jerry, and just before they left the room, Gibson said, "This is Emma, Chloe's security. She'll do a good job."

Ten minutes later, once we knew that Kace was busy with Emma, we transferred across the hallway to Kace's room and were sitting nervously waiting for news of what was happening in the bar. Johnny had hung back because he was usually always with Gibson, and was the more recognizable of his two body guards. If Kace had been watching us, the chances were he'd have spotted Johnny previously.

After another argument, it was agreed only Gibson needed to wear the wire because it would record all the conversation and there was no way Gibson wanted anything taped to my body. Besides if anyone was to leave the room during the altercation it would be me. The detective complained again that everything we were doing was highly irregular and had to be managed properly so that Kace couldn't accuse us of entrapment. He had to enter his room of his own free will with Emma.

The victim would never be put in front of her abductor in normal circumstances but nothing that had happened since I had left Kace could have been described with that tag. I knew this– they knew this, and the huge risk they were taking to catch him wasn't lost on me.

Kace had been very clever and although there was CCTV footage of him in the hotel, the only sighting they had was him putting 'Something in a blanket in the trunk of a car, hired in his name.' Circumstantial evidence at best, my apartment investigation had thrown up no evidence either. There was no clear CCTV footage of him taking me or of being in my building, but he was picked up on some cameras close to my place at the time, and no finger prints. None of that was enough to convict him of anything.

Twenty more minutes passed before Johnny's finger flew up to his ear. Turning his back he listened for a moment then turned and stared at Gibson.

"Affirmative."

"Emma's worked her charm they're heading for the elevator. It's show-time."

Fighting my body's response to the shock of hearing Johnny confirm they were coming, I hung on to the sleeve of my coat. Gibson pulled me in for a hug and kissed the top of my head, quietening my wildly rapid heartbeat enough to focus on him. "You sure about this?" I was petrified. The shock of Johnny's voice saying something so simple but so final, suddenly made me feel unprepared. Gibson hugged me tighter and gave me a resolute stare. "I got you, darlin'," at his words I trusted he did, but the anticipation of Kace's imminent arrival was terrifying.

CHAPTER 35

ANTICIPATION

Gibson

Mulligan refused to leave the room but agreed he wouldn't show his hand until the time was right. In civilian clothing he could have been anyone working for me. Chloe was at the foremost in my mind. God alone knew how she must have felt, standing terrified–waiting for the arrival of the bastard who put her through hell.

No matter what happened, I knew I had to remain calm. Chloe had to witness me taking care of this situation in a controlled and intelligent way, because the last thing I wanted was for her to be scared of the potential for me to become aggressive with her. Above all else I had to demonstrate restraint because I was a better man than Kace.

My internal feelings were that I wanted to punch the fucker's lights out, but not before I squeezed him by the balls and watch him yelp for mercy repeatedly. Kace deserved no mercy but punching him would take me to a place where violence bred terror, and that's exactly what he'd expect of a guy like me. The expectations of others for me to fuck up had been my downfall all my life, until I met Chloe. She has been the only one to realize, what you see isn't what always what you get with me.

Johnny's hand shot up to silence us and he held his finger to his lips. We were on. Chloe was a bundle of nerves judging by her face and how she kept fidgeting she was slightly shaking. I touched her lips with my fingers and stared pointedly at her. "Everything is going to be okay, Chloe." I whispered then I made eye contact to Johnny and inclined my head to guard her.

Johnny moved a step closer to her and dipped his head to speak quietly to her. He knew in this instance, he didn't need to have my back. Chloe needed Lois and him more. Watching Chloe's reaction I noted when her eyes snapped up to meet his, whatever he'd told her was what she needed to hear because a tight smile appeared on her gorgeous mouth and she nodded.

I knew the only time I'd lose my cool with Kace was if he went for her. There was no way in God's earth would I be able to hold back if he tried anything with Chloe. That would definitely be an all-bets-are-off situation.

We heard a couple talking in the corridor and laughter as they came closer to the room. I recognized Emma's voice was outside and then they stopped. I knew Kace was outside and there were only a couple of inches of wood between me and the guy who had fucked up Chloe's life until now, and the last six months of mine. The temptation to lose my shit and go piling in with my fists was so strong that I shoved my hands deep into my leather jacket pockets just so that I was conscious of where they were.

A click of the latch and Kace was hurtled into the room by Emma. Kace lost his footing and landed on the floor in front of me. And, there he was. Kace's voice stopped abruptly when he tumbled to his knees in front of me. Glancing up, his eyes met mine then popped widely when he realized he and Emma were not alone in the room. Watching his frightened eyes do a quick scan of the room I saw the moment when his eyes fell on Chloe. The tense reaction at being in the same room as her was like an electric shock, while his body jerked and his jaw flexed like he was gritting his teeth.

Recovering quickly, Kace went on the attack like most guilty men do when they are caught in a tight spot.

"What in the hell's name is going on here? Chloe! Thank God you are safe. Where have you been? I've been out of my mind with worry?"

Kace was a good actor and began to try to reach out to her, he never got one step off the ground in her direction as Johnny and Mulligan stepped forward. Turning to address me and Mulligan he threw his hands out and straightened his stance.

"You guys know she's got mental health issues right?"

The dude was acting all concerned and smooth and the urge to kick the lying fucker's mouth shut was beginning to overwhelm me, so I began to walk over to where Emma was standing nearer the door in my effort to make space between us. Once I was there I took my hand out of my pocket placed it behind me, then ground my knuckles into the wall out of sight. I had to keep it together for Chloe, but every nerve in my body wanted to tear him apart.

Chloe found her voice and when she did, she sounded so sassy, if we hadn't been in such a serious situation I knew she'd have dropped me to my knees with lust.

"Bullshit Kace. That tact may have worked in a small town at home but these guys are much worldlier and wiser than you could ever know. Gibson may be a rock star to millions in public, but he's my rock star— a decent man. You are not even in the same sport as him, never mind the same league. You're a woman beater and I hope you can live with yourself, preying on defenseless girls like me."

To Chloe's credit she hid what she was feeling very well. It was an Oscar winning performance from my poor terrified girl– the only thing that gave away some of her feelings was that she was gripping tightly to the sleeve of her coat and her finger nails were white with the effort of clinging on. Every fiber in my body was aching to go and hold her, but I knew that would have been fatal, she'd have cried.

"Why did you follow me...seek me out? Leaving you was the hardest and the best thing I ever did. Why couldn't you just leave me in peace to get on with my life?"

Kace was starting to panic—it was right there in his eyes, but his demeanor was reasonable as he tried to deliver a plausible excuse and draw the focus on Chloe's health and personality as the problem. "Listen I don't know what she's told you but I bet it's a crock of shit. Chloe has lived with me for a few years now. This is her usual M.O. Going off with random men, placing herself in danger—she's a sick chick, Gibson. You need to let me take her home."

Chloe's eyes fell to the floor and she looked like she took a hit with his comment. Johnny gave her a subtle touch on the hand by his side in reassurance and she glanced up at him. Witnessing that hurt my heart because I should have been standing holding her while all of this was happening, but she wouldn't have coped if I had, and I was wearing the wire, and if he was going to go for me I didn't want her anywhere near me.

Kace was livid with her, that much was registering with me. Watching his chest heaving as he tried to take in enough air had his nostrils flaring as well. Fighting to control his temper was becoming a full time occupation for the dude, and his adrenaline was flowing judging by the pulse throbbing in his neck. After a second of hesitancy he switched it up and snickered, dipping his head shyly as if he were trying to look embarrassed for her.

Rocking on my heels, I looked down at my feet, trying desperately to remain passive, and when I felt my emotions were firmly in check I looked him dead in the eye, sighing for effect like I was tired, then spoke softly like what he was doing was working. I needed to lull him into a false sense of security.

"Chloe was sick. I've been helping her, Kace. She has no recollection of what happened to her. I felt obliged to help her after all the media attention I had drawn to her. I had no idea she was with someone when I met her. All I know is that I had been with her for a while and one day I went to my gig and when I came back she was gone. Same shit different day in my world. Anyway she was found by the side of Lake Union some days later with a note pinned to her chest saying, 'Guess who I've been with.' They came back to me because one of the bathrobes she was wearing when she was found is unique to the penthouse suite of the hotel I was staying at, at the time. Shame it happened really because Chloe's an incredible girl and I was enjoying her."

A fleeting look of anger crossed Kace's face but he was very self-aware and caught it, then looked back at me with a passive expression again. For a second he seemed to be considering what I had said to him and I saw the injecting of anger when the impact of Chloe being intimate with me hit him.

"So...you're done with her and you want me to take her home? Had your fun but because she's sick you're passing the buck back to me to take care of her? Is that what this is? How did you find me? Anyway, it's typical behavior from someone as selfish as you are. I watched you back in college, I know your reputation with women. Luckily for Chloe, I love her and although it hurts my heart to know she's been with someone like you, I'll do it. I'll take her back...but I'm doing it for her not for you."

Kace began to walk toward Chloe and Johnny reached over to pick a menu off the dressing table effectively halting Kace in his tracks. He didn't realize that it was Johnny's intention to block him and he waited for him to move back. I could see he thought we believed him and he had smoothed things over, then he found a bit more confidence and asked, "So do they know where she was?"

Turning to look me square in the eye Kace looked expectantly as he tried to find out what else I knew. Staring at him with a puzzled expression I asked, "Sorry? What do you mean?"

"The note...'Guess where I've been?' She can't remember where she was?" Looking past Johnny to address Chloe, he asked, "You don't remember, Chloe?" Chloe slipped slightly behind Johnny's body. From his reaction he believed that Chloe had no idea he'd taken her, but then it dawned on him the mistake he'd just make. Realizing what he'd done, Kace quickly backtracked, "No sorry, what did the note say again?"

Mulligan reached over and pulled the handle down on the hotel room door and two huge guys in navy blue police uniform were standing in the doorway with NYPD badges on their caps. Johnny moved between Emma and me while I stepped around him and headed over to Chloe. Mulligan and one of the cops struggled with Kace and it briefly registered with me that he was pushed against the wall with his head to the side, his cheek crushed against the plaster.

Mulligan took a look back at us, "Good job, we have it on tape. Book him: Suspected kidnap of Chloe Jenner in the State of Seattle. You need to liaise with them. Read him his rights.

Mulligan explained again to Chloe, that the evidence they had until today had been circumstantial, but his slip of the tongue in disclosing evidence that was not public knowledge and knowing exactly what the note said, made a case for probable cause, giving them grounds to arrest Kace for kidnapping Chloe.

Tugging her tightly to my body, I looked down and gave her a reassuring smile, tucking her hair away from her face. I could feel the tremor run through hers, so I turned and took Chloe into the bathroom. Once inside she let tears of relief flow and sobbed into my chest uncontrollably, making my shirt wet. Taking a deep breath I dipped my mouth and I kissed her neck, rubbing her back. "It's over, Chloe. You did it, darlin'."

Chloe pushed away from me and gave me a sad, watery smile. "Am I sick to feel sorry for him, Gibson?"

Knowing I would never be able to fathom the workings of a woman's mind, I didn't want to comment. Personally the way I felt, I wanted to run the fucker over with a heavy assed truck, but I sighed and found something to say, "Chloe your dad once said to me that you could always find the positive in any situation. I guess this is one of these ones where if that's how you feel I'd have to agree with him."

Emma and Lois came into the bathroom and

started to help Chloe clean up, telling her how brave she had been. I took the opportunity to slip out of there and saw Kace was still in the room. Stalking over, Johnny grabbed with both his arms around him and I shook him off. One of the officers stepped forward and I put my hands up to show him my intentions weren't violent, shaking Johnny off at the same time.

"Get the fuck off of me, Johnny. I wouldn't waste my energy on punching him that would be an unfair fight he only knows how to hit women. I just want to talk to him."

Kace was sitting on the bed, his mouth in sneer. "Good fucking luck with her, she was never a good fuck anyway. It was like fucking a plank of wood."

My searching eyes flicked in Johnny's direction and he smirked and I swear to God, if it wasn't an ugly scene I'd have burst out laughing. He'd obviously heard Chloe and I going at it. We weren't quiet when we got going.

"Hmm...really? The way I heard it you were the plank of wood. And I know it isn't smart to talk about your conquests so I'm gonna save what I think of my girl's tight little...anyway—put it this way, she's all the woman I need. And, you know what, Kace? I'm gonna treasure Chloe and treat her like the princess she deserves to be, 'cause she is *mine* now. Got that? *Mine.* You lost an amazing woman to your fists and I hope you remember that every time you see her on that red carpet, and when we have our babies, and even when she's famous in her own right one day. Now, if you'll excuse me you piece of shit, I need to take my girl home, she's had a trying day."

As soon as they removed Kace the guys got us out of there. Lois and Jerry had secured the corridor and stairwell on the floor and headed for the car as soon as the ordeal was over. There was so much commotion going on at the front of the hotel, that we had an easy departure.

Clutching Chloe tightly to my body we moved swiftly through the hotel kitchen but this time, Johnny had moved the staff to one side by some steel food cabinets so that Chloe's distressed state wasn't going to be out there in the media. The last thing she needed was any of this being public this time.

Sliding into the back of the SUV Chloe's face still had signs of her traumatic time in the room but, she had stopped crying and was clutching my hand really tightly. Clipping my seatbelt in, I put my arm around her neck and pulled her close to me. Sliding down the seat a little to slouch, Chloe leaned heavily into me turning slightly on her side and spoke to me in a shaky broken voice, "H..how can I ever thank you, Gibson?"

Pushing back from me to meet my gaze with serious eyes she licked her lips and kissed mine gently. It was a touching moment, but something inside told me, that if I tried to tell her there was no need for thanks it would result in another flood of tears and my heart tore every time she did that, so instead I teased her to lighten her mood, "Hmm...let me think...me being a rock star, 'n all, it may have to be pretty spectacular to impress me you know."

Chloe's face broke into the most beautiful smile

and even though her face was blotchy and her nose shining red from her bout of tears, she was still the most amazing looking woman I'd ever been with.

"Well...with you being a rock star, 'n all I'm sure you'll think of something, and drop me some hints. Whatever you want. Just don't make it too freaky because you have to break someone like me in gently."

Sniffing and pretending I was thinking of what to say I kissed her forehead, "Chloe darlin', you're pretty slow on the uptake with that comment, I would have thought you would have dropped that particular phrase from your vocabulary by now." Chloe stared at me puzzled again.

"Whatever I want, eh?" Chloe smirked knowingly and smacked my chest.

"Oh, Chloe." I threw my head back in mock ecstasy. "Fuck can we do this when we get home?" Chloe grinned and I pulled her against me again. "Chloe, right now, all I want is my girl to be happy and for us to put this whole sorry mess to the side.

"We can't forget it, and it's still got a way to go for complete resolution but from my perspective Kace O'Neill has had too much of our time already, so there's no room for him in our relationship any more. I know you may need to talk about what happened, but you have your counsellors for that. I want us to move forward without that guy in my bed on my lap and in my head. Can you deal with that or do I sound the selfish bastard I'm hearing myself to be?"

Pushing herself off of me, Chloe unclipped her

seat belt and slid herself astride me. Taking my face in her hands she dipped her head and licked her lips, then mine with her tongue. Pressing her mouth on mine her tongue penetrated into my mouth and I groaned deeply into her throat. Chloe squirmed on my now thick solid dick. Breaking the kiss she shook her head. "Sorry, I'm not following. Who's Kace O'Neill, honey?"

"I'm not saying you can't talk to me about him, of course you can. I just want to help you move on and live with it, okay?"

Again, just when I thought my little doll was broken she'd come right back fighting with the strength and courage of a lioness. What happened today would never happen in normal circumstances but we weren't dealing with someone normal, and because of my fame it had brought us the privilege of being able to face a horrible situation head on.

Overstepping the mark is a regular occurrence in my daily life and although there are times when I hated the fame and being able to push my weight around. What we did today to keep Kace from Chloe made the last eight years of my life worthwhile.

CHAPTER 36

STEPPING UP

Chloe

Back in Colorado, Emma had me hitting the ground running. Life took twists and turns as I started to take the reins of being the girlfriend of Gibson Barclay. We had finally told everyone we were still together and had been together since the competition and Gibson's team had said it was time we were out in the open. We already knew we couldn't keep my relationship with Kace a secret, because I would have to give evidence in court when the time came, so this information was handled sensitively by Gibson's PR team.

Gibson finally bought a place, a penthouse apartment in a compound where other celebrities lived in LA. Again that was in Jerry's name. We agreed to travel back and forth together between LA and Breckenridge in the mountains.

Gibson and I had a long talk about my fears about his drinking and women and he told me he'd never knowingly do anything to hurt me, but told me he was being honest about when he drank alcohol. He'd sworn off it since the incident with Tori. I felt I could trust him, but I didn't want to leave Gibson to his own devices when he was in LA because Toby also lived in there, and I didn't trust Toby not to get him drunk. That was my one worry and Gibson knew it. He accepted that Toby was a bad influence, but swore never to drink with him. Keeping me with him when he was in LA ensured I could support him with that.

Gibson and the security team had a lot of discussions with me regarding me being introduced into the public domain and I was bombarded with advice about do's and don'ts. I got a distinct feeling there was going to be some kind of test at the end of the sessions. There was so much to learn with all of the information they expected me to remember about M3rCy, the 'Gibson' brand and our personal lives.

When Charlotte told me I had an appointment with the image team I put my foot down. No way was I wearing make-up and stilettoes to go to the store just in case someone took my picture. Although I wasn't a tomboy, I didn't want to spend all the time and effort that glitzy look took. I'd never been high maintenance in my appearance, and I definitely didn't want to look like I was dressed for a wedding every day. I had to fight at times to keep my own identity while the image stylists tried to groom me for the public eye.

Gibson got it. He understood how frustrating it was for someone to tell him what to wear, and when to wear it, yet every few days, bundles of stuff would arrive for him to choose from for the next event or photo shoot.

Many people would be in heaven at having tons of new clothes and shoes, accessories and even watches and perfume. But I was proud when Gibson agreed it wasn't necessary, and voiced that he thought it was a frivolous waste of time and money, when there were people in the world without shoes or adequate clothing in the first place.

Eventually, the image consultants and I found mutual ground. I agreed that I needed help with supporting Gibson at glamorous red carpet events because I felt out of my depth with those, and they weren't my idea of fun. This part of being with Gibson wasn't making me feel any more confident that I could pull being his girlfriend off, but from his perspective, he thought I was beautiful and he wanted to show me off. So I had to put a brave face on it for Gibson's sake.

Gibson was always appreciative of the efforts when we went to special events. He looked stunning in a tuxedo. The first time I saw him I was star-struck. I'd never seen anyone with that much sex appeal, never mind being on his arm.

I have to admit they dress they found me to wear was absolutely perfect. It was a delicate floor length fitted dress with a beautifully sculpted bodice, silver satin underdress with darker silver threads in a lace pattern. The silver pointed kitten heels and matching purse were a perfect match to the dress. A black satin wrap completed my outfit and they had piled my hair up in a sexy messy arrangement of curls.

When Gibson saw me he put his hand out pulled it back behind his head and dragged it around to his mouth. "Hot Damn. Fuck! Chloe. I'm gonna be hard all fucking night, you look incredible. I am so proud you're with me, but I have a feeling I'm gonna be growling like a fuckin' bear all night when the guys in the room are checking you out.

Relentless attention from the media, with references to me breaking millions of hearts the world over, wasn't doing much for my ability to step out in public with the expectation of a welcoming committee. If anything, the women I'd come across tended to regard me as some kind of sex freak who was willing to do anything Gibson wanted in the bedroom. That or they were just downright bitchy and turned their noses up wondering what Gibson Barclay saw in me. I couldn't blame them really it was a thought I had myself on a regular basis.

Every question directed at me seemed to focus, mainly on the size of Gibson's dick or references, inferences or nudges about me being a lucky girl because my man was well versed in the bedroom. The effect my permanent presence had on his male fans was pretty much the same. Men objectified me, directing questions at the both of us, asking what I had that other women didn't. Gibson had a stock answer for that, "Dude, mind your fucking manners. Chloe is my lady she's not an object that you can discuss with anyone, you got me?"

After a few 'red carpet', events I tried to be a little more outgoing and instead of running for the safety of

the venue doors, I learned to take it slower with
Gibson gripping my hand tightly and giving a little
squeeze of reassurance.

Some celebrities were incredibly supportive but
they were mostly men. However, generally, people
became politer and then the weirdness of people I'd
only ever seen on TV, calling me by my first name like
we were already acquainted, set in. It was a steep
learning curve, but although life outside was still
weird, our relationship only got better with every day
that passed and my acceptance of my role by Gibson's
side.

My parents adored Gibson and it was only when
they visited I got the full story of exactly what Gibson
had done for them and what they had all gone through
when I was sick. My dad told me how anxious he had
been and that it gave me even more scope to trust
him.

Ruby came to visit and Gibson seemed warmer
towards her since her visit to Colorado. Ruby, being a
dance teacher wasn't shy, and when Gibson was
singing one afternoon, Ruby went and sat down beside
him, joining in.

Gibson was grinning because she started trying to
harmonize and he found that hysterical and kept
laughing, then trying to continue with the song.
Considering the song he was singing was a heavy metal
tune of one of his favorite bands and the way Ruby
was approaching it, he had a job on his hands.

When he finished he placed his guitar on the floor
beside him and meeting my gaze motioned for me to

come and sit on his lap. As I made my way to him his appreciative eyes stayed on me, but he began to speak to Ruby. "Jeez, Ruby, that was about as authentic as a choir boy signing "Hallowed Be Thy Name" by Iron Maiden."

Ruby's jaw dropped as if she was shocked, then she chuckled back, slapping his arm, and pretended to sound hurt, "Hey that was fantastic. I have no clue what you're talking about. I'm a great singer." Ruby looked up at me expectantly for support, "Chloe I'm a great singer right?"

From where I had been sitting she sounded awful, but I wasn't going to burst her bubble, so when I glanced at Gibson and I saw his smug looking smirk as he waited for me to speak, I knew that he knew, I was a bad liar, "Gibson's a professional Ruby. I think you were very brave to sing with him. Just like Gibson would struggle to perform a dance routine with you."

Gibson started belly laughing and the sound was so sexy. "Ruby she can't do it. Chloe's an honest woman. She hasn't got it in her to lie to you."

Ruby shoved his knee while I was sitting on it and rose up off the floor with an indignant look on her face. "If Chloe's that honest Gibson why haven't you made her your wife? Or is she only honest for selective duet purposes?"

A silence fell and I stared, open mouthed at Ruby, I couldn't understand why she'd come up with something that mortifying to me in front of Gibson. It hadn't even occurred to me that he and I would get married and there she was practically asking him why he hadn't.

Gibson glanced up at me and when our eyes connected my heart began to race because I was worried he was going to make an excuse which might have made her question even more embarrassing for me. Snickering with a slightly embarrassed smile he licked his lips and sucked in a deep breath.

"Glad you brought that up, Ruby. Strangely enough, I was thinking that myself. Unfortunately, Chloe hasn't asked me yet. And, you know— I've been wondering why? I mean I'm a great lay, we're smoking hot in bed, I'm not that bad looking and I still have all my own teeth." Gibson was giving me one of his signature wide roguish grins and he tickled my belly until I curled up on his knee then he slapped my butt lightly. I was thankful he was making light of Ruby's bulldozer of a question.

Ruby placed her hands on her hips and went along with his role play. "Is this true, Chloe Jenner? Fuck girl what's wrong with you he's smoking hot in bed, got all his own teeth and you're gonna let that slip through your fingers, girl? You got to get in quick before someone snatches him right from under your nose."

Gibson squeezed my waist gently and stared at me with a twinkle in his gorgeous grey eyes, smiling seductively at me like what was happening was turning him on. "Yeah, Chloe...you're friend talks a lot of sense. That's sound advice Ruby."

"Chloe?" Ruby was smirking and I couldn't help but grin at how animated she was with her eye brow raised in question and her lips twisted like she was really puzzled.

Gibson nudged me and nodded at Ruby prompting me to say something. Suddenly I felt under the spotlight to act and I was useless at this kind of thing.

Turning my head to face Gibson I began shaking even though it was a role play. I loved Gibson with every bone in my body, so just saying the words to him at any time would have been a big deal.

"Gibson Barclay." The serious way his eyes were piercing mine made me giggle with nerves and I glanced at Ruby, who was still towering above me, her weight on her left leg, a hand on left hip and her other hand across her front leaning on it. Working a swallow, I licked my lips and held his face in my hands making more of a show of it this time. I hated role play with a passion. "Gibson Barclay, I love you with all of my heart. Would you do the honor of becoming my husband?"

Gibson leaned forward and placed his lips on mine and swallow audibly, then drew back to look at me. When his loving eyes met mine again there was a soft smile in them, but he was shaking his head and I thought he was going to embarrass me further with a mock rejection in front of Ruby.

"Chloe Jenner, I am but a man. No man could refuse an offer like that from you. Are you naming the time and the place or am I? Of course I'll marry you." The breath I'd been holding came out in a whoosh and Gibson's eyes widened in recognition that I'd been holding it in.

Grinning at his answer I said, "Whatever you want."

Gibson grinned wickedly and stuck his hand under my T-shirt, sliding his warm hand over my skin. My nipples stiffened and my core clenched as I shivered in reaction to the goose bumps from his touch, smirking knowingly he looked up at Ruby. "I know what I want. If you'll excuse us, Ruby, I'm going to take my smoking hot woman to bed...just to show her how much I appreciate the gesture she just made."

Standing up Gibson winked at Ruby, then lifted me firefighter style over his shoulder and ran toward the stairs, I was mortified. "Stop it Gibson!"

"Chloe. I'm a rock star. This is what we do. Anyway, what would you rather... Ruby knowing I was a red hot male with strong urges to fuck his girl or have people thinking I've gone impotent?"

Hanging upside down I covered my face with my hand but I couldn't help but be turned on by his caveman gesture in front of her. Even if he was joking around.

Spinning to speak to Ruby, Gibson said, "Stay away from that guitar, Ruby, that howling noise you sing will attract bears or hunters around here."

Entering the bedroom, he closed the door with his foot and stalked over to the bed. Flipping me back over his shoulder, Gibson lay me on the bed and quickly lay beside me. "So..."

Chewing my lip, I raked my hand through his hair and he caught my wrist lifting it above my head. Gibson closed the space between us and kissed me hard. We both moaned simultaneously in appreciation of each other. Breaking the kiss we both breathed in deeply, then Gibson spoke, "We should do something special right now."

Staring into his eyes I pulled his t-shirt so that his head was closer and placed a soft kiss on his lips. "This isn't special enough for you any more, Mr. Barclay?"

Gibson considered this and massaged his lips together. "It is, but it's not every day you get proposed to...actually that's not true. I'm a fucking rock star...so that shit happens on a daily basis, but it isn't every day I hear my girl say it. "I want to take you dancing, Chloe. I wanna take you out and be just a normal couple for one night."

Gibson bounced off of the bed and stripped his shirt off of his shoulders, his back muscles rippling as he shrugged his way out of it. "Get dressed," turning to look at me he shook his head,

"I mean put on a dress. We're going out." Gibson disappeared out of sight into the walk-in closet then returned naked from the waist down, shaking out a pair of black dress pants. Beginning to step into them he glanced over at me. "Come on...we're leaving in ten minutes."

Bouncing my way to the end of the bed, I stood up and gave Gibson an incredulous look.

"Where are we going?"

"Town, Johnny's already finding somewhere we can have dinner and dance. I texted him just before Ruby's cat call. I don't want fancy and posh, just somewhere with good food and some sounds I can hold my chick tight to? Is that alright with you?"

Gibson's impulsive move thrilled me, I was delighted watching how fired up he was about doing something without all the planning that usually went into his 'going out'. "Aren't you worried you'll get mobbed?"

Snickering Gibson fastened the button on his pants and pulled up the zipper and my eyes fell to where his hand was immediately.

"Naughty girl...that's for desert. You are going to have to dance with me to play with my dick tonight, Chloe. And no, I'm not worried about going out. With what I have in mind for us, there won't be more than thirty people there at the most. I'm not planning on taking you to a regular dance club. Just something subtle that has tunes we can get lost in for a while. I mean we're in Breckenridge not LA. " I was at a loss how he had pre-empted my next question about attracting attention when we went out.

Gibson's playful mood along with his ass in those black pants was an enticing combination, but I was almost as excited as he was that we were going out. We'd never really had a proper date the way the events had taken shape in our relationship.

Dressing quickly, I came out of the closet to see Gibson sitting on the end of the bed wearing a crisp white shirt, the effect against his tanned skin and dark hair stopped me dead in my tracks, he was bending over, tying the laces of some dress shoes. When he looked up at me, the effect of the sight of him made me freeze.

"Wow! Gibson you scrub up beautifully." Gibson gave me his sexy roguish grin and licked his lips as his sensual eyes appraised me from head to toe.

"Damn, you did *that*, in five minutes? You leave me breathless, Chloe." Gibson's eyes glittered with love as he came over and slipped his hand around my waist and kissed my temple. "Coat. We gotta get out of here or we'll be out of these threads in seconds."

Johnny pulled in front of the cabin and jumped out to open the door. "Swiss...they have a small dance floor and music from 10pm."

Gibson looked pleased and patted Johnny's back. "Come here," Gibson motioned to Johnny to look at me sitting in the back. "Isn't she amazing...gonna need plenty of condoms tonight, Johnny."

Sliding in beside me, Gibson grinned and Johnny laughed, "Chloe...that's one smooth operator you got there, I hope you're wearing your chastity belt under that dress." Closing the door Gibson grinned devilishly and when he saw my jaw drop laughed raucously beside me. "We're messing with you, Chloe. You look stunning."

Watching the confusion on my face he could see I didn't know what to do about the interaction with Johnny. "Okay that was wrong, but fuck, I'm very proud to be with you and to be frank, I either embrace men appreciating how you look or get pissed and run around punching every dude that looks at you. Now I would do that happily if that's what you wanted, but my expert assessment is, that the sooner we front it out in public, the sooner we'll be less of a fascination for everyone.

Johnny pulled away from the cabin and down the snow covered driveway, and despite Gibson's over exuberance about how I looked, I felt we were going to enjoy being let loose.

CHAPTER 37

SURPRISES

Gibson

Joking with Johnny after I caught him appraising Chloe made her feel uncomfortable. Maybe I did it just to see that sexy pink tinge of embarrassment stain her cheeks, it was one of the things I loved about her. Staring back in shock all innocent looking and sexy as sin in response, with her wide eyes popping at me, I didn't miss the way she squirmed in her seat in reaction to my comment about her. It made me chuckle.

When her hand slipped into mine she instantly quietened me, and I felt centered by her touch. So we travelled most of the way into town in a comfortable silence.

One of the things that attracted me to Chloe was the way she regarded herself. How she blushed a little when someone paid her a compliment, or if my eyes connected with hers in a crowded room, and she'd smile at me right before her eyes fell to look at the ground like she doesn't know how mesmerizing she is to look at.

Sometimes when I wake in the early morning and see her lying right beside me with her face completely relaxed, hair tousled around her face and cascading across the sheet toward me, my heart always reacts in one of two ways. It either feels like bursting with pride at my beautiful, brave girl, or it melts with the love I feel for her. Sometimes—when we were in a crowded place it aches because I don't have her to myself, and when she's not there at all, that ache is a burn in my chest.

This morning I lay there for hours staring at Chloe and when she moved her soft sounds had my dick twitching. Sometimes I still couldn't believe how I found her...my *one*. *Mine*. Even after all the shit she'd been through she was still Chloe. A little broken but damn, she was coming back fighting, her strength giving her an assertiveness that I wouldn't expect of her quiet demeanor had I not seen it for myself.

I was a lucky man...very lucky. Everything I had wished for was granted, but if I never sang another song, never walked a stage again and even if I never played another note, I'd be contented because Chloe was by my side.

I have a tattoo of a script I saw on an old billboard for a band I used to like, when I was a teenager. "Heart Strings can only truly be tugged by music." When I had read it I found it so profound that I had a Gibson guitar tattooed on my arm and the words added because I believed that music was the only real way to affect someone inside. All of that changed the day Chloe came into my life. Love tugs the strings, making the music stir the feelings inside me. The way she affects me tugs at my heart strings.

Holding the hand of someone you love...that loves you back above all other people in this world, is a feeling I never knew existed until Chloe. In fact, for all the women I've held in my arms, all the 'free love' that I thought I'd had from having sex with them, Chloe knew more than I did about relationships. She taught me what it was to be intimate... to care so much for someone that they were the driving force behind anything I did from that moment on.

Sitting in the car with her on the way to the restaurant there was so much going on in my head. For weeks I'd been struggling with asking Chloe to be my wife. It wasn't necessary, I'd take care of her for the rest of my life like we were now, but from my perspective I wanted to make her mine, forever.

Ruby played it very cool today slipping it in about me making an honest woman of Chloe and when Chloe asked me to marry her, I felt her little body shake with nerves even though she thought it was farcical, but my answer was completely legitimate. I was ready— for me it has always been her. Chloe was that 'thing' that had been missing in my life.

Chloe was smiling at the tiny white and lilac double fronted restaurant at the top of the main street in the local town of Breckenridge. I thought it set the scene perfectly. Everywhere I looked was beautiful and I remembered why I picked this place as my bolt hole.

Gigantic mountains loomed above the town with ski slopes carved into them all the way down until they almost met the street. Glancing down the main street, it was idyllic, with its thick snow covered streets and antique style lampstands with twinkling lights on the store fronts it all gave an old fashioned feel to the place.

"So...there isn't a chain of Casanova restaurants then?" Chloe was smirking wickedly at the memory of the night we officially met, when Charlotte sent us to the wonderful restaurant with the unfortunate name given my reputation.

Grinning up at me, Chloe was standing shivering with her hands shoved deep into her pockets and her collar pulled up protecting her neck from the icy wind. Her nose and cheeks were already turning rosy red from the freezing night air and she looked utterly adorable.

Glancing down I snuck another quick peek at her temptingly seductive legs in stiletto ankle boots with black fishnet stockings that hinted of sin. This attire was entirely different to the last time I'd taken her out to eat on our own when she was wearing her ass hugging jeans and cropped top with her tiny leather jacket. Pulling my cell out of my pocket I snapped a picture of them and she giggled.

Entering the restaurant I was thankful that they used fold out dressing screens to separate intimately curved booths with round tables. Low lighting and candles made the date all the more romantic for her and our presence was less conspicuous.

Sliding around the booth to be seated, we poured over the menu, choosing to share the simple vegetable fondue. Personally, I could have eaten anything as long as I was able to stare into Chloe's stunning inky blue eyes while doing it.

"So…" Chloe snickered and I grinned as she placed her elbows on the table and took her chin in her closed hands.

"Remember that time we had phone sex, Chloe?" Instantly her eyes glanced down at her glass and she took the stem between two fingers twirling it between them while her lips disappeared into her mouth as she squeezed them closed. She was biting back a grin.

"Mm-hm." Chloe covered her face with her hand still embarrassed about those pictures we sent each other yet I'd seen her hundreds of times close up and personal.

"What are you embarrassed about? That was one of the hottest things I ever did without having sex. I still have the picture by the way." I winked at her playfully and she shook her head. I could see she didn't believe me.

"You have no idea how that made me feel darlin'. Can we do it again sometime? Send pictures to each other I mean?"

Chloe started giggling and brought her half-full wine glass to her lips trying to hide her sudden shyness at being put on the spot. "Whatever you want, Gibson."

"Hmm…that's the second time you've said that to

me today. What else can I ask for? Let me see?" Tapping my chin playfully, Chloe leaned over and wrapped her fingers around my wrist.

"Stop teasing me. What's got into you tonight? You're in a funny mood."

"Not aware of anything getting into me, but I know I'll be getting into you later if you play your cards right." Waggling my eyebrows I could see my corny, crude attempt at humor was a shocker and Chloe's jaw dropped, but she didn't answer because the old waiter arrived with the fondue pan and lit the little warmer on the table, Chloe pulled her hand back and placed it on her lap.

During dinner the banter between us continued to be more and more suggestive on my part and I was completely sober. Chloe had one glass of white wine spritzer, then stuck to water for the rest of the meal. After an hour we'd eaten just about everything on the table and I slid closer to her, pulling her into my side. Chloe's twinkling eyes stared up at me and she looked so fucking cute I had to kiss her.

Once I had started, I was in danger of getting carried away and I still had something left to do before I took her home and ruined those sexy stockings she was wearing. Breaking the kiss I slid my mouth to her ear and whispered softly in it, "Whatever I want, remember?"

Chloe glanced up and worked a swallow then licked her lips. "Hmm...I did say that didn't I?"

Nodding playfully I dipped my head and touched her forehead with mine. "Will you dance with me?"

Smiling bashfully Chloe looked around and shrugged. "I don't see a dance floor, Gibson."

Gibson caught the eye of the old waiter and beckoned him over. "Excuse me, I promised my girl a dance, and I heard you had a dance floor."

The waiter smiled and nodded vigorously, "Qui, it is upstairs."

Taking Chloe's hand I edged out of the seat and helped her to her feet then we followed the waiter to the door we had entered the restaurant through. He opened a door and there was a flight of stairs leading up. Pulling Chloe up the narrow staircase my heart was pounding in my chest. She was about to get the surprise of her life, and I had no idea how she was going to react. Chloe started giggling again.

"What are you laughing at? You don't think I'm serious about my dancing? I'm a great dancer?" Reaching the top of the stairs we stepped into a small room with a highly polished dance floor. Sheer cream silk hung from the windows and the lilac walls with cream ornamental wrought iron candle holders made the room feel so romantic. For a moment I fell into work mode, *shit I hope the press or my PR team never get wind of this. I'd never live it down.*

Chloe was staring into the room looking uncomfortable. "Oh, I hate being the first person on the dance floor."

Stepping closer to her I said, "Well it's only you and me here, darlin', so there's nothing to be worried about. If the two of us dance, everyone will on the dance floor."

424

Sliding my hand around her waist to her lower back, I took her hand in my other one and held it close to my chest but pulling her into my body at the same time.

Chloe looked like she was really enjoying our little interaction. Leaning into her I kissed her softly and drew my head back to look at her. "May I have the pleasure of this dance?"

Nodding she giggled nervously again, "I love when you're playful, it's turning me on Gibson, you need to do this more often."

"Oh, I'm not being playful darlin'. Never been more serious about anything in my life."

Coughing she cleared her throat then made an 'ahem' noise. "Sorry, okay, yes, I'd love to dance with you, but there isn't any music yet."

"Chloe...I'm a fucking rock star...I am the music."

Seeing her chuckle at my comment, I felt so smug because I could almost guarantee that I was going to have the last laugh.

"Are we doing this? Or are we talking about it? Because I'm getting antsy about getting my dancing done before we go home, darlin'."

Looking sheepish, Chloe nodded, "Sorry, Yes please I'd love to dance with you, Gibson."

Taking in a deep breath, I pretended to think about what I wanted to sing. "Fast or slow?"

Making a humming noise, Chloe looked at my mouth then glanced up to stare into my eyes. Where we had a silent frozen moment, "Erm...I'd like to choose a slow dance with my gorgeous boyfriend please."

Without saying anything else, she put her head on my shoulder and I started to move my feet and she followed. I knew the song was a huge risk but it was the one she associated with me, so I figured this was the most significant to us that wasn't mine. I started singing "Waiting for Superman" Lifting her head, she looked up at me and smiled with tears in her doe-like eyes.

Chloe's hot, watery gaze stole my breath and after a brief hesitation I continued until I was approaching the bridge and she smiled just as I sang the line... "And she smiles... and as I was singing a door at the far end opened. Chris Daughtry came in strumming his acoustic guitar and continued with the song.

Chloe's eyes popped wide with a mixture of embarrassment, shock and delight on her face, then she sagged against me. For a second I was jealous because she had that fan-girl-adulation shit going on as she stared at Chris, who was grinning every now and again as he sang his way through the rest of the song.

Before Ruby had pulled her stunt at the cabin and sang with me I had already arranged the evening, but I didn't quite know how to pull it off. Chris and I had been at a radio station interview because we were both headlining a festival on consecutive days. We'd bumped into each other over the years and had tables next to each other at dinner functions in the past.

I'm a fan of his work and he of mine, so when I mentioned the song and how Chloe loved it, the idea sprang to mind to have him sing it live to her at some point. When he told me at the interview he was coming to Breckenridge skiing for a long weekend, I asked for a favor and being the type of guy he is, he was only too happy to oblige.

When he finished singing to her he chatted for about ten minutes then left to spend time with his family. Chloe was absolutely glowing from her interaction with him. "Oye! You weren't like that when you met me. What does he have that I don't?"

Grinning widely Chloe pulled me close but with a hand on my pecs. Tapping them she gave me those big stunning eyes and breathed life into my dick. "Well...I thought you were an asshole then Gibson and I just know that Chris isn't."

"And now?"

Smirking wickedly she fought the grin that was trying to stretch her lips. "Oh, I was right, Chris is definitely not an asshole."

Picking her up off the floor I ran her against the wall, pressing my body flush against hers. My action excited her and I could feel the tremor in her body as I lay against it.

"Well, I'm glad you lowered the tone of things around here because I'm taking you home and I'm gonna get inside you, just like I promised you downstairs. And you can give me your honest opinion on whether or not I'm still an asshole after that. How does that sound?"

"Gibson I like you're thinking, but you're gonna have to work hard to impress me."

Smirking as I lowered her to the floor down my front and over my dick, I smiled seductively and held her glittering, playful eyes in an intensive stare. "Chloe...feel me? Working hard already, darlin'." The joy in my heart at doing something so normal to me, like asking a mate for a favor, had given Chloe an experience of a lifetime, and I felt that it was the first care free night Chloe had, had in a long time.

As we headed home, Chloe leaned in to my ear in the car and whispered, Chris is a lovely man Gibson thank you for tonight. I love you so much...you know that dinner with you would have been enough, right? Watching Chloe's honest face, I knew that it would have been.

CHAPTER 38

A MAN WITH A PLAN

Chloe

Arranging such an awesome date had seemed effortless to Gibson. The simple food and the ambiance of the restaurant were romantic. But most of all, everything felt normal. Like Gibson and I were doing something that was available to most young couples in love. Obviously what happened at the end of the date was far from normal...that was a memory that fantasies were made of. Then again...so was how Gibson and I ended up together.

After we got home there was nothing playful about how Gibson worshiped my body or me his. I was much less self-conscious about how he talked dirty to me when were intimate now. In fact I found the way his voice changes to that sexy, growly, husky one when he's in the heat of the moment, one of the hottest things I've ever experienced outside of the sex itself.

Gibson stretched lazily when I stirred that morning, then curled towards me from behind, pulling me against his hard body and landing a kiss on my shoulder. "Morning, darlin', come over here. I still love you this morning even after you kept me up half the night."

I opened my eyes slowly with a contented sleepy smile on my lips, as Gibson's spikey chin stubble grazed across my shoulder until his mouth nuzzled into my neck. When his lips made contact, it was like a signal to my body, waking it up instantly with all the nerve end receptors flying into action. My nipples stiffened as goose bumps erupted and my core was soon soaked from the tight clenching of it, with each little new nuzzle he delivered on my neck.

"Am I turning you on, Chloe? You want my dick sliding deep in here?" Gibson's hand had moved between my legs and had begun to stroke the length of my seam. When I didn't reply he spoke again. "Well darlin', I got places to go and people to meet today so you're gonna have to make your mind up real quick. In case you forgot you asked me to marry you last night, and weddings take some organizing when you're a hot-shot rock star like me." Gibson said, playfully.

Starting to giggle I turned to look at him, delighted that Gibson was sliding back into the moment after last night. "Oh, they do? Seriously? I mean you got me a passport in a couple of hours. Planning a wedding to someone like you, should be ridiculously simple."

Gibson smirked knowingly but then his mouth stretched into a sexy pant melting smile as he stared lovingly into my eyes, "Well as you asked me...I need to ask you...this wedding... it's whatever I want right? I mean you said that to me twice last night. I know I used one of them up dancing, but I've still got one in the bank right?"

Smiling affectionately at him as I stared back at Gibson's amused, sparkly eyes, they dropped to my mouth and he licked his lips. Watching him and the way he was looking at me made my heart race. *Damn if only this were real.*

After everything that had happened we were finally where we should be as a couple, and any doubts I had about him had been dispelled by his consistent loving support. And, the way he tried to protect me that went above and beyond most men's capabilities.

In my view it was a no-brainer. I would marry Gibson Barclay in a heartbeat, and I knew Gibson had strong feelings for me, but I couldn't really imagine him to be the marrying kind, no matter how much joking he was doing about it.

Nudging me out of my reverie, Gibson whispered sexily into my ear. "Hey, where did you go?" His seductive low tone and hot breath sent shivers down my spine. Snickering, Gibson whipped off the covers and smacked my butt, then rolled me over pinning my hands above my head with one hand, then crawled over me. Taking his dick in his other hand he began stroking it. "I'll ask you again do you want this or am I heading to the shower for a date with my hand? I have to go out in thirty."

What woman could say no to Gibson? So twenty minutes later he was drying himself in the bathroom fresh from the three minute shower, and I was standing by the bathroom door mesmerized, looking a ravished mess after his fast hot and heavy session.

Smiling sexily, Gibson looked incredible with his clean freshly shaven shiny skin and damp hair. Winking as he walked naked into the dressing closet I couldn't stop myself from giving his butt a pat on the way past. No woman would have been able to resist that gorgeously rounded firm rump of his. When I followed him into the walk-in, Gibson half turned to look at me, smirked mischievously and turned back to reach into a drawer. Taking out a folded black t-shirt he shook it out and pulled it over his head.

When his head poked through he looked directly at me, "You need a dress...and shoes...and flowers...get Ruby to help you I'm sure she's great at shopping." Stepping past me he began flicking hangers on the metal pole looking for some jeans.

"Gibson you're acting weird. What's going on? Where are you going?"

"Told you I got a wedding to plan— that is— unless you were shitting me last night, which would be really cruel Chloe, and I never figured you for cruel..."

Taking a deep breath to calm my patience because I was becoming frustrated at him, I waited to see if he would tell me more. I wanted to know where he was really going. Sliding in front of him I caught him by the hips and pushed him back against the mirror. As I did I saw his butt cheeks flatten against it and his face flinched a little at the cold surface hitting his skin.

"Damn, Chloe. This is hot but I don't have the time

to make you scream again right now, darlin'. But...hold that thought. I'm sure once I've been on my errands I'll be able to oblige you all evening if you want."

Swallowing dryly, I stared up at him and his eyes instantly narrowed. I could see I wasn't going to get anywhere, so I growled and pushed myself away from him. Gibson grabbed my wrists and spun me around so that I was against the mirror with my hands above my head. Kissing me hungrily, all the way down my neck, Gibson drew his head back and smiled sexily. "Oh you know what? I've never fucked anyone against a mirror before. Damn, I'm looking forward to that."

"You're not fucking me." Gibson dipped his head and peered up at me a seductive smile on his lips and a twinkle in his eye.

"I seem to remember you saying that to me before Chloe...look where that got you. Are you always this slow to learn? I get what I want. You said that remember?"

"And now you want to fuck me? I thought you were going out?"

"Indeed. I just have to make a split second decision and decide what I want more." Gibson dipped his head and took my mouth with a hunger that had both of us panting. Pushing away from me he growled with frustration and turned to make some space between us. Gibson's thick hard arousal looking painfully stiff as he pulled on his jeans and tried to tuck himself inside and I was stunned that he wasn't giving in to his urge.

Gibson was banging around and I could tell that

he'd sexually frustrated himself, but whatever he was going to do, he was in a rush, so couldn't indulge in his urge. "Where are you going in such a hurry, Gibson?"

"Jeez, Chloe I keep telling you, I have a wedding to plan and a shit load of stuff to organize. Emma and Lois can take you and Ruby for dresses. Don't buy frilly, puffy shit though, because where we're going it won't work." Staring at me for a second he came over and ran the back of his hand down my cheek and smiled at me tenderly, "Unless you don't want to get married to me, Chloe. In which case, I think there is some old law in this state about breech of promise or something to that effect."

Continuing to tease me with the wedding was beginning to give me an ache my heart and a sinking feeling in my stomach, because I realized just how much I wanted that to be real.

"Okay go but one of these days joking with me about that is going to backfire, Gibson Barclay."

Spinning around he moved swiftly back to my side, sweeping me up in his arms. "Chloe, I know it started out as a joke with Ruby, but I don't expect you to have to ask me twice. Besides...I love you...fuck...I *really* love you. So are we doing this or are you gonna piss me off by saying you were only teasing me?"

Gibson gave me a look that resembled a minor lack of confidence then he continued to speak quickly, preventing me from saying my piece. "I mean you could have planned it better of course. If it had been me proposing I'd have put more effort into it— flowers, candlelight, ring, maybe even a tub with floating candles, but hell we've never done any of this courtship in a conventional way, so it's kinda fitting that it was you and not me that took the initiative."

Swallowing hard, my heart pounded in my chest as I watched Gibson's face looking at me completely dead pan and I was struggling with how to answer. "Seriously?"

"Chloe since when have I joked about us being together? Fuck...I'd have married you yesterday when you asked me if I'd had my way."

Hearing Gibson saying those words made me feel like it was all a dream. "When?"

"How does Saturday sound?" It was Wednesday already and I was thinking there would be no way I could figure anything out by then.

"Stop. Don't do that." Gibson's brow creased.

"Do what?"

"All that complicated overthinking shit you do all the time. Roles reversed here. You made the proposal and I'm planning the wedding...with a little help of course. Just don't get drunk at your bachelorette party and turn up at our gig handcuffed to a pole dancer with your eyebrows shaved off, and I'll do the rest."

I had to laugh. Gibson was still Gibson underneath the tender, sweet, wonderful guy, and his alpha male personality pushed its way to the top. Even if it was *our* wedding. Actually I found it very romantic that he wanted to take all the stress from me, but I was a little nervous about what he had in mind for my big day. Our big day.

Whatever Gibson decided would be fine with me

because I wasn't really into grand gestures; if we didn't count the one last night, and anything that meant I spent the rest of my life with him was a small price to pay. Besides I trusted him.

Gibson left and me and the girls all went dress shopping, chatting excitedly about Gibson and me getting married. At first I was feeling pretty clueless about what I was supposed to wear with his vague instructions about what not to buy. Several hours and about forty dresses later, I had decided I looked totally ugly in a long dress and as Gibson said it was going to be a warm climate, I decided on an ivory silk over satin above the knee dress with a sleeveless slightly plunging bodice with material that gathered around the low neckline. It was beautiful, classic and simple. When I described it like that to Ruby, she said, "It's just like you then."

My guess was our wedding was going to be in the hot sticky climate of LA. So I chose some ivory, toeless, sling-backed, strapped stiletto shoes, but I also bought some low strapless ones for the evening; in the event the new shoes weren't comfortable to stay in for any length of time.

Nerves gripped my stomach while I was shopping and I became worried, because when Gibson's fans learned he was getting married I'd have a bounty set on my head, or I'd most likely be lynched before I had the chance to say "I do." I trusted Gibson and the girls he'd hired to protect me, but there was still a part of me that knew that my life was going to be very different as his wife.

Trusting Gibson

When Friday night; the night before the wedding arrived, I was spending it with the girls in the cabin, with a feeling like I was hanging from a cliff by my fingernails. There was no doubt in my mind I'd found the right man this time to be with, but I still had no idea what to expect. All I knew was I had to be ready for take-off by four in the morning. Gibson had been very secretive with the rest.

He had chartered another jet for me and the girls, and Ruby was more excited than me that my wedding was shrouded in mystery. One thing I worried about more than anything, was my big day turning into a media circus with press alerting over exuberant fans wanting to see Gibson, and possibly to kill me. When I voiced this to Gibson, he snickered and was quick to dismiss my worries with a throw away phrase, "No chance, darlin'."

Being approached by fans was one of the reasons I had preferred to have a quiet night at home. We had dinner delivered for us, and although Ruby was a bit peeved that I was spending my last night of freedom this way, and not living it up, she understood that living with Gibson was going to be all about high profile events and committing myself to living the life, not dissimilar to that of a goldfish in a bowl, where anyone could just peer in whenever they wanted to.

During the evening, Emma was bent double with laughter as she tried to tell us about a bad date she'd had when my phone beeped with a message. Seeing Paul's ID come up on the screen still made my heart flip-flop and I turned away from the table for privacy.

**Paul: Listening to 'Something I
Need' by One Republic and I
thought of you.**

Tucking my hair behind my ear my thumb moved
quickly over the keypad and I smiled warmly imagining
Gibson's fingers nimbly twitching like he was playing
the chords and probably not even realizing he did that.

Me: Breathing and thinking of you.

It was true. Every breath I took was hard without
him around. Gibson consumed my thoughts but as
soon as I sent the text I felt it sounded mushy, and I
was embarrassed I'd actually sent something that
needy to him.

**Paul: Jeez Chloe you're getting
cornier than I am! Take me to bed
and text me back.**

Gibson ended his text with a wink and I couldn't
help smirking at the thought of his naughty texts in the
past. It was only 8:15 in the evening, but I needed
some last minute encouragement from him more than
I needed to be with the girls, so I excused myself
saying I was going to relax in the bath and made my
way upstairs.

Flinging myself heavily onto the bed I smiled in
anticipation and texted him again.

Me: Lying on our bed. Lonely!

Paul: Want to play? *waggles eyebrows

Me: Whatever you want. *raised eyebrow

Paul: salacious grin hmm...

Paul: Photos...I want pictures.

ME: of...?

Paul: Body parts. Close ups and we have to guess what the picture is.

Paul sent a text with the caption "I have a burn here." It was just a close up of skin. *How the hell do I know that is?* Then I saw just a tiny bit of definition which I recognized as one of his pecs and I recognized it as the center of his chest. For several minutes the game continued with us both taking pictures of ourselves in close up and I was surprised when Gibson recognized practically everything I sent him, and some of the ones. Mine were all general areas, but the ones he sent me made me blush.

On the last picture I was stumped for what to send so I took a picture of the back of my left hand. It was a close up of just two fingers and I giggled because from the angle I took it from, it looked like the seam of a butt. Gibson's mind—which was frequently in the gutter went with that thought as well.

After a couple of minutes he conceded he didn't know what it was, and when I told him it was the fingers on my left hand another text picture came straight back. When I opened it there was a beautiful white metal ring with a huge round solitaire diamond in the middle. My first thought was *it's beautiful,* my second *it's too expensive what if I lose it?* The caption that went with it said,

> **Paul: Guess you need to wear this
> so I can distinguish between your
> hand and your ass crack Chloe.
> Oh…this one goes on your finger.**

The text finished with a wink, and it made me chuckle. Shaking my head in disbelief, I touched the screen in awe that he'd had the time to choose the perfect ring for me. Swiping the screen I called him, needing to hear his voice.

"Paul Lesley's answering service how may I help you?" His playful, sexy tone made me giggle infectiously which made his low rumbly laugh squeeze at my heart.

"I hope you packed a sexy bikini because I'll want to get a good look at my new wife on our honeymoon before I commit to consummating anything."

"When are we going on honeymoon? I thought you had to work Tuesday?"

"I do, so it's a two day break…the best I can manage right now, but I promise we'll find time for a proper one later. Are you all set? Are you excited? I'm excited…I can't wait for you to get here."

Smiling in amusement at Gibson's excited, enthusiastic questions, I had a little flashback to Beltz because he had sounded a lot like he had back then. Gibson the teenager was the quick talking, smooth, engaging teenager that I fought to hate, except now...there was no way I could ever hate him, because I knew the man behind the boy. "Yes, Gibson I can't wait."

"Cool...gotta go...see you tomorrow." Click. Gibson was gone and I was left holding my cell to my heart, instantly missing him and it had only been seconds since I had felt he was right here with me in the room.

CHAPTER 39

MEDIA EVASION

Gibson

Hearing the nerves in Chloe's voice made me ache to hold her, but I knew she'd thank me when she found out what I had in mind. Lying in bed thinking about how my life was before I met her...well I was at a crossroads and I had found a window where I was feeling a void in my life and was given her number at just the right moment.

Chloe saved me. From myself, from a meaningless life full of excess and low morals, from a life where I never knew what it felt like to truly love someone. Since she'd been in my life, Chloe had taught me a huge amount about myself.

Before Chloe, I'd never given a fuck what anyone thought, or considered the feelings of anyone that came on to me. Sure I cared about people...I cared a lot. I always tried to pay my success forward. All the money I earned was way too much for one man, and although I had a large payload of workers to keep, there was still tons left in the pot to help projects that really mattered.

Three weeks ago, I signed a deal on a new project that I wanted to share with Chloe and I was kind of nervous about that, but I get the feeling she'd be happy about it, so I'm excited to share it with her.

Privilege comes with status and there are a lot of perks to that as well. At first it was like Christmas every day when there were new threads or cell phones, tablets and shit arriving, then I got to thinking that a lot of people would never own some of that kind of stuff. That's when I decided that instead of wearing it once and promoting it, I'd do something sensible with it.

Wonder what some of those designers and corporate executives who took the decision to send their stuff to me would think, if they knew half the shit was being worn in a third world country by people who had to wash their garments in a dirty river. Most of the goods were sold at auctions to provide medical supplies and sheets for the hospital programs in the third world that I supported.

One of the things I loved about Chloe was that she was kind of embarrassed by wealth. She was definitely not a gold digger that's for sure. Accepting of the things that she needed to have, but she was financially solvent in her own right and low maintenance. She never seemed to need anything. I loved the simplicity about her, and how she looked with her casual dress code and her natural beauty.

Reaching for my cell I swiped the screen and her

smiling face looked back at me. She had captured my heart before I'd even spoken to her properly and once I knew her, she'd blown my mind, body and soul apart when no one else had even scratched the surface.

Once the screen went black, I placed the phone back on the nightstand, turned on my side and punched my pillow. The travelling to get where I was had made me tired, so I fell into a fitful sleep.

"Whoop! Get you're hairy ass out of bed and get in the shower, you're a man with a plan and Chloe will be here in two hours. We've got to finish our preparations. The staff are arriving and Chloe's parents are on the terrace being fed breakfast as we speak."

Johnny was pulling the cord to open the heavy black out drapes and paradise inched into the room through the sheer glass in front of me. Clicking the latch, Johnny slid the pocket doors open and they disappeared into the walls. My morning started with an uninterrupted view of an incredible azure, blue expanse of water stretching out before me.

Swinging around to place my feet on the floor, I sat up and I stretched my arms in the air and then stood up. The marble floor felt cool under my feet as I padded my way naked onto the balcony. "Jeez Gib are you gonna put a bag over that or something? You'll put me off my breakfast dude."

Glancing down at my morning wood I snickered and turned giving Johnny as serious a face as I could, "Yeah, sorry Johnny. I forgot you got traumatized by the size of mine. Never mind, you've got a nice personality, buddy." Slapping his back Johnny shrugged me off and started laughing hard.

"Fuck you, dude, just wait until you're an old married man and you're complaining your wife won't put out when I'm out getting laid every night. You won't be so smug then—when your big dick is just an annoying inconvenience in baggy-assed pants."

Gesturing at my dick standing proud, I snickered again, "Johnny...look...it's never gonna happen."

We continued with our playful banter and Johnny inclined his head in the direction of the shower. "Get your ass in there and try and make yourself a bit more appealing Gib, Chloe sees you like that she might run into the rotors on the bird in her effort to make a hasty retreat."

Leaving the room, Johnny stopped and banged on the wood with the palm of his hand. "You did good Gib— Chloe...taking care of her n'all, she's a good girl and I know she makes you happy. Just make sure you don't fuck it up."

Looking him dead in the eye, I nodded slowly at him. I didn't like to be reminded, but I was glad that he thought enough of me and Chloe to risk delivering a warning to keep on the right path with her.

After showering, I headed off to find out what was happening and was encouraged when everyone was completely on the ball. Everything I had envisaged for the day was coming together and I had to keep hugging Cathy, Chloe's mom, who was an emotional wreck but thankfully this time a happy one.

Days to prepare meant there was less likelihood that anyone would have wind of our plans, and this was exactly what I needed Chloe to see I could achieve. I'd hired this tiny island in the British Virgin Islands owned by a media mogul. It was used by a few elite celebrities to recharge their batteries and relax without the world's media on their back. Ironic the owner made his living out of pursuing others, and provided an escape like that.

Sitting a mile long and half a mile wide in the middle of nowhere, the island was the perfect place to ensure that there would be no one to interrupt us. In fact, the only people staying on the island, after the wedding was Chloe and me. Johnny and Emma were sleeping on a charter yacht on one side of the island and Jerry and Lois on the other.

When I heard the chopper had left Tortola ten minutes earlier, I glanced at Cathy and tried to control the bounce in my knee while I sat waiting nervously for Chloe to arrive. "Gibson she's going to love what you've done. I mean I've not seen the whole effect, but I couldn't ask for more of a fairy tale wedding for her."

Just as she finished speaking I heard the sound of the helicopter in the distance. Looking up at the cloudless blue sky, I wondered if the island had the same effect on her as it had on me, when I first saw it.

Shaped pretty much like a rough diamond, it was edged by the whitest sand and the lushest green foliage I'd ever laid eyes on. The three wooden huts on stilts on the water front looked incredible with their hot tubs and oriental style lay out, each with private sun decking. Up at the top set back on a small hill was the rugged looking main house which had an infinity pool and a huge wooded terraced area and a grand wooded treetop view out over the Caribbean.

The master suite I'd been in this morning was where I'd take Chloe tonight and the staff were busy preparing that, but today she'd be in one of the huts preparing for our amazing day. As she flew overhead, the rotors of the bird created a breeze and my open white linen shirt rippled in the wind behind me.

Watching the helicopter's descent I started running up the carved out wooden steps in the hillside to get to the helipad and arrived just as Chloe was exiting the helicopter door. She was hunched over her hair blowing in the wind and an expression on her face that probably mirrored mine. Relief. We'd missed each other dreadfully this past couple of days and I was desperate to hold her.

As soon as Chloe saw me she ran and jumped up onto my body, her legs wrapping tightly around my waist. Cradling my head in her hands, she leaned forward until her mouth found mine. There was nothing shy about my girl at that moment and that made me so hard I wasn't sure I was going to make it to the wedding without making a dishonest woman of her first.

Grinning happily, I walked with Chloe still wrapped around me and her arms tightened around my neck. As soon as the helicopter engine whine stopped she murmured into my ear, "Gibson it's perfect. Thank you, I love you so much."

Giving her a half-smile and feeling awesome that

she approved, I turned and laid a kiss on her cheek. "No, thank you. I can't wait to make you my wife. I half wondered whether to see you or not before the ceremony, but I figured that fate had thrown us together and all the bad shit had already happened, so because we're less than conventional, I had to be here when you arrived."

Once I'd settled Chloe, Cathy and the girls in their huts, we had a team on hand to pamper the ladies and we guys had a relaxing massage. It made me sleep for two hours. I vaguely heard the water taxi arrive. Johnny sat up and nudged me. "Gib the pastor is here, we gotta get dressed." Just as he said it, Jerry came up the stairs and onto the decking.

"Fifteen minutes until dusk, Gibson. Pastor is here. The island staff guys are being taken back to the mainland with this boat and then coming back for Chloe's parents, Ruby and the pastor. Everything is ready." Suddenly, I was really nervous. Really nervous. This was our wedding day and I'd taken responsibility to get it right for Chloe, so I was praying that I'd called it just right and she'd have a day that she'd remember for the rest of her life.

By the time I'd got dressed the last of the natural light was fading and I headed down to the old beat up motor boat that was waiting for me. Within a minute of it pulling away from the jetty it was pitch dark. Instantly, I thought about Chloe and her issues with boats and that made me fearful that she'd fall in the water or some other crazy assed stunt that would ruin her day.

I shook that thought aside and wondered about her reaction to all of it. Planning had been meticulous and when it was time, Johnny and Jerry hit the lights. Directly opposite Chloe's hut, about fifty feet out in the water, I was standing on the deck of a pontoon boat, which was covered in tropical flowers, rigged up with ten thousand tiny, white string lights.

The flat bottomed boat was draped in white and rose-colored silk with the flowers and lights winding up every pole of the structure. Rose petals were scattered the length of the white wash board floor deck. Johnny, Cathy, George, Ruby and Jerry were the only guests on board the boat. Jerry for our security, and Johnny as my witness. There was a roof on the boat offering even more privacy, so even if one of the staff had a telephoto lens the angle the boat was parked at would challenge even the most professional of photographers.

Along the beach were a hundred torch lights each side of her hut and the island's lilac flood lighting on the hillside made a perfect scene for Chloe to step out to. Jerry hit the sound system and "Take Me To Church" by Hozier rang out. That was my one indulgence I'd allowed myself in all of this. I loved that tune.

Watching her step into the boat, I could see that Chloe's hair was down and my heart stopped beating when I held my breath as she settled into the boat safely. It felt like an age for her to get to me and glancing nervously at the pastor. His face beamed, obviously enjoying the whole experience that I was giving her. I was just hoping Chloe's smile matched his.

We'd practiced this...Johnny pretending; to be Chloe, me and the pastor. And I was supposed to stand in a certain spot and wait for her to come to me, but as soon as the put-put noise from the small outboard motor stopped, I headed for the back to help her on, not trusting anyone else to keep her safe.

Chloe stepped off the boat and straightened up into my arms and smiled warmly. "You just can't stop being my hero can you?" Smiling widely, my appraising eyes ticked over her face then I had to kiss her. The pastor cleared his throat and I broke the kiss, put my hand up to silence him, and kissed again more passionately. When I broke the kiss I smirked at Chloe because her eyes were already drunk with lust.

Turning to face the pastor, I caught Johnny shaking his head at me. "What? The dude knows I'm a rock star...he should expect that kind of behavior from a guy like me. I have needs."

Grinning, I took Chloe's hand, stepped back and perused my girl seeing her properly in the light for the first time. Her dress was absolutely perfect. Perfect for her. Perfect for the occasion. Perfect for the setting. She looked effortlessly flawless. "Wow. Damn. Sorry." Clearing the lump that had lodged in my throat, I tried to speak, "Chloe, darlin', you...you leave me ..." shaking my head I had no words because she had called it just right. Leaning forward I kissed her again and a tear rolled down her face.

"I know, Gibson....you...me—I know." Grinning nervously at her broken words, I tucked her hair behind her ears and kissed her softly again,

"I got you, darlin'," Working a swallow I choked and the significance of what we were doing suddenly hit me. The pastor shuffled his feet and flicked the pages of his ornate looking book he was holding and I squeezed Chloe's hand tightly. Immediately, Chloe responded by squeezing mine back.

Neither of us had written vows for each other...we didn't need words...I would have made an ass of myself trying with the flowery-cheesy-shit I kept spouting involuntarily around Chloe, but I did ask to say one thing to her before she agreed to be my wife. "Chloe I will love you my whole life, this is not a promise— it's just the truth."

Chloe cried again and I smiled softly, brushing her tears away with my thumbs as the pastor struggled on, trying to conduct a marriage with two unruly participants. And I don't think he was too impressed when he asked if I took Chloe to be my wife and I answered, "Hell yes!"

When he finally said, "I now pronounce you husband and wife," Chloe and I both took a deep breath and exhaled heavily before laughing at each other. My heart swelled in my chest with pride at my beautiful wife and how she had come so far in such a short time.

After the wedding ceremony, we got into the small boat and headed for the shore. I asked Chloe to look up. Millions of stars twinkled in the huge dark sky, the moon was almost eclipsed in its cycle and the heavens shone brighter for it. "Sorry we're having our wedding at night Chloe, but it was the only way I could give you the stars." Chloe smiled and touched my face then leaned forward and kissed me. Another corny line, but fuck I meant it.

"And, the night time thing...it was a way of guaranteeing that only we know we got married today. We'll tell the world when we get home." When I Winked at her, Chloe's face lit up, delighted that I'd achieved a drama-free day for us.

"This is why you were so confident no one would know when I told you my worries about the media and fans."

New worries about Chloe I had been suppressing, mainly about getting back into my music and all the drama surrounding that, made me feel concerned, but I tried to push them back because I had been blocking some of those things, and could envisage many hurdles to come. We hadn't even started to think about touring again and helping Chloe adjust to the full force of life in the limelight.

What happened with Kace was a major failing on my part but I had learned a hard lesson there and I'd protect her with my life in the future. In the meantime I had to demonstrate to her the gift of love and trust she gave me wasn't accepted lightly.

After a few family photographs with Cathy and George, one with me and the boys, and another Ruby and Chloe we were done. These were the only guest pictures taken. Pictures of Chloe and I were taken by Johnny to mark the day, but to maintain our privacy there was no official photographers or wedding planners.

By the time we said goodbye and watched them pull away from the jetty, Chloe looked pretty tired, she'd had a long day with the travelling. Leading her by the hand from the small jetty up the main house we shared a moment of quiet reflection.

When we reached the bedroom I lifted her up and kissed her hungrily. "Are you ready Mrs. Barclay?" Chloe grinned and nodded bashfully and I dipped down to sprung the handle on the door. The room was lit with hundreds of rose scented candles and a trail of rose petals lead out to the terrace where our wedding feast had been set.

Chloe suddenly seemed nervous and I squeezed her arm pulling her into me. "Too late to change your mind now, darlin'." I teased grinning wickedly, feeling delighted she was finally mine and awesome feeling I had about her was like nothing I'd ever expected to feel for any woman.

"Sit. I have a wedding gift for you." Chloe looked puzzled. Hours of debating about what to do for her had resulted in what I had in front of me. Buying something for her didn't seem like enough, so I had two things that I hoped would show her that I had really thought about it. I was sitting across from her and I slid an envelope over the table. "For you." I said, tapping the envelope and smiling nervously. Chloe tentatively slid it off the end of the table and picked it up.

"What is it?" Gesturing at her by inclining my head at the envelope, I said nothing and she started opening it. Inside was the final agreement on a piece of land with permission to build ten properties to support survivors like Chloe. Before Chloe could react, I pulled the envelope away from her and slid a small package in front of her.

Tapping it lightly with my middle finger, I prompted for her to open it. "Fast Base Tone" by Chloe Jenner. Staring open mouthed in shock at me, she looked like she'd frozen, and my confidence in what I'd done wavered.

"Where...how...did you get this?"

"Your mom."

Chloe's new wedding band glinted by the candlelight as she drew her hand down the ruby red, hard back book cover, staring in disbelief at the glossy picture. Slender, shapely legs in cute ankle boots and fish net stockings donned the cover. Blinking rapidly she stemmed her tears from falling from those gorgeous inky blue eyes. "It's me...it's my legs on the cover."

"Well...I thought if you wrote a book about a girl who became a smoking hot rock chick, I figured there wasn't anyone more smoking hot than my girl... I mean my wife." Winking cheekily at her I could see that she wasn't totally unhappy, but I needed a little more from her to be reassured I'd done the right thing?

"You read it?" Chloe blushed and her face looked horrified thinking I knew the content of the book.

"Is it pornographic?" I asked with a smirk on my face and then wishing I had after seeing her blush, but I wouldn't have disrespected her like that. If she wanted me to read it, she would have shared it with me.

Chloe's jaw dropped her eyes popping widely at me. "No!"

Snickering I sniffed in pretense, "Then I've definitely not read it, darlin'—unless there are plenty of tits and ass...it doesn't hold my attention. I have a deficit remember?"

Chloe knew I was joking but she played along. "Really? I've married a guy who only wants to read porn?" Sliding out from her chair, she surprised me by moving swiftly beside and straddling me, raking her fingers through my hair.

Glancing up at her I caught the sexy way she was looking at me and fought the urge to lift her up and take her to bed. "Oh no I'm definitely not that shallow. I want to watch it as well. Live shows—DVDs—private performances—you name it. I'm practically an expert. If you ever want some research for your...romance books, I figure I could devote some time to that." Standing up, I chuckled and cradled her ass in my hands, then turned and began walking her backwards over to our bed. The food would have to wait.

"In fact, Mrs. Barclay, now that your debut novel is out of the way, I think we should get started on the research for your next one right away." Chloe wasn't protesting and I could feel her body hum against mine with a need that resembled my own.

Sliding her down my hard body to her feet at the side of the bed, I slipped the straps of Chloe's dress over her slender shoulders and watched in awe as the gorgeous dress cascaded down her body, unveiling her as it floated down and crumpled at her feet.

Chloe had been looking down, unaware of the sexy, sinfully innocent picture she made right there in front of me, then she suddenly lifted her gaze and stared straight into my eyes. My hands had been skating up her sides but when she locked eyes with mine, she stopped me dead in my tracks and my heart squeezed with the love I felt for her.

Since meeting Chloe, she'd turned my life upside down in the best way possible because she pulled me out straight at the same time. I'd never wanted anything more than I wanted to be everything for her—to her, and I knew that only time would tell whether I'd achieve that. When everyone else expected the worst from me, Chloe only saw the best. So before I took my new bride to bed, I prayed that the challenges of my work would never come between us in the future.

ABOUT K.L. SHANDWICK

K. L. Shandwick lives on the outskirts of London. She started writing after a challenge by a friend when she commented on a book she read. The result of this was "The Everything Trilogy." Her background has been mainly in the health and social care sector in the U.K. She is still currently a freelance or self- employed professional in this field. Her books tend to focus on the relationships of the main characters. Writing is a form of escapism for her and she is just as excited to find out where her characters take her as she is when she reads another author's work.

Social Media links
Facebook
https://www.facebook.com/KLShandwickAuthor

Twitter
https://twitter.com/KLShandwick

Website
http://www.klshandwick.com/

69229458R00254

Made in the USA
Columbia, SC
16 April 2017